Free Burning

Also by Bayo Ojikutu

47th Street Black

Free Burning

Burning

A NOVEL

Bayo Ojikutu

THREE RIVERS PRESS
NEW YORK

Published in the United States by Three Rivers Press, an imprint of the Crown Publishing Group, a division of Random House, Inc., New York.
www.crownpublishing.com

Three Rivers Press and the Tugboat design are registered trademarks of Random House, Inc.

A portion of this work previously appeared in *Otium* (April 2005).

Library of Congress Cataloging-in-Publication Data

Ojikutu, Bayo.
    Free burning : a novel / Bayo Ojikutu.—1st ed.
        1. African American men—Fiction.   2. Chicago (Ill.)—Fiction.
3. Psychological fiction.   4. Domestic fiction.   I. Title.
    PS3615.J55F74   2006
    813'.6—dc22   2006012663

ISBN-13: 978-1-4000-8289-6
ISBN-10: 1-4000-8289-7

Printed in the United States of America

Design by Lenny Henderson

10   9   8   7   6   5   4   3   2   1

First Edition

For Katherine Anne Grider, 1921–2004

11/06

Acknowledgments

Thanks to Carolyn, Ma, Dad, Bisi, Sherri. You are the source of everything that is right in me. I love you all. Lasting gratitude to Jeffery Renard Allen, Katherine Boyle, Caroline Carney, Achy Obejas, Ted Anton, and Anne Calcagno. On behalf of *47th Street Black,* I thank the *Chicago Reader, New City,* the *Hyde Park Herald,* 57th Street Books, the 47th Street Marketplace, WBEZ-91.5-FM, WVON-1450AM, *USA Today,* the *Chicago Sun-Times,* the *Chicago Tribune* Printers Row Book Fair, the Chicago Humanities Festival, the *Lakefront Outlook,* the *Hyde Park Herald,* and the online literary journal, *Otium* (www.otium.uchicago.edu). Do know that your support will never be forgotten.

I offer respect to this city Chicago, for everything it has been and it will be. This place is not only my home, but it is a tremendous storyboard for fiction. I hope to one day do it some justice.

Free Burning

1

1

COUSIN REMI LIVES on the corner, right before the lake floats away from the city. He rents this narrow crib with three stories stacked to the sky and cracked siding chipped from its frame after all these years fighting wind blown off South Shore Drive.

The place isn't the last on the corner anymore, hasn't been for a year now. I forget the red-and-beige flat built on top of the empty hangout lot where east-west numbers met north-south names. This new tower with the spiked black iron gates protecting its owners from the street crossing, and full Christmas-tree-green grass growing inside the iron. Its lawn is so long and thick seen up against my cousin's half-dead stubble colored like hay and old money. A brick terrace juts out of the third-story front with one to match on the backside, more iron gating both, and a satellite dish spins from the roof to beam in Jesus Christ and J.Lo and young Julio Iglesias, and all such kinds of holy noise, to these red-brick curbside folk.

Now there's another tower built just like the first on the south side of Remi's place, on top of what was once a boarded two-story. Back when Cousin's place was still the last on this

3

side of the block, I could see the shacks coming from east or west on 78th, standing up narrow and haunted and higher than everything else along these rows. These funky new towers cast shadows over the Four Corners today.

These young Mexicans bought the curbside tower to the north. No Latin would even think of crossing north of 79th Street on foot near the lake when we were boys, much less living on these corners. That's not even speaking of the Naperville whites living one tower further south now. We don't see either of them much—we watched as they landed with their big green Mayflower and white Ryder trucks—but they don't bother with the block these days. Just ride in from places far off come evening time, shut their doors and wait for the sun to rise and for us to disappear. Then, come morning time, they start their journey all over again.

I'm almost at Phillips Avenue when I blink and slide the Escort in reverse, wheel into the spot between Remi's place and the south tower. The city fixed handicap signs to mark this space six months back—but I don't care. There's been a blind brown-and-gray woman living right across this street, long as my cousin's been here at least, old lady with two orphan grandkids as gimp-eyed as her. But nobody ever thought about posting caution signs until these people came and raised towers and moved in folks who claim a child with autism just so they can hold a spot out front for the Lexi. When I stop by Remi's these days, I park between the city signs and curse them—"Fucking boo-jie jokesters," I say, "fuck um," out loud. Repeat it every time, just so I remember.

"How long you been here? Ain't hear you knock." We're blood on my mother's side, as Remi's the one child Auntie Denise had before the IC train took her on home. Only male family I've ever known who didn't come from a gangway or the sidewalk corner, or an assembly line; and if he did come from those places, at least he's the only one who stayed. His computer screen flickers gray and white light against tree bark skin. "Shit, close the door."

"Let myself in," I say and shake the key ring in my right fist. "You mind, huh? Busy or something?"

Remi hasn't spun his chair from the monitor. He speaks to the light juking across his screen instead. "Busy for you, cuz? For some other trifling somebody, yeah, I'm busy. But for your trifling ass? Never. Close the door all the way."

He clicks the mouse. "Ain't nobody else here, Rem. Don't sound like it, no ways."

"Your reflection's all on my screen," he says, "and they'll be back."

Silver-framed pictures line Remi's office. The cracked plaster just behind the desktop is covered by Johnnie Coleman preaching about sins dancing down in hell and clouds testifying up in heaven, Billie Holliday singing tears full of blue heron and blood, and Madame CJ Walker burning the naps out of Harlem heads. Near the window, Mahalia Jackson casts alleluia spells and Lena Horne looks all creamy in some flick from the old days and the Joyner girl (not the one with the nails and hair, the other) runs away from herself because she's all that's left to leave. Behind us, Cassius Clay drops Liston in honor of Elijah and Muhammad, letting the world know it'd be best to go on and call him "Ali" proper. Then my man Rich Pryor spills his illness from the stage until all pain and joy leave him numbed by laughter. Just before the wall's end, Mayor Harold breaks the wheels off the city machine—not the real, blue worldwide machine, just this little pissant Chicago version—and Malcolm spouts city rage from up high at the old mosque.

Right before these walls meet to finish the room in cob-webbed corners, Dizzy blows his horn across the way to Josephine half-naked dancing the juke jive. In this computer monitor's flicker, I catch Dizzy's notes floating about, switching her straw-covered hips left and right and bouncing bebop back over our heads.

"Where they at?" I ask and Remi looks over his shoulder at me finally, still without turning his chair.

"Don't know," he says through teeth clenching against bottom lip. "Out on the blocks, I guess. You know how high them niggas be when they come back from hustling."

My cousin's computer screen and these pictures framed cheap to hang from the wall, a dim bulb lamp, the swivel rocker at his desk, two folding chairs, and a phone wire stretching from the back of the desk are all that decorate the room.

"Been at the Soft Steppin?" I see his question in gray and white slipping its way through Dizzy's notes and Josephine's jungle love.

"Where else?"

Remi taps the mouse to the horn blower's time. "Ain't your lady home waiting on you?"

"Not ready to go home yet. Hell, you know what time it is—past one o'clock. Ta's been at work all day. Knocked out by now, been so. She ain't thinking nothing bout my ass."

"Mmh." I hear that sound forced through his throat, and I know the reason behind his questions. Remi wouldn't care about a damn thing but the dungeons, dragons, and white knights flashing across his screen right now if my wife hadn't called over here to track me down. Been with her six years now, and known him all my life—figuring the workings of their riddles is my second nature by now. Tarsha calls Remi to scream when she hurts to be heard, because my cousin was born with these ears, big, soft, and kind. She carries on until her yells turn into weary whimpering words forced through quivering lips and punctuated by a row of sniffles:

"You're the only one who can talk sense to him, Rem," all juiced up and begging, she cries. What was left for my cousin to do but promise to come to the rescue of a poor, thick Oglesby Avenue honey, like a good white knight should? She's my wife, mother of my baby girl, and he's my boy, my cousin and my boy, but tears and thighs still talk to the blue and black soul, blood or no blood.

"Got any bites yet?"

"Shit, market's dry now, Rem, you know it. Look at the news. Read it." This's the same script I offer Tarsha on her Sundays off. "Shit's hard in the square hustle. Only those fucking kings on their hill got it easy now."

"Ain't gotta prove it to me." Remi's medieval conqueror dies on-screen and the flicker stops. He turns from the monitor and pulls the lamp chain until these walls fill with stinging light. I can't see Dizzy and Josephine doing their thing now. "When hypes quit spending loot for the herb cause they're paying it all out for rocks and blows over in Englewood and the stash is so short I gotta use off-brand chicken seasoning to pack my last dime, I know times is hard."

"Thought there was no recessions in the game?"

"Muthafuckin kings, you said it." Remi lights a Newport from his T-shirt pocket. "Went and dicked up the Taliban, so that Afghanistan poppy blows down from those hills to sell cheap off Sixty-third Street. Pure as I don't know what. Kings all getting their cut."

"What time Tarsha call?" I take a smoke from the carton Remi offers, and my laugh floats through dust.

"Ain't talked to her since last week." He lights my cigarette and the flame blocks me from catching the lie in his eyes. Not that I would've seen it anyways—Remi's so smooth, his tales spin circles around his own knowing. The valleys of his cheeks squeeze tight at his mouth to stop the truth from squeezing through, leaving the reaching point of his nose the only limb that gives up the tale. Just that nose and the dark skin crawling on bone around his eyes.

"We're holding up tight though. Her gig is solid downtown, for now. She's making enough to pay rent and keep heads floating. For now."

"You let me know." Remi blows smoke at the knight's bones.

I swallow and cough. "Still got the state check coming in, too, you know. Three more months riding on that for me still. It helps."

"Don't get me wrong. There's still money in this hustle," Remi explains to this hardwood dust. "I complain, and hypes do run to the hard dope these days. Desperate clowns. Enough to make a nigga think about putting cash in a ki, make some real paper. But that's a bloody way, messing with rocks and blow. Still cream to be made right here with the herb. Clean cream, cleaner than some at least. Ain't much blood to this hustle, and enough cash to keep the head on straight. You holler when you need help getting down, Tommie."

"I will," I tell Remi, "appreciations."

I hear Westside Jackie Lowe now, him and their latest housemate, whose name I never keep straight (James-Peter, Peter James, some such biblical founding father concoction). James-Peter is kin to Remi and Jackie somehow—but I don't claim him as my own true family, no more than I do Westside, no matter that I call them both "cousins." We've all got the same blood running in us somewhere, so even when we don't tag New Testament founders from the West Side as true blood, they're still our kin. Calling it out loud like that is the easy way to stop ourselves from getting confused about names and history and such.

Westside is Remi's younger brother by a few years. Same father, different mother. Some ho strolling honey from Madison Street and Independence Boulevard gave him birth. The fool was pushed from a Westside womb, though he's lived here in the Four Corners all his years. He and Remi are barely blood brothers themselves.

"Put that shit down," Jackie Lowe yells over the stomp of boots and gym shoes from their living room. "That's my shit. Yo punk ass ain't do shit for it. My . . . shit—how you gon come up in my house and take my shit after I did the work to get it? Who the fuck you think are you?"

"Fuck you," James-Peter answers. "'Yo crib?' Bitch-ass mark, so what I took your shit. You took the shit from somebody else. So what? Possession's ninety-nine percent, muthafucka."

"How much you want?" Jackie mumbles. "I want my bike back."

"Your bike? Dumb ass," James-Peter yells.

"How much?" Jackie pushes the office door and stabs his head into the private space. He is ruby red–skinned, the melting genes of slaves and Latin kings and Italians and house masters hopping and popping about above his eyebrows and under his cheeks.

He leans on the wall, so close to Dizzy that the jazz man's frame bends crooked against plaster. Westside puffs sweet, cheap leaves stuffed in blunt wrapping. "Oh, my main cuz, Tommie Simms? Didn't see your car out front."

"Handicapped spot."

"A dub," their housemate hustles on the other side of Mahalia's wall. "Give me a dub, you want your bike back, Jack. Now what?"

"A dub? I climbed on the back of that gate and up the porch to get the gawdamn thing in the first place. How you sound?" Jackie turns from his roommate's offer and points the blunt at me, and he giggles. "Told you bout parking there, Tommie. Told you they got a gimp living next door. Get your shit towed fast, boy. Them folk don't care nothing bout no bullshit, raggedy-ass Ford. Got a deal with the city on that spot."

"You're Richie's meter maid now?"

"Hell yeah. Just don't be parking your bullshit in fronta my crib, is all." Jackie laughs louder in his stinking clouds. "Hurts property value."

"I'm gone."

"All right then, Tommie. You ain't gotta go nowhere. Don't be so sensitive." He points at the back of Remi's head. "Chief, we got some skeezes from Seventy-ninth bout to come through, trying to get loose with the fellahs."

"Not from the motel?" Remi asks without looking at Westside. He clicks the mouse to protect this conqueror's new life.

"Naw, Rem-Dog. Ran cross these two at the bus stop off Cottage. Rolled up on um in your Rover. Fresh babes got to slobbering at the lip talking bout where 'y'all going to, who car's this, can we ride with y'all,' testifying on how down they wanna be. Course, I told them it was my boy's ride, and we couldn't get down with them unless they brung the get-down to him, right. They went to get another friend, then they'll be through the spot. *Hehe*—that's how smooth I am, Tommie. You wish you was playa-smooth like this here, don't you?"

"Yeah, I wish." I peek from Mahalia's shadows and the conqueror soon to be burned to ashes by this digital dragon. "Like you. Sure do."

"You told them it was my truck?" Remi's says.

"Of course I did, Rem-Dog. You my dog. Like how Snoop say it—"

"Right." Remi drops his square on the hardwood, squashes it with his shoe sole until ash simmers.

"Fresh babes," Jackie repeats as he steps out of that living room light. "Like eighteen, nineteen years old, no older than that. Just right. Even got a plump one coming for you, Tommie, if you wanna stay. Just like you like um. Had you in mind, Cuz, just in case. Better claim this one before James gets his greedies on her."

"Thick, that's what I like." My eyes swell from the blunt's burn. "Not plump—I like thick women."

"Well go home to your wife then, ungrateful, fatty freak muthafucka. Beggars can't be—punk bitch. We don't love these hos." Jackie sits under Lena, and his clouds turn her even creamier. "Where'd you put the video camera, Rem-Dog? The handheld with the digital view screen and the wrist strap."

"It's like that?" The dragon picks through the conqueror's remains.

"Told you. Straight skeeze-oids. You know how we do."

Remi rolls his office chair my way. "All right, Tommie, get home to your ladies. Holler at me tomorrow."

I laugh, then see in his brown-and-black eyes that my cousin is free from Tarsha's righteous begging now—fresh dreams of burning at the dragon's flames reflect across his face.

"Don't be parking in our gimp space no more," Jackie yells again as I stand and rub the sore hard metal leaves at the end of my back. I pound Remi's fist with the smoking hand and turn away from his computer screen.

"Need be, let me know if you wanna get with me on that thing like we talked about," he repeats, "when you're ready."

JAMES-PETER SITS on the dining room's scuffed hardwood, still wearing his gray-and-brown package-delivery uniform, as I near the exit. This housemate works for one of the big parcels with the globe icons blinking in the corner of its babble box commercials. At least twice a week, I see his truck— gray and brown to match the uniform—blocking these city streets as the apostle makes his neighborhood rounds. He's been with the company long enough to get Westside a part-time job there; Jackie doesn't have his own truck as a part-timer, so he's convinced James-Peter to run misplaced electronic goods straight out the company warehouse.

James-Peter presses Xbox pads to direct and follow blinking TV static. I don't say a word, and he pays me no mind, as the thick air outside Remi's office has him hypnotized already.

Cleopatra Jones watches over us from a faded movie poster taped to Remi's living room wall. Floating before a cityscape background with psychedelic light streams at her back, an apparition cast by a city window, this afro'ed-out mamma totes her .38 piece and juicy hips clothed in leopard's fur. Aiming at the world to convince us to stop running. Submit, before she lays us down for good with either hips or gat. She aims and clings to this peeling wallpaper at once, fading but fighting to keep watch on my cousins, and she follows my steps. So I pay my due respects, nodding at the queen in her get-down getup before leaving the Phillips Avenue shack.

*   *   *

"Is that your Range Rover down the block?"

This little round girl stands on my cousin's porch, bracing to knock as I open the front door. She is shaped like an apple, reverse tapered so her weight rests in her chest and head and in this smile at the core. Her teeth are big and just a bit yellow from corner store hard candy and bubble gum. Clouds of raspberry juice powder blow into my nose as she drops her knocking fist. She's fourteen at best, twelve or thirteen maybe—between rat-tat-tat blinks, her eyes sparkle with the brightness of believing all things whispered her way. Her left hand straightens the barrette at the base of her skull, holding burned-straight, slicked-back hair together so that the forehead juts further than it should on top of her head. Her lids slow and she fixes these pupils on me as she asks her question.

Three more young girls stand at the 78th Street curbside, just in front of the north brick tower. They are no older than the apple on my cousin's porch, just shorties giggling at the old hangout corner, with trick-or-treat bags in hand. They wait for a Snickers bar, or for a package of Now-Or-Laters, or to get down with Jackie Lowe and Cousin Remi and the worldwide delivery man James-Peter.

"No," I answer.

Her overgrown chest sags and I walk past the child, down the porch steps and on to my handicapped spot. I swear that my daughter will never wear such barrettes. She'll never giggle at the Cottage Grove bus stop or on anybody's old hangout corner, she won't be shaped like an apple, no kind of fruit at all, but like a carrot. Straight up and down. Dawn won't ever spit scripted rap to some gimp's shady relatives on Cottage Grove Avenue either. I swear. And her baby eyelids will blink to cover such a lovely color—blink not to hide, just to protect those pure brown circles—without any floppy-eared, pillage-colored crooks ever thinking of whispering her way.

❊   ❊   ❊

THE FOUR CORNERS is Officer Weidmann's beat. The only reason our home even goes by the name is because he cruises along its streets in his red-and-blue-striped CPD car with no siren-lights on the roof. Turning the neighborhood angles to lines like South Shore is space on paper, waiting for the cop to give us shape and meaning. His beat actually forms more rhombus than square in my eyes. Most around here never made it past arithmetic lessons though, so the only shape they know to call it is this basic rectangle: Jeffrey Boulevard to Lake Shore west to east, 71st to 79th north and south.

My cousins and these cats standing on the corners, and the rhyming cats in front of the 79th Street liquor store—blue voices I see and hear so much more of now that I'm not racing to Loop towers every day—they all say Weidmann dropped the square on us soon as he landed his ass on our South Shore way long back. None of them remember when it was exactly that Wee Man arrived, nobody knows from where he came. Might as well be forever and burning hell for the pain in their sound.

They say we'd be free around here not for him. *Free niggas,* they say. Before these cats get to their second swig on the Wild Turkey, I try to explain how this square is a fool explanation conjured in our heads out of fear and apathy and comfort, even as I hear myself sounding like the politician riding a donkey and the preacher on his elephant. Riding and babbling for the cameras' eyes. But I keep on with the sermon, repeat to them how it ain't really Weidmann who traps us here, not here or nowhere else. I say nobody can trap another unless the soul is born trapped and wants to stay like that. Black and blue souls laugh, holding pot stomachs and coughing smoke. In gulps of breath between verse, they tell me I'm talking that college-trained Sunday bullshit. "Dumb-ass nigga," they call me, and they laugh louder.

Soon as schooling ends, they say, all that bullshit ends, too. Look around at our world, see Wee Man riding, feel the lint in your pockets and remember where we've gone in all this time passed since he arrived.

"Still standing on the same corner, with the rest of the blue souls?" they say through gap-toothed smiles "Dumb-ass, mumbo-jumbo-trained coon—that's because this space inside lines is the real world as he draws it round us. Sociology 407 is dead, my nigga, dead and bleeding red."

WE MOVED TO my mother's Coles Avenue low-rise when I was still a boy, and I'd sit up in our sixth-floor window to look at Lake Michigan after all the tree leaves blew off for the winter. Waves of ice floating and breaking on top of each other, headed for the shoreline in this lake filled of water and pus, gray as the cloud-filled sky. Breaking water falling on an almost empty Rainbow Beach—not a thing there except for the litter blowing alongside bare branches.

Out of my eye's northern corner, downtown towers hovered with antennae poking the clouds' bellies, and the O'Hare-bound planes flying near roofs, maybe near enough to crash high steel and glass (just an illusion created by distance, this nearness, I told myself back then. *Haha,* jokes on me. Live long enough in this place and you come to find that all tales are dead Sociology 407 mumbo jumbo). At night, when everything else was black and I was supposed to be sleeping, I'd stare straight at the towers, window lights flashing yellow and red and the tall frames casting shadows opposite the moon, and I'd wonder what lived on the other side of antennae.

Officer Weidmann was around in those days, somewhere prowling and swinging and shooting to remind. Or no, maybe it was just my mother and me on the sixth floor. I didn't think of the sky and lake's meeting place as part of the Four Corners back then at least—or those poking downtown high-rises and their night shadows and blinking lights, or even the windowless wall on the west side of our apartment. They were the end of what I knew, yes, but not a trap, not in those eyes.

The souls I pass on the corner of 79th and South Shore spit some kind of truth in blaming Wee Man for the trap after all then. Their sermon sounds too powerfully good not to be the case, don't you hear? The cop did this to us, and it's his goddamn fault. Goddamnit. I just had that mumbo-jumbo training noise echoing in my head, blocking their message.

* * *

WEIDMANN'S HEADLIGHT hazards flash quick when he's after you. His cruiser has no siren horn either. I should've known that was him from the way the midnight side-walkers slowed to peek from South Shore Drive as we passed. They peeked, then the gym shoe boys scattered into alleys as streetlights turned green at 74th. The cop's Crown Victoria has been cruising after me at least that long, almost half of a mile now.

Blinking orange floods my Ford's rearview mirror and, for a bit, brings sun to this stretch of 79th Street night just west of the Drive. Off-and-on light, until feet scatter about the block. I see the runners, then I don't see anything at all as the cop's warning flash slows just behind the Escort.

I quiet the dashboard radio, though my feet are still tapping to the faded bass jive, and my heart, too. Tapping without music, explanation, or rhythm until the Crown Vic's door closes in my side-view mirror and steel boots click along the pavement as he nears the window.

The cop stops six feet from the Ford's driver side, no matter these cars rumbling past on 79th—they won't run him down, they know better. Wee Man shines his silver searchlight beam into my front seat, blinding until my pupils shift. All I see of him is an outline carved against a deserted frame house and a right arm supporting the flashlight, while the left rises to his side holster. His beam scans the Escort front to back, then front again as my eyeballs cool.

"Drop your window." I spin the panel lever and glass slides

slow, squeaking rubber echoing against the street. "Show me your hands. Keep um where I can see good."

I raise my palms to the sides of my face, use the left to shield sight from his light. "What's the problem, Officer?"

"Put um to the steering wheel and grip," he instructs. The voice is low and empty of the need to make a show of his badge's power. Weidmann's been prowling these corners long enough years to know better than yelling to announce himself. "You ran that stop sign back on Exchange."

I bite my lip, and the tapping stops. It's best to speak no louder than a hum now. "No, I didn't, Officer."

"What?" Weidmann laughs giddy. I grip the steering wheel and its ridges dig at bone. "Gotta come to a complete stop at the red sign. Let the car waiting at the intersection pass before you drive on. So, yeah, you ran the stop sign, sir, soon as you shot out in front of your homeboy's Navigator."

"Sorry," I say. "I got a ticket coming, Officer?"

"Just a warning," he says as laughter runs out of him. "Your license sticker expires next month, too."

"I'll take care of that. Thank you, Officer."

"What? Speak up. Sound like a little girl with a crush on me, whispering soft like that. Makes me uncomfortable to hear a hard leg whispering that way. Speak up, so you sound like a man. Damnit."

"Thank you," I repeat—louder but lacking bass still—"Officer."

He shines directly in my eyes and his outlined hand drops from his hip. "Don't I know you? We had this conversation about whispering and a grown man sounding like he's got testicles before, ain't we? Maybe a few months back?"

"No, I don't think so. Wasn't me. Could've been one of my cousins."

"No, no. I know you, I do," his light flashes against the steering wheel, silver swallowing the twinkle at my ring finger. "Shouldn't you be getting home to your family? It's past midnight. You've got one of these nice little hotties waiting for you somewhere. There's nothing out here for you."

"I know," I say. "I am. I will."

The street returns to night black and Wee Man's outline disappears with his beam. But I don't raise my window until his sole clicking stops seven steps behind the Escort. My heart and my mind start tapping again, and my ring finger joins the organs' tune, two-timing against the steering wheel. I drive on only as Officer Wee Man's cruiser spins and disappears east toward the lake shoreline.

2

THE WOMAN SLEEPS as an angel would. Sweet as her lips spread, she smiles only after her eyes are closed these days, and the sun has faded. But this is the same joy my wife once beamed while we dated, and when Dawn was still fresh from the womb and yellow-skinned, too. Seeing her smile for our child, and even watching her face shine as she slept, these visions once brought me joy. Now I wonder what she sees in the darkness that makes her so happy.

Her head moves under my palm, temples sliding free so that her right cheek presses into the pillow and the smiles fades, or bends into a not as happy place. The nightstand clock reads 1:45 and I smell rum puffing hot from my nose. I cover my mouth with the hand that touched her, sniffing the mint of her nighttime facial cleanser instead.

She'll wake in three hours, minutes actually before the alarm tears open night, slicing my eardrums before stabbing dreams I won't remember afterwards. Maybe she'll watch my chest rise and fall, breathing as much life as what rumbles from her nose now, before the sight of my weight swelling disgusts her and she turns to the clock to wait. Maybe, right before the ripping sound, she will tell herself that my dreams are not as at peace as her own, which she will know because she sees no smile beneath my gaping nose holes.

Then she will listen as 4:44 turns to 4:45, sound cutting past this fat head of mine and on through my skull. I will spring upright in our bed, blood pounding my head. And my tears will pound, too, like this is some new interruption and not the same ringing blade Tarsha has used to end my sleep since last October, though I've had nowhere to go the entire time.

I'll look at her through the slime in my eye corners, and I'll swear for the last time today, that she'll be happy still. Then I'll fall into the sheets and try to breathe life into dead dreams—but I will be chasing a miracle, and not once on these mornings have I been Jesus Christ. I'll force my lids shut as Tarsha stands from our bed, so I won't see the curves broken by sharp-boned lines along her skeleton. I'm blind to her beauty instead as she pushes away from the bed to get ready to get dirty for her boss, in her lonely quest to put Enfamil in our baby girl's stomach and, just on Thursdays, a few meatballs in the spaghetti sauce to dress up our own meal.

One day, I'll get wise and pull the alarm clock's plug from the wall behind our headboard-less bed once Tarsha's drifted off to her joyous, lonely place. By that time though, my mind will be long made and I will care nothing of these obligations, my short options, or of the corners waiting just outside this box. Once my mind is made, all I'll care about is freedom—freedom just for me because living free will be such a self-possessing thing, high and powerful as smoke from the crack pipe. Crave that smoke, swallowing freedom's cloud into my own lungs and, maybe, letting all the rest of them get free off my exhale. Maybe. But I won't give a damn if they choose not to inhale.

Eight months ago, I still worked for an insurance firm, big downtown setup with offices on the hoity end of the city. The eighty-three-story Global Mutual IndemCorp building on Grand Avenue, eight blocks north of—but so many miles higher than— my wife's Loop law office secretary gig. Not the sky-high premium car insurance, door-to-door life policy scam racket. I started out hustling on that low end, no doubt, selling the lie of security to poor fools for a bunch of flimflam artists who folded their crooked schemes into Global Mutual's operation for an eight-figure payday at the end of the Clinton days.

Once the century flipped, I moved to GMIC's big headquarters building, where we offered coverage only to elite hustles: urban condo developments, commercial zone expansions, industrial transport, capital gains investment. Strictly top-dollar clientele we served from that skyscraper rising above the green river's main branch. I had an office on the thirty-second floor myself, just under management and about as high as Four Corner boys from Southern Illinois University climbed in such towers.

Then they went and flew airplanes into the buildings out east. I remember watching the *Today Show,* before I ran out to catch the 8:03 Jeffrey Boulevard bus, how those blasts cracked the company's nut wide open. By the time I got to work, fools in tall temples like GMIC's cried about what they would do if freedom appeared in the windows (up higher than the thirty-second story even) like so. Dark, raging, goddamned freedom, coming at the temple two hundred mph, and a few thousand degrees hot, what they would and wouldn't do. What could they? Cry some more, or run, though freedom flew faster than light, so fast that fools couldn't even see it moving most times? What that window reflected was truth itself, freedom indeed, and that muthafucka was too fast, and on fire. What you gonna do, fool? Jump? Please. You might as well stay right here, watch it come in clear, and count yourself among the blessed first.

Then us fools in the tower got to waving our bloody pale and powder blue flags so we wouldn't think of true fire flying at us, or bother crying anymore. By lunchtime, I paged through the Yellow Pages and, once the satellites were fixed to send their signals again, called directory assistance in search of the unemployment office nearest my bus route. Six years in the insurance hustle was long enough to know how that deal would play out for me. Whenever big-time claims dropped on us in chain fashion—and off the top of my head, GMIC provided eighty-five million in coverage for clients in Lower Manhattan—the company laid off as many in the middle-income bracket as service provision allowed. Then, once payout costs were offset and the claim chain ended, Global Mutual hiked the premiums on all outgoing policies to cover the losses from the devastation chain and still fatten its own pockets.

The last time around, when Hurricane Andrew tore up everything south of the Virginia coast, I was an intern processing claims. I'd taken five steps up the ladder since, so my jig was up no sooner than the smoke settled in the low-down hole. Maximizing the opportunity rendered by tragic circumstance, that is fuel for the wheel's turn in this insurance grind.

I've been out of work since September 30, 2001, and I have three months left standing on the state unemployment check.

"Tommie?" Tarsha's head rises just barely from the pillow, and her smile is all gone.

I snatch my hand from the bed. I've tucked my left hand—with its wedding band gold twinkling even in our room's blackness—between my knees, before her lids open. "Hey."

"Where you been?" she slurs.

"Remi's."

"Oh." Tarsha rubs her face and I smell cleaning fumes hovering around us. Soon as her hand drops to her chest, her eyes fix in the corner near the bedroom door. Thoughts run across the bridge of her nose. "Called over there."

"I know." She scoots closer so her thigh warms the edge of my hand.

"You were there?"

"Went up to Seventy-fifth Street for a minute." I hear myself in bass tone now, squeezed through biting teeth. "The lounge."

"Mmh." Tarsha scoots away and drops back to her pillow, fixing on the clock. "You check on the baby? I hear her."

"Bout to," I say, though the nursery is quiet. I walk to our door, watching the bed until these lids close over the angel's dream stare.

I DO HEAR the child stirring as I walk the short hall to her nursery. Ten months ago, the apartment's second bedroom was my office space. Then this baby child rose from the womb of a woman I love because of the smile she once shined for the both of us.

Her stub arms stretch far as they can inside the crib, batting from within the sleepers to free herself from linen smothering her head. She wrestles, then kicks out until the covers fall empty at the crib's opposite end. She hums a relieved breath, the clean lines of her forehead wrinkling as lids press over her eyes. In her darkness, she pretends to swim inside her mother's fading wet place still. I reach down to stroke her stomach as I stroked Tarsha's swollen belly when the seed rested inside that lake. I pretend that I'm soothing her as powerfully as I soothed the both of them back then.

Dawn's head lifts much as the trunk of her neck will allow, the eyelids stay pressed, and she burps or hiccups, or whines. Not sure which. Tarsha would know the difference, but in my ears the sounds are all the same. I'll call it a burp, as at least if she releases such useless air, then I am bringing her some relief. I lift Dawn from the crib to feel her squirm against my neck and shoulders. I touch the point where the infant neck meets her spine, though the joint grew strong enough to support itself months ago, and I bend the small of my back to fake a rocking motion. The arms and legs rub against me as her squirm cools and I walk to the window chair where Tarsha holds Dawn and brings her as close to peace as she can.

Together we rock and I look through the apartment window, just four stories above South Shore Drive. Nothing rages toward us in this glass: no freedom or truth or fire, no man-made blankets suffocating breath, no leaping, bloodless souls soon to be obliterated or siren-less Crown Victorias. I watch lights flicker red to green on the Drive, signaling commuters who are nowhere near just yet, and I yawn. Dawn's limbs aren't fighting anymore, for she's found peace in my left hand rubbing at her back.

Lake wind blows through the cheap windowpane, and I stand to grab her cover. She kicks my gut to remind me of her emancipating struggle against goddamned cotton. I lean into the chair's wicker instead and scoot her close, hoping that the flow of shared blood is enough to protect her warmth. Black turns to blue over the Drive, and I watch the child's eyes blink open for less than a second. Long enough to see, maybe— hopefully—see me, the source of this temporary soothing. Her lips spread like her mother's. She does feel me, and maybe she knows that I'm never going anywhere, and this knowing brings a smile not quite as thick as Tarsha's just yet. Just enough that I can peek into a toothless hole.

"I'm just as warm as water in the womb, ain't I?" I whisper. Four stories underneath us on South Shore Drive, lights blink signals to the long gone and the lake breeze cools the Corners' darkness.

Dawn blinks again, and I catch light dancing about her eyes. This smart, shiny two-step jigs, and the warmth that I mean to bring gushes up through my chest, and I do feel so good and nurturing again. I start to say what I don't need to say to the child, as she won't understand me anyway.

"I love—" I stop myself to shield her from the blues in the nursery room window, and I wait for the child to smile again.

3

I SET UP job interviews for Tuesday and Friday mornings, never earlier than 10:00 A.M., never later than noon. By eight, Tarsha has cleared all the way out of our apartment, leaving plenty time for me to sheen my bend-down-even-if-it-means-I-bend-over act, the Jesus-fearing, shiny forehead, crimped-cotton look and overly willing words with the hat-in-hand. In these months, I've interviewed in banking, marketing, computer programming, retail management. Pandered after all those bosses without hesitation. "Explored"—I like that word much better than "pandered," for *exploration* seems the act of a man:

"Surely, I am bending and scraping away for your grace, boss, but may I at least explore servitude's various forms? And calling you boss is presumptuous, I know, but the word makes me feel as if I have a place in this world, so please let it ride. Please? Boss? This way, I will at least feel like a man who serves you with honor."

By now I've written an interview script for even the lowest fields. Tarsha's cousin arranged a Public Aid case manager interview in February, back when both car payments lagged two months late. I told that boss how my life's mission was placing all of my skill and education to use in the empowerment of the poor and less fortunate of our community, investing the fruits of my background toward feeding the people rather than growing my own profit. Made a choice, the script went—writing itself by then—to leave the private sector, such that I could bring change to the state of the poverty-stricken horde. *Choice* was script, but that other clever word, *folks*, I've gotta claim that as my on-time ad-lib. Born in the moment because that boss cat seemed a "folksy," down South kind. Told him I hoped to better circumstances for folks from places like South Shore (my home, where my wife's car was two seconds from repossession, but somebody else stood in desperate need of my saving). Those not "blessed" as I, such as my blood cousins and the bloody corner souls who make their way hustling and stealing and pimping and peddling to hypes. Types whose pandering lives I aimed to uplift by passing out welfare checks and soothing fears of surviving thirty days on $560 and a Link card.

Worked like Hollywood—folksy boss cat called the next morning, begging me to bring myself down to the welfare office that very day and begin the saving. "You're just the type of brother we need in this line," he said. But Boss called before 9:30 A.M. and offered $26,500 plus benefits to save them. I told him I had to talk to my wife about his glorious opportunity, and I hung up, laughing as I dropped back to the pillow.

It's just about summer now, and I'm still searching, for the phone bill is a month past due and, after covering our car notes through May, the only somebody willing to extend another juiced-up loan is Lonnie Fairmont's nephew Primo the Shark from 51st Street. Still searching, but only on Tuesday and Friday between 10:00 and noon. Tuesday is $2 for a plate of hot buffalo wings at the Soft Steppin Lounge on 75th Street, Friday is free tequila shots, and noon gives me plenty time to ride out to the northern end of the Corners and catch a seat at the bar.

*   *   *

I'm due at Pharaoh Pugh Insurance Co. at 10:30—that company the cable guide channel advertises with the aqua banner flashing above programming scrolls. White boys in my West Grand Avenue tower would stand in their center hallway circle, guffawing amongst themselves about such crooked operations. How Global Mutual Insurance regularly sold its high-risk policies gone soft to such incorporated ghetto crooks, because Pharaoh Pugh kept piles of hard cash ready to dole out on deadweight policies. These companies' profits had piled on a fail-safe hustle: Illinois law forced bums and foreigners and jigs to sign up for auto insurance coverage if they want to drive, then lawmakers encouraged insurers in tall towers to jack their premiums to the clouds to keep such types far from Grand Avenue. Far away and outside circles where hushed slurs echo under ear-stabbing laughter.

Guffaw circle cats whisper on the source of their knowledge. How most of them made their bones toiling at this sort of crooked outfit out of college, back when the state still forced big-time companies to take on as many colored folk as would fit in the tower in its effort to diversify operations. Back then, the career choice for such quarter-wit, directional schoolboys came down to Cermak Road crookedness or daddy's plaza hardware store—or so they quietly swore between laughs.

I've been on interviews at three other low-tier insurers over these months, but no matter my experience at GMIC, I've received not one callback. While he was on probation last summer, Remi worked for such a company way out in the Hundredths blocks. Cousin claimed crooks with legit storefronts don't care for you to come walking into their doors looking like what you think they want you to be—no, crooks prefer seeing you as what they already know you are.

So I grasp the business this morning. My blazer is tweed, not wool, and the gray of my creaseless pants doesn't match another stitch of my clothing; the wrinkles at my shirt collar gather to choke; I've let my hair grow out to show black bullet points around dull-rounded ears; ash rests in the stretch between my right thumb and fourth finger for the introduction handshake; and my shoes aren't nearly shined.

I see Pharaoh Pugh's offices from the El train's windows—not even downtown just yet, but in the shadows tilting south on Cermak between Chinatown and the Ickey Projects, and I imagine that the boss's name is Leezza, one of these sort of Afro-American women the low-down insurance-scam sharks love to stick in the office's forefront. She will size me up as I shuffle into her lair and slouch into the harsh chair before her throne—no approval will show in her tree bark brown eyes. Instead she will pity my tweed with the seams pulling free at joint-bending points. She'll bite thin lips, suck away at the tickle my wrinkles bring. When I reach to shake her hand and the pinky finger of her left barely touches my ashy web, she'll turn to the window at her back, fixing on the parking lot to spew the snicker she's no longer able to hold. Her disgust will reflect back at me though, back and through me—and it is good that Boss Leezza sees what kind of fool I am. Squirming her thin, painted-pretty brown ass in the right-hand throne of some bloody crook's kingdom. Laughing at me so I'll remember that although Pharaoh needs me to keep him riding on top of his camel—hump full of stolen gold and silver pieces and greenbacks—I will always remain full of just shit, foul air, and useless thought, to them.

The Pugh Company couldn't hire my mother, or Tarsha, or even one of the Cottage Grove skeezes in Leezza's position. Such dark women cry, not laugh, at nappy-headed panderers in tweed getups. They feel me so deep that they must help me sneak inside the company where, on their watch, I'll grow comfortable. Then they'll sense when I've replaced tweed uselessness with the textile of a comfortable, swaggering, corporate buck in the field—likely after cashing two months' worth of steady income. My mother and Tarsha or the bus-stop skeezes would appreciate my comfort so strong that they'd stand me straight, grab me at the hand, and together, at the right hand of Pharaoh's might, we would conjure schemes to tumble him from the throne. Pharaoh can't have our shenanigans—such conspiracy will end this fake Egyptian bullshit, and then what?

So my mother stays lit on the factory floor, and Tarsha takes dictations on top of the boss's desk, and skeezes stand on these Cottage Grove corners, the bright of their eyes bested only by the gap between fresh thighs, and Leezza judges here in the glass reflection two hours early, sitting upon this petty, pink throne. She can't look me in the eye for the guffaw brought by my uselessness. And me, I've got no cause to be angry. We're just filling these roles to make the scamming machine go so Pharaoh stays the king of this Egypt.

*   *   *

THOSE EGYPTIANS WERE some bad mamma-jammas. That's who we're all aiming to be over here in the Four Corners, on the whole South Side—probably over West, too— those old-school Egyptians from the beginning. Not "bad" in that sneaky, plotting to get down and dirty, invading and pillaging and slinking to the back room to truly jam your mamma kind of way. No, those Egyptians were admirably *bad*. The kind of folk that keep Naperville mothers pinned to the window, begging good God for the return of their eldest daughters from the dark city orgy. Only to find that when the virgin does return to Naperville, she stinks of Madison Avenue frankincense and myrrh.

I took a course on Egypt during my junior year at Southern Illinois—the school's mascot was the saluki, dog breed of the kings, and they wanted us to know our heritage. A brother taught the course, one of these dread-head hanging down to his ass, tie-dyed-shirt-wearing cats; as righteous Black knowledge comes all twisted and phony-colored these days.

Tie-dye knew the true word on the Egyptians, though— lectured about how their badasses not only fixed the pyramids, defining physics then confounding gravity, but how they built that beautiful desert cat, the Sphinx, too. Black cat so fine it drove Caesar, or Napoleon, mad at first sight. One of those killer kings put his cannon on the lovely lady's head and blasted her nose right off from her face.

Let tie-dye tell it, the Egyptians conquered the Jews and kept them enslaved so many hundreds of years in that desert sun that the Jew god gave Moses all of His sea-splitting, shrub-burning power just to free them from captivity. Then He promised the Jews Jesus as payback for centuries of suffering. And when they rejected His son, that God cursed His people as payback for the insult. He let the Romans and Turks and Europeans and every other empire lay waste to His people, scatter them about the globe's left curve. So the Inquisitions and Holocaust and pogroms and Hollywood, none of that would've been not for the bad-ass Egyptians in the beginning, not according to tie-dye. I doubt he was supposed to be teaching it to us like so, but he had the knowledge of Egypt behind him. What could some fake salukis do about him?

Tie-dye taught that saluki course so righteous that for a minute, I forgot all about wanting to be an insurance broker. Fuck that, what I truly wanted to be in life was an Egyptian. Had my mind all changed, until tie-dye got to that part about Napoleon, or Caesar, raping all that Egyptian land, and the pillaging of desert women—Cleopatra first—and the children, too, and penetrating the Egypt man's ass not because they wanted to but for the sake of the conquering pain. How the empires battered them bad-assed folk until the Egyptians taught them about true mamma-jamming: how to enslave souls and scare God into Christ-bearing action, and blast breathing holes off glorious cats, and fix upside-down buildings such that they'd never fall, and eighty-three-story towers over sewage green rivers such that they would.

At the end of the semester's final session, tie-dye smiled this twisted off-yellow smile as if he'd proven some kind of circular point, and I ran off to my business class, Contracts 313, escaping Egypt land for good.

❈   ❈   ❈

ALVIN THE BARTENDER serves wings on a plate that sizzles as he drops the order against the Soft Steppin's bar. He wears two mitts on the right hand to carry the wings, and if that plus the wafting sizzle ain't enough to let his customers know, he does warn of the coming burn. Depending on how much money one's spent on his top-shelf liquors, that is. The empty-pocketed fools, Alvin leaves us to our own scalding lesson.

I need proper cholesterol before I deliver this sad script I've written to my wife—the peacekeeping tale, or the maintaining coping indifference one, at least. The El train reflection lied to me this morning. Pharaoh Pugh's boss's real name was Mr. Ramsey, and he didn't even bother with any demeaning comedy. Just rolled proper consonants once my begging ended, then chanted his flat, melody-less tune about the secretary calling soon. A callback definitely won't happen now, seeing as I suspect the mocking Boss Leezza reflected in the train window was actually the boss man's secretary.

My glance switches between the bar's whiskey-smeared wood and the swirl of rum in my glass as heels sound at my back. I look into Alvin's security mirror as Roy-Roy Murphy's shiny forehead dips from the corner peppermint light. He walks on cowboy boots, his left side swaggering low with each step while the right stays even with the neck as if one heel is taller than the other. In the window opposite the lounge's far corner, I catch the headlights of his white Bronco resting with driver side titled to street pavement and the passenger lights raised upon the 75th Street curb.

THIS IS THE same Roy-Roy who brings his downtown people to the neighborhood every Saturday night. They sit over in the Soft Steppin Lounge's far corner booth where years back, Blindman Willie Coles scribbled blues riffs on brown napkins. Now in these hip-hopping/fake R & B days, King Lonnie Fairmont collects profits from his street hustles and talks his way between thick thighs from that booth. From this blind king's peppermint-lit corner, nine in the eve until at least eleven, Roy-Roy and his downtown folk gawk at us, Roy-Roy's eyes widest of all, as if he's never come across anything of this sort in his life. No matter this is what born him.

Roy-Roy grew up just around the block on 74th Street. Our mothers used to get blasted together in this Soft Steppin Lounge. Old Four Corner honeys showed up here to sip and step and frolic giddy about smoky walls after cashing their checks on the month's first Friday. Only difference between Roy-Roy's mother and mine was that she raised up her son to be one of these curly-haired, shiny foreheaded church boys. Mrs. Murphy's favorite hangout after getting funky at the corner lounge was Mount Zion African Methodist on 78th. Come

Sunday, you'd find her and her church boy Elroy at Mount Zion sipping the wine of Jesus until the both of them were blessed plenty good.

Roy-Roy works for a company down in the Loop now—a *multinational corporation* is how he likes to refer to it. With offices in London, Paris, and New York, to go along with the one in the red building on Van Buren and Wabash just before the El tracks. They're supposed to be top-dollar consultants, Roy-Roy and these downtown folk. Software, information technology, some such jive. But I figure Roy-Roy is really no more than a data processor who spends his workaday life inputting digits into a computer mainframe, pressing buttons just right to keep the machine turning its blue wheels. One of these cats keeping the head held high while getting by. He never earned a degree from a real college—Roy-Roy went and got himself a computer certificate from one of those technical institutes advertised on the cable TV station. Fake schools full of ashy automatons who woke up one morning after staying out all night, stirred by that bit about the future requiring mechanical answers to scripted questions.

ELROY MURPHY GROANS and climbs onto the stool at my left and points at Alvin without greeting him. If the bartender minds, he doesn't show it. "Jack Daniel's," Roy-Roy says, "make it chilly."

I bite into a lukewarm wing, watching his curled hair waves breathe mist thick as the menthol smoke that rises around us. "What's up, Roy-Roy?" I ask.

He points at me now with no peppermint smile or half-assed nod. "Tommie." The data consultant sips his whiskey without paying.

"Catch the game last night?"

Roy blows on the Jack Daniel's surface—I don't know if he's cooling liquor or amusing himself with the brown waves his breath makes. "Which game?"

"I don't know," I say, "who was on yesterday? Sox?"

He growls and sips. "Hate baseball. Damn nonsense sport."

"Use to play in the park all the time over on Jeffrey. What're you talking bout?" I point at Alvin. Only after I've caught his attention do I hope that my gesture isn't as sharp and cold as Roy-Roy's. "Let me get a Heineken."

"We was kids." Roy-Roy glances over his shoulder as this chocolate-skinned woman with hair dyed red takes a stool at the bar. "I don't watch baseball."

"Neither do I."

Roy-Roy laughs as he watches the woman. "So what you ask about the game for?"

"Thought you was a fan," I say. "Seem like the baseball type. Just making conversation, besides."

"Then talk about some real shit."

"All right." I pretend to fix on a lady in a gray dress with the hem at her ankles. I watch her walk near. But for Roy-Roy I watch, not for her or myself. "How's the wife?"

"Fine." Roy clears his throat until this wet gurgle is gone.

"Good. Your boy?"

He shakes his head. "We've got a girl. You know that." His whiskey glass is near empty.

"My fault. How's your little girl then?"

Roy-Roy points with a twenty-dollar bill between his middle and fourth finger now and the bartender's head shines above eyes free of disgust. "Another whiskey. You want something, Tommie?"

"No." I turn him down no matter the dust coating my tongue begging for something stronger than German swig. Offering is just Elroy's way of bribing me to shut up—I used to do the same while working in the tower, once the Grand Avenue beggars started pulling at my suit jacket. Their ashy lips flapped after loose change, and I'd pay as much as I could spare, long as they promised to give me peace. But this bum's silence won't be bought so easily by slick Roy-Roy. "I'm straight."

He holds the quiet—silent but for the screeching and hoofing over our shoulder—holds it long as possible, and I watch disappointment frown across my mouth in Alvin's mirror.

"Asked about your daughter."

"Oh, didn't hear you," Roy says. "She's fine."

"Damn." I wipe buffalo sauce from my mouth. "Family ain't nothing worth talking about neither? You ain't shit, Roy-Roy."

"What?" Alvin delivers the Jack Daniel's and my beer and we both pay him quick this time. Roy groans. "My bad."

"What you sit down here for if you ain't have nothing to say? Plenty tables in the corner, gawddamnit."

"First open chair I got to."

I puff saucy air against my top lip. "Had a rough one today?"

He glances this way without answering. "Are you working yet?"

"Kinda thing is that to ask?" I say, and I laugh to hide my stutter.

"Fools who got jobs usually don't spit empty questions on the table." He tosses a dollar-bill tip to the bar without looking at Alvin, waits for me to do the same. My eyes dart to the bar's far end instead. "Niggas forget the nature when they ain't doing shit. Woke up at six this morning, Tommie—that was thirty minutes late, okay? Just time enough to wipe the crack of my ass with a face towel, rub Q-tips in the corners of my eye and suck on a Altoid before racing myself to Bedford Park."

"Thought you were downtown?"

"Not since they bought this new site." Roy-Roy blows the drink's surface, then swirls floating ice cubes with his fingertip. "You know where Bedford Park is? Neither did I, till the man told me that's where I had to go. Spent ten hours of the day in front of a white-and-green screen, reading numbers that didn't add up to no kind of sense except for in the wallet of some joker in Delaware, out there where the only thing near black as me is midnight shining against a horse's ass on the riding trail. Numbers get to dancing across that monitor by two o'clock, get to turning blue in my eyes. But they still don't add up. And the man tells me I best come up with something to say to him and his people by the end of the day to make it sound like there's rhythm to the dance. That it ain't even no dance at all, but a march, and I know exactly where those digits are headed— straight to the Dover ass riding trail."

"This's how you like to make cordial conversation, talking this kinda shit?" I bite the wing bone and sip Heineken. "De-pressing, chief."

"Musta forgot, Tommie, all this free time on your hands. Ain't been no change out here. Shoulda known. I'm the one asking fool questions? Rough one, you say? Today, this rough day, is just like every other rough day following and marching."

"And dancing. You sipped on a few before you got here?"

"No." He flicks the empty wrapping of a long vanished straw with his middle finger and smiles as paper bounces against the bar mirror. "You making fun of me?"

"You sound drunk."

"These are my first two." Roy hiccups before choking again. "Swear."

"What about Saturdays?" I ask. "Come in here with them folk from your gig. They're from your gig, right, the blond Suzy-Qs and all the rest? Looking happy as a fish in clean water entertaining them peoples. What kinda two-faced bullshit is that?"

"You forgot it all," he laughs. "Man gave me all this, built up this show in my honor. If I wanna keep playing his part, can't leave him out here suspecting he's supporting a skank ho who won't do for him back. He ain't gonna keep no skank ho on center stage, you know. Best way to let the man know you're his good boy is by cooing in his woman's ear—once she knows a Black man's love, then he knows you're his forever. Those Suzy-Q's are kinda hot, right?"

This approving smile spreads his lips again. "Little skinny from what I recall." I wouldn't recognize that this snickering sound comes from my own mouth not for the bar mirror reflection. "You're sick."

"The whole setup is sick. You know, too, Tommie. Wasn't you a philosophy major down in col-lege?"

Funny, this way folks who never finished degrees at a real school say "college"—slicing the throats of the words in the space between consonants. "Sociology."

"That's some sick shit, too, so you best know the deal."

"You got a ja-hb for me in Bedford Park or what?" Roy-Roy pays me no mind. I don't even think he heard me, for he's swerved the stool in a half-circle to face the 75th Street door.

"Ain't that your ol girl?" he asks.

I cough and grab the cushion tears. "Tarsha?"

"If I was talking about Tarsha, I woulda said 'ol lady.' 'Ol girl' is your mamma, 'ol lady' is Tarsha. Show some respect. Don't be falling off the turning earth just cause times is hard. It's all a revolving door, Mister Sociology Man."

I pay Elroy no more mind. I spin my own stool as my mother saunters onto the dance floor alone, pointing at familiar souls as she steps smooth and soft before settling in King Lonnie's empty peppermint-glowing booth. My mother points my way only as I walk to her corner, and her green smile shines brightest of all now and I feel better, I do, almost better.

"What are you doing here, Mamma?" I slide into the booth. "You know you don't need to be in no place like this—Tarsha sent you?"

"Mmh." She lights a Newport and drops the carton on the table. Once her hand is free, she scratches her forehead without puffing and embers barely miss her slicked-back hair strands. "Hey, Tommie, how are you this evening—thanks for asking about me. Such a rude nigga boy I raised up here."

"Come on, Mamma." I drop my hands under the table and leave them in my lap. "You want a Coke or something?"

"You know I can't drink that sugar bubble mess. Makes my sides hurt." The cocoa skin at her jaw pulls smoke into her mouth at the synthesized drum's time. "I tried, you know. Did the best I could."

"Lemonade, then? You want some juice? No bubbles." Newport smoke slips into my nose holes and my eyes swell and temples bang, begging for oxygen. "Where's Dawn? You said you'd watch the baby for me today."

"Outside in the car."

When I was a boy, this knot would grow in my belly and twist into coils the longer I paid mind to my mother. By the time I hit sixteen, the coils'd spread up to my chest and lungs, tangling my heart until inspiration came to me: the only way I could save myself before my spine, brain, and balls knotted up like hers was if I took the fool woman by the neck and squeezed two fisted at her throat. Not all the way, never all the way, just until I'd choked all the stupidity and waste from her.

Been fifteen years since that inspiration sprouted, yet I haven't brought myself to healing action yet; she raised me to love and respect her especially when she is wrong. Besides, I barely notice the twisting of muscle and vein these days. "You left her out there by herself?" I grab my right kidney. "What the fuck?"

"I ain't crazy, nigga. Only came in here for a minute." My mother's eyes skip across the lounge. "Wallace is in the car."

"Don't know no Wallace. Where'd you park?" I push myself halfway from the booth.

"Just down the way. On Euclid."

"Who the fuck is Wallace?"

"Stop acting crude." Her cheeks pucker. "The gentleman who spent Thanksgiving with us, you remember."

I don't bother asking why this Wallace clown is a "gentleman" where I am a crude "nigga" twice over. No need, for I know the proper answer. "Who is Wallace?"

"Dawn's just fine, Tommie. Don't be rude. Get me one of them juices while I go to the bathroom." She walks past the bar and disappears inside the toilet hall, and I order her drink.

If she'd processed my hair so I could slick it back from the forehead and borne me without this wolf's tail dangling between my thighs, I'd be Doreen Simms' twin sister. Even I see it. The same peanut head shelled in brown skin spotted around the lips and the eyes. The body spilling over the sides without falling to the ground, supported by a pouched belly that leaves her waist unseen. Chicken legs, long and bowed to give her solid height though the rest of her seems meant for a short woman. These are all mine. Everything except that ass jutting behind to balance the belly and hide the waist from the backside, too, swinging bar to door as she steps smooth and soft to the ladies room—though, no, I don't see my mother's behind, nor the wannabe Soft Steppin players watching its sway.

Seeing so much of myself in the old girl choked at my throat when I was a boy. Choking fool faith from me while I'd listen to my factory-floor uncles' moans from her bedroom come Saturday nights. Yet there was no fighting truth—I've been a cartoon of my mother since seven years old. Everybody saw it clear and said so. One of those uncles claimed my mother spelled Tommie with an "ie" instead of a man's "y" because she knew how woman-ie (that fake uncle's word for me) I'd end up soon as I popped outta her.

The Ford plant started making my mother go to meetings when I was in junior high. I had no clue why then—all I knew was Ford put her on the midday short shift, and she'd come home, run and sit in the bathroom for a half hour, then run right back out the apartment door. Meetings started by six every evening, and she couldn't be late. She carried a slip of paper she'd never let me see good as she walked through our door. Around nine, she'd come back home smoking on her Newports with that same paper tucked in a battered blue book the size of the mass Bibles at Queen of Ascension. A few days after I turned eleven, she tried running to the ladies' room then leaving me lonely, but I grabbed her right arm and wouldn't let go. The old girl had no choice but to take me where she was going.

So she walked me shamefaced into this blazing white room way in Uptown, full of skinless, empty-eyed folk gathered in a too-neat circle and talking about burning desires and reflections and a good and favorable Lord, Jesus and Savior. Blessed full of gratitude, all of them claimed they were. Even my mother, once her stare emptied out as she sat in the circle's first curve, she was there among the gracious blessed. Maybe I went as blank as that while sitting with them, too—no mirrors hung in the white room for me to see. None except the old girl's face dotted with eyes deep and empty. They talked about how today was a new and better day and everything was okay in it. I heard that word, *today*, plenty—and *bless-ed* even more— counted one spoken for every minute we sat with the fiends.

She was on circle Step Five that evening, "admitting to God, to yourself, and to another human being the nature of your wrongs."

And on the way home, she did fess up, said her foreman'd caught her sipping Boone's Farm on the plant floor six months before, caught her more than once, actually. "Just trying to make it through my shift was all," she said. Ford forced her go to the group meetings simply because her foreman'd pressed the issue after she wouldn't give him no ass right there next to the press machine. My mother wasn't really one of those Uptown circle fiends then, hell, no matter what the factory said. Just rolling with the assembly line to keep her job, and trying to avoid fucking that rat bastard all the while. She swore it to me from the Lincoln's driver seat, and I did believe in her no matter what.

One of my uncles from the plant come telling me later that the old girl'd gotten caught doing a little more than sipping from a flask. Said she was smoking that base, too. Figure she'd stopped giving it up to him—punk nigga, should've whipped him right on the spot for lying on the old girl like so. No matter, she isn't tricking off these days, not now—the old girl hasn't been to an Uptown circle fiend meeting since I finished high school.

I started making peace with truth at nineteen years old, just about the same age as she was when she gave me birth. By then, I counted myself among the lucky to know my true root—half of it at least—felt it *blessing* me with this powerful edge on most souls around these Corners. The fact that the two of us were spitting images didn't have to mean that I looked like a Four-Cornered South Shore honey. The woman's lived this dirty down life of hers, and the world's beat her cold and hard just like it does my factory-floor uncles. So it's not me but her who the world has flipped all upside down.

"HOW'D YOUR interview go? Did good, right?" She sags against the booth's back cushions.

"You wash your hands? Damn." Alvin's waitress drops the lemonade glass in the middle of the table. I toss the five onto her tray. "Waiting on my change."

"When'd you get like this?" My mother draws the glass near her chest.

"You're welcomed." I slip a Newport from her box and hold the stick to the ceiling light. "For the juice."

She blows at the dance floor and repeats, "How'd the job interview go?"

"Said they'd call me back."

"That's good, right?"

"Give me a light, Mother." She touches the tip of her fading square against mine until a line of smoke rises between us, floating in green mist.

She blows and makes her frustrated sound, this low hysteria trailing full of g's and u's—gu-gu-ug-gu—even her frustration choked. "A callback is a good thing, right?"

"Just waiting. When I hear something, then I'll know something."

"You best let me know then. Like I say, I can talk to the floor supervisor if this other don't work out." She holds the glass to her glossy lips, but lemonade swims at the rim without seeping through. Her eyes slide about the room before she drops the glass to our table. "Need to update this place. Shit, could be 1972 in here still, I swear. What's wrong with Alvin's cheap ass?"

"Need to make sure Dawn's all right. Shit ain't cool. What, Tarsha had you come up here to get me?"

Her eyes don't return to our booth. "Your wife'd have to send me some place to check on you? What're you trying to say? I can't keep up with my own boy?"

"You knew I was here? On your own?"

She points at me now. "Today is chicken Tuesday. Where else you gonna be? Work?"

"Buffalo wings, not chicken. Buffalo—" The waitress stops at my mother's shoulder, about to drop my three dollars and change next to the Newport box. "That's mines. And could you wrap that plate of wings, up next to that greasy-headed cat at the bar. Them's mines, too. Tell him he can have my beer. I paid for um already. Just give him a glass."

"Chicken's probably cold by now." The young waitress tries to sound accommodating, but the act doesn't work and her words sting.

"Buffalo wings, I said. Don't matter," I tell her, "we've got a microwave at home." I take my three singles, forget the five dimes on the platter and watch her leave.

"You're a mess," she says.

"You shouldn't even be in here, Mother. Ain't right. You know better." I crush my cigarette in the table ashtray, at the far end. I hate Newport's stinging smoke myself, but wasting this square means Doreen has less tar to singe her own lungs' lining. "Let's get Dawn. Can't believe you."

"Yes you can."

The plate of wings and a Styrofoam container replace the serving tray in the waitress's hand. She drops foam in my front and turns the platter upside down so that bones bounces inside. "These are yours, right?" She slides the rectangle toward my bill-gripping right hand and snaps Styrofoam closed.

My mother slips a dollar into the girl's apron. "We gotta do better," she says. "Let me know still, you want me to talk to my supervisor."

I laugh and grab my buffalo wings. "You ready?"

I walk to the lounge door, trying to remember which sucker played the moaning game with her so good last Thanksgiving night that she left my daughter's safety in his hands. I forget to point at Roy-Roy so he can thank me for the Heineken, but I do hold the door for my mother. As I say, she raised me to love and respect her especially when she is wrong.

"I did my best," she says and saunters past, lemonade and menthol wafting in her air. "Always, Tommie. I tried to."

✳ ✳ ✳

I DO REMEMBER this Wallace. Fat-headed bastard ate the last hot dog slice out of the old girl's holiday spaghetti sauce and shot soggy-eyed glances at Tarsha all Thanksgiving day. I haven't seen him since, figured he'd copped his dirty freebies plus a month or so of low-maintenance loving from the old girl and moved on to some other hustle.

But she's letting him drive the Continental now, as she

sits on the passenger side smoking on this same Newport. I lift Dawn from the car seat and rock her against my chest, and I watch the graying conk strands duck-tail at Wallace's neck just above the driver-side backrest. I'm trying to figure whether he's just another cat-daddy from the factory plant floor, or one of the circle-meeting hypes—like the seven-fingered one my mother brought home just before her Ford probation ended. That fiend laid up in her bedroom three full months, waiting for the winter freeze to pass, then bounced back to the streets.

This Wallace is clean though, and mostly clear-eyed—but Remi says the hustlers sell a better cut of dope on 71st Street these days what with the new townhomes springing out of the ground right by the train tracks. Dope so clean you really can't tell who's fiending and who's a square, not just by looking at them, these days.

I whisper in Dawn's ear, and I know that no one can hear me except my child with Luther Vandross' amplified moan shaking the mirror glass up front. "Geechy nigga knows better than to mess with my baby, ain't that right?" Dawn hiccups and I rock her faster.

The Lincoln cruises without shudder over these pavement holes, then turns smooth onto the north-south streets as steering wheel ridges slide through Wallace's loose fists. Dawn drifts off to humming sleep and my mother squashes her cigarette in the dashboard ashtray. I don't even hear the creek of the Continental's rotted catalytic converter from the trunk. Wallace catches my eye in the rearview, and I run from him, looking through the old girl's passenger window to watch these blocks fade.

I went to school right here at Ascending Queen Elementary on the corner of 76th and Jeffrey Boulevard. Gray stone cathedral still rises high out of the pavement to shadow the hoagie restaurants and wig shops and gym shoe joints all around. Stayed at the Queen until third grade at least, when one too many of my mother's checks bounced on the rectory floor, and the nuns busted into Ms. Chaney's art class to snatch me and three other delinquents at the shirt collar, dragged us from their holy finger-painting lesson and slung us on that corner where the Jeffrey bus stops to pick up midday souls. Luckily the old girl worked the 3–11 shift that week, otherwise I would've been on the 11:23 bus home with the other nappy heads. I always wondered whether she rode to the Boulevard to pick me up because the nuns had called her, or was it that she knew her bank account was flooey when she signed that bottom line.

We drove over east to Adam Clayton Powell Public Elementary that morning, where Doreen dropped me with the Mexicans from South Chicago, the stink of dead fish on Lake Michigan's waves, and my cousin Remi. Got me good and registered before noon, just in time for recess, then she left me on 75th Street to finish school training.

There was a newsstand off the corner of 76th and Yates in front of the currency exchange. And that beauty shop next door used to be an Islamic bookstore, before they laid the cable TV wire under the Drive, when fools around here still read: *Ebony* and *Jet* and the *Defender* and *The Final Call,* at least, they read. All the newsstands and bookstores are gone around here now.

Me and Remi once tried to rob the old man who hawked his sheet rags from that corner. Would've got way with it, too, if the Muslims hadn't chased us down to 79th and Yates. The *Penthouse* with Vanessa Williams bare-assed and dyking in black and white had just come out, but we didn't have anywhere near four dollars between us. And we were too scared to mess with the big magazine rack farther east at Woolworths, and we knew the newsstand man was old and that his business barely survived from the Fruit of Islam sweating him to keep his line of gossip sheets and smack mags from sidetracking converts on the way to the Qu'ran.

Remi pulled his box cutter and hopped behind the stand, took that old man by the throat and told him he'd stab him through both gray ears if he peeped, while I snatched an *Essence* for my mother, *Globe* for Remi's old girl—if we got caught, at least we could say we took something for our mothers—and just one copy of Vanessa getting filthy. We ran east (though nobody chased just yet), because no matter how much the Muslims hated the old man's newsstand, those bow ties would be coming for our asses. FOI believed in sending crooked shorties to jail quick as possible, just to get us good and ready on the road to conversion.

We didn't even make it a half-block before the Fruit huffed at our backs, hollow heels clicking 79th Street. But we were twelve years old and full of stupid speed, so the Fruit didn't catch me until the funeral parlor parking lot on 79th. Knocked

my skull upside a hearse hood and took back auntie's *Essence*
and our *Penthouse,* left me with the *Globe* because I'd stuffed
that paper down into my drawers. Bow ties never did get Remi
though—Cousin knew all the corners and alleys cutting through
South Shore even back then.

I courted Tarsha on that porch in front of her granny
Allen's crib right on Oglesby. Brought Ding Dongs and cans of
sugar pop and chicken sandwiches from 79th Street in bags so
greasy that carrying them left puddles in my palm. Popped up
on that porch every summer break Saturday, ringing her door-
bell with a rusty elbow because both hands were so full and
slimy wet. Glee lit in Granny Allen's face when she answered,
first because a man stood on her porch with treats, then
brighter glee as she swirled thick chocolate and leaky cream
about her gums; she shined on as she scanned me up, down, all
around. Smelled me, too, the old woman did, before calling for
her granddaughter.

"This one of them good ones," Granny Allen'd say before
swigging grape pop fizz and closing the door behind, leaving us
on the porch. Before long, Tarsha's girl neighbors and boy
cousins would appear from all the look-alike houses on the avenue, run out to Granny's yard, where they'd skip about and
sing and throw and shine same as the grandmother shined. For
in their young, dumb eyes, too, I was one of the good ones.
And the two of us together were so good—"see how she smiles
at him, LaLa, see." Tarsha and me were queen and king, as-
cended to a porch that jutted out from just another bungalow,
above them all.

Tarsha and her people don't even look me in the eye much now, and I sure ain't one of the good ones. Just another no good, jobless bastard, another mark from another corner, standing with his shiftless boy cousins. Granny Allen's gone off to someplace where they don't sell greasy sandwiches on boulevard corners and folks call grape pop "soda." That's how Tarsha rationalized it when they found me wet-eyed in the corner of the old woman's wake service.

Her little neighbors from our courting block have all grown and moved away, except that there ain't nowhere outside this place for them to move—so, though they thought they'd grow and go, they all stayed in the Corners. They just don't skip or sing or throw anymore and there's no shine to their smiles, because we ain't queen and king, and there's no lives to begin. Just these houses of chipped brick where the souls stay to keep watch.

I swear that I caught a glimpse of another Century 21 sign on Granny's lawn. "They're selling Miss Allen's place?"

Wallace touches the dashboard to quiet Luther's moan just a bit. "What you say, Tommie?" he asks.

"I'm talking to my mother." Don't care how rude I sound now with our ride almost ended.

"She's asleep."

I hear her snore and watch her head bounce against the window glass, and I look at him in the rearview mirror. Here, it's the geechy's eyeballs running now, out to the braking taillights in our front.

I lift the baby and twist her at the waist. Her tiny eyelids don't even flutter.

"Wake up, Mamma."

"Said she's sleeping," Wallace snaps. "Had a long shift. Let her rest."

"What?" My voice sounds over the ditty's slow fade and the skin of Dawn's lids twitch but stay closed. I press my knee into the back of the passenger seat and the old girl's head rises from glass. "Wake up," I say again.

"What's wrong?" She yawns.

I rest Dawn against my left shoulder to support her with my strong hand. "We're almost home."

Wallace stops the car across the street from my building, taps worn brakes without squeaking the pads or jerking my baby at all. "Turn into the driveway, guy. Got my baby and the car seat with me."

He eases into the driveway stretch and the steering wheel glides through fingernails pointed like crowns. The conk's duck-tail raises from the backrest and Wallace looks into the rearview glass again only to shift the mantle and allow himself an angle on what approaches.

Doreen stretches, then rubs her eyes until she's clearheaded enough to light another Newport. For her, I say thanks to the driver and unstrap Dawn's car seat.

"Tell the wife we said hello," duck-tailed Wallace says, smacking gum I didn't know that he chewed while my mother blows smoke into the dashboard vents.

"Take care of yourself, old girl," I say and we climb from the Lincoln's rear, the belt from Dawn's car seat dragging against dirty Detroit carpet, then driveway asphalt.

I watch as Wallace reverses onto South Shore Drive without

checking over his shoulder. Then I walk toward our building lobby, strong hand pressing the child into my chest, while the weak drags a chair with a loose strap behind. In Dawn's ear, I repeat my spur-of-the-moment edit to my coping script, polishing its delivery for the child's mother. "It's gonna be all right, baby. Remember how we pretended we were king and queen of Egypt, sitting on your granny's front porch?"

4

BEEN STARING AT the telephone since Tuesday, reclined before Oprah and Jerry Springer and Rikki Lake. The world is halfway done turning now—so many hours spent fixed in this place that the lunatic noise of the nineteen-inch box still rings inside these ears.

The living room phone has rung twice since I reclined the waiting chair. The first was a saleswoman calling as Oprah soothed the tears of a woman with a face of sun-burnt cancer scars. Telemarketer Mandy offered a seven-day, six-night vacation package to one of these Mexican heavens, or to Hawaii. Or that wasn't what she sold at all maybe, just the sexy benefit of my enrollment in this layered pyramid scheme, or of my potential decision to purchase the newfangled products she hawked: digital camera, coffeemaker, CD burner, time share. Something for sale.

"I do appreciate your offer, Mandy. Sounds enticing. And you read so well. Impressive. I've looked at those digital picture-takers in the past. But I'm going to have to say 'no' at this time. Perhaps later, if you call again." Mandy speed-read the reluctant buyer lines, but I'd tired of her. "Times are hard, Mandy—I'm waiting for another call." Oprah and her singed patient reappeared on the screen, and I hung up on Mandy.

The next call was a collector for one of my defaulted Visa cards. Once the man—voice part Gestapo, part pea-cocked rapist cackle—once he announced who he represented, I dropped the receiver to my knee so that his threats on behalf of God, country, company, and fiduciary responsibility echoed off the joint. These credit card hawks have time, money, and rage to waste—but there is no need in hanging up on them. Hanging up only turns them hateful. I pretend to listen instead, because then the shakedown hawk thinks he's got me cornered and his bloody purposes are served such that he's forced to spare a bit of mercy. If he grants me more time, the hawk can always call to insult and abuse again, and that's all that he truly wants. Very worst thing I can do to his mad ass is pay my debt—and I want to hurt him so badly, but these pockets are full of only lint.

So I rest the cordless at my knee, avoid the hassle, and stave off the headache until I make out this new raging bit: "Global Mutual Incorporated at 312-583-0150 as reflected on our records," he says, "let your employer know what kind of a delinquent you are. Shall we—you don't want the boss to know what I know, do you?"

I lift the receiver from my knee, biting bottom lip as plastic touches my cheek. "It's Tuesday," I say, "ten-thirty in the morning. Why do you think I'm home; why do you think I'm always here when you call, muthafucka?"

I let go the laughter and press the phone's off button, for the shylock's shakedown man gave my question too much pause.

*   *   *

THESE DOTS IN my eyes turn purple and blue now. I want to nap, but I'll sleep too hard and miss the rest of the turning, maybe miss Pharaoh Pugh Inc.'s call. I tap my knuckles at the edge of the living room table where the phone base rests until my hand swells and I am fully awake.

The phone rings and my knee bounces from the chair upholstery, tumbling the remote to our dusty carpet. I forget the TV opera and grab the receiver.

"Cuz—" Remi yells through my ears as dragons roar from dungeons behind. "You ain't say nothing. You supposed to pick up the phone and say something. What up, chief? You busy?"

"No."

"Where you at?"

I choke on warm air. "Where'd you call?" The roar is quiet as I swallow. "I'm here. At home."

"Called your cell phone. You ain't pick up."

"It's off," I say, "been off weeks now. You know that—call the home phone first besides."

"Yeah. I forgot." He quiets the game. "What you on today?"

"No—" I bite my tongue, figure Tarsha might have arranged this call. "Waiting on this job."

"Oh—I'm interrupting your progress?"

The soap's commercial break ends. "We've still got call waiting. If I click over, and it's Pharaoh, I'll get back with you."

"You still waiting on them?" Remi hits the receiver against some hard plastic, maybe his computer table. Not sure if he does so on purpose, but the empty chime echoes inside my ear. "Thought you said that interview didn't go like you thought it would."

"It didn't," I say. I force my pinkie finger inside the ear hole.

"So what you waiting on?"

"Their phone call. So I know for sure."

The fingernail shows wax as Remi barely breathes into his end of the conversation. "You need to come by the house when you get time," he says finally.

"Your crib?" I laugh. "For what?"

"Got something for you—how long you gonna wait for them people?"

I choke. "Till they call, what else can I do?"

I miss the opera's teary resolution, tragic exposition, bloody closure, followed by another commercial break. I'm not sure what happened, really, just hear string music lingering through the dishwasher liquid advertisement.

"Need to come by," he repeats, "get on with this."

The Visa collector's spiel about shame bounces against my knee. "But my old girl—"

"What about her?" Remi says as my voice trails. "Auntie still trying to get you out at the plant? Ford Heights is the end of the world, you know that by now. Slow death in pink smoke for fools and machines. That's a square chump's life out there—it's your end."

"No, I know," I try again as my leg twitches. "But my mother—"

"No disrespect to auntie. She's gonna be shitty, no doubt.

Shamed for both us," Remi says. "Tarsha will be, too. But we gotta live, what else can a brother do out here?"

I try to breathe, but choke on the apartment's air. "You remember how I used to go to Uptown with her, to the meetings?"

"The fiends? Back when auntie was sipping that syrup," Remi hums. "Our old girls were wild, Cuz, that's how they do round here. You're just lucky you found you one with some sense to marry off Oglesby Avenue. No disrespect to auntie— what's that got to do with this? Your old girl was a lush off wine, just like mine. So? If we all used strung-out family and lushes as excuses to stay away from making our way, then somebody else'd be left with the hustle, putting this paper in their pockets. You ain't talking sense to me—ain't nothing but a few bags."

"I'm talking plenty sense, you're not listening," I snap without meaning to, and shame jumps from my knee to the middle of my throat. I swallow. "Figure this gig's in the bag, Cuz, that's all. That's why I'm sitting here waiting."

Laughter sprays his end of the conversation. "Been a week, nigga. You already said the interview didn't go good."

"I know." I rub my forehead though it does not hurt. "Got a feeling, that's all."

He puffs air to end his laughter. "What kind of fool-ass feeling?" Then, he whispers, "Best stop that feeling shit. Got something coming in tonight."

The babble box offers laundry detergent for sale—Tide or Cheer, one of them, colors flash by on the screen so fast that it's hard to take in the cleansing magic—followed by Metamucil. The phone's call-waiting alert sounds. "Hold on."

As soon as hello slips through my lips, the second line disconnects. Tarsha calling, or my mother maybe, checking what I'm doing with time. The two of them take turns phoning around the end of *As the World Turns,* out of concern or curiosity or disgust, one or all. They used to force circles of noisy breathing and nothing-saying conversations October to just after the holidays. Whether they're protecting my pride now, or if they figure I've got their round-and-round pattern down pat, or if they have nothing to say so long as they know that I'm still here breathing and reclining in front of the box, I'm not really sure.

I switch back to my cousin. "Gotta go, Rem, it's them."

"Oh yeah?" More breathing fills his pause. "You were right? About Pharaoh—"

"Told you, nigga," I say.

"Handle your business," Remi says. I see his smile forced across stretched brown skin. "One love."

"I'll let you know," I tell him and press the off button before promising, "I will."

I sag deep into the reclining chair and drop the cordless at my knee again. Scoot up just so to catch the very end of my opera. Once this tale ends, I shut the television off and listen as threats and lies and string music fade against the apartment walls. It's almost time to pick up Dawn from my mother's, and I don't care for the story that ends Channel 2's daytime hours at all. The show's actors are no worse and their tales no more simple than the rest. It's the soap's cockamamie name that puts me off. *The Guiding Light,* they call it, without explaining how the hell Channel 2 knows what we're looking for.

* * *

"TOMMIE . . ."

Tarsha's hands press into my back so hard that I'd tumble from the bed not for grabbing our mattress's corner. She surprises me this morning—she hates for my eyes to follow her about the room as she gets ready for work. My crusty-eyed watch, she says, reminds her too much of our condition, festering in yellow behind glaring black dots.

I press the lids into my face and scoot myself to our bed's center.

"You're awake, Tommie?"

She pushes me twice, then not at all. I miss her touch. "What's wrong, Tarsha? You need a ride to work?"

"I knew you was awake."

"Now—yeah," I say. "Turn off the alarm. Damn."

The room is quiet, except for her huffing and the bounce of hot air against my top lip. "You've got an interview this morning."

I blink, can't figure her words for question or reminder. I turn to lie on my back and light fills the room, so I answer. "No, I don't."

"Time to get up."

This light gleams to bring sweat, even through shuttered lids. I squeeze them tighter. "Yeah." I swallow. "How come you was pushing on me?"

I feel her legs swing from the bed. I peek, and she sits at the edge, swaying. "I'm tired," she says.

Air slips inside my mouth to join the funk between jaws. "You've got a few minutes, baby. Come back to bed."

"I'm tired," she repeats. Tarsha's weight leaves and the mattress floats higher, though I know better than to watch her walk from the bed.

"It ain't too late," I say, words stinking worse than breath. She shuts the bathroom door as brush bristles scrub against her teeth and water splashes in the porcelain sink.

I watch four minutes blink by on the nightstand clock and shower water rains barely long enough for Tarsha to lift the nightgown from her body. The toilet flushes and she cracks the bathroom door—I lie on my right side and glance through eyelids barely open. But I see only her shadow in the bathroom's soft light.

"Why'd you wake me, Tarsha?"

"I need to get in there early this morning," she says. "Remember, the baby's got an appointment at the doctor at one o'clock."

"I know. Mamma's taking her." I yawn.

"Oh," Tarsha speaks so low, the sound don't echo, "your mother. What're you doing?"

"Not sure. Maybe go by Remi's." My lids open wide to allow full sight. "Why'd you wake me up?"

"I didn't. You were awake already."

"Really—"

"Weren't you?"

"No." I turn away to watch a spider spin from the ceiling light dome. "Not really."

"I thought you had an interview."

"No—today's Wednesday."

I glance over my shoulder as Tarsha slides herself into nylon pantyhose, golden to match her skin. "It's getting hard, Tommie."

Breathing hums low from my throat. "I know, baby. I'm trying."

"At your cousin's place?"

I laugh. Her words aren't funny, at all, but I laugh. "I've got business over there."

Tarsha laughs back, same tone and pitch as mine. "Ain't nothing but crooked trouble and waste at Remi's."

"Sound like your grandmother," I say. No laughter now.

"I know times is shitty." Tarsha's voice isn't loud or angry at all. Her mouth just moves to connects dots with black lines. "Back around Christmas, you still tried, I know. I remember the blink in your eyes and your teeth and your collar as you went out to interviews. In that ice. You tried hard then. Just didn't work out with them people. Market is wrecked all around, ain't no use for us to pretend any other way. But you gotta try, keep that crisp in you, else what do we got? It's too hard on your own."

"*Crisp.*" I laugh now. "Keep hope alive."

"Ain't joking. It's getting hard."

"I'm still here, and I am trying." I sit at my edge of the bed, palms to the mattress like I'm going to push myself to foot— but I'm not going anywhere. "Hard thing, hearing 'no' from every which way. How long's that supposed to keep going?"

"Not for me to call, or you. Just gotta keep—"

"Said I am. Said it *crisp.*"

Tarsha's fully done up in her gray suit, tailored close to her frame. "What's at Remi's place?"

"Trouble, waste, and crooks. You know, that's your boy, the nigga you call begging for help. You hit it on the knob. You don't hear me arguing with you."

Tarsha walks to the dresser mirror and watches herself, or me maybe, in the corners of the glass. "So how are you trying over there?"

"Either it's Remi's place or my mother's factory." I prop one leg on the bed to turn myself halfway toward Tarsha. "You know me: better to dirty myself than to go get myself dirty."

"What's the difference?" She glides gloss, all wet and shiny, on her lips. "I've never known my husband to be dirty either way. Those are cop-outs, Tommie."

"That's my choice now, only one," I say. "All that your shitty market's left me with. These are the breaks."

"Can't stay dirty long," she warns.

"I know. I won't. I can't. Promise."

"You don't bother talking to anybody before making these decisions?"

"Tried," I lie, because before her palms pressed and the alarm stabbed twelve minutes ago, I hadn't made any kind of decision at all. This decision has been made for me now. If the unexplained touch at my back wasn't enough, then those words, "cop-out"—two curse words—sure as death called it out for me.

"All you act like you really want to know is where I've got an interview lined up. Only interview I've got coming is on

Seventy-eighth Street this Wednesday morning. So I'm telling you now."

"Gotta keep trying for us, Tommie." She lifts a perfume bottle to her nose.

"What do you want me to do?" My wife sprays herself with budding garden scent and turns from the mirror to watch me as I spread myself on pillows. I see the yellow of her eyes beaming this condition, her concoctions, and some kind of conspiracies in the mist of her fragrance such that it all glows together in nightstand lamp red. The apartment is silent until our daughter screams from my office and Tarsha walks to the bedroom door.

"Ain't nothing I do right by you no way."

She disappears into the hallway to tend to the child, and I press my eyelids closed to hide from the nightstand's light. It doesn't work though. Darkness is dotted by the clock's red blink.

5

WESTSIDE FIDGETS AS Remi counts and separates green-brown leaves. His eyes dart into the kitchen's corners to chase the mice that slide beneath their Yugoslavian landlord's old appliances. Once the mice disappear into their holes, Jackie's watch darts overhead to this dangling ceiling fan and gray light fixture, as their kitchen isn't just haunted and rodent infested, it's filled with high-flying fleas.

Jackie swings at the beasts, arms springing from his body to trail after his eye, fingers spreading at his palm, grasping to trap what haunts him against his sweaty skin. Remi says that I shouldn't take his brother's jitters seriously, swears Jackie gets like this whenever he's too close to the product. Says that Westside's smoked so much weed over the years that his brain sets off nervous charges once his nose hairs ruffle with the sweet high stink.

But I can't help but take Jackie's spasms to heart as he's put those wild eyes on me from the table's stove side, and his pupils spin about holes. Turning me around and upside down inside this jaundiced stare before his arms spring my way, stretching

68

so the fingertips close six inches from my nose. I'm not sure whether I'm a rodent, ghost, or rat to Jackie—haven't quite decided which is safest in the mind of a mad man. A rat, I figure, must be the worst of all: ghosts are already dead, and flies have no tails. So I sit on the door side of the kitchen table as Remi counts and measures the product between us. Just in case I am a rat to Jackie Lowe, I've got a hole nearby for escape.

"What you looking to hold?" Remi sips bottled water as he seals a Ziploc bag half full of leaves. "Start off with a pound or one and a half, or you think you can carry two and make it right off the top?"

Jackie's fingers snap, means he's done spinning me for a moment. "Who's he gonna move two pounds to? Nigga don't know nobody like that. He's just a square—nothing but a mamma's boy. What you know, fool?"

I laugh—wouldn't feel so comfortable if his pupils still turned me upside down. "Suck on a pipe, crack monkey." My laugh rises until I sound like the GMIC white boys inside their thirty-second-floor circle.

Water spills from Remi's lips. "Would y'all shut the fuck up—ain't it enough I got one retard hype living here? How much you looking to hold, Tommie?"

I drop my arms to the table. "Two. I'll carry two pounds." Remi seals two half-full freezer bags and pushes them my way. I slide one underneath my windbreaker, but Jackie isn't finished.

"Just a square bastard."

"We'll see."

He laughs. "How you gonna let this guy hold on to all that, Rem-Dog? Where's his cash? Where's his customers?

Who's he know—who knows him? I can go on down to Social Security for a charity job. Thought we was running something real here."

"He's family," Remi snaps. I stuff the second bag past my jeans waistband.

"So what? Thought this sissy had a square job coming, like a square negro mamma's boy should. That's what he said," Jackie snaps. He scoots his chair back from the table.

Remi's fingers stop halfway through sealing a baggie, waiting. My legs turn away from them so that my feet tap toward the door, and Jackie swats at flies over us. "Didn't work out like I thought," I say finally.

"So what?" Jackie repeats. I rest my legs underneath the table circle and Remi finishes closing the baggie. "How's that involve my business?"

"See, that's our problem," Remi says. "Any other group, you say 'family' to them to explain a situation, and that's the end of the conversation. Ask them white folks, the Irish and the Italians, the Mexicanos and the Polish. Niggas, you say 'family,' and they stare at you with glass eyes and complain about charity. There can't be no charity when we're talking about family. It's just 'family,' that's all."

Me and Remi went down to Southern Illinois together back in 1990. Stayed in the same dorm room for two years, tried to get into this cornball Black frat together—until Remi hustled his way into some side-loving with one of the brother's ladies in our dormitory laundry room, kept her moaning loud enough for the whole campus to know how they got down. Before that, we would've made it in with the real square negro mamma's boys for life.

We started out freshman year taking economics classes. By the beginning of second semester, Remi was running with the Asians and the white boys up from the St. Louis suburbs, because they always kept their pockets full of money and my cousin had herb to sell, sent downstate in nickel and dime bags by one of his 79th Street uncles. The Carbondale police were locking Remi up every first and third Saturday of the month by our third year, dropping him in that jailhouse at the far end of campus town where the rope still swung north to south from the ceiling, ghost's tar neck dangling about in its noose. By spring break, the downstate cops told the university they'd have to drag that wannabe wicked gangster from the deepest part of the old Mississippi if the university didn't get his dope-peddling ass far away from their town. Sure enough, a counselor from the Student Affairs office drove me to bail Remi out at the end of March, counseled cuz good and plenty in the backseat of a Taurus before dropping him at the Carbondale bus depot to catch the first Greyhound back to 95th and the Dan Ryan.

By the time I came out in '95, Remi and his uncles had the Four Corners all locked up as far as the weed market, and cuz rolled those blocks in an older model of the same Bronco Elroy Murphy parks on 75th Street outside the Soft Steppin. He rides in a shiny Range Rover now, and he's the last of them standing—two of his uncles are locked away, and the other two dead the same way his old man is dead. Gone and dead to him.

Remi still curses me for staying at SIU after they put him out. Fool didn't look back over his shoulder in that Carbondale Greyhound station, so he missed my eyes wet and swelling full of disappointment in the closest thing I've ever known to a brother. Disappointment, because Remi was so stupid—or just bright enough—to chase the free honor in dirtying himself in this life instead of letting the double-talk schools and churches and jobs and families run scheming scam on him until they had him buried under dirt. While I stayed downstate, crying because my cousin didn't take me back home to the Corners.

"Forty hours from my degree, just forty from walking across a stage with the cap and the yellow strings hanging from my head for mamma—rest in peace—like you done for yours," he sobs once Westside's herb takes hold of him. "I got took, and you're the good square, Cuz-o." And he shakes his head as he breathes that pinprick "-o" through the tiny hole between his lips.

"YOU PREACHING TO me, fool?" Jackie snaps. "It ain't like this sissy is your mamma or your sister or no blood like that. You full of shit right now, Rem, this square ain't nothing but a dime-a-dozen cousin. Go bout giving this kinda charity to the other eleven of um, then what we gonna have left here?"

Remi rubs the stubble at the top of his head. "Blood is blood, Jack, you can't take that." He sorts weed into smaller pouches. "You gotta get out of this petty nigga thinking. We're trying to grow something here. Black folk don't know how to grow, Jack. Black folk too busy biting one another at the back."

"I got money riding on this load." Jackie gulps from cuz's water bottle. "What's he got? Helping his ass don't grow nothing for me but the empty in my pockets. That's business. Call it family, call it whatever you wanna to make you feel good about this shit. I see a spade, I call out spade—if we got a welfare spade in the family, and I give him something without seeing nothing back in return, a 1992 Ford-driving, no job-having, Public Aid applicant taking help out of my pockets, then I call that charity. And this ain't no good time to be messing with my pockets like that. Stakes is high."

"I'm gonna make your money, Jack," I say, just so I won't disappear in the hole with the kitchen rats, "and I'll be back here with your cut. I've got mouths to feed at home, and I'll remember who helped me take care of them. You sit tight, give me a few weeks, and you'll count thanks in green. Just shut the fuck up for now."

"You think those Irish and Jews give charity to their welfare cousins?" Jackie slides near the table and rubs his palms over fresh weed.

"None of them peoples would've never had to be on welfare in the first place." Remi speaks only after the pause is interrupted by sirens racing 78th Street. "That's the whole point. Like Tommie says, he's gonna look out for us when he's set his papers right. We help him get settled, he kicks us down on the long end. That's how we grow this family-style. Gotta learn some time. Only a small-minded nigga whines over losing a penny today when he's got a quarter coming around the next corner."

Jackie's laugh hisses from the throat. "Best be a half-dollar round there, and that corner best be coming around tomorrow."

"It will be." I swallow from the same water bottle, tasting their crumb-filled backwash. "Damnit."

"That's what I wanna hear," Remi says. "Ain't nothing but family up in here, no time and place for bullshitting and non-sensing."

Jackie stares without fingertips popping or eyeballs rolling. His lips part and curl to close on air, yet he makes no noise. I feel my brow frowning as this stare lasts. His lips spread and curl again, wide and slow.

"Black-ass rat," Jackie mouths.

"Show family love," Remi orders.

Jackie's arm coils through the mounds of ganja leaves and plastic bag rows with an open, wet palm. I stand over Remi and take his brother's hand, leaning across the table to half hug Westside because I do appreciate this charity.

Jackie whispers in my left ear. "You know we're just making your ass into a dope dealer. Just like us, Cousin."

Underneath the love of bloodless brothers, Remi smiles and weighs bags on a cooking scale. I sit back down under the high-flying fleas to listen as he and Westside Jackie school me on peddling weed in the Four Corners.

* * *

WALKING EAST UP 79th Street, you do want to count yourself among these hustlers. And your trade doesn't have to be of some criminal sort. The true players here on the strip, they make a hawking scheme out of all things. Gym shoes, painted gold, videotapes and CDs, newspapers, vinyl bags with stitched designer tags, cigarette wrappings, freedom, time. Doesn't matter that we're already wearing fresh Nike soles, or that our skin shines in this spring sun, and we smoke prewrapped menthol with a half-full box poking from T-shirt pockets. Doesn't matter that we don't read anymore and the tape-playing machine is broken, and fresh labels already dangle from our behinds. Doesn't even matter that we walk this strip without a real place to go, on a clock all our own.

Seventy-ninth Street forces you to move with the hustle's limp. Not because all the rest walk like so—some slick-Willie pimping, others wounded, all working up some jive drama script for the strip—but because so many souls work 79th on a May day, you've got to bend that left knee to dip down, then hitch back up on your right to make your way without crashing into others practicing their lines.

Over here is nothing like the strips downtown, where folks march fast as legs move them—fast and slow all at once. Those people are headed where they don't want to be without any other choice in life but going there. Marching lines straight and ordered. Northbound against the curbside, southbound against the buildings, marching and hustling in their own way, to some bosses' time.

But 79th Street's sidewalks are too narrow for such downtown order. Our blocks were built for the Jews and Germans and Polish long ago, those tiny, straight-line folk. Now one jive soul heads east, walking directly toward another headed west. Folk dip and limp and slide their way through just in time, some imagined time. When the sidewalk becomes too clogged, the hustlers walk out in the middle of the street and force the cars to limp and slide on by.

*   *   *

JW'S CLIPPERS buzz as shears sizzle against my hairline's kitchen end. I look over my shoulder to the shop's middle mirror, expecting to see the tool smoking in JW's hands. But his lips streak a smile that stretches yellow cheeks as he yanks the metal teeth from my head. He holds a brush high up over my scalp, though he hasn't used it on my head. Instead, the barber turns the brush to the bristle side and scratches the matted patch of his own braids. The buzz becomes a low ring as he grips the clippers' plastic base and scratches harder.

"Turn round, cat," JW says, his knee propped against the barber chair lever, "ain't finished."

One ceiling fan wobbles stray hairs above, another spins slow and useless high over the fifteen uncut heads waiting in the shop's sitting area, packed against a 79th Street window. Frowns tear into most of the faces as their eyes fix my way— their frustration burns in the mirror reflection. The few happy faces are fixed on the broken vending machine and dry water fountain behind the first barber's chair.

It's the hottest day of the year so far, sun boiling steam out of the lake to choke us dead here in South Shore—everyone without central air will surely die, at least. All that JW's shop has for cooling air is this dusty wall unit facing out onto the rot alley and the condemned building next door. Yet the AC's not running today. JW's uncle says that its engine gone up to be with Marvin Gaye, Malcolm, and St. Michael; the barber in the last chair says the machine needs a freon recharge; and JW just wipes his forehead with the backside of the same hand that grips the bristles he puts to his head. On the wall behind the first chair, an electric cord hangs from the quiet air unit, unmoved by the breeze blown by fans.

I watch the last barber use a rusted straight razor to shave his customer over the sink. JW's uncle sits in his customer chair, no matter the uncut heads sweating in the waiting area. He's the owner, and this is his break time. The uncle reads one page of the *Sun-Times* over his left leg and fans himself with the rest of the paper on his right.

"You gotta turn round, Tommie," JW begs. "Got customers waiting."

I touch my neck and sweat sizzles at the burning place. I yank my fingers away for effect. "You're tearing me up back there. What's wrong with you?"

He pushes at my shoulder with the clippers. I half-spin to face the uncle, who watches me now, just above the rim of black-frame eyeglasses. "I got peoples waiting over there, Tommie, good-paying clients now. Everybody ain't patient. Work with me here."

"What's wrong with your clippers?"

"I dropped them earlier." I turn over my shoulder, looking for the punch line in the barber's face. Yet his eyes are the same deep black as his natty braids and lip skin. "Been making this noise ever since. Like they bout to explode or something. Like something's broke up inside."

"You think? So you're just gonna test out this broke shit on me. Tear up my neck?"

"Turn around, Tommie. Got folk waiting." JW spins my chair so I face the air conditioner as rot steam seeps through its vents.

I relax against the backrest and watch the crowd in his uncle's far mirror.

Herringbone chains shine on every third throat, and two young players in the front row wear cell phones strapped to either hip. Against the vending machine, a tall boy leans low from the neck so that the fan's slow whirl won't crash his head as he whispers, whistles, and points at the young girls strolling past on 79th Street. He wears a do-rag to cover wild curls, backed by a white sheik towel hanging to his shoulder blades. His gray basketball jersey reads "Archibald" then "1." I believe that I've seen him in the *Sun-Times* sports section before. He plays ball for Simeon High School or Dunbar maybe, and he'll be a star one day. Well he's a star now, in the Corners, but one day, the blue folk swear, he will *blow up* worldwide.

This honey from my South Shore High days, three years younger than me, sits in the back row. Fine as ever, hair shaved low with waves flowing ear to forehead, ear to neck. She holds a boy child with a brown afro growing bush wild and loose all about his head. I figure him for her son, for she rocks the child against the cleavage peeking over the top of a Sean John T-shirt. To her left, a burly dark jokester from the liquor store corners wipes his forehead with a monogrammed handkerchief. This blue-black soul is her man, I assume. I'm not sure which of the three have come here for a haircut.

JW trims my hairline, and I lean upright from the backrest.

"Them jobs burn," I repeat. "My money's just as right up in here. I'm paying fifteen bones like all the rest."

"You don't tip good, nigga," JW says, still without laughing. "Never have."

He puts the brush bristles against my scalp's base. Soon as I feel their sting against the burning place, I push his hand away with my left elbow and jump from the chair. My loose hair tumbles to the floor tile and lands still, no matter the fan's wobble. I rip the smock at the neck snap and toss it against the middle chair's backrest. What's left of my hair sprinkles the chair lever.

In the uncle's mirror, my hair is close-shaven and even as always, but the burning place tingles with static's pain. JW's charred black lips smile empty in reflective glass, showing teeth yellow to match his skin. "What is this? That hurt, JW. You ain't cutting me right. And you smiling bout it? My money's the same as these other fools' money—fuck this. I ain't paying for a nigga to slice and burn the dome."

"Sit down, Tommie," JW coos, the corners of his eyes on the waiting area. "Got folks waiting here. This ain't cool— what you so agitated for, my man?"

All fifteen faces frown together now, the uncle still watches me above his plastic spectacle frames, and the second barber holds the straight razor at his hip, switchblade ready-made.

"Ain't your man," I say as sweat drips from my scalp. "You ain't fading me like usual. Keep talking about who you got waiting for you. But I'm sitting right in your chair. Ain't paying you to jack my locks up."

"But I'm done already, Tommie." He bites the bottom black lip. "Just gotta fix the line up. Why're you tripping?"

"Back of my head's on fire. See this?" I lean toward the uncle, who closes his *Sun-Times* without looking at my neck.

"Sit down, Tommie." JW pats his smock in the middle seat, like he talks to knucklehead children throwing tantrums during their very first haircut. "Come on."

"Fuck that," I say. "Fuck you." The waiting area fan blows a quiet "oooh" all about the shop. The barber's black eyes fix my way, and his lips curl beneath his nostrils. His clippers buzz louder than the jive talk radio station fading in and out through stray signals over the second chair. Puffs of smoke rise finally from the tool's plastic as we stare each other down. The last barber watches in his own mirror, wiping his razor with a white towel over the floor, not over the sink, for his client's head waits there.

The honeys, herringbones, and hoopers wait to see who between us is the punk in this shop, hot and frustrated frowns replaced by wide, waiting eyes.

It ain't me. I can't be a punk, not if I'm gonna sell around these corners. But the fan's wobble slows above my head and sweat stings my eye much as this clipper burn does at my neck, so I walk the two steps toward JW, my eyes on his black lips until I lean into ear.

"Come holler at me in the bathroom," I say, cooing almost soft as JW.

"What, fool?" JW voice is loud and showy now. "What kinda gay shit are you on? I look like a homo?"

"Yeah, nigga," I say, and the grown-up fresh honey from South Shore and JW's uncle both laugh. "Just come holler at me in back. Might have something for you. Straight this away."

"I got customers," he repeats.

JW pauses over my shoulder, then drops the sizzling clippers at his station as he tiptoes two steps behind me. I walk past the short chairs, and the waiting eyes, and the uncle's rim-top-peek, and the third barber's clean glistening blade—all of them follow us into the shadows just past the bathroom door. I stop behind the shop pay phone with its shriveled cord receiver hanging crooked from the hook, and the lineup columns of blue-black men's heads fashioning the same thirty-two haircuts these barbers have been offering for the last forty years, and the wall poster of this eggnog-skinned, mystery race woman wearing only a purple bikini and seated crooked upon a high chair. She clenches the ends of long black hair with puffy pink lips, and her hands press the wood seat between perched legs— as if she is ready to propel herself upon customers headed for the bathroom, or maybe she is protecting the sight of her crotch from onlookers in these back shadows. Here in the corner at the shop's farthest end, I turn to JW, who closes to one-half steps from my unfinished hairline.

"Think we can work something out," I whisper. "Got a hookup on some action you might want to put a little something on. Some real business you'll like. Got plenty."

I pinch my forefinger and thumb together and bring them to my mouth to kiss and suck the tips. JW's burned lips let go a cackle as he glances at the purple eggnog woman. "What's wrong with you, Tommie? You know your cousins don't get with me like that. You know how much I owe them cats—both of them say I ain't good in their books no more."

I bring the thumb and forefinger to my mouth again and puff air. The barber's eyes light. "I said *I got plenty,* fool. *I* got the hookup. You're talking to me, JW, if you want to get down now. Look like you could use you a spliff. I'm talkin bargain prices. Nine and a quarter for a dime. Can't beat that price for this kind of business."

The shop's corner is quiet but for the radio jive crackling. "What are you talking right now, Tommie?"

"I'm talking whatever you're talking," I whisper. "You let me walk up outta here clean and forget about the loot I owe you for burning up the back of my neck, I'll put that fifteen I owe you on a dime bag and two-thirds of another, long as you get up with me later tonight. Then we're even till you get up with me next time. And you will get up with me again, cause this product is on fire. Promise."

JW brings his left hand to his scalp—only now do I see he's still carrying the flat barber brush—and he presses bristles against his knotty twists, I look away from the shadows, and the middle mirror reflects JW's uncle opening the *Sun-Times* in his lap again, to the horoscopes page, and the waiting souls still watching us.

JW drops the brush to his side and turns to the last barber, waving and nodding with his clipper hand. That clean razor blade scrapes against the client's jaw finally. "That'll work," JW says. "Sounds like a solid. You just walk up outta here quiet and I'll hit you up bout seven, seven-thirty."

"Good business," I say, and step through the space between the eggnog model's wall perch, the beaten pay phone, and the barber's hairbrush grip. I'm almost in the waiting area as the uncle fingers his horoscope.

"You working yet, Tommie?" He scratches a graying beard as his eyeballs drop to the center of the lenses.

"Yup," I say and walk past the onlookers as twenty "aahs" uttered as one fade to silence. I wave at the bushy-haired boy propped against his mother's breasts before touching the doorknob.

"Next—" JW calls from the middle chair.

I turn back to the barber quick because these waiting faces aren't quite sure who lost our staring contest. "Hit me round seven, Playa Playa," I say before leaving JW's barbershop.

Seventy-ninth Street sizzles for the first time this season, steaming sweat to pour from my face just in time for more to fall. Soon as I pass the shop's window, I pluck my wallet from the back pocket and spread its lips to look on dust. As I'd sat in the middle chair for JW to snap his smock at my throat thirty minutes back, I'd swore that I still had cash in my pocket—until I remembered dropping the month's last twenty on the Soft Steppin bar last Saturday. I rub the tingling place on my scalp, then my unfinished lining, and I limp east, like all the rest on this hot street, smiling because I've hustled my very first sale.

6

I SOLD MOST of the first pound to Primo Fairmont as payback on two juice loans standing late on my account—squared my credit away with the Shark real nice, just in case times get hard again. Then I moved smaller packets to a peach-skinned pothead from the GMIC tower downtown whose e-mail information I'd been holding since last October.

"Brad—Hey, this is Tommie Simms," my intro e-mail read, sent hoping the company ax hadn't started dropping on thirty-third-floor necks just yet. "Have not heard from you in a bit. How are things up north?"

"T. Simms, my man. No more changes this way yet [Brad inserts his yellow smiley-face symbol here—as this is supposed to be some kind of humor]. Howre things hanging with you, brother?"

When I still worked in the tower, Brad drove an old Ford Thunderbird and listened to the radio station at the FM band's far right end, volume low just in case our division manager crept near his office.

"Just keeping the head above water," read my reply.

"Good to here. Glad your making it okay out there. Stay in

contact. All the best—BR." Brad thought he was done with me, that I'd wasted time messaging him just to say "stay in contact [yellow smiley face]," because I gave a goddamn.

"Came across this sweet honey you'd might like to meet, BR," my final post read "name of Mary Jane Plenty." I'd listened to Brad's circle jive for a full year, lingered in corners with him at company outings, and caught him grooving to the low-down radio bass rhythm. I knew good and well that thirty-third-floor Brad started foaming at the lips somewhere between Jane's "e" and Plenty's "p."

"When and were," his last message read, just like that.

THE SEVENTH FLOOR of the Global Mutual IndemCorp parking structure is the "Blackhawk level," after the hockey team. On each concrete column and emergency exit door, native heads scowl in painted black and red, skin hinting rage underneath a feather headdress that blows with the gusts of Chicago blabber. The native's teeth clench and shine ivory white—some artist imagined this chief as inflicting bloody pain upon "helpless" souls. Either that, or the painting captures the chief in the midst of his own helpless suffering.

Brad Rooks slicks his hair back with gel and a thin-toothed comb underneath the nearest chieftain's face. He's pushed his hairdo so hard to his neck that the hairline recedes and the strands at the dome of his skull thin to bald at the point where the comb curves down with the scalp. Brad's taller than most of the jokesters from his thirty-third circle, but his green pupils rise to the top of glassy holes to meet mine.

His necktie shimmers in the haze creeping through the walls' openings. Brown and gold and silver swirls spinning about this fine silk—he only buys his neckware from Nordstrom's and Bloomingdale's downtown. He fixes his knots fat and extra wide to the throat, too, like the pimps and players and the big-time city hustlers these days. As Brad told me after too many peppermint schnapps last Christmas, "I've got style, much style as any nigger, that kind of true style. Plenty to spare, my nigga." And Brad said "nigger" twice, drunk and comfortable just like that—with an *a* instead of an *er* the second time to let me know how down his style truly was.

He straightens the knot as he steps across the Blackhawk driveway. I lean on the Range Rover's trunk—I borrowed Remi's truck, because if the guffaw circle has to know that I'm living like a criminal, at least Brad will tell the rest of them that I'm making top-dollar cream off this foul game.

"You must be doing better than keeping the head above water," he whispers, "looks like you're big ball-ing."

I look over my shoulder at the white steel, then left and right along the empty driveway and the lines of parked cars with their suburban windshield stickers facing stone walls. My watch says 10:36, too early for Global Mutual folk to head for their lunch hour. Aside from me and guffaw circle Brad and these paintings of Chief Blackhawk, the seventh floor is empty. "What're you talking so low for?"

Brad stops just past the driveway opening. His wingtips nearly brush the ends of my Adidas. "Gotta be careful, Tom, the man listens. He's got cameras and mics and all kinds of shit, peeping down on our asses. That's how he does us now, no?"

"So what you want to meet with me here for? You knew what I was hitting you about, right?" Brad's gut has swollen since last I saw him, full of greasy downtown lunches or too much liquor or cigar smoke, or worry. In the weeks before GMIC let me go, I'd walk past his office to hear the radio turned to the all-news AM station instead of that right dial city jive. Said he needed to hear the updates on the hunt for those godless goddamned bastards, and on our latest plan to bomb the *motherfuckers* in their *coward-ass mountain lairs* as payback—such crusading updates and the Monday pro football reports, Brad tuned in those weeks after the twin fall.

He stopped gelling his hair back then, too, let the strands poke scraggily all about the scalp instead. By my very last day, blond patches peeked from just behind the balding hole in Brad's head. He may be twenty pounds heavier not even a full year later, but at least his strands are slicked back down. "You understood my message, right? You understood *Mary Jane*?"

"No doubt, home-team." Brad reaches into wool pants pockets and jingles change. "Safest place to do business sometimes is underneath his eye. Man don't figure a brother's bold enough to keep it real right in his face. What you got for me?"

"Gotta let me know what you need," I say, because it sounds like the right thing to say. "Shit, I got whatever it is."

"How you selling? Nickels, dimes, quarters, what?"

I laugh. "Got um in dimes, homey." My voice seems to whisper lower than his now. "Best puff for your buck."

"Gimme four dimes," Brad says.

Wind cuts through the Blackhawk walls, and a door closes somewhere, loud enough for blood to jump from my chest and ring my ears. I reach inside my jacket to hide my hands. Brad shrugs. "Fuck was that?"

"Downstairs," he says. "Be cool, fool. How much?"

"A dime is ten dollars, Bradley."

"Oh." His right wingtip kicks parking lot dust. "My partners pick up my stash usually. That's how we regularly do."

"Swift way to do business." I nod. "Forty for four dimes."

I squeeze two small pouches in the jacket's chest pocket. Brad's hands don't leave his pants, but his loose change is silent. His pupils roll to the top of wet green holes. I bite my lips to keep from staring, and this moment lingers too long. "You sure that was downstairs?"

He kicks more crumbled pavement instead of answering, then looks at a brand-new Lincoln when he finally does speak. "Play like they do on *The Wire.*"

"What?"

"Don't you be watching *The Wire,* man? On HBO? That's the best shit on TV," Brad crows. "Just slide your hand my way, like you're dapping me. I'll give you my hand, and we'll grip like the brothers be doing in the Towers. You'll press the quarters into my palm, and I'll slide you my scratch. Then, you walk your way, and I go back upstairs, like we're saying goodbye. Just like that."

I nod and repeat, "Swift business."

"Yes, it is." We shake hands. I part the bills between my fingers to make sure he gives me two twenties, then slide the take into my jeans pockets. Brad stuffs dime packets next to his pennies and nickels without peeking at the packets. "I'm gonna test how good this stuff is, then you and me, maybe we keep doing business on the regular together."

"Can't get no better in the city. Guaranteed," I say.

"How do you know?" He smooths the ends of his locks to the nape and guffaws in his sole circle.

"Cause that's how we do good business." I press Remi's key chain and the alarm remote echoes. "Spell-check your e-mails before sending them. The shit looks bad. You still represent the company after all."

"Fuck you, square. Go get a fucking legitimate job." Brad walks along the Blackhawk driveway, steps slow and fakes a half-hustler's pimp. "Make sure you drive out the back on the Clark Street side, not Dearborn. They've got cameras over on the Dearborn end, always watching."

I close the driver-side door, but I watch as Brad pushes the chieftain's emergency exitface without a security alarm sounding. I hear him laughing still—

"Be careful," he says. "The man's watching. You remember how it is up here."

BEEN SUPPLYING GUFFAW circle Brad with two quarter bags, sometimes more, every Tuesday and Friday these last three weeks. I don't know if he really smokes all this ganja, or if he cops off me only to run into the thirty-third-floor executive bathroom stall to jag himself off, silk Bloomingdale's drawers all heated pretending this sexy, black shit.

The trouble with small packets is there really isn't much

money in peddling for the start-up dealer. Once you cut the portions generous, seeking to build your clientele base like Brad and JW, you're looking at maybe fifty dime bags, a few nickels, and even fewer quarters out of a pound. There's a profit margin of two hundred fifty bucks for the peddler who actually flips the cost on a load; next to nothing for all that hustling. Lucky that I've got Remi covering me this round, cause the Ford note and phone bill are due and I need my full stack.

According to Remi and Jackie's lesson, it's wise to crap-cut this second pound, seeing as I've got my core customers well on the way to locked in on the supply. Use enough parsley flakes and fertilizer and tea, bag it nice and tight, expand my base, and this next pound will make me a solid two Gs, or so the lesson goes. Somebody up high is profiting hundreds of thousands off my desperation—I know as I've been on the top floors. But I don't plan on becoming a greedy-type hustler. All I need is my two Gs. Gotta pay bills and still have enough left to flip my next bag.

Tarsha found the second pound in my pants Sunday morning and threw a two-hour fit. Can't blame her, no matter that she used to smoke more than a little bit of ganja herself before birthing Dawn, and forgetting she'd already signed off on my decision to enter the trade because things were "getting so hard for her alone."

I understand that it's different seeing these brown leaves in a plastic baggie all twisted up in your husband's drawers, tossed inches from our bedroom door. Inches from the place where she dreams, and just six feet from Dawn's nursery, the truth of my crime slapping her upside the head. Truth there for even our child to discover on top of this filthy hallway pile, high above the depths to which the world forces a soul to sink while pretending to provide for his people.

Tarsha coming across the second pound on her Sunday off is all the worse. We don't go to church anymore—haven't been since the first Sunday after doctor told us Dawn was on the way, and then only for good luck. But her granny attended the 8:30 A.M. service at Second Baptist every week without fail when she was alive, and Tarsha remembers. There ain't no blessings in getting caught doing filthy deeds. Especially not on a day set aside for atonement, tithing, and thanking Him on high, like granny taught us.

"If somebody busts up in here to find that shit in your drawers' stains, sitting so close to my baby girl—"

"Shhhh!!!"

"You know they'd have to call Family Services on us like we was living in the projects. Them peoples'd come up in here quick fast and take Dawn for good. Then, what would we be?"

Her point doesn't end the fit, but it might as well.

Everything in the Corners comes with guilt's weight, that's how good souls stay in line and why poor boys don't bother complaining, even take pride in the swing when their necks are in the noose. Maybe it's all of our fault together: mine and Tarsha's and God's and granny's and the terrorists', and my mother's fault, too. But mine especially for carrying guilt on these shoulders and sticking my head in just as the world's rope tightened. This weight can only make me fall faster, and yank the yellow twine harder.

*   *   *

ALL THE PAYDAY loan and quickie cash storefronts lining these odd-numbered blocks between the lake and Washington Park should've put Primo Fairmont's loan-sharking racket out of business—just like the corner store lottery machines did his uncle Lonnie's numbers game back when we were kids. But the last time I saw Primo, he claimed money was still coming in mighty fine. I figured this was just his wannabe big-balling talk, until the Shark got to breaking down the scheme's economy: (1) he's got so many debts left outstanding with points collecting as the weeks pass, so many fools scared of his knuckle-and-bat Vicelord crew, that debtors beg to pay at least something on the points to keep their bones unbroken. All these fearful welchers on the blocks puts regular cash in Primo's pockets, and (2) what with so many more welchers let go from steady employment, the banks, credit cards, currency exchanges, and even the storefront quickie scams still aren't keen on doling out their loot, not to the desperate horde.

So they bring their grubby hands to Primo, willing to pay heavy points on a few dollars just to make it through another day. Since these souls have no income, Primo knows they're sure to default on their installment payments, forcing them to reach out for another loan at higher points. The third time around the default circle, the welcher catches a beat-down—broken ankle and elbow guaranteed, or maybe just the ankle if the welcher has at least a Jackson and a Lincoln to put on the points before the Lords get to slamming. Either that, or the welcher finds an odd-numbered hustle of his own, all proceeds going to Primo until the Shark's mostly paid back. Then the welcher can keep on scamming, free to put money in his own pockets. Or, maybe he starts paying back his legitimate bills. Primo smiled bronze teeth as he explained this part of the sharking economy.

He originally made his cash dealing dope, back before ready crack rock arrived on the South Side and all the blocks around here turned bloody in '87. Once the rocks hit and the Vicelords chased Primo out of the dope hustle, his uncle Lonnie from the Soft Steppin Lounge set him up as a shark. Now, Primo's branched out and got a few Vicelords swinging bats for his points and some side pocket money of their own, for even dealing ready rocks ain't recession-proof these days.

THE 55TH STREET Green Line station is the very last stop where you'll catch white folks riding southbound. At 55th, the university students spin through turnstiles and sprint to Hyde Park, and the gray and polka-dot people who refuse to let go of their neighborhood hobble from the platform; they head east like the students, just not as fast with their backs hunched low on their canes and walkers. Those from the Back of the Yards huddle at the 55th Street curbside, too, unmoving eyes waiting on buses to carry them far off to the west.

King Lonnie told me to meet his nephew here—said there was business Primo wanted to talk, said he figured I'd feel safer at the train station than anywhere deep inside this Washington Park. I just finished repaying the Shark with part of a bag after leaving my debt and its penalties swelling for months, so Primo could still crack my head to send a message to stray fools who figure they could get away with skipping on his points. Those like me, getting over because they look like well-meaning sorts temporarily down on their luck. Or he could have my ankles broken to soothe his own ego. King Lonnie knows his nephew's shark ways, so he arranged this meeting at the last safe Green Line stop before the tracks break and divide.

The El cars shake the station's cracked ceiling, and a line of city workers and college professors and downtown secretaries peel through the platform exit turnstiles, off to their corners and huddles and yards until the Shark is the only rider left. Primo's eyes scan the scene behind gold-rimmed glasses: the two CTA cops near the door; the old man mumbling to leaking plaster five feet from an untouched pay phone hook; and the child in the opposite corner who slides change into the fare card machine, then follows instructions blinking on a digital screen with the middle finger of her right hand. The Shark watches without ever twisting his neck, but when his eyes find me standing against this northbound turnstile, he nods.

He wears a Dr. Seuss hat the same brown as his skin, standing high on top of a lean frame to brush the ceiling cracks without toppling from his head. His suede outfit is clean and brown, too, and his skin drips train station sweat. The little girl at the fare machine stops reading as Primo passes, dropping change as her lips fall open.

Primo stops before passing the northbound turnstile, leaving low metal bars to separate us. "What up, Thomas?" he coos. "You've got everything together, I see—"

"What?"

His eyes slide side to side behind sparkling frames. "Ain't seen you looking this happy since Lord knows. Making a little paper in the game is treating you all right I see, brother. You look like a free man standing here, instead of another grinding fool scattering between train rides."

"Appreciate that," I say, though I don't at all.

"Just took a ride from downtown, and I still don't know where all these trains take folks. Why they gotta have separate lines here and there, Tommie? All of um full of unhappy muthafuckas scurrying to the middle to grind themselves. If all these souls are gonna be unhappy every day of their lives, how come old Richie Daley just ain't make one train to carry their unhappy asses all about together? At least then everybody'd know how everybody else is unhappy, too, no matter where they're coming from."

"See you had plenty time to think on your ride," I step away from him as I speak, until my back touches the wall. "Saw Lonnie on Seventh-fifth the other night, he said you wanted to talk to me. Some kinda business."

"Like I say, I hear you and your cousin are making nice papers over there in South Shore, moving those dimes."

"No," I peek at two CTA cops near the empty ticket booth. The fat partner pats the little girl's head as she pushes through the southbound turnstile. "Just getting by. I paid back what I owed. Everything after that is scraps."

"I hear you." Primo steps closer to my turnstile, but there's no space left for me to back away now. "You're all good in my book."

"So what are you after, Primo?" He pushes the brim-less hat back to the end of his skull.

"Ain't after a goddamn thing. Just trying to figure why they call the trains so many different colors when every one of them ends up in the Loop." Primo catches the CTA cop in his spectacles and nods. "In the back of my mind, I still call um by their rightful name anyways: A-train, B-train, 1-2-3-4. Simple like that. What they trying to hide nowadays with the colors?"

"Ain't my call to say," I answer and slide off the wall. "I'm just here cause King Lonnie told me you wanted to holler."

"Guess we'll never know," Primo says. Another south-bound train rumbles above and souls file slow through the bars. I watch the procession, figure Primo will do the same, but he's busy spinning the northbound turnstile in hand, turning and spinning until the entrance locks. "I'm looking to do some real business here, Tommie. I see making scrap change is treating you right. Making you feel like a real free nigga. I like for a brother to know how good getting down is for the soul. Want brothers to be profitable here, see, not just scurrying around like rats to make a living."

"Make something," I say and then, "but I did like the view up there back when I was riding those trains."

"I hear you." He laughs. "I'm putting up a proposition, Tommie. You got the hookup on the bags from your people down on Phillips, and these are your people, I understand. Family and such. So you're gonna look out for them same as they do for you. I know. Blood's everything—like my uncle. You get those pound bags through your blood connection at whatever price y'all got worked out and you bring them in to me. We work out a fair price—me and you like businessmen, up under your discount, and I'll move the poundage for you. I got street guys looking to do work, ready to make some change themselves under me. You're a good boy, like you say, you liked your east-side view. That's the life you know: that righteous, good living, for square rats. You don't wanna be running around these corners slanging garbage like no thug. This way, me and my people do the heavy work for you on the front lines. In return, I cut you in. Say fifteen percent off the top of what I turn on each bag."

I see the CTA cops strolling the sidewalk and wait for a northbound train to rumble into the station before I speak. "I cut you a discount on my cousin's bags, take the loss up front, all to move some bags based on a promise that you'll turn a profit and put a portion back in my hand on the back end?"

"Call it deferred moneys," Primo says as the sole rider unlocks the north turnstile and slides past us without blinking. "Just like you accountants do your business downtown. You only got profits cause you know it's coming later on."

"I'm in insurance," I say.

"All the same game. Your insurance company had accountants in that tall building up on the floors higher than yours. Making more loot than you did, and with a better view, cause they took care of the back end, made sure you and the CEO kept getting paid even when the front of the pot showed no dough. I read the *Trib*, too. That's how they get down in the Loop."

"And up," I say.

"Best believe."

"Thought you was done dealing a long time ago?"

"I was," Primo says. "I am. This ain't nothing but some weed I'm trying to move here. Help you out to help me out, so I can help my people out. Got mouths to feed, souls to please, too. Even when times is hard, Tommie. Especially now."

"You're really asking me for a favor, Primo, when it comes down to it—" I say. "How come you don't go straight to Remi and Jackie?"

"That's your family, brother, not mine. They cut you a deal to get you started, I know. That's what blood family's for. Now I'm looking for the same consideration from you here."

"They're *my* family," I tell him.

Primo laughs, more blood than breath now. "I hear you, player. Uncle Lonnie vouched for you though, told me the good word about Thomas. The king said to look out, no matter that you was a penniless, square muthafucka riding late on your payments. Back when I wanted to let my guys get loose upside your head, he put his voucher in your name. His word carries weight with me, means I gotta look out for you damn same as I would my own family. Blood flows both ways in a better world, no?"

"No," I say. Primo tries to look mean as he spits this spiel, eyebrows curled up like he's about to pull a bat from underneath his top hat and put it into my skull the same way his Vicelords should've done when I still owed. But I paid up already, and the CTA cops are near. "You coulda gone to Remi and them."

"Yeah," Primo says. He pushes the hat toward the left

now. "But me and you got history, dealt before in the past. I can't say that about your cousins."

"I welched," I say. "Owed you for months."

"But the king vouched for you," Primo repeats, sweat pouring hard now.

I step away from the turnstile, walk a half circle from the wall so I'm staring at the right side of the Shark's suede getup. The clock above the opposite exit reads 6:58, and the last rush-hour Green Line rumbles to the platform. A student runs through the metal, his face red but still dry, and his plain tie flaps over the shoulder. He slows to stare at us—at Primo's top hat at least—slows just before peeping the CTA cops and turning to run east along the Boulevard.

"I'm gonna have to get with my people," I say, certain that I'm looking into his spectacles as the words pass.

Primo laughs. "They taught you good down on State Street," he croons.

"Grand Avenue," I say. Primo's skin cools as his teeth show. "I worked on Grand, not State Street, not in the Loop, up north, for an insurance company—*corporation*—chief."

"Chief? Name's Primo, Smoove, fool."

Laughter shoots too fast for my lips to stop. "Primo what?"

"Fairmont is my uncle, the king," he says. "I'm his sister's son. They're Fairmont, my last name is Smoove."

"Primo Smoove—" I say and catch the laughter in my teeth now. "You just thought of that while you were on the train looking down?"

"That's my old man's last name. Family ain't nothing to

make jokes out of, is it?" Primo says, his stare blank. His right hand reaches for me. "It's all good though—"

I take Primo's hand before turning to the fare card machine myself. "I'm still squared away on that debt, right?" I ask.

"Said it's all good, player," he answers. Primo Smoove lets go of my hand and walks toward the exit, where CTA cops wait. "You talk to your people like you do down in the big corporation buildings on the north side, and we'll get together and do some real business together."

"On the back end," I say and reach for my wallet.

The Shark in the hat walks through the train station doors, headed the same way as the student in the flapping tie and the old folks on their walkers, and I forget all about his proposition and how I'm a square rat and he's suede Smoove. I hear a southbound rumbling near. I buy my fare card and run through the turnstile to hop this Green Line El before it makes its break east to the Corners.

7

RAISE UP YOUR goddamn hands. Now, clown! To the sky, the both of them," the voice bounces against brick walls along 79th Street, megaphone-boosted. "High and slow—"

I don't know where the sound comes from exactly, but I do follow its order with both hands. Folks stop on these curbsides all around me, their eyes wide to keep careful watch or to protect me from the stray bullets that fly about from cops' Glocks on lonely corners, *accidentally* aimed at dark bodies; or maybe they watch full of simple curiosity. My Ford's rust flickers with swirling red, blue, and silver lamps aimed from the top of three cop cars that form a triangle to block 79th Street.

The cop with the megaphone stands taller than them all, propped on the running board of his cruiser. "What's that poking from your pants?" His voice slams along the block. I look down, and plastic barely juts from my belt line. "Don't touch it, don't even think. Keep the hands raised and drop to your knees, slow as you raised them skinny wings!"

My left knee hits the pavement first, and a moan wells up from the curbside folks, a rising chorus of disappointment from this audience, like my surrender is beneath their expectations. What would they have me do, ignore the megaphone echo and squeeze one of these raised palms into a fist that jabs at dim sky, drop the other arm so that my submission appears an old-school Black Power death pose instead? Why can't they rise up themselves? There's far more of them on these curbsides than there is me, more of them than there are cops even, more of us together than there is everything. But this is the two-faced way on these blocks and strips; I notice only now, as I'm the one falling down to my knees. If they rise from these curbsides, chase away the megaphones and Glocks and the flashing siren lights of silver steel, then who will be left to blame—or judge— after all the wee men are gone, and nothing changes?

I drop my right kneecap to the 79th Street sidewalk, and the cops swarm me. One of the three with pistols drawn is dark-skinned himself. He comes at me from behind and presses steel just under my ear before reaching into my jeans and pulling loose my last pound of ganja without bothering to show me a cock-searching warrant.

"Shit," he curses in this rhythmic tone of a Stony Island preacher. He holds my cousins' bag over my head for all those swarming me, all standing in the triangle, and the folks on the curb, to see. Another disappointed group moan rises, and he forces the pistol harder until my head tips toward my shoulder "What's wrong with you clowns? Making a joke out of us, boy. When are you bastards gonna learn?"

The moan of the curbside folk fades. Guess they're all tired of me, so they start to move on about their hustle. The dark preacher cop got the last word in and the show is over, just like every other 79th Street show before it. He drops my hands to cuff me at the wrists so his unit fellows can drag me into the triangle. Remi and Westside Jackie's pound bag swings from his gloved hand, and he smiles and my pit swells and sours. By the time we reach the swirling lights of the CPD car, the corners are empty, and the pigs pat their black and blue brother on the back.

I listen to a rookie echo my rights through the megaphone. Listen and understand that the only somebody left for me to explain myself to is the judge sitting high up on top of the ends I'm trying to hustle this path to earn.

❊   ❊   ❊

I'VE NEVER seen Wee Man this close up before, not even when he stopped me that night outside Rainbow Beach. What they say about this cop out on the Drive isn't so obvious to the eye—his face is actually that of the bird painted on the green bills and the flags waving about from stems. Eagle or hawk, whichever they call it. They say he's a devil in front of the liquor stores, spoken in whispered tones because Four Corner folk don't like it known that they mention him by right name. But his is the mask of grand soldiers, heroes, and knights from the bloodless black-and-white war movies. Weidmann looks more like the eagle general, John Wayne, than he does Lucifer sitting in this interrogation room.

His head slopes down from a pale gray crown to the falling edge at his bushy brows. He's forty-five, maybe fifty by the sag to his cheeks, but his eyes shine searchlight bright from his skull, set close enough that there's really only one pupil rising from the nose's pyramid to beam its watch. The stare aims above me as his beak nose pecks ahead with its stabbing tip, pulling the rest of the face to attention at some point he finds between my eyes.

"Where I know you from?" His voice is full of mush—sauerkraut, chewed bratwurst, and chopped onion—but his words are street jive, could be spoken from one of my cousins' mouths.

"Don't know, Officer." I look away, to the spiderweb-laced corner of this beige room just outside the precinct cells.

"Got to be somewhere. I know I've seen you before." His left elbow rests on the fake marble table between us. The overhead lamp brings beads from the chalky hair stubbing his head. This light doesn't burn me at all, but Wee Man sweats. "You used to play ball over at Hyde Park?"

"Hyde Park? No, I went to South Shore."

"You played ball?"

"Football?"

His head shakes and he slides a palm against that up-and-down slope to dry his skin. "How could I remember what you look like running around with a helmet on your mug, hmm? Basketball—"

"Never played hoops," I mumble, "Officer."

Weidmann stares past me, through the two-way window lining the room's back wall. "Recognize your face from somewhere, Tiny."

"Tommie," I correct, my voice more harsh than is safe trapped with the eagle general, "Officer."

"Just a joke, friend. Lighten it up some." Weidmann smiles

and his teeth shine lemon lime. "I know this ain't your first time locked up, big fella like you. Can't say I remember picking you up before: that ain't what I know you from. But I'm sure you ain't no first-timer here."

"Yeah, I am actually."

His teeth hide behind crooked lips. "Oh, damn, am I speaking political incorrect again? Could've been the case you were a crook, I ain't seen your file, but if I actually say that, then you'll run to the judge and claim I was treating you prejudiced. Calling a crook a crook based on his looks. I picked up another clown dealing weed last month. Crook pulled that same crock, and walked. Now, my captain tells me I shouldn't go about stereotyping crooks: all crooks are innocent, even when you catch them with the bag, right? Gotta remember that. Tricky goddamn law."

"Can—may—I make my phone call, Officer?" This chair of steel and hard plastic squeaks against the floor, though I don't mean to move myself. I can't tell the real color of the table, the floor tile, or my chair, only these beige walls. Everything else glows in the lamp's pink red.

Weidmann laughs without smiling. "Your fidgeting way makes me nervous. Sit still. Phil told you he'd arrange your call soon as the pay phone freed up. Got a line full of bee-atches teary-eyed and whining out there already, waiting to call out for help—collect. Till it's your turn, Tiny, you just sit tight here, and be cool. You know we can get a lawyer if you don't have the money to afford yourself one. That's your rights by law. Tricky law. My guys read that part after they caught you slinging out on Seventy-ninth Street, I know. Between the bond money you'll spend to get out of here and any decent lawyer's hourly rate, you're out four times the money you were going to make on that plastic baggie. Selling a five-hundred-dollar bag of weed to make the system two thousand dollars richer. And you blame us for your woes? Bad business, son."

"I'm not in any business, and I wasn't carrying anything." I speak loud again and squint, but Weidmann still fixes at this point on my head.

"Relax. Thought you needed to call your lawyer," Weidmann reminds. I swallow the vomit churning in my throat. "You played football in high school, not basketball?"

Though our chairs rest on even floor, he looks down on me now—I swear his eyeballs swoop from the very top edge of the whites. I fix on the wall at Weidmann's back. "What, Officer, what do you mean?"

"You sounded like you don't care for hoop much, like I insulted you taking you for a basketball player."

The longer he stares, the louder the blood at my temple pounds. I pretend not to notice. "I played football, until my sophomore year. At South Shore—"

"Played four years myself. Roosevelt High, up on the North Side. Still follow our Bears like religion. You?"

"Not so much, no."

Weidmann moans again. "You know who my all-time favorite Bear is, to this very day? Harlon Hill. You heard of Harlon Hill?"

"Can't say I have, Officer." My ass squirms steel. "Nope."

"Played wide receiver, just like me—fastest guy I've ever seen on the gridiron. This's before Papa Halas let Galimore and

Sayers and Payton and them country field boys—don't get offended, son—in the game. My old man took me to see Harlon Hill play at Cub's Park back when I was eight years old, his last season. The guy was still a wing-footed god, I tell you. I'll never forget. Greatest of them all, for my money."

The door opens and dotted white light swallows the beige walls. The preacher cop from 79th Street enters, part-waddling and part-limping, until he stops in the room's cobwebbed corner. He doesn't look at me or Weidmann, but at this fake marble table where my hands rest with fingers spread. The eagle general holds his chin again. "We've got a phone open for you."

"Hold on a second, Phil, we're coming." Weidmann presses his hands against the chair's arms to stand but holds himself in this squatting position. More laughter slips from his scowl. "I know a lotta guys from around here who used to play ball—football, basketball, pastime, whatever—when they were young. These guys, their dreams pan out to be full of hot air, so what do they do with themselves? Hit the street, selling bags and blows and rocks, make shit of their lives. I don't get it. And I don't mean some mediocre benchwarmer jerks here, I'm talking big-time: all-city, all-state. Busted an all-American two guard a few years back, selling smack over on the East End. I had dreams when I was a kid, too, wanted to be Harlon Hill, man, like that wing-footed angel. Woke up one day, and forgot what I was dreaming about just long enough. Then I went out and found myself a job, became good police. How come the rest of us forget our dreams and survive decently here, while you all forget yours and make yourselves into shit?"

Silence is lit in hot white, floating in the ceiling lamp's glow.

"Got any good thoughts on this, Phil? Apparently this clown don't," Weidmann says.

"He's a clown, what should you expect?" Phil steps out of the corner and the bald outline of his shadow touches the table's end. "Don't know, Mike. Ain't figured these clowns out myself."

Weidmann seethes. "What's to figure?"

"Like I say, there's a phone open for this guy." Phil grabs me at the shoulder and I stand, though he doesn't pull at me really. Phil's hand drops to squeeze at my elbow as we walk into stinging light.

"See you around, Tiny," Weidmann says.

"Yeah." I answer low, so only the preacher cop will hear.

"Better watch yourself, jack," Phil advises as we turn from the interrogation light and Weidmann. The room's sting fades.

I hear fresh tears from somewhere unseen in the precinct house, louder than the ringing phones and the rap of chained crooks and beggars, and the sirens' call. Phil's fingers dig into the bone as he drags me, and for the first time since I dropped to my knees on 79th Street with a pound of leaves poking from the waistband, I think of my mother and of Tarsha—and above this noise, I hear a baby crying.

*   *   *

"WHERE'S TARSHA?"

My mother wheels the Continental onto Cottage Grove and the catalytic converter churns behind us. "Had to stay late downtown." Her answer begins and ends with a click of the tongue against the roof of her mouth. She doesn't look at me as this clicking disgust sneaks through her teeth.

"You went and left the baby with that Wallace mutha-fucka?"

"Watch your words." She adjusts the eyeglasses at the bridge of nose. "Need to show the man some respect. Kind enough to watch a fool's child while the fool's out playing like he's street trash. What you think I shoulda done, brung a nine-month-old girl to the jailhouse to see her daddy swinging about monkey bars."

"What're you talking about?" The light at 76th turns green and I wait for her to press the accelerator. I tap her shoulder, point through the windshield, and she drives. "What monkeys? What swinging?"

"You didn't come up like this. Can't say what happened to you, but this ain't what was supposed to. You owe me seven hundred fifty cash for that I-bond. Hurts my heart to speak of these things."

"Can you believe it? Seventy-five hundred bail on a five-hundred-dollar bag of weed. Don't make sense, the schemes these people got." My mother's knuckles show rust stains from years of scraping against Ford parts. Calluses line the sides of both palms where torn gloves have left her unprotected. "You shoulda asked Tarsha for the cash. You know you coulda—"

Her tongue touches the roof, just once now. "Girl's behind a desk all day, your dumb ass is locked up on Sixty-third Street, her child cries for milk in my arms, and I come begging for seven-fifty to bail you out of a cage. How does that sound?

Like some monkey shit, right? If you were my man I'd let you rot at the ass in that cage, or swing, whichever came first. What you think she woulda done? How're you making me look here?"

"She's my wife." I kick the car rug at my feet, hard so the mat flips to the raised rubber side.

"And I'm your mother. What're you thinking about?" She turns to me though the Continental squeezes between an early-morning Number 4 line bus and one of these army tank Hummer trucks. "Since you wanna act like some kinda street player, instead of like the young man I bled for just to send to col-lege, you need to get this lien took up off my car, too, right after you pay back my seven-fifty. Since you wanna play like you're a nigga without sense."

I blink. "You talked to Remi, Mamma?"

"Who?" Frustration gurgles instead of disgust. "Who'd you say? Remi? I shoulda known. Blessed De ain't round to know what her nappy-head bastard got my baby into now. Sad thing, the heifer's soul could still be looking down on all this madness she left me with."

"I just asked if you'd talked to him."

"I knew that fool was behind this. Hell naw, I ain't talked to his ass. Let me come across him now, I'll go up the left side of his skull like I shoulda done you back at that jailhouse for all the thieves and whores to see. You know better, Tommie, I raised you the best I could. That boy don't know nothing about nothing better. Heifer Mamma was the wildest thing I ever known, wilder than I ever was. She wasn't never even trying."

"Auntie's dead," I say. I touch her knuckles on the steering wheel, these ridges where rust flows into scales. "Just thought he could help you get your money."

"Crooked, no good bastard. Ain't he done enough?" Mamma's eyes fix on Jeffrey Boulevard as she slips a Newport between her lips. When she wheels onto 75th, the converter roars loud enough that I'm sure the car is soon to stall. "You trying to put this on somebody else? It's you who owes me. You can't make that go away. Didn't I tell you I'd talk to my supervisor?"

I hear her *tiss* inside my own mouth. "Remi ain't got nothing to do with this. You know I wasn't dealing or no such bullshit. They planted that bag on me, that's how the devils be doing. Goddamn. You know it."

"Who are you talking to?" The Continental stops at Exchange Avenue. "Raised nothing but a lying, crooked, ungrateful, rude, common, foul-mouth thug. I'm the one who just bailed you out—we gotta face up to the truth here. Need to send you down South with your daddy, boy, maybe that'll straighten you out."

"What?" I can't stop laughter from spraying the Lincoln dashboard "Even if you knew where that muthafucka was, how you gonna send me anywhere? I'm thirty years old."

Her right hand touches her heart, but my mother laughs, too, full of blue hate, as she cranks the Continental ignition. The engine roars, louder now. "What you think them peoples gonna do once they get their hands back on you? Hell or prison, one or both, they're sending you someplace, that's for sure. They can send you somewhere for their own good and your own mother can't to save you?"

A red-faced hustler in a backwards Kangol struts South Shore Drive, casting his shadow on the intersection as my mother drives near Rainbow Beach. I only see his side and back, but I swear this is Westside Jackie waiting on me—I recall him wearing such a hat over on Phillips Avenue. I sink in the torn leather seat until my head is lower than the window and my knees press the rug's rubber border.

"Might's well sit up straight, pretend like you still got pride. Way too late for shame."

"Nothing to be shamed for," I say. My mother moans. "Got no cause for shame" is all I can say, repeating my own proud lie.

*   *   *

A MESSAGE FROM Pharaoh Pugh Insurance Co. waited on the voice mail this morning. Their secretary's name was actually Gladys. Like Knight and the Pips, Gladys.

"Call us at 312-586-0165 to set up a second interview with Mr. Ramsey," Gladys' message says, "if you're still interested in our company. A-S-A-P." She spells it out for me just like that. I can't figure her late call for irony or insult though. Had the Pugh Company's preferred candidate taken a better offer downtown—where that candidate wasn't as preferred, suited, or qualified as me, but where the dollars stacked higher than on Cermak Road—or had Gladys waited until I was completely unemployable to phone for the simple sake of jabbing insult into both of my forehead temples? Whichever, I scribbled the number on a piece of napkin that I've already lost, and erased her voice.

* * *

WEE MAN CHASES through factory air. Not even a symbol for the cop, but Wee Man himself—his head at least, with the body of a bird. Feathers the color of tree bark at the torso, and shining white wings spanning seven feet tip to tip. A long metal weapon shows in his claws, mostly unseen for the rustling feathers. A school of birds flap about at his back, too, wings nowhere near broad as his own, but they're all after me: red, blue, black, silver, gray, this school of bird-pigs.

I look down from this sky of storm clouds and exhaust, as I'm airborne, too—look down on 78th Street, where Cousin Remi's home hides in tower shadows. I stretch arms at my side because I've got no wings or feathers, just bare limbs beating purple wind. What I see is still 78th as I know it, one identical block of the street after the last. I smell the lake in this air, somewhere ahead, dead fish and shoreline industry stinking and hovering. Lake Michigan waves crash just in front of us as I peek in our front.

East, toward the water's outline, my arms beat, and I feel swelling at my armpits from flapping, and I fly till I ain't flying no more. I land on the real 78th Street now, but they're still after me. I can't move, though the only thing in my front is the lakeshore and one last shack like my cousin's. I stand in place, naked ass waiting for Wee Man and his birds to swoop, and I know they're about to get me—why else chase a wingless, flying fool through clouds? His water blue eyes and beak angle in, wings eating toxic clouds, and that long metal is snatched from feathers and wielded in yellow claws. He aims for my head with his pitchfork—what can I do but wait for the bird-pig to drop me into one of the potholes, this fate I've got coming to me?

But they say you can't die in your own dreams, that even the freest mind's got no concept of its own end. Dreams themselves die over time, but never you in them. If this is so, heaven's got to be a crock—somebody's all too conscious, simple, and wishful thinking. Dreamt my fair share of dreams, you see, can't say I ever died in any of them.

Wee Man swoops, stabs me square in the scalp. Stabbing, then scrapping and ripping apart: pain, plenty pain, and sadness in these dreamy tales. The pitchfork tears from my head and Wee Man and his bird-pig army fly beyond me, the lead eagle dropping his weapon so that his claws are free to carry his bounty. The flying pig has snatched away my hair. Bushy curls and naps that covered my head as a young boy dangle from his claws, clumped and sewn together wiglike and dripping red into the waves. My head stings and leaks as I touch the scalp. Only stubble and blood left here, the remnants of a crown, and this black-red stream flowing into my eyes.

Now, I run to the lake. The last of Wee Man's bird-pigs disappears in the East End clouds, but I don't chase after them. They got what they came for, and my little boy's afro is too far gone to take back. I run only because I'm free to move now, run to the lake as it's the only place in this dream different from 78th Street. Just this water and the purple clouds above it. I can't get back up there, as the flying part of my dream is done. Not chasing or escaping anymore, just feeling the breeze my escape stirs, cool to soothe the sting at my temples. So much blood flows into my eyes that waves smash black and red beneath my lids. I keep running though, along Rainbow Beach sand, where the fish stench chokes breathing. And I stir, enough to blink away blood drops and remember that my mother never taught me to swim.

Water touches my feet in these holes where the beak pecked, and more blood runs from the heels. The beacon light still blinks out at the lake's end, though night hasn't fallen, and the water won't even flow red now. This lake is too strong for my blood, washes it all away. I blink again and two small hands push at my chest, and I stumble from the lake because her touch and the blinking remind me that dreams do end. Life just can't inside them. I never learned how to swim, so the stirring of my wife's hands at my sternum saves me.

DEATH CAN BE a saving thing, too. That's how I heard it from the folks at Granny Allen's church; of course, none of them telling it like they know about dying one way or the other. Their speculation just makes damn good sense running through my head with the granddaughter's words.

Never figured living in the Corners would come to this. Had to nap to prepare my mind for concocting a new script. "Ten years you known me." I only recognize that I'm yelling as I watch Tarsha's face cringe at every third syllable. "Shoulda come to figure I ain't the type to be about no half-ass bullshit. I look like a blue-collar factory nigga? Ain't bout to be one to pay your rent."

"My rent?" She laughs this spiteful laugh. "Didn't figure

you as the type to stand on a corner dealing dime bags neither. Takes a special kinda genius, I guess . . ."

"Shhh!" I point to the apartment's thin plaster. "Wasn't standing on no corner. Are you sick?"

"Are you?" Tarsha laughs, truly amused this time. "What the hell were you doing?"

I sit in the reclining chair. "Not a damn thing more than what we talked bout me doing already. Talked in circles, here, there, then talked it here again. Round and round. But if it's all right over here, girl, it can't suddenly be all criminal when the conversation comes back around. Makes you out to be a phony hypocrite in the circle. You sound like I was out there selling crack."

"First of all, the shit was never 'okay' with me. Don't insult me. You said you were doing it for a minute to take care of what was standing overdue, nothing more."

"Ain't been no longer than that. Nothing but a minute has passed here—"

The roll of her eyes hypnotizes. "I'm talking," she pierces my ears, and the walls, and my trance, too. "Second of all, you might as well been dealing crack. Ain't gonna have mercy on you no ways."

"Who? You?"

"Them—they ain't got mercy for you. They don't care nothing bout the substance, long as they found it sitting snug against your ass."

I smile, mean for it to show full of wickedness. "If I'd been moving rocks instead of a little smoke, I wouldn't look so useless in those eyes, I bet. You woulda liked that cash, no? If I gotta go down, might as well get myself good and filthy dirty on the way, phat paid, do it right. That's how y'all think over on Oglesby."

"What the hell are you babbling?" Tarsha sits on the love seat to my right, blue suit cringing around her waist and skirt riding to her knees "Shut up talking garbage to me. I'm done with you."

I laugh, nowhere near spiteful as her, not in my ears. "For good?"

"That what you want?" Dawn cries in the kitchen high chair. "Keep talking. It's hard out here on your own, damnit."

Threat, plea, or warning, I don't know. These are my wife's feelings, not mine. Years joined at a tin band covered in twinkling paint, and she could mean all three at the same time. "Yeah," I blink long, "you would've had mercy on me if I'd gotten real dirty paid."

She jogs off to the kitchen to tend to Dawn's afternoon hunger, true mamma that she is. I recline my chair and turn off this five o'clock news and its long forgotten script.

While I was in Carbondale, Tarsha finished her schooling commuting to Chicago State's campus way out on 95th Street. There should be no shame in that place; Chicago State is not much different from Southern Illinois based on what I've seen. But I went away from the city to get a degree, and that means something special to those who never leave. I can't blame Tarsha for the rage from those thick lips then. In the Four Corners, commuter school honeys are supposed to go wrong before us campus town clowns. Maybe they end up with three illegitimate babies running around a one-bedroom apartment, broke and wanting over on the South Side's East End, taking scraps off their sugar daddy to get by. Those that do make it on their own—because they are "all alone," right, "and it is so hard"—survive on noble, low-end scraps, head held barely above the water's surface to allow themselves a trickle of proud air.

My wife came up over on Oglesby, the Seventies blocks of that street, where weeds grow from cracks in the concrete, and they've got as many cardboard box-tops covering window holes as they've got glass. A Chicago State honey's Oglesby Avenue, where tire rubber rips and screeches and sirens whirr and wail and that *pop-crack* sounds one after the other come summertime, until you pray to Lord Jesus that it's just the noise of cheap firecrackers, though the Fourth is still almost a month away.

I never told Tarsha about how I sat in a white Uptown room just to the left of my testifying mother and her blue book and the fiends. If I had, at least the woman might understand where I went wrong, and she could figure some kind of sense out of this. Maybe. But her granny Allen was a good Baptist—the rock of old Oglesby Avenue—whose deadly vice was Hostess snacks, and I was their good man, and Tarsha was so fine and thick and sweet to the eye. Never, ever told the child a damn thing that would've made her think twice about letting me lose myself in those chestnut eyes, or between bare hips as she swallowed me. Maybe my mother was only on Step Five, but she didn't raise a fool here.

Been different since I came to understand our togetherness as a trade-off. Took me five, six years to understand that this union is just like everything else: I look at her and I love her, and she loves me back, and we loved each other for years and it feels good and she keeps looking so good and sounding sweet and pure. No matter—can't keep loving another soul in this place, then get love in return, without the question of payback rearing. That's the only way you know it's real in the Four Corners:

"I love you, so let's buy rings."

"I love you, baby, so let's sign these papers."

"I love you, let's get jobs and cars and, one day, a house in the South burbs."

"I love you always, love. Let's drop a seedling, so it's not just you and me loving, and let's buy our offspring new clothes and cornered playpens of mesh bars and let's buy her some factory milk and diplomas and degrees so she knows to grow into a carrot in this world, not a plump-bottomed apple, and let's turn the office you used to make a living for us into a baby room. You won't be needing it now. Our life is already made."

LET MY MOTHER tell it, this is what she stayed drunk and high on a Ford assembly line for anyway, to numb the pain of her own eyes crying tears just to clean her seed of weeds and cracks and broken glass. I was supposed to come back from Southern Illinois different and better than this—me and Cousin Remi both, degreed to the hilt. Educated and offering salvation to the hustling masses in civilized, golden chalices: not weed smoke. And then to get caught on these very corners, getting down, dirty, and more broke than paid, just the same as all the rest of the wounded cousins? Embarrassing the woman and shaming souls full of hope, no different from a couple of 79th Street thugs—"hoodlums," like Granny Allen called them. After that old Oglesby Avenue woman went and convinced her girl child that I was a good negro, and the downstate folk exiled Remi just so one of us could finish schooling right. All this trouble borne, just for me.

My own bones should be full of as much shame as Tarsha's and my mother's are of purple rage. But to be honest, I ain't hurting at all inside this skin. Reclined in my good nineteen-inch babble box chair, these bones aren't even aching from a night spent propped against a cracked cell wall. My mother and Tarsha can stay mad all they want then, and swim in shame on my behalf if it makes them feel bless-ed about how I drown. All I know is what's reflected on a television screen—that love ain't real around here until you go to the loan shark and accept his points to buy trinkets that make this reflection shine.

8

W E LIVED IN A first-floor crib off 71st and Merrill for a bit, just outside the Corners. Auntie De would come by to watch me while mamma was working at the plant back then, leaving Remi with his uncles to learn the East End hustle.

Auntie couldn't keep a job once summer heat hit good, so the fine Blackbird's time was always free come June. She'd sit with me until her attention wandered from the TV screen, or until the phone rang with one of those guitar-strumming, jive-humming cats calling after her love. Once wanderlust hit, De'd take a walk to the corner store—a full hour's walk, though the Asian's rotten joint wasn't but four blocks from our place.

"Just goin to smoke on me some squares, and get a fresh pack," she'd say, though our living room's walls and couch pillows and Montgomery Wards drapes already stunk with the funk of Camels and Cools, left by uncles from the plant floor and the mack-daddy booths. Mamma'd never uttered a cross word to those men as they lit fire to our breathing air.

"Why you gotta go, Auntie?"

"Just bout to take me a walk real quick. Catch some air.

Sides, don't wanna smoke up you all's place. You know how your mamma be. Don't be telling her I left you when she come home neither. Promise to be good and I'll bring you something back. You want something brung back, don't you?"

"No—you got two more cigarettes in your box. I see um. Mamma don't care about you smoking up in here. Why you gotta go, Auntie? How come I can't walk with you?"

"Just getting me some air, Tommie," she'd say with this smile juking and hiding across ruby lips, and freckles lighting at the tip of her nose. "Sure you don't want nothing brung, my love?"

"Just come back home, Auntie." Then De'd leave for her walk, that not quite empty box of Newports pressed against her pokey left nipple.

Once the *Tennessee Tuxedo* rerun ended on Channel 60, I'd know thirty minutes had already passed by; and because I didn't care for punk-ass *Underdog* afterwards, I'd prop myself at the front window and count each minute slow. Time floating in pasty clouds up high, until the silver-and-red IC train shot by on the 71st Street tracks in my left eye, headed from Indiana to downtown through Stony Island then back again to the Sticks. Every summer day, minutes raced with the Four Corner fools to catch up to that sleek caboose headed northwest. Folks running past me, but never fast enough, for the midday train always left a few puffing dust on those tracks.

I pressed my head against hot glass on this June day, counted ten cabooses passing, and Underdog and Woody Woodpecker and Popeye and the Avengers, all of them had finished screaming about saving my world from the UHF dial, and the sun tilted just a little bit from the lake so Merrill Avenue's brownstone cast enough shade to cool the forehead. Auntie De still wasn't nowhere to be seen, and mamma wouldn't be home from the South Chicago Heights plant for another two hours.

My eyes strained from sun magnified by window glass, and thoughts spun dizzy inside my skull. Mamma'd always told me to wear a hat to protect my dome from that heatstroke pain brought by high sun, cause it burns like crazy even through glass come the summer months. Then again, my dizziness could've been brung by the bloody breath churning between chest and thighs, panting to see Auntie's De's nipples poke from the thin T-shirts and Woolworths bras she wore in June-time. Sharp and high on her body those triangles, and so unlike her big sister's cones rounded and dull from pressing against assembly line levers.

Maybe sweet auntie had just caught the Jeffrey line bus to pick up her Social Security check—all Remi's old man'd left De with, let mamma tell it ("May be all," auntie'd screech back, "but it's a hell-a-bit more than . . .").

De had such trifling ways, like they used to say between our blocks. Mamma claimed the reason I'd turned out such a bright baby boy and Cousin Remi came up an alley thug was that my old girl loved me enough to prop nipples between my lips; where Auntie Denise was always too selfish to stop running and wine-ing and smoking with crapshooters and gray-haired slicksters to think of cleaning up for Remi to sip good nurturing himself. At least that's what she'd tell me whenever I'd start talking that ungrateful nonsense of mine.

Remi, he got the mother who wandered about cracked streets but kept her nipples primed and pointed and let him hustle the corners with the real players because it freed her to do her June-time thing. Me, I got the woman all dull and scarred from struggling in machine fields and returning every day to this smoky-aired, muthafuckin home of ours. This nurturing mother who left me pinned to the window glass, watching trains and folks running in vain and waiting for some sign to point out love's return, but finding only shadows trailing behind fading light.

Sounds shook the window, any sounds, didn't have to be that *pop-crack* from the blocks behind, could've been tires tearing concrete or steel against steel or ambulances racing to Jackson Park Hospital—or the echo between a fading cartoon and an Apple Jacks commercial, maybe. I'd imagine the quaking as the noises of love's end. Mamma and De were all gone from the Corners, I knew—dead and gone to me somehow, someway. My head pressed harder against that window, and I knew I was alone. Sweat dripping the forehead, skin tingling the crotch, feet tapping hardwood, all alone in body.

I felt another train passing north, and it wasn't three o'clock just yet, so the floor supervisor had yet to find my mother overdosed in front of the catalytic converter belt, and Auntie De had wandered too near the train tracks somewhere out there. I knew that such a death had only come for auntie because I'd wasted seed the night before, dreaming of her pointy chests. Spilling incest all over my He-Man pajama bottoms and She-Ra bedsheets to stain. The window glass rumbled as death had snatched auntie as she walked to the corner store because I'd violated her—and she had to pay for my sin. She was the adult, who should've known better than wearing see-through shirts with menthol boxes pressed against breasts full of unsipped milk. Bringing that tingling between a boy's legs until a bloody boner popped out of my drawers to almost match her sweet perfection.

I lit a match from the booklet auntie'd left on the cocktail table. Lit it to see, or to pay honor to my missing loves. Lit that fire to shine them both a clear path to escape death and come back to the Corners. I watched the flame stroll down to my fingertip, where, just before heat blackened yellow palm skin, the flame laughed at me—wicked, knowing, and low—and jumped off its match stem, freed itself all on our living room wall.

Soon as the fire touched plaster surface, a million more laughing, dancing flames shook flickering asses against white plaster, and the room went up. I ran to the kitchen, fire chasing at my tail, coughing and still hard for my lost love, as sun-shaming heat grew and spread to full life in the apartment. I took a safe watching place in the kitchen, far enough away that smoke hadn't swallowed air just yet. Stood on top of my favorite eating chair to see the burning through that doorway; watched our lamp shade melting and plaster peeling down from the ceiling, saw how those white walls turned gray and then black as sky over the nighttime lake, just before paint crinkled and smoke swirled without choking my safe corner just yet. Close enough to let me see the bristles of mamma's shag rug float from the floor though, before the burning paused its mocking to gulp away debris. My hard nut wilted only as flames jumped up to the living room window so the IC tracks, and Merrill Avenue, and the neighborhood folks chasing after trains, were all gone from my eyes.

I stood on my tiptoes gagging and slobbering by then as the legs to my sunny side table melted, and its glass top crashed. That fire didn't dare touch our thirteen-inch color TV screen though. Its smoke swirled all about the brown cabinet and marched up to chomp away the rest of the carpet, then stopped right before the last of the afternoon cartoons—*The Amazing Spider-Man*. Flaming, mock laughter quieted long enough to let his intro music play:

> *Spins a web . . . any size . . . catches thieves*
> *. . . just like flies . . . Lookout . . .*
> *Here comes the Spider-Man.*

I never thought of dying on top of my favorite eating chair. Death may be a villain in a smoke-white hood but he can't come for dizzy twelve-year-old knuckleheads, not while the Spider-Man song plays.

Auntie De and her new sugar daddy busted in just as the living room couch disappeared, and I'd hopped up to the countertop as my favorite chair had turned hot to the soles. That sugar daddy ran through that gray-orange cloud with his head down—all I saw coming at me was a black bald spot rimmed in gray and his forearm shielding the face from smoke. Snatched me up off the counter and wrapped my ass in his leather trench coat, he did. Why was sugar daddy wearing a trench in hot June daytime? Cause he was a true player, pimping South Shore's Four Corners, ready to do anything—live or die, run or burn—to get between the thick legs of my auntie love. That's why.

Thank God for nigganess that burning day. Sugar daddy grabbed me up from that counter and ran down the three-flat entry steps, out to freedom on Merrill Avenue.

By the time my mother showed up from the plant, the fire department trucks clogged our block between the tracks and 72nd Street: more swirling, mocking, hot lights. Our potbellied landlord leaned against the busted light post in his front yard, smacking tobacco against his right-side teeth, one eyeball watching me hide snug under Auntie De's arms, while the other peeled on my mother crying to the cops at curbside.

The top of my nappy afro nudged against perky heaven, right there next to sugar daddy in his smoldering trench coat. He hadn't shed a lick of sweat yet, not running into those flames, not running out, and not even standing in the late-day funk of our blocks. The man was still doing whatever he had to do to make my love into his own—where's the sweat to that for a hero in a burning leather trench coat?

My mother stood with us finally, took me by the hand and pulled me from her trifling sister, just so slightly, but not strong enough. Leave it to me, nothing would ever take me from second heaven, not even the old girl's resurrection off the factory floor and return home. But it's never been left to me. I let go of De as tears streaked from mamma's eyes, and the *gu-ug* sound whimpered from her rust-chapped lips. Then the city firemen crashed out our living room window, that hole where I'd propped and pressed my head to wait. Black hero bats shattered glass, let smoke free to swallow the sun left over home.

*   *   *

THE 3:54 IC train did run down Auntie De not six months later. Auntie and sugar daddy'd gone and gotten lit at the Soft Steppin Lounge, then took a walk along the tracks. Drunk fools stumbling along so bubbly, half a block from the next odd-numbered IC stop. That silver-and-red steel train came speeding along its southeast-bound way, as they do midday, ripping through the streets fast enough to sideswipe auntie into the Clyde Avenue wig shop.

My mother blamed my sugar daddy hero, rambled on about how he'd slap auntie upside the skull whenever she'd get to spitting her fool back talk. *Maybe De'd started flapping her sassy-ass mouth out on 71st after sugar daddy'd covered for all her drinks, maybe he'd got his full of her nonsense.* This was how mamma's teary speculation ended: sugar daddy, fed up and floating high off that freebase while swimming low off sauce wine, pushed my love into the IC, after timing its approach just right.

I didn't buy it first off, not at all, not the hero who'd saved me from flames just because he wanted to impress Auntie De. Why would he hurt her? Steal those sweet, pointy nipples full of fresh love from me, sure, but just to leave her mangled and chopped in window glass? Never. My mother rolled eyes full of salty water and crust at my fool argument. *Haha,* she laughed in her breath-choking way. *You never underestimate the doings of a sugar daddy nigga,* she said, *especially when he's already gotten all he ever truly wanted. They're beasts,* she told me, *all of them.*

And after he didn't show for auntie's homegoing, what could I say? That's what mamma and them called De's services,

just like folks would call Granny Allen's burial years later—
high-low holy rollers dropped my wife's grandmother under
dirt and had the nerve to name it a "homegoing" party. Bunch
of fools full of pain pretending that it ain't right to cry for an
old woman's cancerous bones sinking deep down in the ground.

Homegoing at least seemed a proper name for auntie's
services. Love never seemed like she belonged to this place no
ways. Maybe wherever the IC train took her off to really was
something more like home for auntie. Still couldn't blame
sugar daddy, not my hero—sugar daddy knew to save me from
the flames and push De into that train. It's a rare thing, for a
soul to understand the difference between one who belongs in
the Four Corners and one looking to go on to rightful home.

*　　*　　*

THIS LAWYER TARSHA sent to the 63rd Street precinct
house reminds me of the claims adjuster who filed that paper-
work to cover up my mother's negligence, saving me from the
Department of Children and Family Services. Punked our fat-
rat landlord out of the suit for damages he was ready to file
against us, too. This insurance man conned his bosses into replacing burnt-out possessions floated into the Merrill Avenue
dusk, too, although my mother had stopped paying the premiums months before. He was a true savior. I believe she went
ahead and gave him some once the claim was settled.

I'd thought of becoming a lawyer as a child because it
sounded like an accomplishment she would've found worth all
of her sacrifice. All that selflessness so her baby boy seed grew
into a legitimate hustler, attorney-at-law. Sounded good and

worthy. Then I burned our home and came to find that lawyers were only the middlemen between us and the true saving we needed in this tragedy. The real scam at the end of our salvation back in 1984 lay in the con an insurance man ran on his bosses, all to benefit poor fools and for the happy moaning place found between her legs—so that's what I became in life, an adjuster.

Tarsha's lawyer blocks the sliver of precinct house light as he walks into the interrogation room, and he has the same acorn-shaped head as that adjuster from years back. He bounds as he walks, moving on his tiptoes as if dropping soles to the ground will force whatever stick that straightens his back deep into the crack of his ass. He nearly leaves earth with each step, knees springing his body high so the eyes peer and shift over and above the rest of this room, over me most of all. When I was a child, my mother took me to Great America with Cousin Remi and one of my factory-floor uncles. Soon as our canvas soles touched hot funhouse concrete, I bounced as Tory B. Moore bounces now, gazing at roller coasters and merry-go-rounds without paying mind to the world around.

Tory Moore is short and slight, a wisp blown into this place by the breeze—wicked or clean breeze, I can't say, for we're locked inside airless space just now. So slight that he wouldn't be here for my eyes to see, what with his orange skin swallowed by this ceiling lamp fluorescence. Wouldn't notice him at all not for his bounce.

The main difference between this cracked orange nut and our old claims adjuster is the eyes. The lawyer's pupils shift about the interrogation room, left, right, and through me as he drops his briefcase across fake marble, into this very same chair where Officer Weidmann sat a week ago. He's hiding his true reasons for coming to this 63rd Street cop house, thinks I believe that he has only arrived to protect me from the barbs of Wee Man's new questioning. That insurance man from 1984, he looked straight into my little eyes back then; and I saw him looking at me and understood that once he'd finished with his hustle, silence at the end would certainly make everything all right in our lives.

Either this new school savior is a fool or he takes me for one—which my pride tags as a form of foolishness—for he should know that I fully grasp what truly brings him here. Tory B. Moore is a contracts consultant at Tarsha's firm. Twice a month, he visits her Loop office for meetings with the single-breasted suits up high and, while waiting to ply his jive trade, he strikes up friendly conversations with the office ladies. So impressively thoughtful and provocative this lawyer, or so Tarsha gushes, for such a gold-shitting machine figure. Even asks about the baby's well-being, always remembering my child's name, no matter the weeks passed and attention divided—

". . . is Dawn walking yet? . . . talking, too? . . . no, I don't know what she said this morning . . . what a genius child . . . takes after her mother surely—"

Tory fakes this pitiful, temporary blindness at the .4 karat diamond hiding between the folds of Tarsha's left ring finger and the dim of the waiting room light. Talks more phony jive just before asking about Tarsha's husband—the provider of this dull gem—always sure to ask about me, because he's a mighty slick acorn head.

She doesn't have to say the words, but listening to my wife speak of him, I know Tory's morning visits and his deep questions are the highlight of her days in the tower. He probes her, then listens intensely, sensitively to her answers: how else to explain these gushes as she recalls? Although Tory Moore remains astute enough of the feminine ego to balance the interest he affords every one of the office ladies, his eyes only stop shifting to fix on the slice of lace slip in Tarsha's lap, peeped just over the top of her desk monitor. Meanwhile, he reminds them all, if they or their families ever find themselves in need of legal assistance of any sort, his ribbed business cards are posted at the main reception desk. His Dearborn Street firm is stocked with an army of attorneys available for pro-bono or reduced-rate work, and his primary concern is forever the community, and will remain so, no matter how high he climbs. And he's already sixty-six stories up, see, pretty goddamned high. He'll never forget from whence he came, he reminds as his neck cranes just over that monitor.

So Tarsha took herself to the Loop last Monday morning, just as handcuff marks started to fade from my wrists. Got herself sprayed and painted, hairdo freshly straightened the night before, to share with this acorn the tale of my shame:

"*What can you do to save my family, Mr. Moore?*" she whimpered, just like she begged Cousin Remi on Soft Steppin Saturday nights. "*If the authorities want to pursue this case, maybe they'll come to take my daughter away, and my life— my family. You told us you care so much about the community, that you're one of the good brothers. And I seen you speechifying on the cable access channels and marching next to Jesse Jr.*

and the preachers, not even next to them really, but a few steps in front, power signs raised to the sky, haberdasher hats crowning heads to hide cracked nut peaks like it's still 1964. You claim by any means necessary you'll do what must be done on behalf of a poor family in South Shore, there in the projects, over on the West Side. Wherever. You say you started out in the Reagan era representing the desperate and trapped from these streets, fighting in the PD's office for folk who didn't possess the crumbs to afford a proper fucking—excuse my foul language, Mr. Moore, sir, I'm from Oglesby Avenue, this's how we speak with our own—a proper muthafuckin-over by Cook County–style justice. So please, Mr. Moore, save me, save us. In return, what you see down here, it is all yours."

The sound of lovely tears melts a heart beating from worlds trapped by pavement blocks—any four-cornered block, I'm here to tell you. I know, for Tarsha once whimpered like this for me, sometimes when we'd got done loving, sometimes during.

Tory saw enough of what it was that he wanted over the monitor, and here his middleman ass sits in the 63rd Street precinct question-asking room, across the table from a fellow South Shore (or some trapped place) fool whose handcuff cuts healed a week ago only to reappear today. I see them now, at the same place where ivory cotton decorated with shimmering links drape on Tory Moore's wrists. And I do hear what Tarsha says, and doesn't say, about him. I've always listened.

No different from the leather trench-coated sugar daddy and even that saving insurance adjuster, and completely opposite to our potbellied Merrill Avenue landlord, this hero has come to save my life, all for the price of taking love from me: Auntie

De, mamma, Tarsha. Dawn, too—yes, one day some hustler will slither near to save me for the price of my child's soul.

"How're they treating you, Tommie?" Tory Moore's voice is a pierce whine, the noise of an orange-faced man from the South Side faking a Dershowitz Brooklyn accent through nasal passages.

"Since I came in today? Just fine." I rub my left wrist, then the right. I'm soothing the nerves clenching and running up to the messy weight found inside my head. "Last week, I wasn't nothing but a piece of shit jailbird. They change it up on you once they peep you got the loot to post bail and family looking out for you and a lawyer to stand in. They know you're not out here like a crumb-less bum now, and they ain't getting away with their bullshit, so they straighten theirselves out, you know?"

Tory sneers as he spreads his briefcase open. "No, I don't."

"Neither do I." Under the interrogation room door, this crack of gray light blinks. I see it as I stretch my neck to peek over his left shoulder. "I was just saying."

Spit gurgles in his throat. "None of them touched you, threatened to touch you," Tory croons, "raised a hand as if they thought about touching you, then changed their minds. Tortured you or told you to imagine the torture they'd exact upon you. Think carefully, Tommie."

His brown eyes dart about the room's corners, then along the two-way mirror at my left. "I didn't fess to anything," I hum. These eyes switch to me for a bit, shining satisfaction, and I feel proud of myself because my savior approves. Until they dart to the corner again. "Only thing they told me to imagine was the harm I'm doing the community. Only thing hurt was those cuffs slapping my wrists to stop the blood flow. See—"

I drop my arms to the fake marble, pulling my sleeve back to expose wounds, but three fingers rise to the lawyer's lips. He wears a diamond-crusted, platinum-gold wedding band squeezed to the ring finger's hilt.

"I want you to think carefully, Tommie. I understand some time has passed since the arrest, almost two weeks. You've gone through quite a bit, my friend, definite trauma. The mind tends to deal with such experiences by burying the particulars, even in the short term. But I want you to think. Remember that pain on your wrists. Seeing those marks, I feel you hurting. That pain and how you were blasted with light as they surrounded and hounded you on—Seventy-ninth Street." He reads from a crumbled sheet long enough for the bottom margin to dangle from the table. The lawyer spreads the document's top ends with the same fingers he used to shut me up. "You remember every word these police spoke to you, take your time going over the nature of these conversations. Each curse and every lying promise, every hateful bit of hypocrisy. You don't forgive them for anything. Bubbling gratitude and easy mercy are the African American man's great weaknesses, you know. Remember over these next few days, so we can clear you of this nonsense."

Lies? Yes, this lawyer is hitting it right on with his speechifying—I see why Tarsha worships him once or twice a month—acorn head is tearing the mask off their lies. Even if Tory only reveals truth to me so that my wife will thank him by twirling about on his face, he's breaking it down for a brother.

Not for him, I would've gone away peacefully, bowed down in gracious deference if that script had damned me for life for dealing weed on 79th Street.

"*Good police you is,*" I would've slobbered. Maybe I would've sung a down home chitlin song for Officer Wee Man and his birds and his law, and the judge who'd send me away, too. Because I need to see the light creeping from Tory Moore's back and forget the shift of his eyes to remember that it doesn't matter that this acorn has thoughts only of the gap hidden by my wife's T.J. Maxx lace or that he's been there and done that (as the Soft Steppin pimps say), up high in the executive bathroom's last stall. His lust for her only means that me and Tory Moore are down for the same cause.

Eyes shifting with this gray light's blink, my lawyer empowers a fool with brilliant, churchy words, and he at least tells me the real deal here in the interrogation room. And he's to be believed, for only a true savior from some place just inside Four Corners appreciates beauty like her trapped beauty.

"When they come in here," Tory Moore says before bringing three fingers to his mouth again. "You shhhh. Don't say a word. Let me do the talking. You just listen to every word spoken. Carefully, use your best, good mind. You listen, and you remember."

I haven't completely figured out this latest hustler who's jived my love away from me, but I promise to do as he says as Officer Weidmann and Phil do the flatfoot march through the interrogation room light. I vow, and I say "thank you" to this lawyer, my hero.

9

WEIDMANN HIDES IN the alley's shadow. The cop's always somewhere he's not supposed to be, wouldn't be, if the world were right: cruising down boulevard blocks, flying about in dreamy sky, popping out of garbage pile shadows. If he came at me face-to-face, I'd know good and well to turn the other way and run for dear life—not that I could save myself even then.

I catch his outline poking from the alleyway as I stumble from Tory Moore and the precinct house. I know this is the cop lurking before I hear his voice. "Quite a joker you got yourself there."

"What?" Weidmann shows himself out of the alley and stands so that part of his body blocks this path to the 63rd Street bus stop. He leaves just enough paved curb for me to slide past, and just enough covered by his east-leaning shadow for me to understand escape as a dare.

"Said that's quite a joker you brought in here. Fancy joker of a mouthpiece." Weidmann smiles, stretching the sloped outline of his head. "Where'd you get that guy from?"

I don't move until the cop turns himself toward 63rd so that we walk together. "Family friend," I say.

"Mmh." I hear the clicking of his boot heel trailing behind as we pass the gangway opening. "Didn't call for all that showtime crap though—this situation doesn't need to be as serious as a thousand-dollar clown. That's about how much fancy trousers is running you a week, I know."

Spite sneers through my lips, though I don't mean for it to show. "It's covered. He's a friend of the family, like I say."

"Just mentioning for your sake, Tiny. Dealing weed's not so serious in our world, is it? Unless somebody's looking to make it serious. You were carrying a lot of the crap, but it's a first offense on record. Better to save your big joker for a hand when you'll really need um, I figure. Got a real war coming soon, gonna wish you still had a big joker to play on that bloody day."

I peek over my left shoulder, searching for Phil—this has to be one of their corner shakedowns. No matter that we're far north and west of the Corners, this cop is playing me for a hype. "Are you supposed to be talking to me right now?"

"What?"

"After I execute my right to a attorney, doesn't that attorney have to be here for you to even talk to me?"

"Mouthpiece charging you all that money for this advice?"

"I didn't need a lawyer to tell me that. Learned Miranda in my criminal justice class," I say.

"Oh. Col-lege boy. That's right." The cop blushes and smiles. "Funny. You wanted to come into the business?"

"No," I say because I can't stop myself. I blink and the darkness behind my lids lies and tells me that I'm not so scared of this bird-pig. "Wasn't nothing but an elective."

"*Elective, execute.* Those are fancy-sounding words." I recognize that Weidmann isn't wearing a uniform as his fingers pull at his windbreaker's Velcro and fiddle about the insides of pockets. Swore that I glanced a twinkling badge and nightstick slung from his hip in garbage pile shadows and heard those same boot heels clicking from the 79th Street night—not this orange Chicago Bears coat, half-faded blue jeans and K-Swiss sneakers cloaking the cop in Southwest Side sameness. "What've I said to you? Spoke not a word except to give you a compliment on the lawyer you chose, for what comes down to such a tic-tac-toe case."

I chuckle. "Not my call to make—what this is and isn't."

Weidmann pulls a White Sox cap from his pocket and slides it over the forehead slope. "Whose call is it?"

"I don't know." The 63rd Street bus tumbles east. "Like you say, this is my first time offending. Not sure how this's supposed to work out. Guess it's all on the judge."

"Mmh." Weidmann steps toward St. Louis Avenue and watches this bus fade as black smoke rises and circles. He squeezes both hands into his jeans. "That supposed to be a smart-ass answer?"

Two Mexican women appear on the opposite side of the steel pole, their arms and backs drooping toward the sidewalk with the weight of plastic Aldi bags. Weidmann speaks his words barely above a mutter, but yellow rage flashes in his forehead before he pulls the cap low to cover his brow. I watch another bus tumble near, still blocks west of us. I wish it closer, but traffic blocks the 63 line underneath a viaduct.

"No. Ain't meant to be."

"Cause a smart guy with some advanced education like your big joker mouthpiece back there, he woulda asked me about the easy way out of this situation by now," the cop coos like the factory-floor players used to coo my mother on our burned living room couch, before they disappeared to her moaning place. "And I woulda explained to the smart guy what he already knows too well: there ain't no court, no judges, no shiny jokers, no law here, just two fellahs standing on a street corner talking our way through a situation."

The 63 bus eases through the overpass as the streetlight turns, and a jet floats overhead toward Midway, its fuel tanks' roar unheard as if the plane flies higher than it seems. Weidmann's words are a hustle in my ears, for even near the airport, everybody scams to get by. Got no better choice than to roll with his game though; my bus is coming to take me home. "So what's the easy way, Officer?"

Weidmann laughs and looks at the Mexican women. "Knew it from the first time we sat down together, you're a different type."

"What's funny?"

The women drop their grocery bags to concrete and stare, nostrils furling at the burning fuel as another jet passes silently, and the 63 rumbles in our front. "Just that most from over your way woulda snapped by now. Gone about putting me in my place for dissin' um. Ain't that how you all say it? Called me, my partner, my country, all kinds of piece-of-shit motherfuck-ers. How do you all say it: '*muthafucka*'? Snapped me up good for doing you like this, playing you for a soft mark. Anybody else woulda let me have it by now. Funny, you don't see the need to dis my white ass. Must be the col-lege schooling."

"Told, you, I took Criminal Justice. I know my rights. I know how it works. Why would I curse you—so you can whip out your pistol butt or go up under your armpit for the billy club and bust my head open? Ain't like I'm bout to fight back. Once I ball my fist to steal off you, you turn that butt around, and take me outta here. Legal execution, like you say. What place is anything out of my mouth about to put you in?"

His smile fades, and Weidmann peeks at the bag ladies. He loosens the windbreaker, then stretches his arms to full span, and I think that he's about to flap across these three feet of pavement; but I don't run, no matter the pitchfork he hides in cotton feathers. No, I can't run, and instead of chasing after me, Weidmann turns a slow one hundred eighty degrees with the jacket opened. The women laugh foreign laughter as he lifts the windbreaker tail to reveal himself, raising the material at the low end of the spine for a glimpse at his ass. He twirls once again, slower, and there's no nightsticks, no pistol butts, no pitchforks hidden on this cop. He's clean in his brown shirt buttoned to the rim of his Adam's apple. When his circle is done, he steps toward the steel pole and his whisper slices at my ear canal.

"I want this to be easy, Tiny." An American Airlines jet flies above us now, and this bird does dive as it approaches Midway's landing place. "We know you're a guy trying to make some change in a chump's hustle. Unlucky guy definitely, who got hemmed with a nice amount of illegal substance. But a down-on-his-luck-first-time-chump guy who a judge will look up and down, then hear the mouthpiece's fancy rhyming pap about col-lege and getting laid off from a good job with a family at home, and the judge is gonna see that hungry crow look in your eyes, hungry and sad like the one I see right here. He's gonna cut you slack, seen it two thousand times. You'll fuck up again: I know—the judge, he knows, and your prick-lick mouthpiece knows, too. It's just our calling to feel like mercy'll give you the opportunity to do good and right. We ain't fooling nobody but ourselves. Shit, deep down, you know you're gonna fuck up again even. These times is hard, ain't getting any softer soon. What can you do but keep hustling in a chump's game?"

The bus touches this curbside, unloading its final passengers. "Learned my lesson, Officer," I slobber, "thank you. I don't wanna go through this trouble no more. Got too much to live for."

"Hold that bus," the cop points at the 63 driver with his left hand, whips out his badge backed in black leather to flash against the bus's windows. "Yeah, yeah. I don't see any reason why we should sit around and wait for you to fuck up on a pink judge's time. I say better to wipe this slate clean. The better and real easy way, I say."

It's me smiling now. Fool thing to do, I know, allowing this stretching at the bottom of my face where gratitude breaks into the jaw until the corners of Weidmann's smirk dulls. On 79th Street, I know the players don't smile until the crap's bounce falls still on one side, and even then, their smiles won't shine with joy. Nothing but a half-cocked grin those players show, left side turned up to the nose and the right fixed even with the jive. I bite my bottom lip. "How much?"

"Mmh," Weidmann glances over his shoulders. "No real price. Everything really ain't about dollars, Tiny. That's another col-lege lie. All I want for us choosing to leave mouthpieces and judges and courts and the twisted system out of this business between two men, all I want is for you to set up a meeting between me and Remi Simms."

"Trick on my family?" I laugh, can't help it even as passengers' eyes glare down from the bus windows. I pause as another jet floats north to south, taking off now, and I pray the cop forgets himself in its flight.

"There you go again," Weidmann pushes the cap's brim so that most of his forehead slope shows, "talking two steps ahead of the game. Who said anything about 'trick'—that's not a good col-lege word, Tiny, that's Seventy-ninth Street jive. I'm just telling you to set up a conversation between me and your relative. You don't gotta bring him over here to the station, I ain't looking to sit down over on Jeffrey Boulevard. So we pick a neutral spot: restaurant, bar, downtown, shopping mall in the burbs, someplace clean. You set the meeting up, and long as your dope dealer kin sees things the way how I see things and he's willing to talk, you won't have to worry about retaining that thousand-dollar mouthpiece and I won't have to sit down with any big prick-lickers anymore, cause we're all squared away."

My conscience whispers into the right ear, opposite the cop, advises me to ask for a guarantee, writing on paper to turn words burned and blown away in airport heat into promised scripture, but I blink as I listen. And by the time my eyelids rise, Weidmann's gone from 63rd and St. Louis, returned to the shadows behind his cop house.

The passengers on the 63 still watch me, pent-up frowns bringing the red of lost patience to their cheeks. The bus driver stares my way, too, with his knuckles wrapped around the door lever. Walking the bus's steps, I notice his is the darkest face on the bus aside mine, and I recognize him from some place. Maybe he drove the Jeffrey line when I was still riding to Grand Avenue. Or no, maybe he's a wannabe mack with his city paycheck cashed and rolled in silk pants pockets like the rest of the weekend players at the Soft Steppin Lounge.

"You riding, or what?" he asks.

I jog the two top steps before he bends the door shut, and his bus tilts up from the street pavement. I pay my fare with the last dollar-fifty in torn cotton pockets, before answering, "I'm riding."

✳ ✳ ✳

MEETING AT THE Greektown Gyros joint on Jackson and Halsted was Remi's idea. There's no free legal parking around the fried take-out hole, even past midnight—Jackson Street is packed past the Jackson Hotel just to the east. Olive-skinned party girls and boys from the brown brick clubs lurk around us in their BMWs and Audis, them and the bums on foot rising from the alley bins and out of the flophouse next door.

Most don't eat in Greektown this late; party people just snatch their gyros and burgers and salads of shiny purple and green in brown paper bags with stained bottoms near bursting, then run back into the night. But there's still so much noise made inside this place, what with customers yelling over the countertop to echo outside, answered by cooks' grease-burned yelps, and sizzling grills burning whole lambs to char—so much Greektown music that this is the best late-night meeting place south or west of downtown. Nothing spoken softer than a scream is heard here.

Remi pulls the Range Rover just past the Jackson flop-house, at the Kennedy Expressway overpass. Stops inches from a hydrant where this bum in a torn winter cap turns his back and squirts himself against red metal until smoke rises from the pavement cracks. The man raises his head to midnight sky to thank God for relief, and I turn to Remi. My cousin touches the bill of his LA Dodgers cap, straightens its left cocking, then reaches across the gear shifter and taps the back of my head; for luck, or for blood love, I don't know, but he taps twice before pushing his door open and running across Jackson Street. I watch until he passes the empty Crown Victoria cruiser leaning against the curb where Jackson and Halsted meet.

I turn on the hazard lights as Remi disappears, but my hand isn't clear of the dashboard before Westside breathes deep and pained in the backseat. He slides across leather and rests himself behind my seat, and I remember the lesson from the old mob flicks, the good ones. That gangster counsel about never letting a snake slither at your back, cause he's only looking to suck the sap from your spine. I remember and turn myself so that my left kidney rests against the door as I watch these cars and semis fade north on the Kennedy.

"Always knew you was a fuckup," Jackie says. I peek over my shoulder, and the man in the winter hat has disappeared from the sidewalk, leaving only his hot stream. "Remi always talking shit bout me and James—but I always knew it'd be you who'd fuck us up in the end. Tell him that all the time. Fool's always taking your back though."

My gut wants to tell Westside about the hell he can burn to char in, remind him that he's the bastard son of a three-dollar crack whore, and part retarded on top of it. But sitting on Jackson across from a flophouse while my cousin meets with Wee Man the bird-pig, and I wait with this wild-eyed born fiend at my side and a stream of pee flowing and burning under us— "Remi shoulda listened to you" is all I can say.

"Damn right," Jackie taps the back passenger window with his thumb knuckle. "Wouldn't be in none of these problems if his ass'd just listened. Gotta be smart and careful who you get down with in this game, if you wanna make it—you know how I figured you didn't know a goddamn thing about being smart and careful?"

"How's that?"

"Got too many questions floating around in your eyes." He laughs and hits his window and the passenger door shakes my spine. "I see them. That kinda fool-ass curiosity makes me figure you for soft around the trigger finger and at the balls. Even when you really ain't—but you are soft, I hear it, I see it in you. Too many soft candy questions passing by those eyeballs. Means you're wondering about the ways and means, bringing worry to your own head, and worry to a real nigga like me who sees question marks floating through you. Be worrying a bunch, don't you, Tommie?"

I lift myself from the seat cushion, stretching for a glimpse of Remi or Weidmann's forehead slope through the joint's window, but I find nothing but glass and party folks lined up for lamb meat and hamburgers as I rest my back against the door and forget Westside's question.

"Thinking and worrying right now, ain't you?" he says.

Jackie drives a knee into the passenger seat's backrest and my seat tilts to the dashboard. "Yeah, thinking. I do a lot of that."

"You thinking and worrying types make a real nigga wonder. And if a real nigga's wondering, how far he's got to go before he turns to worrying his damn self? Real niggas like me can't be worrying, cause it takes us to do the things thinkers is too busy worrying about to get done. We bone the fine young thang with her legs spread open, we pop a cap in a shit-talking mark, take the last dime off a punk muthafucka, while thinking niggas is sitting high up there, all hard-dicked and insulted and broke with your heavy thoughts."

"That's me." I look Westside in the face for the first time. "Damn shame to admit it, but you got me right."

"Muthafucka," Jackie's eyebrows furl to swallow his pupils, "you trying to be a smart-assed nigga or something?"

"Not at all," I say. "You got me pegged. Sensitive, poor, and hard-dicked."

"Was bout to say." Jackie's knee moves, lets my chair drop to the truck's floor. "Cause for all that goddamn thinking, you thinkers is some dumb asses. Cracking dumb jokes bout somebody's livelihood which you done fucked up, pretending like you the smart muthafucka when it's your stupid ass who got us out here on Jackson and Halsted past midnight. Should be out hustling a way to get the loot back you lost while you was busy thinking dumb ideas."

"I was wrong." I look away from his yellow rage, out to the fire hydrant, then left to Jackson Street as an empty late-night bus passes. "Should be enough for me to admit that."

"Ain't bout being wrong, that shit's given." Jackie lowers the back window glass to spit slime that bounces off the hydrant before splashing in this stream. "About doing dumb shit like riding up to 79th Street and selling a big bag to a fool who cuts hair for a living. If your eyes didn't have so many thoughts and worries running across their view, you'd see obvious shit. Anybody who clips hair for a living ain't but tantamount to a bitch himself. And you ever known a bitch without a big mouth? Might as well've called up the wife of that cop who's got Remi in the gyro shop, told her you had a pound for sale in dimes and nickels. 'But psst, Mrs. Po-po, Misses Bridgeport-Redneck-night-crawling-hammer-cocking Po-po, psst, listen up—don't tell your husband. I'm just letting you know, Misses, in case you maybe wanna smoke on a little something with me.' What's the first thing she's gonna do once her head hits that pillow next to the Mr. Po-po she been taking that one-and-only nightstick swing from for twenty years?"

"Talk."

"You're damn right, 'talk.' Trick off on your dime-bag ass."

"So, what're you saying?" I ask. Jackie's eyes drop to his lap, and breath comes from the drooping gap between his lips.

I figure him for sleep or passed out, until he rubs the right socket. "JW from the barbershop's the one who put us out here?"

Jackie laughs. "Him or somebody else you did business with. Can't deal with all niggas, cause a lot of these niggas is bitches out here; your boy in the middle barber chair for example. Can't deal with most bitches, cause so many of um got big mouths, lips stay spread and flapping to match their fat kitty cats."

"Who're you supposed to deal with then?"

Jackie stares at the hydrant for quiet seconds. "I—shit, who did you sell to?"

"Nobody but who I already told y'all about," I say.

"Well then, you're answering your own questions. It's all shooting craps in the alley." He turns to the pavement. "Musta been one of them putting word out on you. Maybe ol boy at the shop, maybe Primo. Hell do I know? You only dealt a few weeks before the po-pos hemmed you up. Musta been some tricking going on somewhere. It's the dumb nigga who leaves himself open to getting tricked on."

"You made your point?"

"No," Jackie touches my left shoulder, mocking the love tap Remi placed at the back of my head. "Ain't no points been made till my five-spot, or my pound, get put back in these hands. That's what matters. Only reason you ain't took the whipping you got coming is if I break you off like you need to get broke, how I'm ever gonna see my proper payback? Remi talking this *family* bullshit. Any other muthafucka who'd got us all exposed like this, we'd be burying him."

"Then you'd never get the money you're owed, right?"

"What did I just say?" Jackie taps the window glass three times with his thumb knuckle. "Shut up with your stupid questions."

"I'm gonna take care of what I owe," I tell him. "I ain't running off on my debts. I remember."

"Nowhere to run," Jackie's laugh is full of salt now. "Remi talking his *family* bullshit. Wouldn't be on Jackson and Halsted in front of the roach motel, and he wouldn't be sitting at po-po's mercy, not for family. Niggas ain't got family, that's what being a real nigga's all about. Best know that by now."

"You're right." I grind my teeth.

"Shut the fuck up with your comments—you worry me," he says. I don't hear his thumb tapping now. His knuckle hits against whistling air where the window is barely opened. "You hear me? Don't say nothing else to me, goddamnit."

I swallow and touch the dashboard radio controls. Midnight on Fridays is the low end of the radio dial's late-night rap hour, and the Rover's fixed with this beating sound system. Fake crooks rhyme loud and long to echo inside our space. Murder, debt, and such real nigga shit—hos and blows and mofos, all to these looping, heisted beats. I watch Westside's head bounce to the drum track, and feel my own feet tapping against Remi's driver-seat leather, until I turn to the pop station way up the dial. More echoing mofos, with less bass now; I keep turning, just to the left, where I find WNUA's elevator melodies.

Jackie snaps at the synthesized lullaby. "So you dumb *and* a faggot, both together? What the fuck?"

My toes don't tap now, and it's not long before Jackie's head falls into his chest. I wait for the backseat snore, then answer him in a whisper just low enough for hollow strings to hide the sound of me.

"I know I worry you, mofo," I reply. *"It's cause I got these thoughts, and you see um shining, not floating, in my eyes. Scariest thing this world done ever known is a nigga with thoughts. Your punk ass's just another mofo going with the flow of some other man's show. Should be worried—when my thoughts bring me to flipping this world all on its head, you're going down with the rest of the mofos. Who's the dumb ass now, worrying bastard—"*

"What?" I look to the backseat, and Jackie's head is still bent to his chest, and his snore sounds louder. Watch and wait for him to say something more until I hear the tap of soles escaping against pavement.

Remi runs from Greektown Gyros' rear door, darting across Jackson Street just in time to miss the grill of a *Tribune* paper delivery truck speeding east. He hops inside the Rover, landing on my ankle before I turn myself to the windshield. He swallows three chunks of pissy air, but it's not before he catches his own breath to speak that Jackie's snoring stops.

"Goddamn," Remi yells, and the sound of the word swallows Elton John's piano keys.

"What?" Jackie says again as he looks to the gyro joint, then to the hydrant.

Remi kicks the Rover accelerator to the floor and slices us in front of the eastbound headlights on Jackson, glaring over his shoulder at the restaurant as he drives. When he finally turns to his front at Jefferson, the funk of lamb meat cuts from his nose. "That cop is a beast."

"Told you," Jackie chimes. Remi screeches the Rover to a red light stop. "Wee Man ain't no punk. I tried fucking with him before, over on the blocks long time ago. No happenings."

Cuz's breathing slows as we pass the El tracks. "We've got troubles. Wee Man says I gotta start giving him names."

Jackie's laugh is full of hiss. "You're supposed to sell us out to save this toothpick bastard. Ain't that a bitch—you're about to do it, too, aren't you? For him? You'd best remember I'm family before he is. You're my big brother, don't forget—"

"What are you jabbering about?" Remi turns the truck right, heads south on State. "Don't nobody care about your name; they already know where you live. Cop wants to know about the real players, supposed to give him those names. Tell him how they're holding, where the stash sleeps, which honeys hold the keys to that big-time dough: Folks, Lords, Latins, Hustlers, Stones, all of um. Long as they're getting down any-place near 79th Street, Wee Man wants my lips to speak loud."

"You told him you don't know a damn thing, right?" West-side pulls at my shoulder to draw himself near the front seat. His head, neck, and half of his torso are between us by the time he lets go. "We ain't bout to go out like no rats just to save this candycake ho, I know."

Remi picks teeth with his pinky finger and laughs. "This ain't *Law and Order,* nigga." At Roosevelt Road, he turns back toward Lake Shore. "Ain't nobody taking statements to build no court cases. Remember where you live, *lil bro.* Wee Man's M.O.'s been the same, long as you known—cop's trying to make himself some side cream, shaking down the big players."

"What's our take?" Westside asks.

"Our take is this fool's ass." Remi adjusts the mirror, then points at me as he stares at his own reflection. "Police got himself a whole crew of street beaters ready to do shakedown work on the Corners."

"That's what he told you?" I ask.

They laugh until Kenny G. is only a radio whimper somewhere inside the Rover cabin. "Shut the fuck up. I keep telling him," Jackie says. "Could you please tell your boy to shut the fuck up?"

"Wee Man's ill police, Cuz,"Remi explains instead. "His old man was a ill cop back in the day. Granddaddy same deal, a sick slicker in this jungle, all of um into a little bit of all things dirty. Only difference back in the day was his daddy and granddaddy had to act like they were on some righteous, public service kind of hero patrol. That 'just say no,' kiddies' shit. This Wee Man in '02, he don't play like a goddamn thing. Everybody accepts this is gangsters' kingdom we're living in now, no mystery—so here he go, stank ass right with the rest of us. Fucking and hustling and slinging and stealing and rolling round. Everybody knows. What the hell is this on my radio?"

Remi dials back to the radio's end, where the rap hour bangs on. More rhyming thieves delivering love poems about this bloody, real gangster shit. He raises the volume and our heads rock beyond control. The commercial between songs breaks open enough space for me to answer. "Sorry, y'all," I say. "Didn't want to cause you any problems—after how you looked out for me. Y'all always looked out for me. Tried to. Ain't trying to put you out like this."

Jackie's knee jabs my back. "Keep telling you to shut the fuck up." Westside leans over my right shoulder and whispers against the ear, more hissed mumble than words. "Who's the dumb ass now, cuz?"

REMI LEAVES JACKIE on Phillips Avenue, then swings the Rover back north toward the Drive. I figure he saw Westside's knee digging at my back, or heard the hissing breathed through yellow teeth in the rhythm of the rap hour. Or saw his brother's stubby knuckles tapping and fingertips snapping all about the backseat, disturbing the Rover's ride with their search for ghosts and fleas.

We sit in front of my home now. Twenty stories of blankness, except for this pink lamp beaming behind glass, up too high to be Tarsha waiting on me. In the space between our building and the taller scraper next door, I look out on the lake—no, out on that black line where water and sky end— and in this place, the silver beacon light blinks and wobbles. Off then on and off again, floating on water and falling out of sky all at once.

I feel Remi staring at my left side. He sucks air deep into his stomach while I count the eleven stories to the lamp, and I look north to brace myself; I know he's soon to smash the right side of my face with his steering wheel fist. When no pain comes and the lake light blinks on, I turn to the driver seat to find Remi leaning toward me, his eyes swelling. He can't bring himself to hit me, so his anger dances through the Rover's windows.

The bass drum dies with the rap hour's end, proof that it's past one o'clock. Remi's mouth opens, looking down to the gear shifter now so I won't see the pink lamp or lake light reflected in his eyes.

Then he mumbles, "I got you in this."

"What?" I say, though I do hear him.

"I got you into this," he repeats. "Offered you this bit to get down with me, damn near begged you to get on."

"So?" I say. "You were trying to look out."

"No, I wasn't—look out for who?" Remi turns the steering wheel though the idling truck stays still. "I was thinking like a street nigga that don't know better than eating outta trash bins. You got a wife and baby up there, I know that. They're yours. I coulda done right with myself, too—I tried, always figured I coulda—"

I never told Remi how I waited for his mother in our Merrill Avenue street view. When I speak Auntie's De name out loud, his eyes still glass over as he stares at plaster. Figure he blames what came of us in Carbondale on the bloody difference between his old girl going home and mine coping and living on in this world. He's never said so with his own two lips, but I've seen auntie's drunk ghost sweeping down to haunt him as I say any of these words: college, tracks, Greyhound, mamma.

Westside hints around this pain I bring his half-brother. Jackie isn't one for subtlety, and it's none of his Independence Boulevard business anyway, but he's found some kind of truth here. Where James the package delivery man or Westside Jackie mentioning their mothers don't trouble Remi at all, the sound of my lips spouting the word turns empty glass windows into eyes full of slow-floating clouds.

I look away so I don't see Remi's eyeballs trailing after her soul. "You made it, you did it, so now you can't afford to roll like I roll," he says. "Fucking around with me—that family you made, you can burn it up in smoke just like anything else touched by hands."

"Life ain't always how the other man sees it," I say. "You were trying to keep me together the best way you knew how."

Remi lets the air from his stomach. "I know what I was trying to do."

"See." I chuckle. "Ain't always how the other man sees it."

Remi smiles and leans against the window. He picks his bottom lip, then points my way. "Don't you never let me hear you apologizing to nobody who ain't got it coming to him never again. These muthafuckas ain't nobody to be shucking and jiving for."

"What are you talking about?"

"Westside Jack," Remi leans and talks loud over Mariah Carey's screech. "You don't got nothing to be saying 'sorry' to that fool for."

"Wasn't really apologizing to him," I say, as I only remember asking Remi's forgiveness. The beacon light shines without pausing now. "Part of that was his stash—figure I owe him, too. Partway, at least."

He taps my shoulder again. "I'll take care of Jackie. What's the point of calling somebody family if you ain't gonna back him when he's got the devil chasing his ass? Jackie's from out west. Fuck him. Better remember that."

"He's your brother," I remind.

"Halfway. Besides, I ain't heard nothing bout no Satans chasing after Jackie Lowe," Remi adjusts the rearview mirror, then peeks over his shoulder as he talks. "Devil's interested in good souls, you ever noticed? Chases good ones, and lets all the rest be. Nigga like Westside ain't worth a damn to Satan. Until hooves and horns get desperate and start coming after lunatic crack-clowns, don't ever let me hear you saying 'sorry' to a bastard like him again."

I relax my left cheek. "I owe you, Remi—"

"You don't owe nobody, except them." His words swallow the freon breeze as he points through the Rover's roof. I'm not sure if he's aiming at our fourth-floor apartment or at the clouds, but his fingers jab at the hard upholstery leather. "I'm sorry, Tommie—"

"What'd you just say about apologizing to bastards? *Damn.*" I say.

"Tell Tarsha I said so."

I step out of the Rover cabin, but Remi doesn't drive away until my fist touches the building's door handle and my stare drops from the fourth-floor window. Down and away from the meeting place, and I've repeated to myself that I will repay them—my cousin and Westside Jackie Lowe both. But these thoughts float across my eyes in the lobby's glass reflection, warning me to be careful promising payback on the Four Corners. I already owe too much to too many souls here.

$\underline{2}$

10

M Y WINDOW LOOKS on Kung Pao's Carry Outs west and the elevated Red Line tracks to the east: three stories above these streets connected and dissected by a road that slices diagonally and then straightens to the south. A row of shops housed in commercial flats—every one of them as crooked and faceless as Pharaoh Pugh Insurance—stands on the other side of Cermak Road and Wentworth Avenue. This last cubicle with the view from Pharaoh Pugh's corner window, this is my workstation now.

Gladys Tucker makes jangling noise as she navigates the path between our walls. The receptionist has a brickhouse walk, mighty feet slamming against the floor through flat-soled shoes. Her arms are decorated wrist to elbow with gold and silver shackle bracelets. Must be her grandmother's costume jewelry, left to the woman in a last will and testament as some lame-ass excuse for a heritage. Tarsha's grandmother used to wear such jewelry over on Oglesby Avenue. We could always hear the old woman coming two rooms away, good and plenty time for me to snatch my right hand from between her grandchild's thighs.

Clanging and jangling seems more fit for women of those times.

Either Gladys wears these shackles to honor her grand-mother, or she jangles to warn us she's coming near so that we know to pretend to be busy growing Pharaoh's insurance crops. Her jangling, then, could be some merciful way of saving our livelihoods.

Her music stops. I look away from the take-out joint and Gladys leans at my workstation's edge. I pull the roller chair to my desktop computer and tap two keys to clear the screen saver. A cough spits from my lips as I forget to breathe before speaking.

"Hey, Ms. Tucker," I cough again, "how're you this after-noon?"

"Bless-ed," Gladys says, and jangles just so slightly as she answers. Good Christian woman I've come to know her to be over these two weeks, Gladys is always "blessed," far as such things go in scam joints diagonal to Chinatown take-out restaurants. I keep asking only to make certain that today is but another day—if Gladys is still blessed, then I can go on scamming.

At 8:48 each morning, she posts herself at the Pharaoh Company's door, counting heads as workers file into the office and glancing at the clock up high to match and record our entry. Blessedly, she returns to this post at 1:20 each afternoon, near the end of any good worker's lunch hour. Then she jangles about cubicle paths at 4:45—like now, checking a new set of information: which workstations are already cleaned of piles, who zips and unzips bags and locks drawers, and, most of all, which desks sit cleared of all but settled dust. The receptionist recognizes her full blessings for serving Pharaoh Pugh and his office boss, Ramsey, well. They keep the peace and order in Chinatown.

I'm nowhere near as appreciative of adjusting claims as Gladys is of her overseer responsibilities. I'm just another ingrate soul who finally answered the job call because the lives that depend on me left no choice but answering. Merciful grace opened cell bars, so I've gotta make something out of this time granted. If I sit around waiting for the next pitchfork—just like old Weidmann said I would—then what point was there in escaping those flying pigs in the first place?

"Can I help you with anything?" I ask.

"'May'—may you what?" Gladys laughs. She's got this lounge vet chuckle, older than her forty years and gruff from lungs full of stale menthol smoke. "Aren't you the new one here? How are you going to help me, pray tell?"

"Just asking," I stare at her block of a body and flash my good boy grin, the one Roy-Roy uses on the blondes in his mack-daddy booth. I know it'll work, though Gladys' yellowish strands are South Side fake and barely seen in the ceiling fluorescent.

"Such a nice young man," Gladys says and smiles back, because my grin does touch her. Each of her teeth are perfect square blocks, too, and as shiny white as her skin is plant-soil brown.

Gladys has invited me to her Sunday service three times, though I've worked here only these two weeks. I haven't figured yet whether she's trying to save my soul or get inside my drawers—something in her eyes as she makes the invitation, something like this leer that creases and crawls under her brow as she leans on the cubicle edge just now—could be either or both inspiring her. I wish she'd understand that maybe I'd visit her Trinity Baptist if I didn't think she wanted to fuck me; or that I'd get down with her on the sly if she'd stop putting God in between us. If she doesn't come about a clue before asking again, maybe the next time she invites me to Sunday service, I'll tell her I'm Muslim.

"What do you see out there?"

"Where?" I ask, and Gladys points at Kung Pao's. "I don't know. Just glanced quick. Not long enough to see nothing one way or the other."

"'Anything,'" she says. "Southern Illinois is a better school than that, Mr. Simms. You are better than that."

I ignore her. "You just caught me mid-glance."

"While you were looking at—"

"Nothing," I say again.

"Right," she mocks, "nothing."

"Maybe I would've seen something if I hadda looked longer."

"If I hadn't interrupted," she moves her right arm to the back of her neck, jangling as silk hugs these chests.

"Exactly," I say, meaning to mock her, but Gladys laughs because she's got something to pass on to Mr. Ramsey now. "But I only meant to be glancing out there for a bit."

I prop my left hand against the keyboard so the computer screen's blue twinkles against my gold-silver wedding band for both of us to see—though the light does nothing except turn her leer into eyes rolled deep into painted lids. She passes the cubicle wall, approaches without noise, and I see the ring of faded skin on Gladys' fourth finger. After inviting me to Trinity the first time, she confided that she's been divorced some thirteen years. But the wedding band hasn't been gone so long; her ring finger still bubbles from corroded metal. So it's not me or God that Gladys chases in cubicle paths and church pews. I'm not so arrogant to believe otherwise—can't speak for God, but I ain't so cock-foolish, at least. Gladys doesn't chase after a damn thing, no, she's just seeking to escape these odd and lonely years.

Pretty lady, this receptionist, especially once she lets the leer go from around her eyes and her smile beams through ruby lips. She doesn't need the makeup decorating her skin, but this is what dark women from her time do—paint themselves as clowns and jangle about pews. No matter this rouge mask she smears on her face to serve Master Pharaoh every day, there's no hiding these lines carved from crying and straining and forcing and trying to forget and remembering everything. Fashion Fair ain't covering that, no more than it covers how Gladys is built like a bungalow, or that she is what they all become—what Tarsha, too, will one day be. Made up, lonely, hiding nothing from everyone, and stacked strong like a wall full of painful life and sex.

"So what exactly did you want back here, Ms. Tucker?"

"Am I bothering you?"

I feel my forehead wrinkling. "No. Just thought maybe I could help you out."

"Told you, that's *my* job," she says, touching the framed

picture of my Dawn hung on the cubicle cabinet. "Making sure everybody's okay around here."

I won't tell her that I stay at my workstation staring at my watch because I know she's waiting by the exit door. She knows it well as I know the only reason she comes back here to say anything about it now is that she feels some holy tingling between those legs squeezed in her knee-length skirt, tingling along with boredom and her responsibility to Ramsey. In this office, on these late-afternoon jangling rounds, I'm the only thirty-year-old deskbound claims adjuster with a sack full of life unlived waiting on her.

We both know that my mornings go by watching souls file from the Red Line platform to the Cermak bus stop, off to their own paths and fields. Then, for three hours, I stare down on the bald domes of old Chinese men at the corner of Wentworth Avenue, arguing mah-jongg and fan-tan in raging Mandarin while pointing between each other's eyes. All before one juggles game pieces for mocking show, and the other slings American dollar bills wrinkled in crisp balls at the first. Then I spend an hour with the phone pressed against my ear, listening to tales of stupid tragedy, full of more debt than blood, and an hour searching the Internet for solutions that I've never bothered to remember, before I watch the clock's arms tick away remaining time. Waiting for Gladys to jangle her way southwest and invite a heathen to salvation.

"Just taking care of the business, Ms. Tucker." I watch her trace the dust caked in Dawn's frame with her faded ring and middle finger. "Like I'm supposed to."

"I know," Gladys wipes my computer monitor with a pink handkerchief, and smiles. "Just checking."

"Thanks."

"No need for 'thank yous.' That's the job—how they wrote it up at least." She lingers on her wristwatch's face longer than it should take to read. "It's ten past. Come on now, Mr. Simms. They don't pay us enough to put in bonus hours here. This isn't downtown any more, you know?"

"They didn't pay me enough down there neither."

Gladys laughs again, fake amusement echoing about empty workstations. "'Either'—at least you had a better view though." I'm not sure which of us she's mocking.

"Grew up on the lake," I say, "looking at water's overrated. Puts you to sleep, unless it's in the middle of a storm or something. The waves, you know—whitecaps crashing on the shore when the wind kicks up."

"Oh," she says, and her bracelet shackles sound again as she walks past the cubicle, away from me now. "See you tomorrow morning, Mr. Simms."

"Eight-forty-eight." I zip my work bag, full of not a damn thing but office air, and roll back to the window to look on Kung Pao. There are no old Chinamen arguing on Wentworth. Instead, I watch the brown and pink and yellow bodies rise the Red Line staircase, bouncing with each high step. Once they reach the station's platform, their legs skip from climb to run, chasing after the rear end of a train rolling along the tracks with no thought of stopping. Nothing stops—not that last car, not the folks running afterwards.

※   ※   ※

THE TEMPERATURE DROPPED twenty-five degrees this morning, the way it does in the city even in the middle of blazing summer. The low-end station dj claims that it's seventy-three somewhere in the metro area—but that somewhere is nowhere near this lake. My skin dots as wind cuts between the Drive's skyscrapers. These goose bumps show all along my arms, and my teeth chatter until my forehead temples fill with ache. Feels like it'll never be hot again in the Four Corners, yet the radio news predicts Sunday temps in the nineties. But this Wednesday could be the end of September on the lakefront looking at this weepy sky fixed over us.

I watch in my driver-side mirror glass as Primo Smoove steps out of his Impala approaching the Ford as the 75th Street red light lingers. Maybe the temperature in Washington Park is seventy-three degrees, over there near the end of the Green Line tracks; Primo wears a thin white underwear shirt, the kind with the straps at the shoulders like a woman's halter top. His white cotton blazes in this rearview mirror, yet a wet splotch shows where his gut and chest meet. His skin sticks to this wet place, showing its brown color through the fibers: one brown spot surrounded by clean blank dryness.

The 51st Street shylock straightens the haberdashery on his skinny head—not a flashy gangster hat with a fedora feather poking from the left side, but one of these crisp camel-hide jobs like Harry Truman wore as he dropped atom bombs. When the brim is an even circle on Primo's head, he taps my window, though the glass is already partially open and we've been staring at each other since his lizard boots kicked out of the Chevy.

"Pull to the side," Primo says and points to the elementary school building just past the streetlight. I do just that once our streetlight turns green—pretend to so for some other reason than because Primo told me to in his Green Line roar.

I wait outside the Escort as he walks near again. Primo rubs his exposed arms, hugging and protecting himself against the lake breeze while I let my teeth chatter so that I won't laugh in his face. My mouth does go silent as his arms flex though; Primo's skinny as the steel gates protecting Rainbow Beach from the Drive, but his limbs are all muscle and stretched skin. From pumping iron during his last trip through Joliet Correctional or swinging bats on the welchers over west, Primo is an atom-bomb-hat-wearing, wood-bat-slinging, mahogany statue, and I have no clue what he's doing in my Four Corners just now. Laughter leaves me.

"You can't call me when you're in trouble, Tommie?" He lets go his left arm to push his eyeglasses' bridge close to his face. "Thought we was better than that, thought you was my guy?"

"What?" I hug myself, and stare at a concrete crack that streaks from a pothole in the Drive. "I don't know what you're talking about."

"This trouble you're in over here. Four, five miles ain't a long way for word to travel. My ears stay to this ground, my nigga. You didn't think I'd find out?"

"What's to find out, *my nigga*?"

"You got busted like damn near a month ago." Primo's

teeth shake until he rubs naked arms faster. "Knew you wasn't bout this game. Too ripe—tried to help you. How long was it you was slinging before they picked you up even?"

I roll my eyes out to the lake's gray waves. "Folks are talking about me on Fifty-first Street?"

"I heard about it at least," Primo says. "You got a court date coming? They'll probably let you ride, square like you. Heard they got you with damn near a pound in your drawers though. It's the 'Intent' they use to fuck a nigga up. 'Possession' ain't shit, they'd let you ride off that for sure, but you can't go claiming you was strolling Seventy-ninth Street with a pound in your sack just looking for someplace to puff on a spliff, can you? Probably just put a square such as yourself on probation for a year, maybe eighteen months. You've got no priors, right?"

"It's all took care of," I say, and there is a giggle left beneath my tongue. "Brought in a lawyer—he handled the business. No charges ever got filed."

"Shit." I follow Primo's gaze, find his eyes fixed on the roof of our building, just north on the Drive. "What kinda lawyer you get?"

"Family friend," I say. "A brother, too."

"Good . . . downtown Stein woulda cost you plenty. Oughta let me use this nigga next time po-pos come bothering with me."

I let the giggle loose. Sounds louder and lasts longer than my intentions, until I turn to my driver-side door at last.

But Primo touches my shoulder, grabs me without holding on. "How about that other thing?" he asks. "You ain't got nothing for me."

His eyes beam with pitiful begging. "I'm lost, Smoove. I

paid you back long time ago, plus interest. You said you up-
dated your records. What else am I supposed to be holding of
yours?"

"My books is always current." He rubs the right eye underneath his frames, but the begging remains in his stare.
"Don't front on my business, Tommie. You know I take care of
operations."

"I paid you in full," I repeat and turn back to the Escort.

"I'm talking about that other," he says, "that business we
rapped about. Your cousin's stash? Said you'd help getting me
back on."

"Oh," I say. I remember the northbound turnstiles on
Garfield Boulevard, trains rumbling, the pay phone and the
child proud of buying her first fare card. "Can't help you,
Primo."

He steps closer. "You talked to Remi and Jack?"

"No," I say, "I'm out the game. Like you say, this hustling
ain't right for squares."

The wind kicks up off the water and swirls in front of Powell
Elementary where I spent third through fifth grades. The lake
gust is taking note of my jive, letting me know that it will
be back around later even if the Shark won't, swirling while
weighing the truth in my words. "Said I'd help you out, just
like before."

My teeth chatter louder, but I feel strong at their bite. "I
asked for your help? I don't remember that. I thought you
came to me?"

The skin at the end of his eyes turns downward, insult replacing begging. "Muthafuckin man got done using you and

put you out on the street, and you didn't have nowhere else to go. Who'd you holla at when the bills came due? Lemme see: your mamma? Your wild-ass cousins? Your daddy? Your broke-ass skeeze at the crib? Hell, no. You brought your ass way down to the Green Line and hollered at Primo Smoove, nigga, cause you knew I'd be there for your bitch ass. Funny how fools forget: mighty convenient, mighty comical, broke frontal lobe, fool-ass niggas."

"I paid you your money."

"Then I came back to you," Primo says. Both fists clench at his sides and goose bumps rise out of these rips. "Trying to look out for a brother and do some kind of righteous business."

I stare at the potholed crack now so he won't see my eyes rolling. "What do you know about helping?" I'm whispering—but he stands close enough to hear my words. "Righteous? That's a kinda funny word to hear coming from a shark."

Primo's not looking at my roof now, or at the sky, or the schoolhouse. He stares to his right instead, watching wind whistle. "Fuck you say? What you call me? Ain't hear you."

Red beats behind his spectacles. "Don't be disrespecting my wife," I run from his stare now. "Ain't no cause to go cussing my family neither."

"The muthafuckin audacity," Primo moans. "What kinda nigga is this here? Got the nerve to be calling me out my name, to my face, after I saved his ass. *Family?* Nigga, what? My uncle vouched for you, I listened, looked out for a fool when you was down, turned a blind eye while you strung me out like a skank ho. Fuck I look like? Shark, you said? You come back-talking me now, bitch? You wouldn't be standing here right now, not on two legs at least, not for me. Now you wanna come outta pocket—fuck that—outta muthafuckin school on me? You wasn't talking this rude bullshit when you was in need. Talked like a sissy mack daddy then, tryin to sweet-talk your way between some of mine. That's what you think you done here, fucked me in the ass?"

I touch the car door handle. "Look, Primo, my bad. You got me—been a bad week. I came wrong. It's on me. I'm done with the weed though. Straight up."

"Don't try no reverse psychological bullshit on me now. Too late for that. Nigga, I went to college, too. Fuck I look like to you?" Primo snatches the spectacles from his nose. His eyes are rimmed in sweat, no matter this breeze. "You ain't seen shark, boy. You're a square—you don't know shit. You see a shark, I see a victim."

"Put your glasses back on," I say, more begging than commanding. "I said I'm sorry. I'm done dealing, but maybe I can talk to my cousin for you."

He slides the spectacles onto his nose slow anyway. "A vic is what I see. Fucking pussy. You say I'm a shark—bet it up—Jaws don't forget, muthafucka." Primo backs northward to the Impala, staring and pointing. "Shoulda never come out on these streets, boy. You ain't ready for this."

Primo's lizard boot stretches into the Impala and he closes the driver-side door, but I don't move. I'm thinking back to Intro to Animal Biology, recalling whether Primo tells the truth about sharks and memories; but we didn't make it to the chapter on fish before semester's end. Birds and ants had mighty recall powers according to the textbook. No matter their tiny heads. Elephants, too—elephant memories last forever.

Primo steers the Impala over this pothole crack, lowering his passenger window as his tires brush the tips of my Adidas. "I'm driving past a vic and a pussy. You fucked up out here now, Tommie. Best take yourself on home now."

"My bad," I repeat. But Primo rolls his eyes, then turns the Chevy just in front of a street construction truck that's come to fix the Drive's pothole. The Shark whips his steering wheel one more time to cut back west toward the Green Line's end.

I look up, two blocks behind Powell Elementary and up. Not as high as the Shark stared, but my neck cranes in search of the fourth floor. Wind whips and raises goose bumps at my jugular and I open the Ford's door. Once I find what should be our apartment window, I sit behind the steering wheel ready to circle myself north on this cracked street corner.

*   *   *

WE DON'T say much to each other these nights. When I was still up high in the Grand Avenue tower, we'd sit on this same couch as Tarsha interrogated, until she'd snatched at least one foul tale from my thirty-second-floor day. No stopping her back then, not until I let go some rage—gotta talk about it to soothe it, baby, she'd say. The catharsis of closure, this same logic Oprah Winfrey uses every morning on cancer-scarred vics. I never noticed anybody getting over pain by putting it into words at nine A.M.—and I watched every day while I was jobless, waiting to see the salvation of one soul or the resurrection of some pitiful mark's hope-filled sense of life. Watching and waiting for Oprah to close the deal. Never happened on any of those one hundred and ninety-three days, just so many goddamn words babbled.

Once I'd finish recounting my shame from the guffaw circle, Tarsha would feel obligated to share her own hardship story from the Loop reception desk. Which saggy-jowled executive had her (a) fix a fresh pot of coffee, (b) run down to Krispy Kreme and grab a dozen glazed for the ten-thirty meeting, then (c) ordered her to leave the conference room because the subject on the table was too sensitive for a treat-delivering reception girl's loose ears.

"Just drop the donut holes there in the corner, Miss Simms,"—she'd mock from high inside nasal passages, North Shore style—"Leave them there for us, and my cup of dark here in front of me, and scuttle on back to your phone-answering desk. And, oh we appreciate you, kind missy, for the glazed donut holes. Thank you so."

I'd stare at the television screen across from this couch and lose her words' meaning somewhere after the donut hole. Watch her reflection in a nineteen-inch screen until her hands started moving with the rhythm of the garble, and peeked to my right to catch her skin turn from beige to red. Never knew whether she'd get that hot and bothered by the pitiful way of her day—and if so, why she put herself through reliving the insult for a deaf and blind fool—or did her sweet face swell with blood because she knew swinging hands, a raised voice, or an exploding head be damned, none of it inspired me to hear a word spoken after the glazed hole.

Survivor is on the nineteen-inch now. The contestants eat a snake chopped alive but still slithering, because doing so somehow decides which of them will make it out of the Serengeti victorious. I glance at my right, watch Tarsha pinch her lips together with thumb and forefinger, sealing the mouth to kill her bright smile, or whatever it is that seeks to come out of her.

A cell phone commercial interrupts the show. I listen for Dawn fidgeting in her corner playpen, mad that her mother won't breathe a word to her daddy, because baby girl's always on her daddy's side. So I've convinced myself. I swear that I hear one of the plastic playthings shaking in mighty violent protest before the commercial ends, and I remember that my mother still keeps the baby on these Thursday nights.

"Think we should call and check on Dawn?" I ask. The sound bangs my own eardrums.

Tarsha's hand moves from her mouth and a frown creases her forehead. "You need to relax," she says. "It's TV night."

She stands so that the cotton nightgown slips from her waist, walks off to the kitchen before the hem hits her ankles. My fingers touch my lips, not to trap anything inside, I don't think—thoughts, maybe I'm holding thoughts inside my head, though I've never known bright ideas to slip through the mouth. Thursday used to be Date Night, before Dawn. Then, as Tarsha weaned the baby from nipples, we called it Quality Time Night and never felt obligated to leave the apartment, as long as we spent the passing moments with each other. Just the two of us, as the sap song goes, or as we used to sing it.

After my GMIC gig ended—or like tower Tom Brokaw says, post-9/11—Thursday came to be Fight Night, the evening for Tarsha to let loose bloody disgust our Four Corners leaves inside her, and I'd spit it right back out of bloody pride and ego. Even Fight Night was better than what Thursdays have become since the New Year. "TV Night," she calls it. Our quality time is spent on a cockamamie program set in the wilds of the Motherland: folks eating snakes alive to survive. Thursday is *Reality* TV Night now, let the truth be told.

Tarsha returns, sipping Snapple fruit juice from the bottle. She sits in the crevice where upholstery has yet to rise up from this couch cushion, and the nightgown hem rides back to her knees. The commercial break doesn't end until she leans her elbows against thighs and lets go the Snapple on the cocktail table and the right hand is free to pinch her lips again.

"I need to relax?" I ask. "Look at you—you see yourself?"

"What?" She barely lets go to chuckle. I'm not sure whether it's the snakehead this redheaded contestant spits into a mud stream that tickles her. "I'm watching the program."

I rub the base of her neck just above the gown's stretched collar, touch the peach fuzz growing unseen there. She doesn't flinch. "How was your day?" I ask.

She glances across her left shoulder quick as one of her dry-eyed blinks. "Fine."

"Mmh. Let me get a taste of juice."

Snapple rumbles my gut—it's Tarsha's favorite drink, but this fake sweet saccharin sickens me, and she knows it. She hands me the bottle anyway, without glancing from the screen. I hold it in my left hand as the right rubs on her peach fuzz harder, and I sip.

My gut gurgles without hurting really, and I bounce the

juice bottle against my lap. I look down to find a joy-filled limb poking from my sweat shorts. Poking and bopping against the bottle, and bringing waves to the saccharine surface. I let go the plastic only to feel blood echoing at my thighs, down through the crotch. I squeeze her neck, but she flinches away and waves me off with the lip-pinching hand.

"Stop, Tommie," she says, "the program."

"Just trying to talk to you."

"Oh," she drops the hand to the cushion underneath and sighs. Soon as *Survivor* breaks for commercial again, she scoots near along the couch backrest, leans this way so quick and oblivious that I'm barely able to snatch away the hand I use to touch her. "Sorry, baby," she speaks soft and sweet and believable enough. "Got caught up with *Survivor,* is all. How was your day? I didn't ask, did I?"

"It's all right." I'm not so good at sounding pitiful, especially not as my eyes bounce from her to the throbbing at my lap, back and forth without stealing her attention. "It was fine, just another day."

She half smiles, fake and not so warm now, without looking from my forehead. "Nothing interesting happen?"

"No." My eyes linger in the lap for a bit, making certain the full poke is still throbbing. "Just another day. More fools crying and little girls screaming and little boys burning, more old ladies left lonely, everybody making claims about it. Ain't nothing changed."

Tarsha frowns and rests her head against the living room wall. "So," she says, "you're okay?"

"I'm fine." Before the answer is all the way out of my mouth, she leans on her thighs again, fixed on the nineteen-inch.

I can't wait for the next commercial break, not with the tip of my limb tapping against the end of a stomach full of sickness. I knock at her spine just below the place where I'd rubbed her hair, knock twice before she turns to me with nostrils furled inside out from breathing the funk of her own disgust. She tries staring at my forehead again, but I point to the blood hope pumps into my lap. Her nose unfurls and she pinches her lips, not in time to hide the first shakes of a giggle.

"Oh." She reaches between my legs for the Snapple, takes the bottle from my thighs and sips before turning back to the show with this plastic rim holding her mouth together.

My wife drinks slow in front of this spectacle of folks chewing living serpents and this clown to her left who throbs and hums some make-believe sap tune. She swallows the last drops and though she does finish long before her program ends, it's not until credits roll that she stands from the living room couch and turns herself to me. My right hand plants in this unmoving indent where the woman ignored me. She looms for a bit. Then she bends over for the hem of this wrinkled gown, pulls it over her knees and up to her belly, hitches cotton at the edge of the c-scar where that Indian woman doctor sliced her open to snatch free Dawn's head. Tarsha holds the hem here, and my own stomach numbs from the gurgling and this bloody muscle beating. She wears no underwear beneath the ripped birthing place, never wears panties on Reality TV night—she knows the faint smell of her still keeps me in this place, drunk with joyful days long past even as she ignores me for the babble box.

She reaches behind her back and turns the television off, holding the gown above her waist with the lip-pinching hand, and she gyrates slightly at the hips, head still twisted over her shoulder toward the screen. Some Hindu mating trick learned from the stomach-slicing doctor? I don't know, but fresh blood rushes into my crotch, and the gurgling noise I know now is that of life, not processed saccharin, running through my coils. As I understand this, Tarsha straddles me and uses that breath-taking clutch between thumb and forefinger to slip me inside.

This is what has done it for us all these years, used to do it for us back before TV night at least. Sweet friction makes so much sense between these legs, much more sense than it does at her left side, in front of a television screen, or watching her before sunrise smiling in the middle of dreams in which I'm not to be found. Sweet friction makes me smile, a true spreading of the lips, drunk and stupid happy. The woman always has the one-up, yes, here she is always in my dream. Shown in a black TV screen, over her rising and collapsing shoulder, this vision of a smooth-skinned back with cotton wrinkled between crack and spine, arms spread and palms pressed against the living room wall for leverage as she slides along me. This *is* me in the vision, I guess, though all the evidence I find is the reflection of sweat shorts pulled down and knotted underneath my mother's knees.

No matter, for this is such a joyous vision. Even if I do hear hollow plastic rattling in an empty playpen, and I can't see any part of me except for bony legs. Even if Tarsha has won the

contest and the smile on her face as she rides and slides now is
only crooked smirk to the glee that burst so bright on Oglesby
Avenue when Granny Allen's jangling was nowhere to be heard.
Even if sweet friction really scrapes at me, and her womb lips
blink around my limb to wet themselves with tears as fake wet
as her smile is crooked. Or if I start to go soft inside as I watch
her back slide in the blankness, hear her puffing more than
breathing and feel the drip of her labor fall from the brow as it
drops near my bitten lips. On down into our laps where—
together with the fake womb tears—it still ain't nearly enough
to lubricate us. No matter, there is true joy here, I swear. She feels
it and puffs it free. Me too, I hear it and I feel it, low in my gut.

"Feels good?" she asks between puffs.

"Yeah," I say, "see."

And it is the sound of my own word—*see*—along with this
dream of us in the nineteen-inch, all together with scraping
friction, that lets loose relief just under the place where that
doctor ripped out Dawn's head. Now, I can go limp without
shame, and Tarsha can slide back into her indent so that I see
my full self in the television set, twisted-up shorts just under
knees knocking together. She lays on the couch backrest and
lets go her hemline to wipe her forehead and her smile straightens just a bit because there is relief. We do feel this together.

11

THE WIND STINKS of city funk as it cuts through my cousins' living room. This air has blown over from the lake, seeped through door cracks and uninsulated gaps between windowpane and sill left by their crooked Yugoslavian landlord. Their shack won't let the breeze back out either. Phillips Avenue is a one-way trip, even for the funky east wind. Sweat runs from my eyes and on down the spine from this hot funk wind. It's not the stink of fish floating on Lake Michigan, as I know my dead fish breezes. This smell is more poison rot than death.

Its mildew crinkles Cleopatra's poster edges. I press the paper's yellowed corners into plaster, yet it does no good. As soon as I let go, her borders climb back up wallpaper flowers, tearing tape from the surface and touching the tip of her leather boot.

"Damn—" James-Peter's voice echoes from the room opposite her wall.

The package delivery man tosses his Xbox controller against the television, but plastic bounces and the game cord yanks the joystick back to his sitting place on the dining room floor. He kicks the joystick toward the game console.

"You all right?" I ask.

"Fuck this!" he snaps before inhaling. "Thought I had this muthafucka beat, joe—"

He's playing Virtua Fighter or Vendetta or some other game where killer cartoon heroes spill maroon blood before Hong Kong's bright stereo roar.

"How come I can beat all of y'all, but I can't do a damn thing with this cockeyed computer villain?"

James stares at me, the vessels in his eyes beating darker than the high-definition blood that gathers in the light show. He pinches his nostrils closed—I'm not sure whether he smells the trapped rot now, or if he's holding a sneeze. He chokes and coughs, lets go his holes to breathe, then bangs the joystick against hardwood with his free hand. He stares until I understand that he's waiting for my answer.

I sit in the folding chair opposite his game console. "Artificial intelligence," I say. "You know the Japanese put working brains in these games now. Ain't like Atari no more."

"Atari?" James laughs and drops the joystick one more time. "Now those was the days, the real shit. If you could beat a live soul in them games, you good and well knew you'd beat the computer. The bastards is cheating me?"

"What?"

"That's the only reason you go and add fake intelligence to the game, so the machine can cheat you," he says. James-Peter smooths the moustache penciled above his top lip side-to-side, then flicks the line up to the nose so hairs are out of place again. His brown delivery uniform is opened to the stomach to reveal an untucked graying T-shirt though the ends of his uniform top are still stuffed into pressed brown straight-legs. "How am I gonna spend money to buy something, only for the piece of machine shit to cheat me?"

"God bless America," I say.

"Thought you said them Japanese did this."

"I did." I laugh before choking on this air myself. "God bless Atari, then."

"Yeah." James presses the console's rest button. "*Atari.* Ain't heard nobody mention them in a minute."

A shadow leans across the hardwoods. I look away from the screen, over James' shoulder and toward the kitchen. "Remi around?"

"Had to make a run, way out south. Roseland or somewhere."

"Jackie, too?"

"Yeah. They went to handle the business." James points to his joystick. "You wanna play?"

"I'm not real competition."

"I know," he says, "tired of losing."

I force a frown and lean the folding chair against its back legs. "When are they supposed to be back?"

"Had to meet Wee Man," James says. He lowers the skill level to intermediate. "Probably be a minute."

"Oh yeah?" I pretend not to notice his eyes following me in crooked corners. I reach for the second joystick. "Set it to two player."

Digital lights flash schizophrenic and alive now, and I am in control of the game. The tip of James-Peter's Grandmaster's foot connects with my intermediate fighter's left temple quick, the heel with the right temple, and blood spurts from holes unseen as my fighter wobbles in a tumbling circle yet stays standing.

The Grandmaster puts the heel of his palm into my intermediate's forehead, a tongue wags from my man's mouth, just to show blood dripping here. The fighter—funny thing to describe this beady-eyed, 2-D victim—drops to one knee and seems to bow, but I push joystick buttons just so as James' Grandmaster lunges to roundhouse my swelling dome. My intermediate springs to foot and takes a kung fu defense stance from the Fred Williamson movies, just in time to block James' spinning kick and send his Grandmaster killer back two stumbling steps. The screen bursts in purple and orange, all in celebration of this incompetent fighter standing tall and defending himself. I turn toward putrid wallpaper so my smile won't show, but my lips stretch before my neck turns and he sees me. I figure James for throwing the joystick, or flicking the power switch in frustration, but I still haven't accomplished a thing but bringing a battered intermediate to foot.

"Been trying to figure out why Westside talks so much smack about you," James says.

I press the red button and my intermediate swings a blow so short-armed that the Grandmaster stops in preying tracks to laugh before slapping my fighter in the chin. "Jackie talks shit about everything—that's him."

"No. He talks a lot of shit, but the nigga really don't like you." My fighter drops to surrendering knee again. Takes a minute for me to remember which button to press to stand him up. By the time my thumb touches the red circle, the fighter bleeds from the ear. "Think I figured out why."

"Fuck Jackie." The Grandmaster pounds me into video-game ground with the sole of his kung fu shoe.

James hums. "When you're around, you remind Remi that Jackie's dick ain't suppose to be up his ass." The Grandmaster bends to bloody ground, puts his right claw to my dead intermediate's chest. "But when you ain't here, Westside can get in all the sweet ass he wants. Metaphorically speaking."

"The metaphor makes him mad?"

"No," James says, and he's not afraid to giggle in pride as the Grandmaster stands upright with my heart still pumping and bleeding in his right claw—my intermediate wasn't all the way dead after all. I could've stood him up from the ground and kept on fighting, tried to at least, if I'd recalled the proper button. "You're always here—that's why he's shitty. He ain't on top and can't get no ass meat. That makes him shitty."

"I'm in the way?" I nod before my joystick cracks against the floor. "So why don't you go on and give him some, little faggot."

"Nigga don't wanna fuck with me." He resets the Xbox. "It's a metaphor, joe. Thought you was one of those schooled fools, all smart and open-minded. Don't get mad with me. You're done playing, right?"

"I'm done." I slap my right knee. "Bout to watch this cock-eyed computer player whup your gay ass."

"I see why Jackie don't like you," James-Peter repeats, then smooths his moustache line. "Bitch-ass, hating nigga, always in the way cause you can't do nothing better than interrupting somebody else's flow."

"You won, ripped out my heart and left me laid out. What'd I interrupt of yours?"

"It's a metaphor," he says, "just talking. I thought you went to col-lege."

I stand and close the chair, walk back to the living room to breathe more funk. I lick my fingertips and press the poster's corners into wallpaper mildew again, and she does stick there for a moment, just that long, before paper wrinkles up to her ankles and the tape sliver falls from wallflowers.

This sharp gust blows Remi and Jackie through the front door and the tape blows off to someplace that I can't see.

"Can't keep on like this," Jackie says as he slams the door at his back. "That beast is choking at the throat, Remi. Ain't no point to this—we can kill ourselves all on our own."

"What else we gonna do?" Remi sits on the living room's pastel flea market couch and glares at me, waiting on answers. "What else can we?"

"Always gotta be some choices." Westside walks a tight circle as he talks, his head to the hardwood. I'm not sure if he knows I'm here. "Bastard cops had me on probation damn near a year last time. Now he's putting a nigga in another corner—that's how they do you when they think you've got empty choices. Get your life all twisted. It's just so often we can stand on these corners. Hustlers put one and two together, too—they ain't dumb—come after payback outta us. We better have some kind of choices. Dying at a hustler's hands ain't gonna be slow as it is dying with Wee Man choking like this."

"This is better, dying slow?"

"Ain't saying that—ain't even my point. Slow ain't as painful as going fast, is all. Barely even know you're dying this way. Big corner hustlers, they make it hurt so there's no doubt left." Westside pulls the shred of a toothpick from his mouth. The wood sliver clicks against the floor, disappears with Cleopatra's tape sliver. "Ain't like we're getting anything out of this no ways. Wee Man's juicing us for the fingering, putting us out here bad on the streets, sending us home without a thing but some cheddar cheesies in our pockets. We're rats, and they all know it. Who wants to do business with a bunch of rats? Can't trust a fool who eats cheese for a living."

Remi shrugs. "So what's our choices then? This's the price—"

"Price for what?" Jackie walks toward the Xbox room. Hong Kong's sound and schizo light flashes against the corner edge where Westside leans. "I did my time. Now for this punk muthafucka here? This is bullshit. 'Price we gotta pay' ain't a legitimate answer. I've known it all along, even he knows it. Don't you, Tommie? This is bullshit, ain't it?"

I stare at the living room's opposite end, where I can't see Remi or Jackie or the lights flashing, just stare and listen to blood shed in stereo. "What's Wee Man got you all doing?"

"Ain't none of your concern," Remi's voice is softer than the video-game echo. "We've got this. Ain't your concern."

"How come you're protecting him?" Jackie says. "He ain't innocent no more, nowhere near. Why's he gets to keep squeaky clean ears and the gig with the wood desk and the computer screen and the wife and the shorty in diapers? Living up high on South Shore Drive."

"Fourth floor," I say, "ain't so high."

"Shut up. Up higher than this, ain't it? We all wanna be some Afro-American negroes, too—how come he's the one who gets to keep his ears clean?" The wall stops flashing with the crash of James' joystick against the television screen. "He best can get dirty. Cop's got us rolling out to the hot spots, scoping out those scenes for him cause we're the in-niggas with all the dime to drop—at least, somebody told Wee Man we've got this dime. We get to the spots and point out the young clowns holding the cream or the rocks or the powders. Few hours after we point the finger, him and his crew jump on the dealers from out of the street corners, unmarked and plainclothes, beat um down for what's stuffed in their socks and their drawers.

"If the pea-heads ain't holding on to enough to make a cop happy, Wee Man'll take him hostage, Glock pressed to his nose. Like he done that Hook from Stateway in back of his cruiser a few weeks back. We saw it, was sitting right there next to old boy. Even if the loot ain't enough to satisfy the cop, it's always more than enough to make a big baller kill, so Wee Man forced pea-head to call up Chief Hook round the way and have him drop a garbage bag at the Stateway gates for the police. Or else Wee Man was gonna pop a hole in that pea-head, pin it on the Chief Hook, and keep the rocks in the boy's pockets. On our way out of the projects that night, what did we see sitting up against bricks but a fresh Hefty bag of dope? Am I lying, Rem-Dog?"

Remi watches light flash in the corner without speaking.

"Few days later, they find this project Hook stuffed in the garbage bin behind the Gardens, both his hands and his nuts cut off and all the blood drained out of him."

"No choices," Remi says finally.

James-Peter walks from the Xbox room and stands opposite Westside, pinching his nostrils without choking. "Heard there wasn't nothing in ol boy's pockets when the garbage men found him neither," he says.

"Fuck no." Jackie laughs soft. "Big Chief Vicelord took back all his product before pea-head got done screaming and bleeding. You know it."

Remi's head drops. "Ain't fair, the way they got us out here."

"Damn right it ain't fair," Westside snaps. "That's all I been trying to say. Why my shit gotta be dirty while your cousin stays up mighty high and pretend pure? He got us in this."

"Y'all don't need to be doing like this for me," I whine full of gurgling pity. "Ain't worth it."

Remi laughs alone and waves an open right palm through the must. "This ain't got nothing to do with you no more, hell, only got to do with the rest of us far as Wee Man needs us to finger these fools. Cop got himself a cash hustle juicing us. I ain't going down outta principle. They're gonna squeeze all the blood that flows out this scheme, and if they need our fingering to cut it open, what else can we do here but keep pointing and slicing?"

The living room is quiet for a bit. I find the tape sliver in this silence, fluttering against the tip of Jackie's gym shoe with wind blown underneath their living room door. Only this piece of tape, talking its happy jive against a swoosh sign, knows what to say.

"You're gonna go next time. Your ass needs to see how it is. Ain't no jokes to be telling, shit ain't funny. Ain't always gotta be the dirty one neither, ain't on me—this bullshit." Westside Jackie bends over to flick the clear tape from his gym shoe. "Gotta be choices," he repeats.

*   *   *

"HERE'S THE PROBLEM right here." Weidmann folds the *Sun-Times* so the newspaper forms a two-sided tablet on top of the Crown Vic's steering wheel. "Right on page two. Didn't Kup's column used to be on page two of the *Sun-Times,* good stories like that? Fuck. News is one big problem after another now."

Phil the preacher cop peeks over the raised lid of his giant off-brand slurpy, his shoulder pressing into the passenger seat upholstery. "Mmh. That still the morning paper? You're just now reading it?"

"Noontime edition," the driver says. He points at a black-and-white half-page photo of some pasty-faced, scraggily haired crook with a cracked pencil moustache and dented jaw. The crook in the page-two photo wears an orange Cook County jumpsuit and stairs empty-eyed into the camera.

"Damn. That's Fred all right," Phil whistles, "goddamn. Fred Conley."

"Shame," Wee Man says. The right side of the bird-pig's face turns red as his head shakes slow against the seat rest. "You know I went to Academy with Fred, right?"

"I know. You told me. Thousand times this last month, you said it."

"Fucked up seeing it in the paper. They've got him looking like a criminal in here."

Phil's teeth click against his lips and orange chunks of fake slurpy leak from the corner of his mouth. "Shoulda picked-up the *Tribune* instead. Tried to tell you, Mike. *Sun-Times* is bogus for that."

"Wouldn't have made any difference. Story's all over the place." Wee Man's chin digs into his chest. "Would've used the same friggin picture even. Maybe they woulda showed it from a different angle is all. Still the same damn story."

Phil sucks the end of his slurpy drink. "Wouldn't have been on page two like that in the *Trib*. Not right out front. Fred might've made their metro section maybe. You woulda had to search through all them other parts if you wanted to find him, that's for damn sure. All the good shit about the profits, and mergers, and the interest rates, only thing bad in the front happens far off in some bad-ass place that was born bad, near about to die besides. Chi-town bad don't happen on page two in there. His picture wouldn't have been so damn big in the *Trib* neither."

Weidmann unfolds the noontime edition so that the two-page headline stretches from his door to the dashboard in block print: VET COP INDICTED ON ABUSE CHARGES.

"Don't matter." Weidmann's left thumb covers the pasty newspaper face. "It's everywhere. Fucking shame, man. Wasn't supposed to go down like this. A rotten orange crook. I went to Academy with Fred Conley, you know? Came out in '72."

"I know," Phil says. He pulls the straw halfway from the lid's center hole, then jabs the tube to the cup's base bottom, then again, faster, fucking plastic for more wet bits. "You said. Shame."

"Abuse? It's a joke. Goddamn ridiculous. They've got idiots all across the city buying this diarrhea."

"Sure you want to talk about this in front of these ones?" Phil lets go of his straw and points wrinkled fingertips at me and Remi in the Crown Vic's backseat.

"Fuck it," Wee Man says without pondering the preacher cop's question. "It's all over the place now. Top page is always extra thin. Can't hide what's right on page two."

Sunlight disappears from the cruiser's backseat. We're facing south on Stony Island, just past the meeting place of 71st Street, the repaved IC train crossing, and the eight-lane Stony highway with its strips of flashing drive-through banks and chicken nugget restaurants stretching along the path.

The sun still fades through the preacher cop's passenger window, and an automated construction rig drills holes into a black concrete slab in the lot across Stony Island's lanes. Weidmann's driver-side glass is opened quarter way as sweat shines from high on all four of our foreheads, even in the rearview mirror reflection. A developer's sign rises just barely higher than the tracks' warning lights, almost blocked by the angle of Stony's grassy north-south divider. Coming Soon: Starbucks Coffee, it reads.

We're parked on the southwest curb, waiting on some Blackstone king to pass by in his newly minted AMG Mercedes Benz. V-8 or V-12 engine purchased special—at least, that's the word on the street. This street-hustling king—who came up on Stony Island under the wings of Big Lester Hooks and Otis Ray, those old-time gangsters long damned, according to my cousin—purchased his Benz-o just this past weekend. But Weidmann needs to know the car in his own eyes, so he can follow the king to the pot of cracked gold at the end of his path.

"There's no rhyme, reason, or excuse for a cop to go about abusing any buzzard who's already locked in jail. That's what it says right here: the guy'd gone down already, had a rap sheet long as the New Testament. Hell, he was Fred's arrest, his case, this clown. Fred was working it. He knew better. I know that for certain fact.

"Say this was some rook. These ex-gangbangers the city's training—like there's such a thing as a Disciple giving up what he does out here—or a Mexican, or one of your brothers, or even some Okie recruited to the Academy straight out the Marines. Then I could see it. Abuse? They taught us in the army that the whole point of service was keeping things what they are. We were over in My Lai to protect the balance, keep it top up, bottom down—same thing got reinforced in us come the Academy. The seed was planted from 'Nam. Fred, too, he was over there. That's what our calling is, maintaining peaceable order, so it lasts. All that we can be, all it's ever supposed to be."

"Fred might've been Marines, though. Marines is something totally different," Phil interrupts. Weidmann's eyes roll in the rearview—both slopes of his face are red now. "*Semper Fi.*"

"Attack, attack, attack. Always on the attack. Compensating, like there's something to prove to somebody." Weidmann digs his chin deeper into his chest through the blue patrol shirt. "I aughta know—Fred was Army, man. You know they created the Marines for the Irish and Italians and Polish just off the boats. Ignorants who couldn't understand any commands in the language except that one: *attack!* Then after all them learned the language, the Marines were left to the Okies and gangbangers."

"Mmh," Phil utters. "Now, they're all cops."

"Could understand were it one of em," Weidmann starts speaking before "cops" is finished slipping past Phil's slush-covered lips. "But if you know good and well things are just as they're supposed to be, then there ain't nothing to be compensating for. Just is what it is. Ain't that right, college boy?"

Weidmann turns to the backseat. The color in his face cools to its natural pale as his eyes fix on me. I look away, to Phil's plastic cup rested above the dashboard scanner. I draw my knees away from the preacher cop's seat. "What?" I say. "I don't understand, Officer."

"You understand me perfect, son. You took Criminal Justice down at college," Weidmann croons. "If things are what they are, ain't no reason to go about overcompensating for what's missing, right?"

I look away from the scanner, to Remi. Cousin bites his top lip and rubs the corners of his eyes as he stares past me to watch the sun fade.

"Depends," I say. "It's all relative, Officer."

Weidmann laughs and grabs for the empty cup. "Am I fucking saying that big word right, college boy? *O-ver-comp-en-sat-ing?*"

"What's missing can only be what somebody don't see. Got three million eyes in the city," I answer.

"Six million," Remi says, without turning away from the eight o'clock sun. "Three million sets of eyes, seeing six million different sights."

"Well," the preacher cop sings, "thought you said college boy took up Criminal Justice. Sounds like some phil-os-o-phiz-ing right there."

"I went to college, too," Remi says, and the car is quiet until Wee Man sips the bottom of the fake slurpy through Phil's straw, sucking plastic and backwashed bits of air through the tube.

He looks back to the newspaper, his thumb sliding from his blue brother's face. "I want to say I don't believe this crap. Fred knows better. Read this they put in the *Sun-Times,*" Weidmann points at words in columns. "Look, 'duct-taping one's eyes open and forcing his head into a bucket of ice water.' 'Roping another one's scrotum to the blades of a ceiling fan turned on high.' 'Sodomized a suspect with the handle end of a Louisville slugger.' They put a baseball bats halfway up this kid's ass—that's some sick shit. How'd it fit? We didn't learn these things in the Academy or in 'Nam. How does any of this conduct protect the way of things? Forcing the low lower ain't no better than forcing them to the top.

"Maybe they found Fred was slagging some columnist's gal, or that he didn't care for Jews, so they cooked this up. It's out of whack. I know Fred Conley—this's got to be some kind of payback. They went and created this pap, like a fiction tale."

Preacher cop lowers his window and tosses the slurpy cup

onto Stony Island's sidewalk. "I'd be with you, Mike, except for they got your guy on surveillance camera. I saw one of the tapes. Clear as day, it's Fred roping up those balls. Real deal, partner."

"Damn surveillance cameras." Weidmann's head shakes left to right now, until sweat leaks past his ears. He forms a fist out of his word-following hand and bites the skin beneath his thumb. "Every fucking thing is out of whack."

"Let it be, man," Phil says. "Sad story, but it is as it is for now. This time next year, we'll hear another tragic-ass duty tale, then run across the street to grab a latte right on the corner. Say lattes wash all trouble away, till the mind is clear. Say it's a peaceful drink."

"Who says? That's some more sickness." Weidmann sniffles. "A Starbucks on Stony Island? World's gone mad all around me."

"Shi-it. Bout time they brought something over here to keep folks awake. Fast food, liquor store, church, pork loin shop, everything else on Stony is meant to put you down. In a year, we'll be able to run across the island and buy us a latte. Things are changing for the good."

"All right, Reverend," Wee Man says as he stares through his driver-side mirror. I glance over my shoulder just in time to see a Grand Am turn left underneath the city sign with the eastern arrow crossed out in red, just south of the tracks. "I'm tired of waiting. Don't they see the signs?"

Weidmann churns the Crown Victoria's ignition and presses the accelerator in one motion. The cruiser whirls away from the Stony Island curb and Remi is forced to look at me as the sun finally disappears behind the corner chicken nugget shack. He stares this way and I reach for the backseat door handles, trying to keep my place The bird-pig U-turns beyond the traffic divider and twists eastbound on 71st Street, chasing this illegal Grand Am, with hazard lights rat-tat blinking in silence.

"WASN'T NOWHERE NEAR what you all made it out to be," I say. It is me avoiding looking directly at Remi now, though I do see him rest his head against the Range Rover's passenger window in this windshield reflection. "Two of them seem like a couple clowns, truth be told."

"You think so?"

"Far as I could tell it," I say. I press the radio controls lined along the steering wheel's edge, lowering the hum of this unknown R & B tune, though I don't have much more to say.

Wee Man and preacher cop Phil dropped us off at the White Castle on Stony Island, where Remi'd left the Range Rover just underneath the Chicago Skyway's rise. I steer us east now back on 79th Street under the blue dark of summertime.

"Wee Man got impatient waiting for nightfall, that's all that saved you from peeping the scenario," Remi says, he turns the hum louder. "Once sundown come, their real-deal nature rises up out of them. Become like pigs in blood, my nigga."

"Pigs live in mud," I tell him. "Wallowing in mud."

Remi laughs—I see his teeth in the windshield. "Been sleeping, shitting, fucking in that mud for thousands of years. Got to be some blood in that mud, Cuz."

"Been a long time," I agree.

"Ain't no lie," Remi says. I look away from the stoplight at 79th and Jeffrey, just down the way from Ascending Queen, the last school I attended without Remi. Or the last until SIU's rep rode him out to the Greyhound to catch a ride back to 95th. We finally look at each other without blinking or turning now, and my cousin speaks, "Damn shame what goes down when you give a gangster mud to do his thing up in. Can't help but get it bloody. They sit up and tell you the other mutha-fuckas is criminal. Dope slingers, thieves, terrorists, whatever the fuck, and you look at these muthafuckas, and they do look like some sick bastards. Then you look at wee men with their badges and uniforms and billy clubs. What you gonna do when they get to dropping bombs on them sick-looking muthafuckas in the mud? What you gonna say—they're just the pigs, serving and protecting us, doing their job."

"Making sure the things stays what it is," I chime. "Like the cop said."

Remi turns to our front, peeps at his own reflection now— if he sees it like I do—either at himself or at the silver and white full moon beaming on our ride. "You ain't see him with the sun down. Fuck Wee Man."

MY COUSIN SNORES against the passenger window, and I've turned from our path, driven west past the Skyway. Not ready to be at home in the Corners—not yet.

I see her, where Cottage Grove meets 79th Street. She stands underneath the glass bus-stop protector, though there's no rain or wind or evil to be shielded from on this night, none that I know. I almost miss her for the UPN TV-show advertisement posted inside her bus stand. These reds and oranges and brown clown-show colors blocking my apple from street sight.

Until I catch these eyes. Even from here, as the Range Rover tumbles over potholes, my apple's stare shines a silver brighter than the streetlamps washing 79th Street in safe orange-blue. Her stare reflects this full moon over our heads as she stares at the corner grocery store shut closed across the street.

I cut across 79th Street's yellow-dot divisions and pavement holes, as no eastbound traffic approaches, and ride the Range Rover against her curb. The truck's moonshine white glides into her path to face headlights far off and streetlights blinking yellow and red. This is the first time I've seen the trick-or-treat girl from Remi's porch in months. Remi and Westside spout off on how they still deal with these fresh Cottage Grove skeezes—Westside Jackie's word, *skeezes*.

What I see at the bus stop though, peeking from behind stupid TV-show signs, is still an apple. She wears a tiny T-shirt cut short at the end of her chests to show frayed pink cotton dangling over a belly that spills baby fat from her waist. She's smiling as the Rover approaches the bus stand. But my apple walks two steps back from the driver door as I glide near—she loses her balance against the bus-stop bench, then bounces on her right Reebok heel to catch herself. Her bubblegum smile is gone by the time my window drops.

"Hey," I say, softer than the low-end Midnight Love grumbling from the dashboard, soft enough that my cousin still doesn't stir. My apple smiles without teeth. "You going home?" I ask.

"Naw," she says and retakes the two steps toward the curb without tripping this time. Her teeth pop bubble gum unseen for glossed lips. "Headin out."

"Want a ride?" I ask.

She looks at the cage that secures the corner grocery's pitch black windows across the street, then left and right along 79th Street. I hear a bus rumbling in front of us, not sure if it's a CTA carrier on 79th or Cottage, as I'm too busy staring into her yellow smile and these eyes. "Naw. I'm good, man. Bout to get up on this bus coming. Should be mine, right."

"I don't know." I try to hold on to brown circles twinkling silver. Our Dawn could grow and have my apple's eyes, nothing more—not this fresh Cottage Grove body tapered and jutting and hopping along the block on white sneaker heels. These apple eyes will blaze beautiful and pure in my baby though. My child won't be standing underneath any corner-side glass protectors. Never—Dawn's eyes will just outdo moonlight no matter that it's full, just like this child's.

She looks away, at the all-night Number 79 coming from the West. "You remember me? From Phillips Avenue," I ask.

She takes a half-step back, scans the Rover's white steel, then peers into the truck. She catches Remi, or his reflection, and teeth return to her smile. These block teeth aren't rotten up close, but they're not white either, they don't shine, and there's a sliver gap between the two front bucks. But her smile is sugar sweet. "Oh yeah," she says and points at Remi's head rocking against glass. "You're old boy's cousin. The one they call the square. On the porch."

The Number 79 has eased through Cottage Grove—its

headlights burn against the rearview mirror, blinding, so I see no twinkling in my lovely apple, no bubble gum between her teeth, no more. "Yeah, that's me," I say.

The Number 79's horn sounds and fog drops out of a sky gone darker blue. The child runs to the bus' parted doors and I look away. Not before I watch the back of her disappear in the driver-side mirror though, just as Wee Man watched that illegal left turn over train tracks.

The bus driver lifts her fist to pound the CTA horn again, so I circle from the curb over these yellow lines and untreated gaps that trail from the Skyway and White Castles and the Island. Remi's head stirs and his eyes blink away wet sleep—we're driving back the way we came now. I press the Rover's accelerator until the summer fog and blinding bus headlights fade in my cousin's rearview mirror.

12

THE OLD MEN spit their curses in English on Wentworth this afternoon. Their last mah-jongg round usually finishes by 3:00, leaving me to look down on balding head patches as players settle the game's debts. Remi explains their racket as a Chinese take on dominoes; fitting tiles together on top of a flat surface until some shape or order appears. The fastest to create the most logical design gets the biggest cut of the pot. So these old men crouch in alley openings circles and in Chinatown lounge corners, fixing their tiles until the loot from the day's pot is nearly spent. Then the boss man takes his cut of the winnings for the privilege of letting them play on his street. That's the characteristic that separates mah-jongg from dominoes in the Corners, according to Remi—on the Corners, boss would take his cut from the front of the pot before any wannabe players claimed winnings. Otherwise, he'd never collect a dime without threatening to shoot or cut, Remi says. My cousin believes this because he's never had his own window view of Wentworth. Remi doesn't know that Chinatown is just the fifth corner of the city.

Today, the mah-jongg boss is dressed in a black single-breasted suit with matching tie, bought off the discount rack. He doesn't yell, and his skin isn't its usual flaming orange—in halting English, he spits no more than an idle "damn" and a trailing "shit." No poking of the chest this Thursday, and no ball of green bills thrown at the sidewalk.

The winning player shrugs to answer these low curses, and the boss looks to the sky, uttering "goddamnit" twice to his Buddhist heaven, though he sounds like a hustler fed up with Jesus on 79th Street. The boss's gaze drops to the sidewalk and he crosses Wentworth without spitting another word to the player, who's left to scratch his rim of hair strands. He's still scratching when a navy blue Taurus pulls to the curb, its rear passenger door opened before the front wheel stops an inch short of the old man's house shoes.

"Mr. Simms, you have a client," I turn to my desk phone at Gladys' call—the clock on the base reads 3:25. I don't schedule Pharaoh Pugh's customers this late. Past three o'clock is time for watching collections and cleaning the mind of cubicle jive, so that I can make it through the rest of these days. I look to the edge of my walls and expect to find Gladys standing here smiling that Mississippi smirk, crooked and full of jokes. She knows better than bothering me with company business this close to 3:30. But I'm all alone in this wing, with the munch of Dale the adjuster one cubicle over, his teeth grinding Jays potato chips from our office vending machine. "Mr. Simms?"

I press the reply switch. "Ms. Tucker," I say, breathing hard and heavy as if I've rushed from some far-off place, no matter that she knows I'm sitting right here staring into my window view. "Who is it?"

She pauses, mumbles words I don't understand away from her speaker. "It's a Mr. Lowe—" she says finally.

I let go the switch and roll back to my window. The old man in the house slippers and the dark blue car are gone, leaving tire streaks on concrete. I reach toward the receiver, ready to tell Gladys to send this client away for another day, but I smell bowel-bubbling cologne and catch this backwards Kangol hat colored purple just over the wall wobbling near my workstation. Only now do I take "Mr. Lowe" for Westside Jackie.

Jackie doesn't pause at the wall's edge before he enters—he's wearing his delivery service gray-and-browns and wiping lunchtime mayonnaise from the corners of his mouth, and he cares nothing about my permission. He drops into the chair underneath Dawn's picture and slides to the edge of my desk, blocking escape. In case it came to my mind. He taps the cheap plastic under my elbows and looks to the ceiling, searching. "What is that noise?"

I point to the wall that supports my desk. "Shhhh," I spit.

"Tell him to shut up. Don't he know this's a place of business?" Jackie's words echo and the munching noise stops mid-bite. My neighbor barely breathes now.

"What brings you this way, Mr. Lowe?" I ask.

He slides the Kangol halfway around his head so I don't see the kangaroo hopping across purple fur. "Just checking on you, Cuz. I talk so much noise about your job, figured I'd come check it for my own self. Least I'll have a vision in my head when I get to running my mouth from now on. Words don't mean much without the visual."

I point to the wall again and roll my eyes. "We've got a variety of automobile coverage policies that you might find suitable, sir."

Jackie laughs. "I don't got a car. Drive a package delivery truck, not a car."

"We also offer comprehensive homeowners' coverage and renters' insurance packages."

"Don't keep much of nothing in need of protection. If I lose it, it's gone, what you gonna do?" he says. "We're covered."

"Life insurance—up to one hundred and fifty thousand dollars."

"That's all my life's worth?" He taps the desk again. "Kind of bullshit?"

"In 2002? With this policy, your beneficiaries will have more than you'll likely ever earn lifting boxes, Mr. Lowe. As long as when you pass, you do so under legitimate circumstances."

"That's all the favor I've gotta do for somebody else to benefit?" His laugh leaks beige lettuce as he stares at Dawn's picture. "Die legitimate?"

"And pay your premiums on time."

"Ain't that bout a bitch?" I wonder if the old men have returned to their corner. "Living ain't worth a dime unless I'm paying your boss a cut. Then, I die, only to make somebody else happy and rich while I rot. Everything's a racket, can't beat it for trying."

"Or dying," I say, "this racket."

My neighbor peeks past the cubicle's edges. Peach lips spew vending machine breath. "You all right, Tom?"

"Just fine," I say and wait for his head to disappear. But the adjuster stands and looms over Jackie, swirling his snack between gums. "I have a client."

"Oh—I don't mean to interrupt." The adjuster reaches into the cubicle, offering his palm to Jackie. "Dale Gefangen, pleased to meet you."

Westside Jackie stares at my neighbor, the bottom of his jaw quaking with laughter. He snatches the Kangol from his head, offers Dale his hand, and swallows. "Jack Lowe," he says. This is the first time I have ever heard Westside refer to himself as such—I imagine him delivering parcels and telling lonely old brown-and-gray ladies at their door fronts that his name is "Jack."

Dale lets go Westside's hand and rolls his eyes toward my window view. "Tom, finish telling me that story from this morning."

I push a stack of claims toward the keyboard. Westside's jaw quakes harder. I tap the desk, then use the same finger to point at Jackie. "You see I have a client."

The adjuster leans farther into my cubicle and his shadow touches Dawn's wall. His tie is loud paisley, and his pants are hitched up high along his spine, though he wears no suspenders and his belt buckle hangs beneath an unseen stomach. The only difference in our cubicle uniforms is the scraggly hair streaking about his scalp to reveal snow white patches above a wrinkled forehead. "The one about the crooked bum from this morning.

You remember. This gentleman will get a kick out of it. I'm sure you'll love this story—"

"Jack Lowe," Westside repeats.

"I'm sure Mr. Lowe'd enjoy it," Dale says and twists himself such that his leg touches Jackie's chair, and he and Jackie and the chair and the cubicle wall and my daughter's picture form a guffaw circle of their own, though only Dale lets go laughter.

"Tell us about this crooked bum." Westside leans forward in his chair. His lips shake between his words. "I want to get a kick."

I drop my forearms on top of the desk and lean toward Jackie. Yet I speak loud enough for my colleague, who's quiet as he looks over Westside's furry purple kangaroo. "There was this claim, you see, came across the desk my third week here. Seems a guy—drifter guy in his forties, in and out of jobs with a wife and a bunch of bad kids—twice every year, he'd get into a car crash, major body damage, always rear driver side. Guy's clearing six-, seven-, eight-thousand-dollar checks from insurance coverage every rip. And if a damage estimate fell short of that figure, he'd come down with some extra injury. Neck, back, blurry vision, those hard-to-prove pains. Busted out with a foam-at-the-mouth seizure a few days after one accident, blamed it on postconcussive trauma syndrome and walked away with twelve hundred more from Allstate. True hustler, this cat."

Dale laughs louder. "You'd be amazed the conniving that comes across our desks, Mr. Lowe. So many scheming crooks."

"Sounds to me like an unlucky type," Jackie says. "What do you want him to do? He gets hit, he gets hit. Happens all the time."

"Only so much bad luck in this life for anybody," Dale says. "This guy was a bum. Tell him, Tom."

"I'm trying to." I swivel away from the computer screen. "Come the third time in '02, this guy gets hit by one of our policyholders, and our supervisor drops the case right here for me to look after. Find out this joker's on all kind of meds long before these so-called accidents started: Depakote, Prozac, Dilantin. Guy'd wake up and see the sun shining, figure it was a good day to get paid, skip his morning meds, and go for a drive in the city. Pull up to some good-looking expressway entry, always up north or out in the burbs, and wait for just the right car to come near the merge. Time it perfect, and once he knew that other driver'd discounted his merge attempt, this bum'd shoot in front. The other car'd slam him square in that safe spot—nice, safe, and three G's in damage at some crooked auto body shop. Assert he had right-of-way and the other guy was speeding, and because his damage was in the rear and he was always nice and bloodied by the time he filed his claim, the insurance company'd cut its losses. Figured writing him a check would cost less than the court hassle or investigating the background."

"That kind of money adds up twice a year," Jackie nods, "if you're tucking it away."

"Told you that you'd get a kick, Jack." Dale laughs again.

I lean toward the window. The mah-jongg boss speaks calmly with another player just outside Kung Pao. "In the five years he's filing his claims, he buys three different used beaters, never more than five hundred a pop. So you figure that's two accidents per pieces of shit. Crooked shops were estimating damages five, six times the car's worth every trip in return for a cut of his payout. For no repair work. You're right, the game is a racket. Once he collects two checks, he junks the beater for parts and pockets that right along with his insurance payoff."

"Everybody's gotta run a racket," Jackie says. Dale's laughter is helpless and short now.

"Yeap." I point at Westside again. "But we weren't having that hustle garbage up on Grand Avenue. Why treat it any different in Chinatown? Supervisor put me on it, and I tracked the dates of these so-called accidents, right? All of um in December, about a month before Christmas, or in the six weeks after April fifteenth."

"Shady bum." I'm not sure whether Jackie's speaking to Dale, or to me.

"Shady and habitual," I say anyway. "Add his timing to the medications, and to the repetitive circumstances of these events, and I had his drifting, hustling ass boxed in, see. Turned my investigation over to my supervisor, and Pugh didn't pay the fool a dime. My office will be back on the thirty-second floor somewhere, right, Dale? Before you know it."

The adjuster bites the last chip he finds hiding between his teeth before answering. "I'm sure."

"You're proud of tricking on a fool who's trying to make his cakes? Long as you get the payoff for turning him in?" Jackie says, his sound not so proper now.

"Am what I do," I tap keyboard buttons. "Right, Dale? That's all we are—"

"Right."

"But we are at least. End of last week, the guy tries once

more after coming up short with Pugh. And he was a unlucky clown, no question. Ran another beater out in front of a SUV at the North Avenue Kennedy entrance. Timed it all wrong and the truck hit him hard enough to spin him into a semi headed south. Ended your boy upside down, head smashed between the guardrail and his car. Now, the guy's wife was paying on a life insurance policy, something like the one I'm looking to sell you here, Mr. Lowe, to cover herself and those bad-ass kids who sent him out to this dead man's hustle. Thought they had a cool fifty thousand coming. But the guy who sold her the policy didn't read Mrs. Loon Bin the clause about dying legitimate—we've got shady jive suckers in the insurance racket, too, see. Supervisor turned my investigation over to her insurer's reps Monday, and I guarantee his litter won't see a cent. Not a chance. They'll still owe the mortician a grip for burying the fool. Watch. That's the job. Is what it is."

"Winner of a story," Dale says as he grabs a full potato chip from his desk. "Best I've heard in some time around here. Hell of a tale."

"Thanks," I say and hear something between my mother's frustration and a guffaw behind my lips.

The adjuster's crunch is partially muffled by the wall, just under Westside's cackle. "Great job you all got here," Jackie says, "bunch of haters."

"Remember, we've got that four o'clock meet with Mr. Ramsey." Dale walks on, staring at his watch as he follows Gladys' usual path. I spit in the garbage can beneath Dawn's picture. "What's the business, Cuz?"

Jackie pulls himself near the desk's edge. Our knees touch and his whispered wind cuts my earlobe. "Time to pay what you owe me."

I roll toward to the windowsill. "What?" I whisper low as lips will allow beneath an open ceiling. "Ain't got that on me—won't no time soon, Jack."

He laughs as the words skip with my heartbeat. Laughs and leaves this fake love tap on my shoulder. "I know, Cuz—times's hard all around. Nobody has nothing these days. That was more than a G's worth of ganja you got took off us though. Half of that was mine, ain't no new business coming in. Nigga can barely eat right about now. Damn roof's about to go."

"The times," my heart hums, "some kind of times. Been so for a bit."

"Considering for the state of the economy, we gotta be creative in how we settle our obligations these days. Debt still needs to get paid, no matter how bad this shit stinks. It's still gonna be here. Collectors coming for your ass, guaranteed—"

"I've got not a goddamn thing to give you."

"Don't be so rude. I'm looking out for you, trying to, and you're cussing and using words like 'ain't' and 'nothing' and telling me what you can't do. You talked to the bill collectors like this when they got to ring-ringing while you was unemployed? I thought not. Who owes who here? I'm trying to help." Dale glances into my cubicle as he passes again, walking circles inside the square office. "Everything don't come down to money. I don't need no degree to see past that. This is about the principle of the debt."

"Money or a bag, that's what I owe you."

"Just said this has got nothing to do with loot. You ain't listening, Cuz. Principle of the debt: you repay what it is you owe in whatever fashion the man who's due wants it back."

I smooth my tie against this wrinkled white shirt, feel paisley stitching raised against bad silk. "Depends on what you want."

"Always something bubbling up in this mind, see. I need you to come by our place tomorrow night, all right?" Jackie says. "This Wee Man bastard, we gotta take care of him."

I turn on the clock radio so that synthesized city blabber drowns the cubicle breath. But Jackie doesn't give a damn who hears us now. And I smile, mean for it to condescend, but he doesn't get me—or I don't get him—so he smirks back.

"Who?" I say. "What're you talking?"

Jackie crosses his leg and kicks the desk just inches from my left knee. "This Wee Man, I've been watching him since you got us into this mess. Kicked it with the cop and his boy Phil Friday on the blocks a few times. They're both some funny muthafuckas—they know how to get down. Sick old bastards, these guys. Both got a taste for ganja trimmed in powders, and young girls. Especially Wee Man with the young girls. Can't say the guy hates Black folk all that much. Cop keeps a fine tar baby in a four-flat right down the block from your place."

"'Phil Friday'—?"

"Bald-head, flat-foot Phil. Call him 'Friday' from the kid- die story. Like the little boy who takes care of the sailor lost on the island. Told you I ain't no fool just cause I didn't go to college."

"I see."

"You'd better." Jackie spins the chair, so half of his words spew into Gladys' hallway. "Remember the bus-stop shorties who came through a few weeks back? I think you was over there when they showed up. One of um was real cute, kinda plump with barrettes in her head."

"I was there."

"Ran into those girlies again at the arcade, told um to come by Saturday so we can get down like how we got down last time. The kick is I got Wee Man and Phil and some of their crew stopping in around eleven that night, too, cause we're supposed to have gifts laid out for them. That's what I told um, and I ain't a liar—all I need you to do is be there early, get yourself a good hiding place with a view, and run the digital."

"Camera?" I cough.

"Gotta put somebody behind the lens to zoom on their faces."

"Who you gonna turn Weidmann in to? Don't nobody care if this cop's getting off with no Black girls. All that goes on out here? Try to give it to the CPD, they'll burn the tape to ashes for him once they're done laughing at your dumb ass. That's how they look out for their own."

"There those thoughts go swimming across your eyes." Jackie follows the float with his pointer finger. He stabs at my right eyeball when he's done. "Ain't looking to turn these pigs in cause they're doing us wrong. What, do I look like a Black Panther, or the niggers in the pictures on Remi's wall? I don't care nothing about who he's fucking, as long as it ain't me. But don't be a fool for them, Tommie—the last things these folks want to see is more Chi-town cops ass-out on video getting buck up inside some skeeze from Seventy-ninth and Cottage.

Seeing it makes a joke out of all the bullshit they've been busy telling us all this time, col-lege boy. Ain't no more laughing left. He's married, got kids I bet, a church and a redneck neighborhood to live up to. Wee Man's supposed to be out here serving and protecting wife and children and God, not getting jungle cracked with a bunch of niggas, not on the television screen.

"You make this video of cops getting down with these little girls—and he's gonna get down, no doubt. We let him know we got him on high definition, say we'll send this tape to Connie Chung and put him out here just like that last sick muthafucka with the baseball bat on her news show. And we'll do it for sure, unless he cuts us in on a solid piece of the loot he's shaking down all over town."

I want to reach around the wall and steal an unbroken potato chip from Dale's desk. "All my debt will be squared away?"

"You just be at the house, about nine-thirty Saturday"—Jackie chews peppermint gum that pokes from underneath his tongue—"and we'll handle this cop like he's got it coming to him."

"And my debt will be covered?" I repeat.

"All squared away." The gum is a ragged ball showing in the gaps between the bottom of Jackie's smile. "Long as I get mine from Wee Man, you're all good with me. I can't speak for Remi. I guess you and him got that worked out on your own anyways. I'm just trying to look out for you, too, family."

The clock radio reads four thirty-five in numbers blinking with the blare from radio speakers. Down on Wentworth, the black-suited boss is long gone, and somewhere in the office, Gladys' shackles jangle not quite so faint. Dale's munching breath is quiet now. He's finally moved on to the meeting with Mr. Ramsey, or snuck away with the day's early escapees. Jackie stands from the client chair and leans near my daughter's picture. "You'll be there?" I think he means this as a question. "Saturday. Nine-thirty?"

Westside opens his right hand to offer peace dap. I take it. Don't want to, but Jackie still blocks my escape. "Saturday night," I say.

"Till then, Cuz, you still owe." Westside bites down on chewing gum to save rubber from falling to my rug before his purple kangaroo wobbles on from these walls.

I look to Cermak Road through my window view, where little heads rise to the El platform and traffic churns about and these trains rumble near, full of fake gold and noise. I search for the tire streaks and almost don't find them but for the narrow end curve where the Taurus ripped east off of Wentworth without me hearing it go. Once I see that streak, the receptionist's jangling quiets.

Gladys leans at the usual place, her arms folded. I turn to the cubicle opening and the corners of her smirk stretch thinner than these pavement marks. "Remember our four o'clock office meeting, Mr. Simms," she says.

"Yes."

"It's almost time to go home," Gladys says.

"Yes," I say, swallowing my mother's frustration now. "Almost time."

13

HER BODY IS still an apple come morning time—sweet fruit, just as I remember it. She waits at the bus stop over by the nursery and the liquor store/corner grocery, the Shop 'N' Drop with the half-empty shelves and lottery machine ringing and spitting numbers long after dark. On Cottage Grove Avenue, where the Korean woman hides behind bulletproof glass, pressing buttons to make the numbers lotto go and swearing that one day the black box will spit and ring right for all who pay to play.

That joint is just the same as our store on 79th and the Drive—the one where my mother sent me to buy her Seagrams pints whenever factory wannabes visited—so I know it well, although my apple stands two miles west of the Corners. All at once, her soft fists push open the store's smeared glass door and unwrinkle the bills her kin pulled from pockets and purses once she announced that she was headed to Cottage Grove to catch the Number 4. They give their cash to my apple to spend every time she goes, praying on that sweet ringing day when it will all come back to them: spare bills and then some, come back all at once. Just as the bulletproof woman promises in her broken jumble of conquering tongues, which even an ex-slave only grasps with ears pressed against double glass.

"Pay it out," she yells at my apple. "Pay it out. God bring you back. You people, you keep come here—" These words our apple understands clearly, for she knows and the grocer knows. We all know the reason, "He bring back."

"God is fair," the grocer continues, and my apple wants to ask this woman for the full name of her God. But the yellow woman's palms are so shaky and sweaty as they slide through the slot to reach for Uncle Jo Jo's twenty, and she never steps away from the protective glass, and her eyes shoot around the store quick, fixing only on the do-rag slicks and gym shoe boys who come and go through the store's front door. So the young girl figures this grocer's God must be same as the one in the early books of the Bible, from back when old folk still made her sit in Sunday service and listen to the old preacher reading, with one eye on his scripture and the other on the curved lift at the low end of her spine, poking from a creaky pew. With that vengeful God, you always get back what you pay out, a few hundred times over.

Best keep close, shifty-eyed watch knowing that, your shouts left wet by the sweat from your tongue and bent by the fear in your bones. Nothing else you can do but shake, sweat, and shout if you already paid out bullshit to conquered souls for Wednesday's Big Game ticket.

UNCLE JO JO'S lottery number shows from the young girl's back blue jean pocket now on this stub rising above her denim stitching. I press the green button to zoom in, just as Westside showed me to do. My apple sits down in the living room, in one of Remi's folding chairs, elbows and forearms rested at her thighs so that her pockets peek from the space between back-rest and seat, as I imagine they peeked from the dirty preacher's pew.

26 - 6 - 7 - 12 - 11 - 14 - 36 is Uncle Jo Jo's Big Game play tonight. Some series of birthdays or Old Testament passages or a combo spat arbitrarily by the black box machine, or just some old digits that jigged through the little girl's mind as the Korean screamed from the safe side.

"This my number," my apple snapped, because there was only so much foreign jabbering she was about to take two blocks from her own home. She read the dancing digits out loud. "Take it down right, just like I said it."

"You pay."

"I got yo pay. Here," she slid Jo Jo's dub through the slot, and my apple took the ticket, double-checking the numbers' order before turning to half-empty shelves. And just under her purple Kool-Aid tongue, she murmured "bitch" and spat on that smeared glass on her way out.

SHE DECORATES HER hair with orange barrettes this sin-ning Saturday night, one to hold the bun in place at the peak of her scalp, the other to keep her bangs from falling over fore-head acne. I perch on this chipped wood dresser turned into the doorway of James' second-floor bedroom to afford myself a full view of the living room happenings. They can't see me for the upstairs shadows beneath this ceiling drop, and the camcorder's red power light is covered by tape to block any reflection. I hold my elbow in my left hand, sure to keep the right wrist steady, and I watch them through the pop-out view screen. This is how they'll look on tape, or so Westside told me. "Just you be sure the picture is clear," he said.

Haze rises with the dust above their circle—my apple is in the middle of it all, or so I imagine. They pass a joint counterclockwise between them, but she pauses before taking the stick, stares off into the ceiling, searching, though she only finds cobwebs. My eyes pretend this at least, for the view screen actually reveals her snatching the joint from James and sucking deep on the twisted end, then puffing gray ganja balls from the tiny hole in the corner of her lips. Her smoke trails and settles above these six heads to float off with the haze. And when she does finally look to the ceiling's corner, the view screen catches her eyes—dry and glassy now, not twinkling or lingering, but rolling to the fellow bus-stop girl at her right. This is one of the same little shorties who waited at the 78th Street corner as my apple knocked last time.

Eyes roll quick and disgusted, because maybe she does see a saving answer in the cobwebs and thinks about as much of it as she does of the Korean behind bulletproof glass or the preacher at his podium. Or maybe my apple just doesn't take kindly to the thought of passing Westside's joint to her girl just yet, wants to keep puffing and dragging and lingering herself.

My apple—Kamisha is her name, I know now—her two bus-stop girls, Jackie, James, and Remi make up this weed circle. The rest of them sit on the living room's dusty hardwood, legs crossed in laps like a bunch of nursery school kids listening to their very first tales. Kamisha sits above them, in the folding chair.

Westside hung a stained polka-dot bedspread over one living room window and a baby blue comforter over the other. I zoom on both, just testing, then back on the joint, in the other bus-stop girl's hand finally. This girl is not as much the smoking veteran as my apple. She lingers long enough for fire to burn her fingertips, and when she puffs on the twisted end, she chokes. James snatches the joint as the bus-stop girl spits smoke into his lap. He pulls his own easy ganja clouds as my apple reaches down to pat her girl on the shoulder, soft and soothing—she's soothing the both of us, sweet child.

I catch Jackie running his finger under the halter top of the skinny, crooked-faced Cottage Grove girl. She leans his way and tongue kisses his yellow cheek. Jackie pays the child no real mind, although his finger stays underneath her bra strap. His eyes rise to the top edges of the sockets, fixing on my place in the landing shadows. The free hand points to the top of her head as she licks him; this is our zoom-in signal. I press the green button and the ends of this girl's face, her twisting tongue, and the red rims of Jackie's eyeholes fill the screen.

Metal clangs at my back. I turn to the uncovered window in James' room, point the lens at the north brick tower. Peer down and inside the Chicanos' home, where shimmering windowpanes put the stainless steel and marble kitchen on clear stage for the digital view screen.

※　　　※　　　※

NEXT DOOR, THE tower's owner—fake Mexican Ricky, I call him—is my age, maybe a few years younger. He stands over shining kitchen appliances turning burner dials that control no real flame, for his stove is electric. Ricky stirs beans and green and orange vegetables in the pan, no meat, and wears Coke-bottle glasses over tiny eyes. This is how I know he's not a Chicano, not like any of those I knew over south of 79th Street: the meatless pans, the flameless stove, and the damned glasses. More pots and pans dangle over his head, hung from decorative wood support beams with silver hooks—again, like nothing I've ever seen near these Corners. Wind seeps through their kitchen, knocking silver hanging pots against each other hard enough to make this clanging noise, but not so hard that they threaten to fall on Ricky's moussed head.

The view screen shows a woman now, dancing from the shadows behind this kitchen. Samba music plays somewhere in their tower. Been playing all along I guess, but I only hear it now as I record Marisol. She passes the kitchen counter, and Ricky stops stirring to watch her, too, his eyes watering with the onions he's chopped beside these burners. Or maybe he cries because he believes Marisol is teary-eyed beautiful in this place, or because she is so thin and pale yet without the arroyo hips of those South Chicago women who walked way north to pick up their niños from Powell Elementary. Marisol looks nothing like my pretty high school chicas either, the ones who sauntered about south of 79th Street come morning time, headed to Bowen High School with the Menudo book bags slung just above butts shaped the same as this unchopped stove-side onion.

Whatever he sees is somehow worth tears. He watches Marisol dance the samba, the onion is in pieces now, and he did it, and the only damned thing it's good for is cooking. The view screen shows him wiping underneath the spectacles and reaching to the pan at the far left burner to flip his tortilla, smoke rising from dough turned brown. I back the lens from their kitchen, record the red, white, and blue flag sticker posted in the corner of the windowpane, just above a sign announcing that their shiny brick tower is protected by a Brinks security system, for all Four Corner hustlers to beware.

*   *   *

JACKIE TOSSES THE crooked-faced girl's halter top under the movie poster. He pulls a tiny breast from her pink bra and plays with the tip of a nipple with his fiddling hand. I press the green button as Remi finishes dragging the joint and skips over James to offer it to Kamisha. He blows a kiss her way before letting go.

The camera has caught enough of Jackie—and Remi now, too—playing with the crooked-faced girl. But there's one more window left uncovered, here at the end of the second-floor hallway. This is the most important view, or so Westside says, out on Phillips Avenue and the curb just before the handi-capped space. I need to catch the license plates and the faces outside the shack, zoom on them good because faces and num-bers are the true proof. The dirty deeds inside are the showtime part, just enough to turn Weidmann's skin vomit pink if he asks to see the tape. But his face and the municipal license plate numbers, backed by true dark shame in South Shore is more than enough to snatch Connie Chung's eyebrows up to her temples, turn her legs all quivering, and get us paid in the Four Corners at the expense of this cop's soul.

Weidmann would know the jig was all done once he saw the proof. Tight plan my cousins came up with here, especially with the Fred Conley spectacle fresh in the city's blue minds. Stupid me for ever questioning them. If we live in a mad world where pigs string fools to spinning blades, then we've gotta get as mad as those wallowing in this mud to get by.

My right arm aches. I rest the camera at the windowsill to make certain the curbside stays in view. My head drops against the dresser cabinet, and I am about to drift all the way into this dream until a car door slams just as my mother calls for me.

"*Nowhere to run,*" *mamma says before the dream ends.*

"*Got us in this, nothing I can do but get myself out.*"

"*Out where?*" *she asks, puffing her own off-colored smoke.*

"*Fools run,*" *I tell her,* "*from these Four Corners. That's how a fool does, Mamma, even if he hasn't figured this place out either way.*"

I lift the camcorder with my sore arm, put the lens on Phillips Avenue, and zoom on the approaching cops. Wee Man's lightless Crown Victoria prowler is parked just south of the house now. I focus on one of the birds who chased me through the sky weeks back. This cop's already standing at the curb as another exits on the street side. They stare at cracked frames and breathe air for a long minute, both waiting as Sergeant Phil Friday slides from the Vic's passenger side, his brown bald spot reflecting moonlight and his smile showing no teeth except for the two vampire bicuspids on either side of the mouth. None of them move far from the curb before Weidmann's sloping dome and eagle beak rise from the street side. I pan back as he circles the Crown Vic's trunk, limping to lawn patches where he pauses to touch the handicap sign post. They all laugh and walk together now. Four hips hitching as if holsters still sling low and unseen beneath beer bellies. Their strides turn into fat peacock struts as they pass Ricky and Marisol's black iron gate.

I switch the lens to the living room as the cops reach Remi's front porch. Jackie licks the crooked-faced girl's breast as she rubs Remi at the crotch. My apple, James, and the choking virgin share embers and blow idle smoke. Not for James fiddling with the second girl's toes through torn flip-flops, they ignore each other.

The joint is in Kamisha's hand as the door shakes. She doesn't bring the ash to purple lips though, or pass the remains on to her girl, or move at all just yet, even as James stands to answer Wee Man's knock. Her nose wrinkles as the knob is turned in the cop's hand and foul lake wind blows these bird-pigs inside. The screen shows Weidmann and Phil Friday whiffing musty funk now, as they look about the room and its broken ganja circle. James stands near the door still, the corners of his face twisted and lost—my apple does smell them, but she lacks the soul of prey.

Kamisha turns to Remi, yet he's busy nibbling for milk that's nowhere to be found inside a flat breast. As Weidmann walks into their broken circle, she looks back to the corner of this living room ceiling. There's no roll of the pupils now, not in this digital view. Her gaze lingers in dust, as if the cobwebs she finds in a wall might protect her from these birds swooping near her head.

WEE MAN GETS down from behind. Must be how he likes his bus-stop girls. Better the shine of their backs and the round of these hips than the brown in their eyes. Kamisha's bent over in my screen, just her and him in this square—oh, and Phil Friday's over in the corner, too, underneath dangling cobwebs. Almost forgot the preacher cop's sweaty, potbellied ass naked on the hardwood floor, hands fiddling with Uncle Jo Jo's Big Game tickets, my apple's jeans spread in his lap as he waits his turn. Boss takes his first, way before a houseboy ever gets a whiff. These are the rules as set up way back in the day. Bet my apple won't bend over for Phil so easily though.

The queen looks at all of this—at me, too—her paper eyes trained on the living space. Remi and Jackie snuck away with the crooked-faced girl and the driver-side cop, back to Cuz's office space to do their thing right under Dizzy and Josephine. James, the virgin in the flip-flops, and the other pig are in the kitchen. They're all running from the queen's watch, but she'll still catch them.

No hiding from that poster, from black-and-white eyes, or from this pop-out digital lens. Bend my apple over all you want then, bird-pig. I zoom on Cleopatra with her .38 cocked and ready, waiting to do these punk muthafuckas in. Prey and birds pretending not to be what they are. Do us all in, with her afro blowing in mighty funk wind.

Wee Man plucks this fresh rock-laced joint from his lips and drops ashes in the tiles between Kamisha's stretched right thumb and forefinger. And my apple's eyes rise to fix on the second-floor landing, though she's got no clue I'm here, can't see the red light for the tape or the green power button for the shadows. No way she sees me—but her eyeballs do rise to the view screen's center. The same way she looked to webs in the ceiling, same way she looked to my cousin sucking a dry nipple.

"I'm here," I whisper to the view screen. "But I've got to pay up. Soon as that's covered, I swear for God I'll come back for you, sweet apple."

Wee Man smacks her thigh and I pan away as she bites thick lips. I fix the lens on her stare, but Kamisha turns to glance over the shoulder, and her tongue pushes purple-stained Kool-Aid air through the gap between her two front teeth.

14

RUST SPREADS FROM the roof and touches the edges of my Ford's hood. I notice its growth only in this orange daytime steam, as the factory paint job is a fading maroon itself. Tarsha calls it blood red.

Remi stands by the trunk, kicking my back tire without paying himself any mind. Twice he does this, then looks over his shoulder, holding cigarette smoke in his jaw and raising his hand for my forgiveness. I don't say a word, not that it would matter. Maybe his thoughts are fixed on the last Newport pinched between his fingers, the red its smoke brings to his eyes, menthol sneaking from nose holes. But I don't bother to ask what he's thinking.

His Range Rover eases backwards into the space just south of the handicap sign. Jackie steps out of the cabin, twirling the key ring and car remote on his middle finger. Cousin stands from my trunk again and walks toward his half-brother, breathing smoke as hot as these orange clouds that won't float on to the east. "Where you been?" my cousin asks, eyes redder than when he peeked over the shoulder.

Jackie bites his bottom lip, sucks away spit. He looks at the shack as he speaks. "You told me I could use the truck."

"Put a full tank of gas back in it?" The corner of Jackie's smirk curves toward his left eye as he pretends to ignore Remi. "Gimme my keys."

The keys still dangle at Westside's middle finger as he looks at me, then at the Escort and laughs. "What's up, Tommie?"

"I'm funny?" Remi snaps before I can answer. He lunges for his keys, only to trip over dandelions sprouting from their lawn.

Jackie's laugh fades into a smirk. "What's up, Tommie?" Westside repeats. "Guess who I seen up on Seventy-ninth?"

Remi turns the lit end of his Newport on Jackie now, aims to stab his twisted lips with the ash. "Gimme my keys."

Jackie looks over my car. "That rust is getting worse. Gonna do something about that shit or what? Embarrassing us out here, goddamnit."

He hikes his jeans above the waist as Remi sucks the Newport again. "You filled my tank at least, right?"

"What do I look like?" Jackie speaks from low inside his gut. "Seriously, guess who I saw on Seventy-ninth Street—"

Remi finishes his smoke and crushes the filter with the weeds and undead flowers beneath his sole. Neither of us answer.

"Your boy Wee Man," Jackie says. "Up there rolling in his cop car looking happier than all get-out. Like today's Happy Po-Po Day on the block or something, him and Phil Friday cruising round together. You ain't tell them about the tape, did you?"

"Me?" I snap. Remi looks up from the lawn quick, then

over his shoulder at Ricky and Marisol's home. "What do I got to do with telling him a goddamn thing? The whole thing is your genius idea how I remember it."

"You dropping word on Wee Man was the kicker," Jackie says. "Remi, you ain't let your cousin know that was how the deal worked?"

Remi looks at the north tower brick without speaking. "Fuck that," I say in his place.

"No—not fuck that." The words rise from Jackie's pit again. "You owe."

"The deal was I make the video, you shake him down to get your loot back."

"Loot you owe. Not him, not the cop—you owe me, my G."

"That ain't got nothing to do with it, not how we agreed. I ain't taking no tapes to no cop, Jackie. Don't play me."

"Shut the fuck up—" Jackie's words echo east along 78th Street, then north on Phillips, and his breath blows hot. Remi turns from us. "You got us in this shit, right, so how you gonna tell me what you ain't doing? What's your position? Shit, you're already played."

"That ain't how we said it in my cubicle."

Jackie manages to laugh and curve his lips at the same time now. "Pay me back then."

I turn to Remi. "What are you gonna say on this?"

He pulls a half square from his shorts' pocket and lights the broken end with a blue-beige flame. "Remember what I told you. You don't owe me a goddamn thing." Then he repeats himself, reversing the answer's order. "—remember what I told you."

"I don't owe you shit, Jackie." I talk loud, so my words might come across as rough. But I hear consonants gurgling soft, with the congestion in my chest. "We set the deal, I covered my end like I was supposed to. If that's how you wanna do it, you take care of the rest of the business."

"Ain't about me. If I ain't helping the muthafucka shake down these corner hustlers no more, it ain't me Wee Man's coming after. All I am is what I'm doing for him. Minute I stop, that cop's coming for your ass, or popping you in the back of your skull when the sun goes down and you can't see him slinking up on you. That's how he'll do you, like a snake, that pig. So who needs to let Wee Man know we got him faded?"

"What y'all want outta me?"

"First, you better buy yourself a gat," Remi says, smoke freeing itself from his tongue, "for protection."

"Protection from who?"

"Then you sit down with Wee Man, let him know about this tape just like we talked about before." Jackie's fingertips count his words against the left palm. "Tell him what we're gonna do with this movie if he won't get down with us proper. That's your message to deliver. I'll holler at Preacher Phil Friday maybe tomorrow, maybe day after, and he'll make the meeting happen. You just be ready."

"In case of what?" I snap again. "Y'all don't play me."

Remi and Jackie glance at each other, and cuz speaks for both of them. "In case some trouble pops off, and we ain't round to look out, and the sun is down. Before you hook up with Wee Man, I'll set you up with Lonnie Fairmont, get you a gat at good price. Smooth piece of steel, something a player can trust."

I laugh and shake my head. "That's exactly what I need."

"You trying to tell sarcastic jokes again, muthafucka?" Jackie speaks too loud and Remi pats him at the shoulder. The south neighbors' Lexus pulls in front of the handicapped sign, idles for a blink, then parallel parks just past their tower. The family exits from the shiny ride together; mother holding the hand of a toddler boy whose eyes don't move about his head. Father carries paper grocery bags and crosses diagonally through the thick lawn until he reaches our sidewalk. Here, he stops, straightens himself, and glares. Not sure, but he seems to be staring square at us—at least, his green eyes don't move about his head as he fixes this way.

Ants crawl in the cracks underneath Westside's gym shoes, and he growls. "I'll be done paying you back now," I say to these bugs. "I meet with Weidmann, then I'm done?"

Jackie laughs and walks back to the Rover, both arms at his side. Their neighbor finishes his crooked line to the tower.

"Where you going?" Remi asks, waving smoke from his head.

"Downtown to the Taste," Westside says, "only four days left, you know, and it's almost the Fourth. Y'all want to roll?"

Remi shakes his head and stands in the handicap space. "Wanna know when I'm gonna be done owing," I ask no one.

Jackie sits inside the cabin now, without closing the door. "What the hell you come here for if you was headed downtown all along," Remi says. "Waste of gas miles."

"Had to step in and check on my niggas. Make sure y'all all right, everything's kosher on the block. Gotta look out for y'all. Who else gonna do it in the end? Them folks in their brick buildings? I'll put some gas in before I come back tonight, Rem-Dog. You know I ain't trifling like that."

Jackie drives off to the north. The neighbor slams the front door at his back once the mother shuts their window blinds.

Cuz sits on my trunk so the Ford's weight shifts on top of tires fixed to the ground. I walk back to his burned lawn and grab the handicap pole to stare at the old houses across Phillips Avenue until sweat drips into my eyes. I blow air onto my top lip and wipe my face with this T-shirt, waving the ends of sweaty cotton to create a breeze. But nothing stops this heat.

WE STARE IN the driver-side glass, me in the backseat reflection. With clear eyes, I see Dawn's car seat, these empty blue cushions and unlocked straps twisted and tossed over the armrest. My sweat falls from my hair, but I don't bother to wipe. I glance at Remi, only because I swear I caught him peeking this way, in the reflection at least.

"You know Lonnie Fairmont, don't you?" he asks.

"Lonnie from the Soft Steppin?"

"Good brother," Remi says. "Done a lotta business with him before. He's got hookups on nice pieces. Won't sell bullshit to you. Top-quality merchandise compared to what else is around here. Looks you square in the face and counts out the cash one bill at a time for you, too. Lonnie's real deal. Won't leave you in a bad situation."

"I was way late paying his cousin two bills-plus off a loan.

Got months behind on his points," I say as rust spreads further along this steel. "Had to drop that ganja on him to square it away."

"Primo? That's Washington Park business. Juicing is his personal thing over there. I'm telling you, Lonnie Fairmont's square dealing, Cuz, especially if you're from over here. These are his blocks, been looking out for fools from the Corners since before the Stones and Hustlers and Lords and Kings. They learned from the man—all the bad-assed shit at least. Damn shame they didn't pick up on the rest of it, the true parts. Lonnie's fair and strong, that's how come they call him what they do."

"King Lonnie?"

"Fair Mountain," Remi corrects.

"King Lonnie," I repeat.

Remi's looking this way again, through the window reflection, his eyes wide. "Your mamma used to always say we favored—ain't never seen it before, myself." He points at the front seat glass, then at his own image. "You do kinda look like me."

"Me like you?" I laugh and watch my right eyebrow bend. "Figure we got the same old man or something?"

"I don't know," Remi says. "How would I? Like they say on the TV—who's your daddy?"

I hear my mother's disgust gurgling, somewhere inside. "Fuck a TV. Lonnie Fairmont's my old man. King Lonnie."

"Lonnie Fair Mountain, king of the Four Corners." Remi squeezes his face, searching. "Yeah, fuck it, goddamn TV lies. He's my pappy, too. Look like we brothers, Tommie. Always figured King Lonnie was some kin to me, him and Willie Coles in the back booth. Means we're princes, the two of us, true princes."

"Must be," I say. Remi smooths the naps to his scalp and I lick sweat from my top lip. "Gonna be kings one day."

"Can't be a king without making it as prince first."

"Damn straight," I say. Clouds move on to let this sun burst over our block. "Goddamn Weidmann."

"Fuck him, too," Remi says. He knows I've forgotten that quickly. "We made him out more than what he is, just like you said. Lonnie Fairmont laid our seed. What is Wee Man but a pig in the mud? To us?"

"Not a damn thing." I follow this lie by fixing wet lips to spit another, "Always knew we were brothers."

⁂

I FEEL THEIR ill stares while waiting in Lonnie Fairmont's corner booth. None of the Soft Steppers paid mind when I sat in this peppermint light with my mother awhile back. Figured I was just another wannabe player then, trying to talk my way up inside one of Lonnie's ladies before the king came to take his rightful place. They knew once Lonnie showed—soon as I smelled him in the air even—I'd clear out to some limp and unseen corner, smiling toothy and congratulating myself for showing the sack to even step to one of Lonnie's honeys. Once we smell the king's sweet tree bark cologne in the lounge air, all the wannabes know that pretend time is all used up on 75th Street.

But for me to sit alone in Lonnie's booth with the man

nowhere in sight, this makes no Soft Steppin Lounge sense. Sour eyes glance, disappointed because they've seen me here so many times before, figure that I should know better. Their stares warn me to come about my good senses. "Lonnie Fairmont calls on your ass—if he bothers to recognize you at all—" eyes remind, "you don't wait on him to arrive. Lonnie ain't never to be waited on, for his is the only clock in this joint."

They don't know I've got business with the man, that he gave me an exact hour to plot myself in his corner booth. Fools can look ill this way all they want to then. They'd best believe I'm right here waiting, on this exact time as it ticks according to the king.

He enters through the lounge's rear, white silk flowing from neck to toe, while the curly crown on top of his head barely rises above these processed dos packing the lounge. The heads he doesn't peek over, his eyes shine through them. Lonnie sees me sitting in his corner booth, toward the front end of the lounge (well as I see him, he does), but the king turns and walks toward the restroom hallway. I look at my timepiece—this watch Tarsha gave me for Christmas years back with the shiny studs for number signs. I figure that a player's player will appreciate its gaudy look, even if he's too much of a player to ever say so. Figure the king'll peep the studs and this gold and platinum painted band, and he'll dig it enough to approve of my attempt.

His chunky weight hitches my way again, each broken step in rhyme with the jukebox jive, and billowing in his silk getup. King Lonnie dips and hitches to hide the limp in his right knee, wound blasted by the .45 of some old-time alley hustler seeking to teach a young king a lesson about respect.

My eyes bounce from Lonnie's face to the tabletop underneath my elbows until he's crossed over the dance floor. He looks more like Westside Jackie Lowe's father than mine or Remi's. Got Jackie's same sort of high bright skin, wet with silver sweat drops between his nose and moustache, along a jaw that barely shows for the swollen cheeks. His eyes are chocolate candy treats filled with peanuts, and the hair at the top of his head isn't relaxed, brushed wavy, or combed straight, much as it's left free to roam. Making a show of its loose way, this perfect mess up high on a redbone player king's head. If King Lonnie was darker by the skin, you'd call this hairdo an afro just like Cleopatra Jones'. But if the king had her color, then he really could have been the one who dropped the seed that came to be us.

"What up, Tom?" Lonnie sits with half of his face on the front door and the other to the bar.

"Lonnie," I say.

He frowns and wipes sweat from his brow with a handkerchief pulled from white pockets. He spits in the cloth when his skin is dried and tosses it underneath the table. This frown still twists his forehead as he looks at me. "What's up?"

"Just trying to get this business took care of," I say. "My cousin hollered at you?"

"Ain't been hollered at in a minute, Tom." Outside of the office nobody calls me "Tom," not to my face. Yet being "Tom" doesn't bother me right now as at least the king knows who I am. "I *talked* to Remi, though."

"He told you what I'm looking for?"

"Need to hear it from you, chill." Gold shows along the bottom row of the king's smile, at least five plated caps shining in this corner haze. More gold shines on the top row, I know, but his lip covers the high part of his smile.

"Trying to get a gat, Lonnie," I whisper under synthesized bass strings. "Don't know why I've got to say it, if Remi talked to you already. This some kind of muthafuckin formality?"

"Watch your mouth, homey," Lonnie says, and my eyes drop to the bottom of their sockets, although all that I see of my mouth is a fuzzy top lip. "This here is how I do business: deal only with words spoken straight outta the speaker's lips. That's how you get at meaning. Only way to know the real deal, chill—keep it professional like so. Best keep watching that mouth till we're done here. This is proper business time."

"Got you," I try to sound cold and hard, though it's better to act my true self with the king. "Like I say, I'm looking to get some steel."

He rubs the gray strands in his pointy-tailed goatee, nodding in approval or consideration, I'm not sure which. "What kind you looking for?" His voice coos with the lounge mutter.

"Ain't never been much of a toting cat," I say. "Mostly can't call the difference between one gat and the next by sight. They're all killing pieces far as I see it."

"How you gonna look to buy something you don't know nothing about, then go and tell the man you're buying off you're ignorant of the product? I could sell you any kind of cockamamie crap now. How do you know one way or the other?"

"I thought you said this was proper business time?" I ask. "Told me to take this serious."

"Come again? I am serious," he says. "This's exactly how proper folk do business out in the world, just with 'g's' at the ends of their business words: hustling, and fucking and stealing and shamming. Correct punctuation written into their contracts, too."

"My cousin says you're a square-dealing brother."

"Shit." Lonnie hisses as he laughs. "How's he supposed to know one way or the other either? Mighta been running game on that young 'un all along, still doing it."

"I'm from Seventy-fourth Street." I shake my head at the waitress shadowing our table. The king orders two Hennessys with Coke. "We all know Lonnie Fair Mountain over here."

He rubs the goatee harder. "Nice try. That's 'King Lonnie' to you."

"We know him, too."

"Trust me, chill." This hiss is louder than the mutter. "You don't know shit—just told me so yourself."

A Jackson 5 medley plays on the jukebox now and little Michael's falsetto does make me sound rough, in my own ears at least. "About guns, no, I don't know a damn thing. But I figure if one nigga sells such a goddamned thing to another, he'd best be truthful with his customer. Otherwise, he's putting revenge right in the other man's hand, and pointing the way to his own end. Why would you go about cheating your buyer when all the cat's gonna be aiming for afterwards is that throbbing vein running under your hairline?"

King Lonnie pulls a gray strand from his face, blinking

without flinching, then he speaks. "You wouldn't, chill. You ain't hard."

"I wouldn't." My palm brushes against my own hairless chin. "Many in here would, though."

Lonnie's tongue pokes the inside of his cheek, stretching fat wrinkles. "That's a better try," he says. "Like that in you."

"So which way should I go, Lonnie?"

He leans across the table as the waitress comes near with the drinks. When she breaks her stride, cursing about how she's forgotten napkins, he talks. "Depends on what you're looking to do, chill. First, you gotta figure out if you're really meaning to shoot the thing."

"It's a gun."

"Your mamma taught you better than to interrupt when grown folk're trying to explain something, I know." Lonnie leans on the booth's backrest as the waitress drops two nose-hair burning Hennessys mixed with just enough Coca-Cola to turn the bottom of the glass black. Once she leaves without quoting a price, Lonnie uses both forearms to pull himself toward the table. The spit of his words splashes in my drink.

"If you're looking to stick up a joint, maybe the 7-Eleven or the liquor store—not that I'd advise such nigganess—but if that's what you're planning on, you just want the gat to be big, clean, and black so it reflects the ceiling lights and makes the clerk go sour-balled as he hands over his register loot. You ain't looking to fire the thing, just something to take the courage outta the muthafucka so you get what you're after. Don't even really need the bullets, cause it ain't about shooting off. It's about letting it swing in that light."

"Gat don't even need to be real then." A female dancer wastes Michelob on her sequined dress to Lonnie's right, but she keeps shimmying in a clean circle. "Long as it looks scary."

"It's gotta be legit, Tom, and on the real, I just say you don't need the bullets to make a bigger point. Was a *disclaimer,* like how y'all explain downtown. This is the end of my big point here: you go up in that store planning on not popping off one of my pieces, only to come face-to-face with one of these Chinese behind the counter. Them and the gas station Arabs got no fear of your Black ass, and none of your big, shiny black gun neither. World's been stealing from them, poisoning their children, dropping bombs on their heads since when they put us in shackles, before that even. What they got to be scared of a nigga or a gat for? The muthafuckas invented gun powder—"

"Remember Marcus from off Seventy-seventh?" I hear myself talking in the space between songs. "Took his ass up in the Chinese joint—or were they Vietnamese?—up in their place in the Sixty-third Street mall, talking that bullshit and waving a gat at those people. Owner laughed, pulled a bazooka cannon from under the counter and put Marcus' ass to sleep quickfast. That's how they retold the story on Channel Two right before the reverend went to march on Sixty-third Street and his people busted out all the Vietnamese's windows."

"Marching for hype-ass Marcus Tate." Lonnie swallows most of his Hennessy. "Now what's the worth of such nigganess, Tom? Just to get locked up or blasted, or to end up marching against a muthafucka who got two billion countrymen at his back? All over twenty-five dollars and some stale-ass Reese's Pieces?"

"Do I look like such a hype?" Lonnie rubs his hairline curls without answering. "Well, I'm not."

"Didn't say you was. So what, you're looking to pop some fool cause you found he's messing round with your lady?" Lonnie reaches over his shoulder and touches the woman with the stained dress. She leans down so the king can whisper in her ear as he offers a fresh handkerchief. He points at the bar for Alvin to send another drink. All this while the wannabe who's supposed to be grooving with the lady dances his own careful steps with floating menthol smoke.

Lonnie turns to the table as our waitress delivers an opened Michelob for the woman, again without speaking a word. "You want a gat with kick then, something gonna put that clown in the ground off one blast, so you'll have time to figure what you're gonna do next: run, or pop your lady, too, or put the muzzle in your own mouth. Long as that clown is good and taken care of first, clean and quick. But that ain't worth it neither, chill. If she's with another cat, she ain't yours no way, and if you went about shooting all the clowns who'd get down with her while your back is turned, you and your old lady'd be the only two left living in this place."

I blink visions of Tory B. Moore through my head. "Old lady ain't cheating on me," I tell myself, and the king. "We're married, got a daughter."

He stares at a point on my forehead to stop his eyes from rolling. "Good," the king says.

"Sounds like you ain't interested in my business." My tongue burns with the Hennessy. "Remi told you what I was looking for. What'd you have me sitting here since seven-thirty for if you ain't looking to make a sale?"

"Never *want* to do this, chill. It's just what I do to put change in the pockets." His stare is nowhere near me now. "Kind of caliber you want?"

I drink and burn and swallow more pain. "Forty-five, I don't know."

"That's a white boy's piece. Hefty enough to let um forget how my ding-a-ling is supposed to be bigger than his, play like it's myth. And if it ain't, forty-five packs the blast to do something about flipping up truth."

"Don't need all that," I say. "Got any twenty-twos?"

"Got anything you'd ask for." He lets his eyes roll now. "But that little 'pant-pant' noise your lady makes while you're up inside of her, playing like she's cumming—that's a twenty-two, all harmless and hollow. Your honey don't mean to be faking on purpose, she just can't bust no real nut cause she ain't never been inside it. If those little 'pant-pants' was true cum you bringing her, she'd be laid out like how you're laid out after you're done in there. No disrespect at all. Ain't no 'pant-pant' you're letting go inside of her, is it?"

I want to tell him that, no, it's relief, more a puff than a pant. But Lonnie is the king, Lonnie's the player. "I bring noise, King, not that it's for me to be saying out here."

"That's what I'm talking about. That's life, and when you let it out in that place, it's all done. Your woman ain't been in no true womb since she was up inside her mamma's at the start, so what's she know for life spilled?"

The sequin woman doesn't dance with her wannabe anymore. She leans on the wall behind the corner booth, sipping Michelob and watching Lonnie.

"Tech-Nine?"

"Now that's better. That there's a real soldier's gun. Nines are for a nigga who knows he's a nigga and wants all to know he's a nigga, so there's comfort with him and his crime—cause he's just showing um he's exactly what they good and well knew he was all along. You heard the rappers singing about them in their ditties, right?"

"I'm just looking for some protection," I say, "just in case, Lonnie."

"Why didn't you say so? I asked you what you wanted to do with the piece, didn't I? Only way to go is a thirty-eight, if all you want is some protection."

"Thirty-eight Special—"

"Saturday Night Special," he replies, though I wasn't asking. "Gat tells no big lies, just pull it and 'pop.' No questions, and no refunds neither. Got plenty thirty-eights for you. Over here, it's the way most go. Why didn't you say so from the first off, Tom?"

"How much?"

King Lonnie shakes his head, and his jowls keep trembling even after the rest of him is still. "Remi's my guy, and your other cousins—Jackie and James over on Phillips Ave.—I'm solid with them."

"Remi's the only one I'm related to."

"What?"

"Remi's my cousin, like you say." I stare at sequins as my mouth moves. She swallows her Michelob without spilling and eyeballs the back of Lonnie's head. "Rest of them is just peoples." The woman peeks at me, and I look away quick. "How much for the thirty-eight, Lonnie?"

"Four-fifty."

I reach into my jeans pocket for the roll of bills cashed out of my last paycheck. Four hundred and fifty is a third of the check, but the currency exchange gave it to me in fives, tens, and twenties so maybe I won't look so spent after I'm done counting. One third of my net these days and one fifth of my pay down on Grand Avenue—and there's still light bills to pay and Enfamil to buy.

Once I've counted the last ten, Lonnie stands and walks across the dance floor without speaking. Our eyes trail him as he turns into the bathroom hallway. He disappears and the woman stands over his side of the booth as if she wants to sit. She thinks better of it. Her dress reflects green, and I blink.

"He say anything about me?" she asks, before dropping the empty beer bottle next to his Hennessy.

"What?" I ask, though I do hear her.

"What's that fool sayin bout me?" she says with fake bite.

"Nothing," I answer, "really."

"Used to be my man," she explains, fiddling with the bottle rim. "We were together, you know?"

"Really?" I say again.

"Not so long back." Her dress smells from this brown patch sparkling wet between her navel and gut. "How do I look, chill?"

Cigarette lines run next to either eye and the pupils themselves are trimmed in blue-red from standing in poison air, and from burning herself. Her lips are black from the smoke she blows, and her stomach shows a paunch at the beer stain, just above the valley where the rest of her body dips, deep and unseen. Dip carved by too much pork over the years, or, like the fuzz underneath her chin and creeping from her ear holes, carved just by living. "He said you look beautiful," I say, "love."

"I knew he was talking about me," she lies. "Could tell it from how the rolls in back of his neck moved."

Lonnie's done with the bathroom. He slides past sequins and sits without acknowledging her. I blink and the woman leans against her far wall again.

His left hand shows from behind the back, releasing a brown lunch bag that clinks next to my evenly stacked cash. I raise and unfold the crinkled opening—a brown handle, dull and carved at the ends and decorated with blank silver pins is all I see of the king's pistol.

"Got bullets and all?" I ask. "Should come with it for four-fifty, no?"

"Bottom of the bag," Lonnie hisses. I reach past the steel at the handle's down end, find two cardboard boxes. His eyes dart past me as I shake paper until the bag makes popping noise. "What if I picked up your money and checked your count bill by bill right in your face. How would you swallow that insult, Tom?"

"My bad, Lonnie." I let go the bag and steel clinks the tabletop again. Lonnie grabs my cash, peeks at the Alexander Hamilton on top, then bends paper and tucks it away in his shirt's chest pocket.

"You know how to load it proper?"

"I'll figure it for myself."

His head shakes. "Let your cousins show you before you go about fooling with this thing. Nothing to play with there."

I wrinkle the bag's stapled bottom. "How many cartridges you put up in there?"

"What'd I just tell you?" Lonnie's lips stop twisting to let loose his words and he joins all of his fingers to point at me with both hands, palms tapping the table. "Your mother raised you better, and you're from this neighborhood. Act like it."

"Said my bad, man." I slide the bag into my lap and straighten my back against the booth wall so that I sit almost as tall as him.

"How is your old girl? Ain't seen her round here much lately. She taking all right care of her herself?"

His eyes fall on my Hennessy, his spit still floating on the surface. I can't open my mouth until I've sipped, for I've been rude enough already. My tongue doesn't burn as much with this swirling liquor. Either the nerves inside are numb, or his saliva cools the liquid. "My mother's fine, doing just fine."

"Good. Good." His knuckles tap against the table now. "What're you doing with yourself these days? What kind of living you make?"

If I was worth a damn, I'd tell the king that he just took a third of the living I make in exchange for an alley popgun. But he is the king and, right now, I ain't worth a goddamn. "I'm a claims adjuster."

"Insurance?" The king's mouth twists so jowls pull toward his ears. "An adjuster, not a broker?"

"Used to be a broker in a tall building. Downtown."

"What happened?"

"Shit." Luther Vandross plays on the jukebox and the sequined woman twirls away from the man she came with tonight. "Economy and shit."

"What do you wanna be now, Tom?"

"'Tommie,'" my forehead pounds, "with an 'ie.' What you mean what do I wanna be? You trying to say something?"

"The tone?" He crosses his legs under the table. "Ain't doing a thing but asking a question. Should appreciate the fact that another man gives a goddamn."

"Yeah," I say, "my bad."

"Again." Lonnie chews a toothpick slipped from the same pocket he hides my loot inside. "Your bad. Only so many times."

"But I am what I always wanted to be, least far as I remember it."

"A claims adjuster?"

"Yeah," I say. His jowls wrinkle again. "In the business, I mean. Insurance."

"Good for you. Glad you can say that. Nothing wrong with it."

I look over Lonnie's shoulder as sequins walks to the front door with her date, limping on one heel. "Been trying to get in this business since when I was a boy and our house burned down."

"Since you burned it down. Your mamma told me that story. I remember. Over on Merrill."

"However you wanna put it, Lonnie. If you say so," I reply. "Insurance man saved us from ashes. Him and a lawyer."

Lonnie looks at the door. "Sounds good. Don't see it in you

though. Something's in there, just ain't adjusting claims for nappyhead kids with matches."

"Too late to want to be another damn thing, ain't it?" I don't bother waiting for his answer. "Am what I do. What else I'm suppose to be in here?"

"Maybe too late to be, chill," he says as sequins disappears on 75th Street. "Still can't stop you from wanting."

I sip Hennessy as Alvin the bartender pulls the lounge's front door closed. I turn back to the table, and the king waves at a honey leaning on a bar stool. Twenty-five, twenty-six years old at most, with hair stacked and pinned high on her head. She turns all the way to the corner booth and she's smiling and Lonnie's still waving and she's wearing this T-shirt that hugs the deep black hole low on her stomach. His fingers bend at the joints on his right hand as he waves, and she steps carefully across the dance floor.

Lonnie scoots toward me so that she can sit, and I slide the bag behind my back. The honey whispers into his left ear—she's got bright eyes that swallow the peppermint light.

"Candice," he repeats, "let me introduce you to a good brother from around the neighborhood. Hear tell all these young fools put together ain't worth a dime on a dirty rug around here. But this one's a well-meaning brother, at least."

Candice reaches over the king's whiskey spit. I want to remind Lonnie that I'm married, and I ain't a player either, but he knows. I shake her hand and the red lipstick at her mouth parts to show shiny teeth. I smile back, try to, but my grill's been stained off-yellow since I was a boy. "Nice to meet you," she says through this ivory shine.

"Same," I mumble. The wristwatch slides down my arm for her to see my handcuff scratches.

Lonnie takes Candice's hand and pulls her until she's just about in his lap. The king isn't thinking about me—maybe a minute ago he was, but not now. "What can I get you to drink, honey?" he coos.

"A mix: Baileys, Amaretto, and vodka," she says without breathing or blinking to think about it.

The king laughs this horny old-man laugh, all rumbling chest and guts and hot air, and this bass sound booming from someplace deep and empty. "You take care of yourself, Tom. Have a happy holiday weekend."

I frown, but I'm gone from his booth before Lonnie bends his fingers in the opposite direction. I jam the paper bag into my jeans waistband so his .38's tip jabs at the top of my ass and the handle pokes out of me. Still, as I walk from the corner booth, I keep my back to the wall, just in case.

Nobody pays me mind though. Over my shoulder, Candice sips from the Hennessy I left on Lonnie's table, for she's thirsty and the waitress is slow to answer Lonnie's call. Alvin wipes his mirror behind the cash register with the same streaking rag he used on the bar top, and the steppers swirl in circles without crashing each other, moving to some R. Kelly moan. The woman and her stained sequins are long gone from the streets outside this lounge. I step onto 75th, where eye-swelling smoke gives way to wet air that sits heavy on top of my head. I turn my gun-toting backside on the lounge, sure that the door closes all the way against its frame.

I ONLY REMEMBER tomorrow is the Fourth while turning the Ford's ignition—this was the holiday happiness the king wished me. My engine rattles, and noise screeches from the radio speakers, but I'm not driving from the curb just yet.

Around the Four Corners, tradition is that if you own a gat, you pop it off to celebrate Independence Day. Can't buy firecrackers in the city, but a gat's waiting in every third corner lounge. No need for crossing the Indiana border for fake bottle rockets if you're carrying a .38, better to pull out that Saturday Night Special and set fire to the sky. Gun-clapping celebration usually starts at the end of June. Those first few days, you'll hear rifle blasts shooting off from all the way over on the West Side. By tonight, the Fourth's Eve, there's no hearing yourself think for cats pulling triggers from their high-rise windows. Folks ain't looking to hurt anybody, no, just getting down for the holiday, happy and free to be.

But crossing the street from the Soft Steppin, I heard no shots around me. Too early in the night maybe, or so many firing all at once that there was no open air to tell the difference between gun claps and quiet. But I roll my window down now, and the rounds do blast from every which way, most of the celebration coming from north and west of 75th Street.

I reach to the passenger seat and take my .38 from the king's lunch bag, along with a box of rounds. I've seen Remi and Westside load many a pistol. I can do this like my baby breathes. Nobody showed Dawn how to swallow air at birth after all, baby's lungs just got to blowing. I close the chamber and spin metal as I pull away from the curb, driving east with my window down and rounds ricocheting.

At Exchange Avenue I turn with the train tracks, away from the Fourth celebration. No souls on these tracks, none to see me rolling—but I kill the Escort's headlights and drive slow along the blocks, scouting. By the time I reach 81st Street, outside the Corners, I know for sure there's no eyes to see, and I hear no other alley popguns clapping to muffle my own. I reach outside my window and point the .38 at flashing sky. No eyes to see, but all of them will hear me. One, two, three, four, I pop off at this loose trigger. Tomorrow is Independence Day and I'd better know for sure that my gat works, just like the king promised it would.

15

WEIDMANN WON'T AGREE to meet unless I'm pointing out a mark for the shakedown. There ain't another damn thing else that needed to be talked about except "making that money"—that was the phrase Preacher Phil Friday used with Remi. "And if you ain't talking about that, then I don't know you. Corner clowns sitting on cash is all I wanna hear bout."

"Telling you, Wee Man'll wanna know this, Rev," cuz said to the cop, at least the way he told it to me later. Chances are Remi called Phil "Sergeant" or "Officer" or "Sir," some such squatting word spoken with breath heavy and humble, and not the rotted "Rev" he repeats to my face. "Ain't no shakedown hustle," Remi tried to tell him. "But Wee Man's gonna wanna know . . ."

"Shut the fuck up," Phil snapped (this part, Remi repeats for effect), "with your stupid ass. We're all about time and money. You ain't talking money, then you're wasting our time."

✵   ✵   ✵

254 | Bayo Ojikutu

I SIT IN the passenger seat of Weidmann's lightless Crown
Vic over in Jeffrey Manor. My window's rolled down so these
dried raindrops won't block my view of the hustlers doing their
curbside thing.

Let cuz tell it, a Disciple name of Nardo "Little Folks"
Wakes runs the Manor for these big-time dealers. Nardo pays
pea-head shorties to call out when the police creep near, pro-
tects the stash in one of these tattered bungalows crammed on
the Manor's main blocks, makes certain all the shorties are inside their homes by ten o'clock come summertime. Ten o'clock
is when the gats start clapping over here, and there's nothing
him or anybody else with rank can do about it but keep another three-year-old from getting splayed on the thin cover of
the *Sun-Times*. Gats gonna clap as long as there's ill money to
be made on these streets south and east, but such bloody bad
press will kill the corner business eventually, far as the hustlers
see it. Nardo Wakes' job is to keep it from going down like so.

Remi and Westside got a beef with little Nardo from a long
time past. Two or three summers back, we rolled to the Armory dance hall in cuz's new Rover, "I Used to Love Her"
beating outta its sound kit to bring all the East End's honeys
running up on us. Remi and Jackie sat in the front seat, mack-
ing look-alike red-faced sisters on either side of the front cabin.
Turned out the female with her head poked furthest through
the passenger side door was the mother of two babies by
Nardo. As soon as Jackie stepped out of the cabin to take her
phone number, this little chopped-off tree trunk character
wearing all blue and green ran up on the truck with the dull
end of a tire iron, swinging Westside to the parking lot gravel.

We tried to help, I swear, but the females let loose high cackle screams, and his Folk partners had the truck surrounded. One of them reached through the driver-side door to grab Remi at the throat, and I swear two or three put pistols on the backseat in case I thought about rising.

Nardo's beating wasn't about love or jealousy or rage or insult though, not far as I could tell—Little Folks even hummed the melody of track ten on the spinning CD carousel as he swung, blank-faced as could be. Never spoke a foul word out of his mouth as he swung either, just dealt his pulp-bloody beating out of Manor principle. And when he tired of swinging low, he reached over the truck and crashed iron against the Rover's sunroof opening, just enough strength left in him to bring glass sprinkling into my lap.

Afterwards, Folks and their females ran from the lot, and we tucked Jackie in the trunk so he wouldn't bleed on cuz's leather as we drove to Jackson Park Hospital. On our way, cops and ambulances passed us by, headed toward the Armory with black siren lights and silent horns.

For the two hundred and seventy-five stitches those nurses sewed to stop Westside's bleeding, and the three bills cuz spent to put glass back in his spanking-new roof, fingering Nardo Wakes is payback. It's not enough that Jackie's been seeing Nardo's old lady steady for these years, not even close. Stealing the redbone loving of a Corner hustler who's left you bloody only matters if your wound leaks blood from the heart, you see. The only way to make balance out of a battered skull is to bash Nardo Wakes' head, either that or to rob his pockets clean.

"That him?" Weidmann points at a dark man wearing a white do-rag and steel-toed boots crossing Crandon Avenue.

"Naw," I say. "I'll tell you. This guy ain't so tall."

Weidmann taps his steering wheel to the tune of the static beamed through his cop radio. "Getting late."

"He'll be out soon. These's his blocks. Gotta be here."

"If you say so," Weidmann taps. "You're the man, Tiny."

I laugh at the cop until he sits straight and his pistol's butt pokes from the heart side of his Bears windbreaker. I look through this window space, at homes rising and falling all along Crandon, and rusted-out Detroit cars parked against each other at the middle of the intersection. Barrettes and banana clips flap in the wind as naps cling to racing heads and feet turn Big Wheel and dirt bike circles to get little people home, or somewhere near at least. The time is a quarter to ten, the sun is all gone, and the shorties have been out of firecrackers for a week now. Joy is done with them now, and them with joy.

"Not in the Manor," I admit. "I ain't shit over here."

"Ain't shit nowhere else neither." Weidmann laughs at himself, alone with his static.

Remi and Westside figured that it was best to shake Weidmann down some place far from his beat, and hidden from the rest of the living world. This is Jeffrey Manor. Wouldn't know it through a Crown Vic window, view backed by blue-black clouds, but the Manor is the opposite end of living in our Corners. We're tucked in the southeast edge of the city, between the end of the lake, the expressway to the south suburbs, and the pink cloud-blowing factories on the Indiana state line. In South Shore, Weidmann could have me popped and dumped in a pothole so fast my ghost would've floated onto the back of some milk carton before concrete dried on the grave. But over here in the Manor, Remi said, there's always doubtful Toms peeking from behind blankets hung from bungalow windows to protect their hiding place.

I feel their eyes with bent brows even now, no matter the hour, beating on top of the Crown Vic to check what ill goes down here. In the Manor, Wee Man gets away with nothing. This ain't part of his beat. Souls scope close to see how it really happens—so they can't buy his bullshit tales. Not until he pulls the stick from its holster and gets to swinging upside skulls, at least. Besides, we all agreed that if I have to escape from Weidmann and this place, I know to run straight north to make it home.

Nardo Wakes crosses Crandon at the block's far end, striding slow from the white houses to the west side of the block, over to the blue on the east. This stub of a man covered in a T-shirt that blazes white no matter the factory haze and the sweat showing on deep dark skin. The right leg of his denim—two waist sizes past his torso—is rolled up tight to his kneecap. He stumbles across the avenue, though nothing rests in the street to trip him.

"There he goes, that's the mark." I roll the window all the way into the door and point to 97th Street.

Weidmann drives toward 97th and I see the red streak slicing down Nardo's leg toward the shin. Somebody's took a chunk out of him as payback for a bloody deed done already. Nardo looks at the Crown Victoria as he reaches the curb, posts himself sideways to watch us roll. He wears a green

Arizona Diamondback visor that shades his head from the night sky. Little Folks cocks the visor rightward before turning to face the blue houses, and he raises his head to the bungalow roofs with his fist half-cupped at his mouth.

"*GD,*" he calls.

Weidmann frowns and I blink with the rumble of Little Folks' call. When my eyes open, the big wheels and banana clips and naps and Pontiacs and bass booms are all gone from Crandon. The cop radio reads nine-forty in digital green and it is empty night in the Manor, empty blue-night dark. The streetlights flicker only on us.

Weidmann puts the Vic in park. "All right Tiny, it's good time. Go talk to him."

I can't help but laugh. "Talk to who? What?"

"Go on up there and talk to your guy. Gotta make sure that's him. Ain't out here to waste time on a bad ID. You?"

"Don't know what I'm here for," I say.

"Then listen to me," Weidmann hits the cop radio's power button so the only sound in the Vic are his breathy words. "Talk to the guy, makes sure he's the proper mark with the goods, and I'll handle him from there."

"I really don't know this cat," I say.

"Thought you said this was your guy."

"That never came outta my mouth." The cop turns to me, his knuckles gone pale gripped at the steering wheel. "That's what you said—you called him 'my guy.'"

Weidmann chuckles full of air and acid. "Your cousins tell me you've known this guy years." He shifts the holster to a space near his underarm. "'From back in the day' was how they put it to Phil. Now you say he's not your guy? Okay, fine, whatever the fuck. To me, he looks like somebody you could know from back in the day, and you look like somebody he knows right now, so get the fuck out of my car and go talk to your guy."

"I don't know him," I say again, but Weidmann presses the power button, raises static loud to drown, as he stares at white frame siding along the block. I don't even hear the car door close as my feet touch pavement. I walk to the middle of the avenue before approaching so that Nardo will see me coming.

Remi talked all that noise about helping Weidmann and his crew do *us* like this. Seeing as the moaning uncles Auntie De brought home had him on the street corner while we were still in knee-highs and canvas, I can't blame him for imagining himself in some kind of union with these hustling souls. Me, most of my uncles worked on the factory floor in the south burbs. So Weidmann shaking corner gangsters should have nothing to do with me, especially not when the take means my debts get paid in full.

King Lonnie would say that I'm looking at Nardo's street corner with my left, nearsighted eye, and that if I peeped what's about to go down through the good right eye, I'd catch the full scope. According to Lonnie, the good lens shows Nardo Wakes is another one of my cousins, part of the tiny popgun army at my back. Yet here I am putting the fan on the Black man, only to blow this pig's shit his way. Most from King Lonnie's day would agree with the righteous sound to that talk. But the way I remember the story, Lonnie once cruised the Four Corners in an old Caddie owned by some fool who tried to insult the king, and the rear window of that sedan showcased a .45 he'd emptied in that gangster's brown-skinned chest just so all would know the score in every corner. Funny how years passed puts contradictions in the place of memories, turns the babble of a corner-side sermon louder than truth.

"What's up, Nardo?" I say, less than six feet from his curb now. He raises the visor to his shaved hairline and the shadow leaves his eyes. There's a scar to match his leg wound running across the forehead, this slice beige and keloid but still streaking. "Everything all right over here?"

"What?" His voice rumbles again and spews GM exhaust. "I know you? What you say?"

"Said all's well—" I talk loud, for Wee Man's Crown Vic is at my back—I peek over my left shoulder first to make sure. "You cool over here?"

"Nigga, what?" The bright in his eyes is gone, leaving this glass daze. "You know where you are?"

"Jeffrey Manor," I say, not so rough this time. I stop walking a foot from the curb. "You don't remember me?"

Nardo's eyes open all the way and his head cocks onto his right shoulder. For less than a second, he does remember my face. He's not sure from where at all, for a smile shows in his lips' left corner. I turn over my shoulder again as he fiddles with an unhooked belt buckle.

In this blink, we both miss Weidmann creeping from behind tree bark grown out of the avenue lawns behind us, or out of the darkness between us and the streetlight's glow, or jumping down from the roofs of the blue bungalows like Spider-Man maybe. The cop wears his baseball cap down over most of his head now, square-eyed sunglasses, and he holds the CPD badge high in the left hand to cover the rest of his face.

But Nardo is a true corner hustler—Little Folks was nearly ready to step off the corner to size me up. But with this badge twinkling at his right, Nardo turns his body parallel to Crandon and steps away to watch Wee Man coming near, his hand at the back of his waist.

"Stop right there," Weidmann walks into the streetlight glow in my front, standing just east of Nardo's curb now. He points at the badge with his full right fist. "Stop. See this? Look real?"

"What the fuck?"

Only Weidmann's forefinger touches the shield now. "Does it look real?" the cop yells.

"It's a badge," Nardo says. There's no rumble in his voice.

"Well then, you should stop moving, you think?"

Little Folks stands so that the heels of his Reeboks tip toward the rainwater that swirls in 97th Street's sewage drain, stands and teeters on that edge.

"Look close so you're sure," Weidmann holds the badge just short of the Diamondback visor's bill, "and read it so you know who I am. You recognize him?"

The cop points to the street, not at me directly, but in my direction. Nardo barely looks away from Weidmann's badge though. "Naw, don't know this mark. Where's his badge?" He straightens the visor's tilt. "What the fuck is this?"

"Gotta talk to you, chief," Weidmann tucks the badge into his windbreaker.

"Chief?" Nardo giggles and smiles my way. "I look like some Indian, homey?"

"I look like your homey, chief? What'd the badge say?"

"Name's DiNardo," he steps into the rainwater as the sewer runs now, "Officer."

"From now on, DiNardo," Weidmann says, "before you go about calling out for your people to get out of these streets, you better find out for sure who it is you're leaving yourself alone with. Is there a place where we can sit down and talk around here, like serious men? Men talk serious around here, right, or is it all corner-side jive?"

"About what?" Nardo asks again. He watches me—this dim streetlight hides the blood in the pig's eyes, and Little Folks hasn't scoped Weidmann's windbreaking wings, so he looks this way as if I'm the danger on his corner.

"Some place comfortable for men, off this damned street."

Nardo steps out of the rainwater, starts to walk from the curb even before he thinks better of it and turns himself sideways again to walk backwards across Crandon, his watch locked on us. He cocks the visor straight at the top of his head.

"Let's go," Weidmann points me toward the white frame houses, "come on."

"That's all you told me to do, talk to my guy to make sure." But the cop grabs me at the elbow and pulls me west. "I'm supposed to be done with this now."

DIM LIGHT FIZZLES high up over the alley, from this streetlamp leaning toward 97th Street to leave these overflowing bins unseen. But the smell wafts similar to the air in the Four Corners, no matter we're more than a mile from the lake.

We've followed Little Folks to an opening between the end of the bungalow row and this house with dangling awnings. Here, Weidmann peeks past the row of houses to check on his cruiser, though I don't think he can see beyond Nardo's corner.

"So what's up?" Nardo asks, sounding fake alley cocky now.

"This is it?" Weidmann looks into the gangway. "What kind of serious business do you do in this place?"

Nardo laughs. "Said you wanted to talk, Officer."

"Turn around, DiNardo, let me see your back." Little Folks rolls his eyes through me as he faces the garbage bin. His hand tilts over his right shoulder as Weidmann pats the space where his spine meets his waist. "You got anything on you?"

"No," he says. I barely see the grin twisting and flickering low on his mouth. "I'm clean."

"What the hell were you back there reaching inside your pants for then?"

"Fixing my belt." Weidmann pulls lining from Nardo's pockets. "I'm clean."

The cop steps toward the alley, stands next to me with the holster poking from his chest again. "You heard about these idiots running around town, sticking up dope dealers and such?"

"Don't know bout that," Nardo says. "Ain't my crowd."

"All right, 'GD.' You do know this is going on though?"

"Not over here," Little Folks answers. "Saw on TV something's going down in the projects. Altgeld, out in Calumet Park, way in Ida B. Wells, heard that's where the action's at, fools getting shot up left and right. Need to tear all them shit places down. Not over here. That type shit don't go on in the Manor, Officer."

"Who's making these moves from what you see on the television?"

"Got no clue." Nardo leans against the bin, his visor strap touching a torn Hefty bag that pours over the bin. "Like I say, I don't get down with fools who do ill like that."

"Especially seeing as this ain't going on in the Manor?"

"Exactly. Especially."

"Could be the reason this nonsense ain't happened over here is that you're the man protecting these streets while the idiots prowl elsewhere. Could be they know not to fuck with DiNardo. How do you all say it—'DiNardo ain't no punk,' right?"

Little Folks smiles and rubs the scar at his cheek. "Could be. Ain't for me to call."

"Or could be true what I'm hearing, too, that DiNardo— what'd you say his last name was, Tiny?"

Rot floods my nose. I spit gray muck to the alley opening. "Wakes."

"DiNardo Wakes—could be the case that what I hear about DiNardo Wakes and his GD crew is true, too. You boys riding around town far away from this place as possible, ripping off, raping and bringing havoc everywhere but in the one place you give enough of a goddamn about not to tear down."

"Which script you reading off, Officer?" Nardo's laugh is soft. "Told you I don't get down like that. Robbing ain't no safe way to make a living around here."

Weidmann lifts the windbreaker from his waist and snatches handcuffs from the belt latch. "Which house is it, DiNardo?"

"What?" Thoughts of running light in Nardo's face, underneath the sweat crying from his eyes. "Ain't do a damn thing but what you told me to. Brung you to the alley to talk."

"So?" The cop tosses his cuffs left to right. "What you're supposed to do now is tell me which house you all stack your shit business in. I know it's one of these."

Little Folks backs from the bin. "I don't know a damn thing, don't get down with foul clowns like that. Can't these days. Wasn't doing a damn thing but walking down the street."

"What 'walking'? You were standing on a corner yelling gang slogans after you saw a police car approach. We've got laws against that sorta behavior in the city, DiNardo. You've heard of Gang Loitering?"

DiNardo looks into the alley's darkness. "I was just walking down the street."

"Don't make me chase you, Mr. Wakes. If you didn't do nothing, you've got nothing to run from." Weidmann steps toward the bin, twirling cuffs. "All you've got to do is tell me which one of these places your people hold the shit in, and you can go on back and stand on your Disciple corner."

"I got nothing to do with hustling, man. What shit? This ain't even your beat. Who are you?"

Weidmann looks at me, confusion wrinkling the bridge of his nose. "Always gotta be the hard way. Never the smart way, always the hard way with you folks. You want that I show you my badge again? Thought we got that outta the way. Give me your wrists—"

"Nigga can't walk down the street? What you squeezing me for?"

"Loitering, like I just told you. Too late now. Wrists—"

"Bullshit, nigga."

Nardo stops moving just past the garbage bin, so deep inside the alley that I really don't see Weidmann swing his handcuffs. Silver does flash just under the streetlight's fizzle though, and the sound of steel slicing skin and bouncing off bone, I hear it. I blink and find Nardo on the ground, his left hand to pavement, right holding the side of his head opposite the original payback scar.

Weidmann closes the cuffs on Nardo's bloody hand. "Get up, Mr. Wakes. Why'd you listen to me? Do I look like I mean you any good? Shoulda run when you still coulda. I wouldn't have caught you. And, what, you think this lame square over here's got the balls to chase a Gangster? A Disciple? He look like he's got balls?"

"Fuck for?" DiNardo holds his head as he stands. His visor falls just under the garbage bin. "Ain't do shit to you, muthafucka."

"Shoulda ran," Weidmann says again as he locks Little Folks at the free hand. "Mighta made it. I don't even know where I am. This ain't my beat."

Weidmann pulls Nardo toward 97th Street without the Diamondback hat. Little Folks looks at me, head tilted to the right again to show fresh blood running from the temple. "What the fuck kinda nigga is you?"

The two are almost at Crandon Avenue by the time I follow, leaving Nardo's protective visor under spilled garbage.

※   ※   ※

"WE'RE GONNA sit here, and we're gonna wait." Weidmann stares at himself in the rearview mirror. "If I don't like what I see going on at your place, I'm locking both you under the first precinct house I come across."

All it took for Nardo to give up the address was the taste of temple blood running into his mouth. Pig told Little Folks to drink it down slow when the Disciple asked for a towel to clean himself. Nardo'd tried, too, after finding that he couldn't use his hands to wipe without Weidmann's steel cuffs ripping his cut wider.

I turn to the backseat to watch his head switch to either shoulder as he fights to move his lips somewhere away from the side-by-side streams that trickle toward his mouth. He stops moving and looks past me, into the open corner of Weidmann's mirror, "I remember you, player. Yeah, in that parking lot. Nigga in the white truck from over there by the lake—" Nardo digs the side of his face into vinyl upholstery, leaving one matching smear on the backrest and another on his cheek. If Weidmann sees his ride dirtied like this before the night is out, Little Folks is dead, no matter that his smeared blood is the cop's doing.

I would spit my own palm wet to wipe the mark from his cheek, just like my mother did to clean my face of Merrill fire soot after the fire—spit on her palms and scrubbed only to smear me blacker. But I'm not here to save a street corner mark, just came to settle debt.

Weidmann's cell phone plays the *Close Encounters* song— the tune from when the mother ship lands on earth for the sake of snatching up one white cat, then breaking camp back to its home planet with the clown onboard. This is the fourth time his phone's rang since Nardo pointed a cuffed hand at the house farthest to the south. His words are more frustrated with each conversation. I figure it's Preacher Phil Friday on the other end of his line—heard him tell "Philly Boy" that he was a "useless, cock-fiddling bastard" after the second callback. He drives slow along Crandon's sewer drain, until we sit three houses from Nardo's marked address. The flip-phone stays pressed to his face until the Crown Vic rests in park.

"I can go now?" I ask.

His tongue clicks against the jaw. "What'd I just say? Want that I should just lock you up, get it outta the way?"

I've forgotten the videotape and my shakedown assignment. "How much longer?"

"Shame if a man needs handcuffs to know how to sit still and quiet. What can you say for that kind of man?" The rearview reflects Nardo's smile, crusted with blood flakes. "Act like you've got sense, like your boy back there."

I swallow whatever I was near saying, pretend to forget it and stare through the passenger window, though its dirty glass is rolled shut. These streets have gone blue to completely black, and the mark I came to finger squirms at my back. I've got nothing else to look for in the Manor, but I stare.

I sniff this salty stink into my lungs, and bile slides along my esophagus to the stomach and bubbles. In the rearview, Nardo surrenders the struggle and digs a deep hole into his head with this handcuff steel, and I know this fresh stench is of blood running free and mixing with scared sweat.

A green van rolls 97th Street before idling to a stop near

the block's end. I catch Weidmann staring west after its license plate disappears in tilted shadows. The cell phone rings again and the cop holds the caller ID screen close to the face. He nods and glances over his shoulder, then at me. "The wife," he says. He touches a dashboard switch and cold wind blows through vents to swallow the stink. "Knows I'm on duty, hell she calling for? Damn." He quiets the ring without answering and listens to radio static crackle.

Lightning blinks as I find a rhythm to this scanner's broadcast, shining to make a joke out of Crandon's leaning streetlamps. I look again, and the sky's blink doesn't come from heaven at all—no matter that the flash fills Manor sky. This silver shines from the top floor of Nardo's crack house. The third burst is reflected blue from the sheets hung over the window, then silver again with the heat of the folks who call the place home. Light blinks one more time, then the insides go dark for good—before my eyes, light blinks at least, for I'm not so sure that Little Folks and Wee Man are paying attention.

Thunder sounds now, this rumble made in deep black to roll through the Southeast Side. A thunderclap, or maybe the screams of godly souls muffled by fiery sheets. I don't look away from the white frame until the van appears from its shadows, headed east much slower than it rolled west. The Ford pauses before leaving the block, and its headlights blink twice, these twin lights full of nothing close to the heat flashed on a crack house's top floor.

The phone rings again and I jump from the seat upholstery. Nardo squirms behind, too, though he sees me watching.

Weidmann touches the flip to squeeze the show tune quiet without peeking at the ID screen. He nods to no one as the van rolls 97th Street on from our view.

The cop snatches Kleenex from the glove compartment dispenser and throws three sheets into Nardo's lap. Then he leans into the backseat with his handcuff keys, and Little Folks breathes and rubs freed wrists. He almost forgets to dab his head wounds dry.

"Go on about your business," Weidmann says as he rests himself in the driver seat and unlocks the doors.

Nardo taps my shoulder before leaving the backseat. I turn enough to see wet red tissue in his right hand—afraid that if I look him in the face, I'll find that same blank mask he wore while slamming Westside Jackie to asphalt. "I'll be catching you soon, joe, over there near the lake. You stay alls well till then."

Little Folks closes the back door softly and walks south so that he won't cross the windshield view or the cruiser's front grill, and he's gone.

"You, too," Weidmann looks me in the face, eagle nose jabbing the end of this cool air. "Minute ago, you were begging to leave, now you want to sit tight with me. What, you scared over here? You need a ride back to the Drive?"

I didn't bring my .38 Special, haven't grown accustomed to carrying like the true players. If I had my piece, this would be a good time to blast this pig. End him nowhere near where he started, no matter the cannon that covers his heart. But Weidmann is army-trained, made his bones blasting Viet Congs from fifty yards away in the rice fields. Me draw against him?

Me, a fool who only learned how to load a popgun from watching chump change cousins, and him, a gangster shielded by badges and uniforms and killing permits. Trained by the first killers to kill first?

Figure I could take him still, if I had the king's gat. Only because Wee Man's not paying my threat any serious mind now. Over in the rice fields, he knew the Cong aimed to kill so he stayed locked and loaded, middle finger twitching ready. When he came back Stateside and joined this force, his sergeant warned that the Black Panthers weren't studding taking out a pig AK-47 style. *Them peoples are ready to kill or die, not really giving a damn which came first,* sergeant warned. So Weidmann better have stayed ready on these streets. In those days, the quick of the draw made all the difference between falling into a grave or dropping to his knees to beg forgiveness next to the pothole in the ground.

Today, Weidmann carries the cannon out of habit, fear, and flashbacks. Only uses it when idiots show they need brushing up on their history. Otherwise, Tech or .45, it's only there to poke from material to make him feel powerful in his own eyes. He knows that we know the score in the Manor, as in the Corners—for we've been watching his prowl—no need for this cop to waste bullets on us.

BUT I AIN'T the Viet Cong, ain't a Panther either, and this ain't 1968. Weidmann is safe with me. My Saturday Night Special sits five blocks away, in the Ford's glove compartment.

"They've got you on tape."

It's Weidmann's head that twitches at his shoulders now, eyes darting through the windshield. "What—?"

"When you came through my cousins' on Phillips two Saturdays back, hung out with them and those girlies, they made a tape. Got you all over it."

"I'd like to see that." Weidmann smiles as he touches the cop radio to quiet static. "This tape, you say."

"Said they're gonna sell it to the TV stations. Like your boy Fred Conley. Put you all over the Internet, too."

"Hell are you talking about, Tiny?" His voice is loud, but its sound doesn't jab or slice like the salt still bleeding n his Crown Vic's air. "When was I ever on Phillips? I don't go over there unless I'm working there. Tape of what exactly?"

Even for the hot pink in his eyes and the insult in his words, his sound is cool. These lies so ice-clear that I only notice them as his cackle fades. "They say they want a cut of your action is all."

"Action. Funny word. Gotta act for there to be 'action,' as far as I know—but I'm not the col-lege boy. What'd I do in this tape, Tiny? What wrong?" He reaches across the front seat, gropes my chest and shoulders. Gray eyes stare at my lap for a long bit, sizing me. Then the left hand, the badge hand with its lingering forefinger, reaches between my thighs, glaring and groping me soft all at once. "Who supposedly made this tape?"

I touch the passenger door latch and hold it without pulling. "They just told me to tell you they had it. Guess *they* made it."

Weidmann laughs. "Had to be somebody behind the camera, making this supposed tape. Who was it, Tiny?"

I lean against the door, handle digging into my palm as he lets loose my crotch. "I don't know—wasn't there. Tell the truth, I ain't even seen the thing."

"So maybe there ain't a tape. Right?"

The freon air blows, more sharp than salty. "Maybe not."

Weidmann grabs the cell phone without opening the flip receiver, stares at its ID screen as he talks. "When I was a kid, where I came from, folks told us not to trust certain people. Be careful dealing with a man who doesn't understand the meaning of the words 'thank you,' they said. I remember the priests' question at St. Bartholomew: what is the quality of your soul if you don't know gratitude? Never figured what they were talking about back then—no bad souls lived on our Northwest Side, you see. I figured those fathers and teachers weren't but a bunch of old fools talking stupid talk. Then I left home, joined the force, and found out there are souls in this world out here even worse than the old fools made them out to be. Men who've got no concept what 'thank you' means, but let the words slip out of their mouths like bad air. Making a lie out of gratitude, even after all I've done for them."

Smoke rises past the sheet's ruffles on the white frame's top floor. "They just told me to deliver the message. Said if you'd cut them in on the business you're doing, a legitimate cut, they'd let you have the tape. Not sure how they're planning this out. All they told me was if I don't make it home in good time tonight, they've got copies going to CNN, FedEx."

Weidmann laughs at my ad-lib hustle. "But you said you haven't seen this supposed tape." His fingers tap the steering wheel. "Don't let these jackasses lead you wrong, Tiny. Get you in way up over your head. I got you out of one case already. Don't make me come after you on a porno rap. I'll make it stick, distributing lewd material without permit."

"What distributing?" I force a giggle. "Told you, I ain't even seen the thing."

"If there's anything to see. Might not be."

"I don't know," I say. "I'm just delivering their message."

"Could be child pornography." He reaches for another Kleenex and his cannon's handle shows from the windbreaker. "Possession of child porn's a Class 3 felony. That plus possession of a pound of illegal with intent to distribute, and you're downstate, my friend. Danville ain't a goddamn thing like any college campus I've ever heard of."

My lip sweats, no matter the vent's air swirling. "They just want a piece. Money's getting made out here, and times are hard on cats. A cut for the tape in return."

The sheet drops from the window looking down on us. Its glass opens and black smoke escapes. "Cut of what?" He fiddles radio dials as a report of shots fired—"shots fired" or "blocks on fire," I can't tell—south of 95th Street screeches through these speakers. "Don't let those fools get you in over your head. It's dangerous out here, and it's the fool follower who ends up hurting time and again."

My passenger door unhinges from the car without swinging open. "Might not be a tape, like you said." My thoughts reflect, swimming across Wee Man's eyes. "I haven't seen it."

The cop glares back at me, and his slope shows sweat. "Get out of here. I've got to answer this call." I push the Crown Vic door and step onto the pavement again. An Impala rumbles by, inches close. "Tell Mr. Wakes I said 'hey' when you see him next."

I walk south, Nardo's way, as Weidmann pulls the passenger door closed. Bile drips into my stomach without gurgling. I check over my shoulder after every third step, but the Crown Victoria doesn't leave the Crandon Avenue sewage drain just yet. I ain't scared though, no, for all I have to do is make it to my Escort, parked in the White Castle lot over on 95th Street. My alley popgun waits there to protect me from bloody fools out for their payback.

$$\underline{3}$$

16

TARSHA'S LAUGHTER SHAKES our doorknob, tilts me back into the hallway before I cross the threshold. I haven't heard this low chuckle of hers—rolling and buckling along the apartment now—in God knows how long.

My watch reads 11:22 P.M., and it's Wednesday night. She has work tomorrow, we both do. Her downtown, me in Chinatown. She's usually asleep by nine on work nights, snoring inside her dreams by this hour. Yet this isn't the laughter of her behind-the-lids joy filling our walls, no, Tarsha's dreamed joy is muttered and quiet. As the sound squeezes the hallway walls before our living room, this guffaw full of hard candy, I recall she last made it as we watched her cousins skip rope from a porch stoop.

I lean at the living room's end, though the plaster wall's edge slices into my spine. She sits on the windowsill, right shoulder toward the view of our parking garage and garbage bins, left jutting my way so that she looks east out on the condominium building that scrapes sky next door. She wears sweatpants with both legs rolled to her kneecaps, and she scratches the left calf with the painted nails at the end of her right foot. Most of her laugh is let loose into the cordless phone headset she presses against her right ear, some trickles out on the parking lot view before the rest circles around us as her skin bubbles red. Tarsha didn't hear the door closing and ignores my reflection in the south view. She's got no clue or concern that I'm home just now.

If it's Remi she's talking to, or Tory Moore calling for his slick purposes this late, them I'm out the door. Back to Phillips Avenue, the Soft Steppin Lounge, or to the Manor, back to them.

I wait for her to end this conversation before I announce myself. She doesn't blink my way until she's pressed the off button and swallowed the streaks of her laughter. "Tommie." A smile waves at her lips—not fake or false or disturbed, just waving there. "How long you been here?"

"Just now." I look over my shoulder, though there is no noise left behind me. "Who you talking to?"

"Your mamma—didn't even know you were here. She asked about you."

"She all right?" I walk toward the TV couch and its blocked east view.

"She had company. Sounded happy."

There's no indent in her usual cushion. I sit in hers, at the couch's midsection. "What she say so funny?"

"Nothing," Tarsha answers. She stands from the window and turns her back to our garage. "You know how she gets to rambling."

I cross my legs, though the position is uncomfortable. "My mother doesn't ramble."

Tarsha's laugh is just inside her throat this time. "Yes she does."

"The shit she rambles ain't so funny." I shrug.

"No." Tarsha walks toward the couch, too, looking down on toes plucking dust from the carpet. She takes the third cushion, to my right, this seat nearest the corner playpen where neither of us rests unless the baby is awake and inside. "I was telling your mother that Dawn walked today."

My mind spins dizzy, but I can still see. Stars bursting red in the television screen are all that moves just now—a nineteen-inch square filled with bursting and shooting. Not fireworks so much, reminds me instead of the Virgin Islands. Looking down from a creaky honeymoon balcony, on poor dark women wearing sombreros with the name of our vacation resort stitched to the crown. Down in that courtyard square island, they twirled circles for the sake of tickled European tourists and for a fellow negro who spied from a balcony. Danced until sweat bathed them, waiting for my pennies to fall, though my hands stayed empty at my sides as I watched. "What'd you say?"

"She took five steps right across the living room floor, I counted. Right before she went to sleep."

"Baby was strong on her feet?"

"Barely a wobble. All the way from that TV to right in front of her playpen. Fell down when she got there, but she even knew how to put her palms to the floor and catch herself."

"My girl," I announce. I laugh, and the sound squeezes and buckles louder than her joy. Tarsha doesn't flinch though. "You took pictures of her?"

"Had to make sure she wouldn't fall and bust her head.

How could I've got a camera? Five steps, she took, too quick, damn near running. Guess her little legs figured if they moved just fast enough, she wouldn't ever drop. Shoulda been here, Tommie."

I look at the screen again and the sombreros are gone. "By the playpen." I nod. "She made it all that way?"

"Guess what noise she let loose across the room?" Tarsha giggles, just before rising from her indent and climbing over the cocktail table. She stands in front of the television, waiting for my answer, her face flashing red. "You know your mother's noise, the one she makes when she's angry with you? Dawn kept gurgling that, three times for each step. Was telling that to Doreen over the phone."

"That's so funny?"

"Watch." Tarsha stumbles short and uneven steps across the living room, hustling so dust cakes from carpet bristles. Her body leans at the waist with the playpen's pull, but she only finishes three steps before reaching its protective plastic. So she stutter steps back northward, her torso drawn by the static still in our television screen. After two more steps toward the box she teeters to carpet, breaking her fall with open palms and knees bent. The whole way, she laughs with herself and fakes this *gu-ugga, gu-ugga* noise. She sounds more like she's choking than she does like my mother, choking and calling for salvation.

I bite my lips closed. "You're not shitty with me, Tarsha?"

"Shitty?" She climbs onto the couch and I slide left so she'll have her usual cushion space. "Our girl took five good steps, Tommie. Fall didn't break until she was ready for it to."

My teeth let go of the lip, and I smile full of weak shame, though I feel the creases of my skin touching earlobes. "I should've been here."

"My baby's first real steps," Tarsha says.

"Five of them." I'm about to repeat that I should've been here, but I stop myself, figuring Tarsha will say the words for me.

But she's looking at the screen as new stars burst underneath misplaced sombreros. This fiesta only reflects in her eyes now. There the red dots go, twirling down beneath our balcony—bursting, bouncing, flashing, and crashing each other.

"Baby still awake back there?"

The smile keeps my wife's face red and warm as she watches the island spectacle. "Told you," she says, "Dawn went to sleep after walking. Spent."

"I want to see her walk." I stand and step around the cocktail table, about to step between these squeezed hallway walls. But I stop at the living room's edge to look at the screen—nineteen inches of blankness now, in my eyes. I lean on the wall's edge and turn to Tarsha instead. Her chestnuts flash red, her smile touching all the way to her temples, and her lips open to make that sound that my child apparently lets loose when she walks: *gu-ugg,* with no choking *a* at the end.

DAWN DOESN'T STAY on her feet in my hands. I lift her from the crib, though her closed lids barely wrinkle at my touch. I stand her straight—pretend to at least, yet her legs hang limp. Bouncing her soles against the crib covers, I do feel the resistance of leg muscles strong enough to support her baby weight. These are strong, proud limbs, though they take no steps for my sake.

I feel the strength in the bottom of the child, but as I move her inside the crib, her knee joints bend to collapse the calves. I pull her upright, for the foot trappings of this pajama suit must be what's keeping her from standing for daddy. I bounce her again, and for a reflex moment, Dawn's legs do stay straight just long enough for me to see. Yes, these legs can certainly keep the child standing even when I am nowhere around. Then her joints flop and she falls to cotton-covered knees. Dawn's bushy eyebrows wrinkle as the lids lift into her head to uncover pupils still faded from her jaundiced birth. Her right hand cups into a fist in this nursery room darkness to pound the crib covers three times.

Her scream comes between second and third slam. The end of sleep hurts the child, much as when Tarsha let the alarm clock rip through our bedroom to stir my obligation. Dawn pounds the crib out of this rage. Maybe baby girl dreamt her first dream tonight, before I interrupted.

I lift her to my shoulder, ignoring the slam of fists against the top of my back now. The nursery's window faces north and east, angled just far enough beyond the building next door that our view is blocked by shadows. I bounce on the tops of my Adidas, then on the balls of the heels, so that we're rocking as we reach the glass. Dawn screams on, no matter, and her tears touch the sore place beneath my shoulder blade. I know for sure her hurt is real. My baby girl is too new for some fake pain hustle.

"Shhh. Hush little—" I whisper in the ear opposite her fist. But I don't sing sweet as her mother, or mine. I point outside the window. "See there."

I'm not sure where my finger aims until Dawn stops screaming and slamming. I find the hole in our view, between the condo building and the end of Rainbow Beach. This gap ripped between sandblasted brick and trees, just wide enough that we'd both fall inside if we could reach it.

"Just the lake," I coo. Dawn turns her head—the neck muscles, too, are strong enough to support weight. I smile as if she knows what I am saying here, and there is a twinkle in her eyes already. Could be a twinkle of understanding, yes, could be. "Daddy came from here, right by the lake. All I know, ain't nothing to it. Daddy never learned how to swim in that lake, love, but it only looks like a hole at night."

I search for the blinking beacon to prove to Dawn that this water isn't the end, scan north and south along the horizon with my fingertip. I find the place where light should float, the same place where I found it through some other window. But the bloomed trees block our view.

"It's there, I swear," I tell Dawn as her neck cranes to follow my empty pointing. We sit in the rocking chair, and she squirms without hitting me.

She smiles and I smile as we lean forward from the rocking chair, my hands underneath her arms. Her feet touch the nursery's rug, but there's no bounce in her joints. Nothing in this place strong enough to stop her just now. The knees bend and freeze so that her body is upright between floor and ceiling. She looks at me with eyes wide and waiting and beaming.

Seen her standing many times—just never taking five good steps. But the strength in her legs is no less lovely, as her yellow eyes fix on me. She wobbles and teeters finally, but I catch her under stubby arms just in time, and I bring my daughter back to my lap. She makes a sound, not screaming or raging at all now, but giggling with wide-eyed play. She will not sleep for at least another hour, and Tarsha will drag herself into the room eventually to rock the child off with one of Granny Allen's church choir hymns. Then Dawn will swim right back inside the sleep that I interrupted, for dreams don't leave her in a blink just yet. I laugh with her for now, much louder than her playpen giggle. She raises her volume to a cackle, and I wonder if my own skin shines bright as hers against this nursery room glass.

*   *   *

"HAVE TO CHARGE you this time around, Tommie."

Alvin snatches the empty glass from my fingertips and smears its resting place with his rag. I press the new cell phone into my ear, though I hear just fine. The connection is clear enough that I even pick up the lawyer tapping a ballpoint pen against his desk. "For what? Ain't even ask you nothing legal yet. Ain't mean to."

"Of course. I won't start the meter until we're discussing your case. Of course, brother." This plastic tapping sounds like his clock's long arm ticking past the half hour. "How are your wife and child?"

I swallow drips of rum from the back of my throat and point to the Martell on Alvin's second shelf. "They're fine."

"Glad to hear it." Tory Moore's words spill from my ears for the swollen-gutted man sitting three stools over to hear. His drunk eyes rise from swirling Jim Beam to stare at my phone. I imagine that my voice spills from Moore's head, too, out through the plate-glass window at his back to rain down sixty-six stories on the steel and glass that line Dearborn Street. "You know, criminal law isn't my specialty, sailed on from that harbor long time ago. I wouldn't be practicing at Austin, Arthurs if crim law was my thing. Corporate consultation, mediation, and arbitration is our specialty. That's what I do, Tommie. Only so much pro bono the firm'll let me get away with. Billables is what they want to see on their desks, billables is what they want to hear about on their voice messages."

"That's your business," I say out onto Dearborn. "How a nigga makes partner in the place."

"Ni—yes. Moving on up, like they say." Tory laughs—at himself, I hope. "There are mouths to feed in places that I care about, as well. This's how I take care of my responsibilities."

"Handle your business."

"Yes," the lawyer says, barely audible in my ears now. "Hungry mouths. Wish that I could occupy all of my billables with pro bono like your case instead, favors for folks for whom I do care. Those in need."

I see Tarsha laughing with him, in my nearsighted eye. No, not laughing, no, she giggles. "Gotta make partner."

"And feed these mouths," he says. "That's all I'm really trying to do here."

Silence spills from both ends and the fat man gulps brown whiskey. "This's what I need to know, E-S-Q-"

"'Tory' is fine," the lawyer's tongue clicks against the top of his mouth. "'Tory B.' even, if you're more comfortable with the sound of it."

I laugh at him, and sip Alvin's Martell. "That's what was on the business card you gave my wife, 'ESQ' at the end of your name. Like a doctor or some such. Some big nigga title."

"Ni—that's what I am," Tory taps louder. "You may call me 'Tory,' or 'Tory B.' though, if you prefer."

"Okay, 'Tory B.,' here's my question." A sequined honey bumps my chest into the bar as some dance floor player grinds against her. I talk low underneath the grinding rhymes, hope this cell phone is powerful enough to carry the sound of me to the top of Tory B.'s tower. "Those charges that almost got filed against me, you remember?"

"The matter that I arranged for the police to quash?" Tory says. "I recall."

"That there case, seeing as you arranged for it to get squashed"—I bite my own drunk giggle—"it can't be brung back up now? I mean, I've got double jeopardy coming to me, right?"

"If the state acquires new evidence, surely, they can pursue the matter further, if they like. *Double jeopardy,* as you say, comes into play only when actual charges are filed and prosecuted by the state, and the state renders a finding the first time around. We were able to circumvent judgment by poking holes in their case. Sent them to backtrack and think and question themselves." His words and breath hum. I can hear Tory whispering to Tarsha like this in the last bathroom stall. "But there's even a price to seeing things go your way. By avoiding prosecution, the legal system disqualifies your case from such constitutional protection."

I swallow most of the Martell. The fat man frowns over his shoulder as our sound spills on the bar again. "System, legal, prosecution: these things is the same things trying to bring this case back up on me. What protections do I got on my side?"

"The police want to talk to you again?" His plastic pen goes silent. "About the cannabis? You haven't sat down with any-one, have you?"

Somewhere, sirens swirls—but Weidmann has no flashing lights on his Crown Vic. "Ain't sat down with a soul, or an-swered questions. They ain't asked nothing to answer."

"Then don't." He breathes hard, and his words come fast and short. "That's what your lawyer is for, protection when dealing with this system. Would you like to retain my services, Tommie? The police department's issued no warrants, am I right?"

"Not far as I know," I say. "Ain't like that yet. Maybe it will be, is all. I'm just asking, just in case something—"

He taps again. "Why would it? We addressed that matter, mitigated then quashed it. Unless there's something more? Do you need to talk?"

I spit laughter too quick to bite. "I called you, didn't I, E-S-Q?"

"What I mean is, do you want to come down to my of-fice?" Tory offers. "Here, downtown. You have to be careful speaking on these cellular devices, particularly in public envi-ronments. I never discuss a client's privilege when a wireless is involved."

The fat man watches in the mirror. Behind us, the dance floor wannabe turns sequins' back to the bar and his pelvis grinds the space between her spine and the crack of her ass, thrusting the woman to the Isley Brothers' hymn.

I forget why I called Tory B. Moore. To interrupt him and Tarsha, maybe. Pro bono, my ass—I've never met a Black man who knew what pro bono meant, no matter how long he's been gone from his corners. How can there be pro bono between us with my wife hiding underneath Tory's desk? I see her, I do, right there below the lids of my nearsighted blink, her sculpted outline crouched before the lawyer's knees waiting for my interruption to pass. After all, she'd just stopped by on her way home from the reception desk, for a taste of good living.

"At the office kinda late tonight, Tory." Liquor pinches my throat. "I was just looking to leave a message for you."

"Billables. That's how they keep Austin, Arthurs running, you see." Tory repeats this line from some tower script, as if it has meaning for me. "How I feed depending mouths."

I swallow the liquor's pinch. "Cops came to me, threatened to bring the case back up, unless I cooperated."

Tarsha climbs from the desk space, rolling those chestnuts of hers and pressing his ballpoint against wood to quiet its tapping. I hear her tongue clicking the roof of her mouth now. "We shouldn't talk on the phone, Tommie. Come down to my office at lunchtime tomorrow. You remember where I am?"

"Yeah," I answer as Tarsha's knee slides the rest of her body between his legs. "How much do you charge for office visits?"

"Hold on one moment, Tommie, I've got another call." He holds the phone away from his face, mouthpiece cupped, but I still hear as he begs her—"give me a moment, baby doll. Respect the poor ni—" he says. "Think he may be in trouble again. Doesn't he stay in trouble? Always?"

"Tell him it's getting hard by myself here," she says.

I almost let go my answer, "But I'm working now. I'm a claims adjuster with the Pharaoh Pugh Corporation." But I want to hear the rest of what they say to each other, too. Besides, she will only answer me with a question: *But what about your third-floor view?*

"Respect him still. I'll be done in a moment," he murmurs. "Aren't we doing enough wrong by this poor ni—, already? Pretend to respect him, until I get him off the phone."

Tory B. Moore is from some four-cornered place indeed, so at heart, he means another dark soul well. Yet because he's from this sort of place, he can't help himself—not inside towers, not inside toilet stalls or underneath a desk, not inside my wife. I understand this because I'm teetering on a bar stool on the northern end of my own oblong square with a two-thirds empty Martell glass in my right hand.

"Tommie," Tory starts, "why don't you come down to the office tomorrow?"

"What's your rate?"

"We'll work something out," the lawyer says. "My retainer for noncorporate is usually five thousand dollars. But like I said, I generally don't do criminal. I'd adjust the fee for such a case. After you've used the retainer, we'd work out a reasonable hourly. All on the side—Austin, Arthurs won't involve itself in such penury matters as a practice. Still must be billable. Accounting and such. I know your wife though, brother, and you and I have dealt successfully in the past. We'll work something out."

"*Gu-ugga.*"

"Why don't I just wait this out, see if they come up with any more evidence. Or a warrant, like you say. I was just wondering about double jeopardy. Figured I was covered."

There is disappointment in Tory's moan. "No, not how the system works. If you need legal protection, we can work something out."

Tarsha's between-the-legs moan is more disappointed than frustrated, too. "Why don't I call you if they try to contact me again? Maybe I'll stop by the office. Dearborn Street, right?"

"Hold one moment, Tommie. That's the other line." The connection deadens, but his plastic taps and ticks even through airlessness. I press the cell phone's power button and slide it into my jean pocket, for I don't want this swollen drunk three stools over to hear my wife's moans.

ROY-ROY'S HEAD is bald now. He wears his tie underneath an unfastened top button so that its silk sways at the Adam's apple. His teeth twinkle behind clean silver metal in the smeared mirror reflection. I'm not even sure this is Elroy Murphy from 74th Street until his right fist pounds my shoulder and he sits in the second of the three stools separating me and the fat man.

These braces gleam brighter at the bar than against mirror glass. "That one's on me, Alvin-o," he chirps, pointing at the glass Alvin fills. "What is that?"

"Martell." Alvin and I answer together.

"On the rocks, splash of Coke," he says and pounds my shoulder again. "Just like my guy's."

"What's up with you?" I stare at his hand, still at my shoulder, waiting for the shady palm to linger to my wallet.

"You gonna ask about my day, Tommie?"

"Hell no," I tell him. I sip my drink. "Told me there wasn't no point in asking about a day. They're all just alike, you said. Asking once is enough. Ever. Remember?"

"Nope, sure don't," Roy says. The lingering hand rests underneath his chin as he stares at his reflection. "You shouldn't ask about any old day, just to go making stupid conversation. Talking for talking's sake ain't worth it. But when something good and special happens, you should talk about these things. They're rare."

"How do I know the difference if I don't ask? Same or special, what do I know coming in?"

"Look at me." Roy-Roy lets his braces show and shine and rubs his hand across the top of a clean-shaved head until he's sure that light reflects the brilliance inside his mouth. His teeth form a block, joyful and white behind barbed wire and silver straightening chips. Roy-Roy's brown eyes twinkle without blinking. "You see?"

"Yeah," I say, "you got braces."

"Got a promotion, Tommie." Roy-Roy touches my shoulder again and shakes me just a bit. He's not wearing his wedding ring—the faded circle bubbles with corrosion on his ring finger. "Made me project manager out in Bedford Park since the last time I was in here. Got the bump-up over two white boys, replacing an Asian they downsized six months ago. Fifteen percent increase to boot. Clocking $76K now, like the real movers."

"Plus you've got full dental coverage," I say.

"Damn right. Benefits up my ass. Project manager's gotta have good teeth," Roy-Roy chirps on. He straightens the tie, though it still dangles from the throat. "Shoulda seen those pale faces—all fresh outta their Big Ten col-leges—when Regional came in and announced me as the newly installed top guy on the project. Bunch of ghosts caught in shock. Got my big dick stuck up *their* asses now. Better bet I'm about to fuck these bitches long and hard, too."

"Better bet." I stir the Martell with a straw from the bar's distiller. "What happened to your hair?"

"Shaved it off," Roy-Roy says. "Got the Michael Jordan thing going. Scalp sleek and professional."

"Congratulations."

He watches me in the mirror. "Now that sounds real muthafuckin happy, muthafucka—goddamn heartfelt. You can't be joyful for another brother getting his? What is this? You're working now, right?"

"Adjusting indemnity claims downtown," I lie, only partially. "Told you that already."

"Well you should be joyful for another man, then. We're all just trying to make it out here." Roy-Roy turns his bar stool to watch this dance floor player grind sequins face-to-face now. "All the doom and gloom flying around in this place. Muthafuckas crashing planes into buildings, muthafuckas dropping bombs on muthafuckas, muthafuckas putting poison in the muthafuckin mail, bow ties talking dumb-ass shit, beards talking wild-ass shit, church talking cockamamie bullshit—"

"What? You stopped going to Mount Zion?"

"Never. Every other Sunday." His eyebrows disappear inside his frown. "That's how I know—if up in the middle of all this—a Black man can become a project manager with a fifteen percent raise and full dental, I'm gonna be back downtown, too, soon enough. Up on the top floor."

"But you said the church's talking bullshit."

"That's all you can say to a brother?" Roy-Roy asks.

"No, I'm happy for you. Need me some braces like that," I say. "I told you 'congratulations.' Meant it, too."

"Everything's gonna be all right," Roy hums with the O'Jays and stirs the drink's ice. "Heard about your trouble, Tommie."

"Which trouble is that?" I ask without looking at Roy or his reflection.

"Come on—I know, brother," he whispers. "Up on Seventy-ninth Street. I know about the trouble with the police."

"Oh yeah?" I clank the empty glass against the bar. "Ain't no big secret, I guess. Can't keep nothing hidden round here. That was me."

"I know," Roy-Roy says.

"I think it's all past now," I say.

He pounds my shoulder twice. "Even if it ain't, it's gonna be all right, brother."

I stare at Roy, fix so hard that I don't see the mirror glass at all. "How're you gonna scrub up under those braces? I mean, no brush can reach beneath the wire. What, your teeth supposed to stay dirty long as you wear um?"

Roy-Roy laughs and lets go of my shoulder. "You want another drink? Alvin-o, get my guy another Martell. One for me, and one for this brother over here, too." Roy points to the swollen man, then shakes his lingering hand toward the third stool though he looks to his right only through Alvin's mirror.

"Make mine a Hennessy," I say.

I wait for Alvin to pour this drink and for Roy to catch the third man in conversation, before I turn the stool to look past sequins and sweaty players, to the peppermint corner.

King Lonnie holds court with an unfamiliar beige cat with his skin-matching necktie pulled tight and knotted thick. He wears a suit jacket of the same color, even inside this hot place. A woman sits beside him, closest to the aisle. Looks just like the man—same bird hawk nose and tiny eyes—except that her skin is two shades lighter. His color matches the suit, where hers is unseen for the lit smoke in Soft Steppin air.

I sniff the drink's surface to make certain that it's Hennessy, and my nostrils burn as I stand from the bar stool.

I tap Roy-Roy and turn toward the dance floor. "Thanks for the drink," I say. "And congratulations. I mean it. Really."

THE KING'S ex grabs my arm as I head to the corner booth. She doesn't wear sequins today, got on jeans and a thin T-shirt that hugs her pot belly. Lonnie's still talking with this couple, so I dance a jig with her. Or I don't move at all really, just rock on the balls of these feet, left to right while she spins with smoke. Spins and shakes a circle around my rocking place. I don't remember this song on the jukebox, but the woman swirls in step with the guitar strum and pounded drums, and her hips follow the crooner's "ooh, aah, baby, ooh, aah" down to the bass gutter. I hold the Hennessy tight, spill not a drop as my feet pick up on the ditty's swing at last. My soles move side to side, just a bit of a sway to go along with the heel-to-toe rock. She leaves the smoke to move close to me, rubbing her stomach against mine, and I feel what's inside of her tapping the hole of my navel, and this bass gutter grumbles. The beige couple leaves Lonnie's booth as the stretch between my navel and crotch swells and hardens. I escape the king's ex without spilling from the Hennessy glass.

"Can I sit?" I ask.

"You enjoying yourself, Tom?" Lonnie caught us dancing in the reflection of the couple's eyes. I can't tell if his question is jealous or mocking. Words crawl from the corner of his mouth.

"Bought you a drink." I slide the Hennessy Lonnie's way before sitting opposite his seat. "Owed you from last time."

"Good whiskey?" Lonnie touches the glass and draws it near his chest.

"Course. Hennessy."

He sips. "Take it that thing worked out for you?"

"Don't know," I say. "Ain't had to use it."

"Good—good." He wears a paisley rayon shirt opened to the top of the chest to show three curled hair strands and a gold ankh tight at his neck. "Ain't looking for a refund are you? Don't do refunds. Bad for business."

I laugh and point to the beige couple back at the bar. "Who are they?"

Lonnie follows their reflection in my eyes. "Can't remember his name. Lydia is the wife. Just moved into one of these redone flats on Yates. Condo unit, they say. Asking questions about the neighborhood. Come in here to find out the real deal."

"Looking for the scoop in the corner lounge's shady booth?" I wave the waitress away. "You tell them to take their asses back to wherever they came from?"

The king's glass clanks empty against his table. "There's a word them hip-hop boys use for niggas like you—what is it?" His finger traces the glass's inner rim. "*Hater*. Like they be saying, 'Don't *hate*, negro, *appreciate. Appreciate and ingratiate*.' Shit, I'm happy to see a brother doing good things with himself and his life. Positive, lets a nigga like me know there's some kinda hope left in the world. Something better than getting locked up for slanging dope and sticking up corner stores."

"I never stuck nobody up," I correct.

"Ain't talking about you," the king says. "Talking about buying condo buildings and dressing in suits, living the life. I mean, I coulda done that, too, still could if I wanted. Shit, coulda been there, done that, and come back right here to sit in this very same place. But not the hopeful way he's doing it. And his wife is fine, too."

"Looks just like him, from what I see."

"You didn't peep in her eyes. Hating makes a nigga blind and bitter, Tom. That brother coulda been me or you. Old girl is fine, I'm telling you." Lonnie turns to the bar, watches the silk and wool covering the couple's backs as he speaks. "Could be you and your wife, buying condos and such."

"Thanks," I repeat.

"I'm serious. All that time I spent talking to the guy, he didn't impress me as one bit smarter than you. In fact, you've got him faded. Guy told me he graduated from one of them Black colleges down in Mississippi. From everything I ever heard, all them places is half-assed bullshit."

"SIU was bullshit, too," I say.

"Point is, there ain't no reason that negro couldn't be you, negro."

"Thanks again, King." But he's not paying me or the beige couple attention. He watches his ex-woman dance. "Got problems, man. Fucked up, big-time."

"Language, youngun." The king snaps thumb to middle finger without looking from the dance floor. "I don't like that word in my booth."

"My bad," I huff. "Just saying. Need word from a cat who's been there and done that, like you say. I'm looking to get out of this mess."

Lonnie scoots himself closer to the table. But he doesn't speak a word. Instead, he tracks the reflection in my eyes. When I stare back, he doesn't move. And when my pupils dart about the lounge, his head twists and turns and trails to catch up.

I fix on the bar, at the couple's tan textile, and I tell the king about Tarsha, and the two pounds of ganja from Cousin Remi, and the arrest on 79th Street, and the shackle marks, and Officer Mike Weidmann, and his beige interrogation room. These things Lonnie already knows, heard voices whispering takes on the story as I approached in the Soft Steppin or along our blocks. I've already mentioned Pharaoh Pugh and my mahjongg view and the sweet apple from 79th and Cottage, and the camcorder lens screen, and how I popped off his .38 alone by the train tracks on Exchange, and the ringing noise of costume jewelry, and the Manor, before the king interrupts to order another Hennessy, just for himself.

The waitress leaves without asking for payment, and Lonnie looks far from the booth. "Tom—"

"What?"

"That's the brother's name. Just now remembered. 'Tom and Lydia.' Nice couple."

"You listening to me?" Lonnie slides scraps from the space between two of his gold teeth.

"Called himself 'Tomas,' like a Mexican. That's how he did the introductions: 'Tomas and Liddy.' She called herself Lydia though, nice and proper. Old girl was bad like that. Told you, but you didn't wanna see it."

"'Tom.' Same thing you call me." I scrape the table with chipped fingernails. "How you gonna forget that?"

"Told you, that negro could be you. But you ain't seeing it."

"No," I say, "my name is Tommie. With an 'ie,' not 'Tom' or 'Thomas' or 'Tomas,' or no beige bullshit."

"That ain't on your birth certificate." He sips the second Hennessy and touches the ankh against his chest hairs.

The overhead light blinks. "Actually, yeah it is. That's what my mother named me."

"Why all y'all gotta jazz up your names to something ain't nobody called you at birth? You hear what my nephew's calling himself these days?"

"Yeah, 'Primo Smoove.'"

He shakes his head. "Make up a cockamamie name, then lie about it. What's wrong with niggas?"

"All right, 'King Fair Mountain,'" I say. Lonnie laughs soft and snaps thumb and middle finger near my eyes. "What about this situation I got myself into. I'm admitting that it's my fault, so you don't go about riding me on how I've got myself all fucked up here. I know that much, I'm letting you have that. You got any other wisdom for me? Was you even paying attention?"

Lonnie leans across the table, gripping the end of his necklace so I can't see the ankh at all. "It's a damn thing about loot. When we ain't got none, we go about assuming nobody loves us, checking over our shoulder and asking folks the same stupid questions two-three times over in different words, because the first answer had to have been spoken from some disgust-filled well of a lie. Everybody's looking to mess us over when we ain't got loot, and we know it, but we can't afford to buy ourselves clear of the mess's way. We just know if we had some scratch, everything would be all good and everybody'd tell us the loving truth. Because not only would they all love us, but we'd love our own goddamn selves. 'Just if we had a little money'—this's how they got poor niggas all fucked up in the head."

"I thought you didn't like that word in your booth?"

"I don't." I wait for the king to say more. He lets go the necklace charm and pushes himself halfway from the booth.

"That's it?" I ask.

He's standing upright and his body faces the dance floor. "You paid for that Hennessy before you brought yourself over here, right?"

I nod. Lonnie walks across the floor without glancing at his ex-lady or at the bar before disappearing in the bathroom hallway.

I'm left alone in the booth again, and the steppers and players and sequins watch me. Even the beige couple turn from Alvin and his mirror to stare into this peppermint corner. I raise my Black fist at them, offer the sign of power and peace. The couple walks on, out to 75th Street without fisting back. Long minutes pass and the rest of the dusty steppers have forgotten me as well.

All except Alvin, who sends his waitress to collect payment for every one of these liquor glasses besides Lonnie's second Hennessy. Seems Roy-Roy left and forgot to cover my tab. I drop a twenty on her tray, tell her to bring back my change. She'd better be quick about it, too, before the king returns— Lonnie wouldn't care for these lounge fools charging a soul who sits in the king's corner. Her stacked heels pound the floor as she rushes through smoke, for the waitress knows Lonnie's rage. My eyes stay on the wood dance floor as she runs, as I've been left to wait and watch the king's beer-bellied woman spin.

17

MAMMA WALKS on 71st Street, straddling the north side of the street along the IC tracks. This looks like her heading east—although this woman slides lazy sandal soles, dragging as my mother begged me never to do in public. She shuffles where there is barely sidewalk pavement on 71st. She dusts up a cloud of pint bottle glass and burger wrappings, and leaves from trees that've been dead since I was a boy. I'm driving from the south, twenty yards behind her cloud at first, wheeling the Ford slow no matter the Cadillac truck flashing its warning lights behind me.

I don't see her often these days. Probably figures I'm ditching on the seven bills I owe. But I've been running around mad trying to cover debt to those who don't mean a damn thing to me, so why would I play shady with the old girl's scratch? Ain't like she's been calling to check on or chase after her one-and-only, besides. Whenever Tarsha updates me on Doreen's condition these days, she says that my mother's somewhere underneath that ponytailed, hot-dog-slice hustler from last Thanksgiving.

I first noticed this woman walking far ahead of the Escort

as I passed Jeffrey Boulevard, my attention drawn not by the clouded drag of her feet but by this high-bright dress she wears. Rainbows cover her body from the neckline to the light brown sliver of foot that shows between hem and flip-flops. Her dress is from twenty-five years ago, at least, and the dyed brown of her hair is faded by lakeside sun and time. Not a full twenty-five years time, just weeks and months gone by.

The temperature is near ninety degrees and the 71st Street pavement shoots wavy orange rays back to the sky for all to see. My mother would know better than draping herself like a Jehovah's Witness dizzy with the love the Lord'd stormed down on them, so I'm still not believing this is surely my mother. I wheel past Merrill near the cardboard-patched brownstone where we lived before, and the Escalade's lights don't flash anymore, just beam, and there's a bending bow to the woman's walk all of a sudden. As the streets and tracks take their sharp dip east headed straight for the lake, I know better than doubting her.

I spin the window handle until glass drops beneath my chin. "Mamma—where you going?"

She drags herself on, paying mind to my voice just enough for the left leg to skip in distraction before the right steps forward. The Cadillac horn sounds and my mother turns to me, her face shining with sweat. "Hey, Tommie," she says, "just on my way home, just walking."

"We live over that way." I point south.

"That way and this way." She nods ahead, into the lake breeze. "Just walking, is all."

"You want a ride?" The Escalade screeches past, tire rubber raising a cloud over this entire block east of Jeffrey. Its driver slurs through an opened power window—something about taking my ass to West Madison Ave. to pick up my whores—before he speeds on toward Yates Avenue so fast that all I can do is flash the Ford's brights at the truck's tail. Sweat pours from my mother's hairline. "I got the air conditioner on in here, Mamma. Come on, I'll get you home."

"Just enjoying the walk, Tommie," she purrs. "I'm all right."

I stop the Ford in her path so she can slide no further. Pop the driver-side door and jog to the woman as the SUVs and beaters and BMWs roll by slow, steel shining and stinging in the sun. She tries to stutter-step juke me, but she forgets to lift her soles. I grab my mother at the elbows and pull her into the passenger side.

She looks at me through wet eyes as I let go. "Trying to look out for your old girl." She bites her bottom lip between all except these last two words, "sweet boy."

I wheel the Ford from the train dust and roll on along 71st. She looks through me though, I feel her eyeballs staring at the IC train headed the opposite way. She dabs her forehead dry with McDonald's napkins lifted from the crevice between my passenger seat and the car floor.

I can't lie, she smells funky, not bad really—my mother never smells bad—just this flat, dull, windy funk blowing through me with her stare. Smelled it on her before, on her and in this air, but I ain't sure what it is. The scent is familiar rot. Like menthol on a chain smoker who ain't had a bath in a week, lingering and wafting, but without the Newport cough.

"Why you dressed so warm, Mamma?" I ask. "It's up past ninety today."

"What you mean, warm?" she asks. "It's what I felt like putting on. What, I don't look good?"

I peek in the rearview mirror. "Look hot."

"I'll take that like you mean I look 'hot,' as in I look 'good.' I know you ain't saying it like so, but that's cause you're blind." She looks through the passenger window and speaks to Yates Avenue. "AC feels good. You got a twenty?"

"A twenty what? Who you talking to?"

"You, my sweet little boy," she croons. "How much you still owe me?"

"Seven hundred fifty bills, I owe. Why're you asking for?"

"How long it's been since I picked you up from that jail?"

"I don't know," I lie, "a month, maybe."

"Be happy I ain't charging interest like how the man and all his bug-a-boos do," she croons on. "Just gimme a twenty. You got a dub or not?"

"For what?"

"None of your business, nigga." The song is over. "Don't you owe me? This'll make your debt seven-thirty and counting. I'll give you credit for it."

I snatch my wallet from the glove compartment and spread it open just over the steering wheel. My mother props herself on her seat's backrest to peek into the leather opening, but all I've got is two tens, a five, and spare singles. I roll all except a ten into a wrinkled ball to stuff into her palm. "That all?"

"You sure it's twenty here?" She stares at the cash without undoing its circle.

"I counted it," I snap. "Check."

She tosses the ball into her right hand and holds it against the passenger door, far enough away that I can't take it back without letting go of the wheel. "That's okay. I trust you, sweet boy."

"You're welcomed."

My mother laughs as air-conditioner vents blow the flat smell of her all about my Escort. "Drop me off up here on Coles."

We pass the bend where the IC tracks dip east and south and disappear. I watch her in my eyes' corners. Her face is dried and she holds the twenty-dollar ball near the vents, cooling her palm with my loot clutched between fingers. "Thought you were going home."

"I am," she mumbles low. "Just gotta stop up here on Coles real quick."

"Fuck is on Coles?"

"Watch your mouth, sweet boy," mamma scolds. She stares through the windshield, straight ahead. "Who you talking to?"

"What's on Coles, love?" I correct, turning the Ford from the IC's bend.

"My business," she tells me, "got to take care of it. Right up here on the corner."

"You want that I should wait here for you?"

The passenger door is opened in her twenty-dollar palm and her words stutter just so. "That's okay. You go on. I'll make it home. Let me walk on from here."

"How come you ain't been calling me, Mamma?" One of her legs is outside the Escort, dirty sole already to the curb.

"Have been," she says over her shoulder. "You ain't never there."

I shift the car into park. "I'm gonna pay you back. You know, right?"

Her leg jitters back inside the car again. "I know. Seven hundred and thirty dollars. When you gonna have it for me?"

"I don't know. Soon."

Mamma steps out of the car for good. "Don't worry, Tommie," she reaches for me with the empty left hand. I touch her fingertips. "Thanks for the ride."

She drags off to the iron-gated apartment building just off the corner. I don't see the gate's opening, no matter this blazing bright sunshine—see no opening nor building courtyard for these bushes growing wild between metal spokes either. My mother crosses the threshold of metal and wild green and disappears. When she's gone, the sun casts a shadow tall and long but hunched near its head. Light stretches the black outline to the corner. But I really don't see its end, for the building's shade swallows my Escort whole.

I drive south and find the shadow's end in my rearview mirror, and I do see past the metal bars, to the source. This black-light stretches from the courtyard's center to the spot where I'd parked. Behind these weeds and bars, a ponytailed head nods as the souls float on by, through an empty door frame and into his hot spot, sliding feet along the ground as they pass.

*   *   *

HEARD THE WORD up at the Soft Steppin Lounge last Saturday. Roy-Roy went and left his wife and shorty for one of the Saturday-night downtown angels he brings to the Soft Steppin: name of Suzy-Q from Naperville. Didn't bother saying good-bye to the family or writing a letter full of bittersweet tears to explain the why behind his escape. Story goes the wife came home with their baby girl in one arm and a box of Popeye's chicken—breast meat crispy and spicy, just as Roy preferred—in the other. She called out his name in their Lincoln Park condo, though she hadn't seen his Bronco parked out front, got no answer except for the boomerang of her own voice. The wife kept calling for her man, even as she passed by a living room with their babble box and high-definition DVD player both gone missing.

"Where are you, Elroy?" the voice echoed, no matter her eyes falling upon the dust outline in Roy-Roy's office where there had been a desktop computer. "Somebody's robbed us blind," she said, standing over the king-size bed with the baby gripping her shoulder and a chicken box dangling from her ring finger. That was all she could think to say staring at an unused piece of luggage, a nightstand swiped clean on the bed's left side, and a mattress stripped of the linen Mother Murphy's Mount Zion congregation had passed on as a wedding gift.

One of Roy's data-processing coworkers called the very next morning to tell her about how Roy-Roy and Suzy-Q split out of town. Who knows whether the processor was intending to do Roy some kind of favor by contacting the wife, or if he was jealous because he'd been digging Suzy-Q himself, or if he was staking his own sly claim on the pieces of a deserted woman's heart. Who can say, one or all of the above? Getting the word from this downtown white knight was ass backwards, this is all that's known for sure now.

Roy-Roy did stop by the Soft Steppin on his way to heaven.

Parked the Bronco halfway up on the curb, just as always. Only difference that Tuesday was all the sequins and players peeped Suzy's brown-haired, thin-grinned mug in the passenger window, beaming out on 75th Street. While her man propped himself against Alvin's bar sipping two Jack Daniel's and chasing his whiskey with a slow Heineken, no matter the giddy, patient blue eyes waiting on the corner for him.

Let Alvin tell it, Roy-Roy stopped in the bathroom when he finished drinking, then stumbled on out to 75th Street without glancing into the king's booth. While cleaning up that night, the bartender found Roy's wedding band on the middle urinal's basin. Alvin wasn't looking to bother the young Mrs. Murphy with such a painful discovery, of course, so he sold the ring to Primo Smoove for two hundred and fifty dollars—just enough to cover the first payment on vig outstanding since May '01.

The wife has seen Roy one time since he split. By this Tuesday past, she'd packed her baby daughter and the Lincoln Park condo and moved in with her sister back here in the Corners. Either to run away from the coworker checking up on her, or from a three-year-old asking "Where's Daddy" in clear private-school English only to hear the question bounce about empty closets and dust-lined desks, or from the spicy chicken breasts waiting inside cardboard on the refrigerator's first shelf, she ran. Came back to the Seventies blocks because this is home, I guess.

So now we all know the story of how Roy-Roy split one day without a word, only to show back up in the Four Corners a week later to pick up his forgotten Wahl clippers. Seems he needed the tool to keep his head shaved Jordan clean, just how Suzy liked it.

Elroy and the wife argued that final Tuesday in the parking lot of her sister's building. The blurb from the shouting match everyone retells is the one where the wife holds their child in her right arm again, the Bible Roy-Roy kept next to his clippers on the nightstand gripped in her left. How she took bound scripture and slung it against the side of Roy's stubbly head as he pranced from them. Then she yelled for all ears pressed against skyscraper windows to hear:

"Thought you was supposed to be a Christian? A good church boy, that's what you told me."

Roy-Roy lifted his Bible from pavement tar and pounded its binding with Old Testament fury. "What, woman? Don't you ever question my faith." Then he spread the pages open to read. *"It shall be as when a hungry man dreams, and behold, he eats; but he awakes and his soul is empty: or as when a thirsty man dreams, and behold, he drinks, but he awakes and, behold, he is faint, and his soul has appetite: so shall the multitude of all nations be.* Looking to feed my soul like folk in all the other nations, like in Isaiah 29:8, that's all—don't question my faith. Ever, goddamn you. My Lord says bless-ed be the hungry man who dreams of feasts. Good-bye."

❖   ❖   ❖

SMOKE RISES FROM the holes in the queen's afro. Fresh clouds floating gray and black into the living room's high corners with Kamisha's cobwebs. But the child's webs are gone now, too, replaced by hole-blasted plaster. More smoking, fingerprint-size openings—there's nowhere for smoke to rise from this high corner wall, so it gathers and forms webs that blink away in the breeze seeping through the queen's room.

Glass shreds cover the hardwood as the last of the smoke disappears. Twinkling pieces scattering all about the floor between the poster's end and the window in this wall facing Phillips Avenue. This window's glass holes don't show smoke at all now. Fresh cracks reach from each fingerprint-size opening to the window's center, where the lines meet before my eyes.

"I saw your mamma." James sits on the fifth step in his delivery browns, right before the living room staircase disappears in second-floor darkness.

"What?"

He leans forward from the step but watches me through banister columns. "Worldwide still got me making AA, NA, and CA with the fiends. Whichever one I can get a signature at, right. Usually go downtown around noontime with the vet honeys from the office buildings—all kinds, all colors, all dressed in their work gear be up in there. Fine as they wanna be. Good donut treats, too, with the strawberry filling inside. Got there too late for the guy to sign my paper last week, so I had to make the evening group out here at Ascending. Saw your mamma sitting right in middle of the circle. Had to pay up a ten-spot before that bastard'd put his pen to my paper."

"How you know it was my mother?"

"Like I said, she was sitting right there in front of me."

I kick window shreds toward Cleopatra's holes. "You're blind," I say and laugh phony laughter. "You spoke to her?"

"Old girl ain't say a word the whole time I was there."

"Then you don't know if it was her, muthafucka." I walk a circle around the rest of the glass, shaking my head as I talk myself out of kicking more shreds or saying that word—*muthafucka*—ever again. "What kinda meeting was it?"

"Told you, I go to all of um. Sometimes I forget which I'm sitting in. Just niggas talking that circle jive. Every trip. All I wanted was my paper signed for the job. I think it was CA out at Ascending, far as I remember. Mostly rock hypes."

"Couldn't have been my old girl then. You got her confused."

"With some of the other fiends at Ascending?" James sucks his lips after he speaks, swallowing the giggle from the bottom of his face, but his skin turns orange and his belly shakes between banister rails. "No, nigga, *you* got her confused. That was your mamma."

"Muthafucka," I say, forgetting already. "Oughta slap you stupid for talking outta turn."

James laughs. "When I get done beating the shit outta you afterwards, it'll still be your mamma sitting in the fiend circle with the hypes and hos, fool."

Another hole smokes from the place where Cleopatra aims her .38. Two show just near her right hip, and one more puffs idle smoke between her knees. I kick the glass from beneath the poster. "What happened?"

"They shot the place up." James looks to the landing that dips above his head and answers shadows.

"Who?"

"Who am I to know?" he says. "Folks, I guess."

I walk through the empty dining room, hear this low breath whispering in the rear. Remi and Westside Jackie jump from their kitchen table huddle as I enter the room. Westside's eyes roll to the doorway and Remi's hand disappears in his lap, reaching for whatever hides beneath the Formica. I step out of Jackie's eye shot and lean against the stove.

"What happened?"

"What's it look like to you?" Westside says through lips grinning and frowning all at once. "What do you want?"

Remi's empty palms return to the tabletop, slapping a tuneless riff as he glances over his shoulder. "Came home, found the place shot to bits."

Air sucks out of my throat and the thump in my chest matches his tapping hands. "Folks from the Manor? Nardo and them?"

"No," Remi's hands find a rhythm. His tap isn't quite as fast at least, and I don't feel my heart beating just now. "Your boy, five-o. Wee Man and Preacher Phil Friday. This's just like some cops. Serving, and protecting, and blasting up your crib when you ain't falling in line."

"Folks, like you said, Tommie. Remi don't know what the hell he's talking about." Jackie sucks his teeth as he answers. Fleas scatter fast and a mouse runs under the stove. "What's Wee Man shooting up an empty crib for? Cops know you're home when they blast, so they ain't wasting bullets on the city budget. Folks did this here, some old street bullshit."

"Nobody sends messages like the po-po. Ain't about taking nobody out. They just letting us know." Remi's right hand taps soft with his words.

"Quit making that noise," Jackie snaps. Remi's hands fall quiet against the tabletop, and he looks at me for the first time since I stepped through the doorway.

"What's Nardo telling us, Jack?"

"Obvious," Westside says. "We fucked up his money. That's all he's saying."

"Message got sent proper whether it was Folks or cops shooting, didn't it? We fucked up—"

"Don't matter," Westside decides. "Somebody's gotta pay for this."

"Even when we find it's Wee Man?"

"Cop ain't magic, he ain't God." Westside speaks too loud. "Like I said, the nigga who did this is gonna get his."

The front door wood creaks, then slams against its frame. Remi's hands reach into his lap again as Jackie scoots from the table. A new murmur carries through the shack, muffled so its words reach the kitchen without meaning. I peek through the Xbox room, and Remi's landlord stands in front of James, jabbing a stubby finger at the staircase as his murmur spews in the delivery man's face. James points the short olive man to the kitchen, staring at the landing to avoid the spit splashing on the fourth step.

The landlord shakes his head, eyes swelling green as he walks through the dining room. "You back there, Ray-me." The words are clearer now, no matter the gypsy accent. He's demanding Remi's presence more so than he's asking for it. "You back there, I know you there. Come out—"

Cuz reaches to tile under the table, then slides his chair toward the refrigerator to stand.

"You do this to my place. What I do to you ever?"

Jackie pinches his nostrils and a snicker bubbles at the bridge of his nose. "What up, Slaba, my nigga."

"You did-it hear me call you that, no?" The landlord points at Remi just like he did James on the staircase. "Why you do this to my place? I let you stay here. My place."

"We pay our rent." Westside laughs. "Eight-fifty a month—that ain't chump's change. You ain't doing us no favors, nigga."

The landlord's finger aims down now, toward Westside. "I do not like that word. You do not hear me say that word. Give you no right to make mess of my place."

"We got no clue who did this here, Slaba," Remi speaks finally, "came home and found the crib like this. How long you been owning this crib? You know how things go down over here. We wasn't even home, Slaba. What you want us to do?"

"You do bad, bad come back. I know you boys do bad here. Always know." Sweat runs from the space between gray strands at the crown of the landlord's head. His finger is on Remi again. "You innocent here? I don't believe. You tell me—"

"No," Remi says. He sits and slides his knees back under the table. "But don't be pointing at me like that."

"Yeah." Jackie's laughing still. "Fuck you, Slaba."

The landlord walks a half-circle outside the kitchen table, stands closer to Westside. He talks without pointing. "You got filthy mouth. This my place here."

"And we pay you plenty rent, muthafucka. Like my man say, we ain't stand outside blasting up the place. What do we look like, some gangsters? If we'd been home, somebody coulda got hurt. One of us could be dead, far as you knew it before you brought your ass in here. You come over here blaming and accusing and don't even know if niggas is okay. Damn."

"I do not say that word." I look over the top of Slaba's bald spot, to the place where raging hair strands fall into his eyes. "You say it. I drive up—next door, nice lady crying in front of her home over here"—he points south through the kitchen's only window, then north—"over here, blinds and doors is closed and shuttered. Big beautiful homes they built here. Nice people want to live in this place by the pretty water. This what you show them—guns, *pow-pow*? You think they come here for this?"

"No," Remi answers again. "Look, we'll pay for somebody to come in and get the plaster fixed up. Windows, too. You ain't gotta worry bothering your cousin."

"Fuck that," Jackie snaps. He points at the landlord now. "Fuck that, nigga—you ain't even from here, Slaba. Probably some kinda goddamn gangster terrorist your goddamn self. Fucking foreign piece of shit."

Slaba's hand pounds his thigh, a one-fisted version of my cousin's table beat. "Don't listen to this bastard," Remi says. "This is on us, Slaba."

The landlord turns to me, pointing with his full fist. "Who are you? You did this to my place, yes?"

"No" barely slips through my lips before Remi repeats— "This is on us, Slaba. We'll take care of it."

"Yes, it is up to you," Slaba drops his fist and walks

toward the kitchen's rear door, shaking his head as he fondles the holes in wood where bullets bounced through. "You look for papers. They come in morning."

"Papers? What kinda muthafuckin papers you talking?" Westside stands to chase the landlord, teeth grinding and eyeballs popping. "You can't kick us outta here. Fuck you talking about? We pay rent here. Eight-fifty every month, muthafucka."

Slaba walks through the alley door, hands stuffed in pockets. "You got filthy mouth, boy."

Jackie stops at the screen door, staring east though the landlord turns to walk north from the alley, toward 78th Street. When he yells, I figure he's still talking to Slaba. "Heyhey. Where you headed?"

"Gotta go," James' trailing voice answers.

"Bring me back something to eat. From the sandwich shop on Seventy-fifth. You going that way?"

"Nope," James says. I stand on the tips of my sneakers to watch their housemate backpedal east, a duffel bag stitched with the company's worldwide symbol slung across his shoulder. "Ain't looking to get shot. All I do is live in this place. I ain't crooked. Just cause I live here don't mean caps gotta fly past my head. Should be somewhere better than this."

"You running?" Westside grabs his chair and props himself against the door frame.

"Slaba's bout to kick us out. All y'all had better find some place to go." James' words fade.

"You're a bitch," Westside says, loud and late. In the kitchen window's corner, the second-floor blinds on the south flat part, then drop to shield those folks for good. Remi taps the tabletop with both fists.

The package delivery man looks past Westside Jackie and the door frame's missing wood chunks. "That was your mamma at Ascending, Tommie. You'd best take care of her now, hear?" Their cousin walks south on Essex, brown bag flapping against his back. He disappears past the third house from the corner.

Jackie slides himself to the table and scoots under Formica. "Bet he took the Xbox, probably got it in that bag. Crooked, thieving muthafucka—it was mine, that thing, swiped it outta his truck my damn self. What kinda nigga runs?"

"Gone off the tracks now," Remi mutters, staring at me, not at Jackie. "Wasn't supposed to come out like this. Point ain't to get nobody hurt. Just looking to live, or make a living. Gotta make this right now."

"Somebody explain to me what kinda nigga runs from heat?" Westside asks the tabletop.

Cuz shrugs without answering as my Adidas soles drop to the floor and I step away from the doorway. But I won't sit with them.

"Everyone I ever known runs from burning." I swallow the end of my answer—"everyone with any sense"—before Westside Jackie shuts me up. I walk back to the shack's living room, empty now but for these smokeless holes riddling a movie poster against the living room wall.

18

THE MOTHER OF Nardo's children told Jackie about Little Folks' trip down I-57. Said the Manor boss was about to put bullets in Nardo for giving up his stash, until Little Folks begged and cried and promised he could make a connection with a cousin in Memphis. Two kis, he swore, just as his saggy jeans soiled—two kis, he could bring it about. "Outta your own pockets?" the chief player demanded.

"No doubt," Nardo said, as their frame house's air stunk mightily from the river leaking Little Folks' leg. That was how the giggling mad woman told the story to Westside Jackie at least, or how he jazzed it up for the retelling to us—this tale passed on out of evil spite.

After chief let him go, Nardo took a collection from all the hustlers short on rocks, put their contribution with every last one of his own cents, and rode south along the downstate highway. Left the city two Mondays ago, according to his lady. If Little Folks has sense, he made it down south and skipped looking over his shoulder, forgot what he left in this purple-skied place and cut all of his losses.

The biggest mistake he made wasn't giving up chief Folks' stash after all—I was there, and Weidmann wasn't offering much of a choice on that. Snitch or bleed to death from the brain were the options in the backseat of a Crown Victoria. But letting the corner hustling pressure drive him so mad that he left his family for two weeks with nothing more than a swollen-jawed mother, the left side of her face etched with the imprint of his own right knuckles after she dared question his business—this is Nardo's true error so far.

We wait for Nardo on the north side of the White Castle lot, and the most foolish thing Little Folks could do now is actually return to the city. Because once the mother of Nardo's kids gets a call from her man letting her know he's almost here, she'll tell him that the children are awake with stomachs full of gassy air and pain because he left no money for food, "so stop at White Castle for ten square burgers with no pickles and extra cheese to fill their tiny guts—theirs and mine, too—and make sure the bread's still hot," she'll say. Softheaded with the guilt still pounding in his right wrist's jammed nerves, he won't question the mother of his children either, just nod and say "okay," hoping to make good tonight, maybe get him some. Then the mother will thank him before rolling eyes and lifting bitter tongue from a jaw still puffy as she dials my phone number.

We face the tracks on top of this hill of weeds, trains carrying boiling muck between the Indiana factories and downtown for sale. To the Escort's right is a mesh gate that seals the Castle's garbage bins inside. Rotted cheese floats in the air although both the gate's latch and my driver-side window are locked. Fumes still seep through the dashboard vents with the AC, and

I hear rustling inside these bins. I figure this is the noise of squirrels scavenging foul dinner.

"They don't come out at night," Westside explains from the passenger seat. "Too many others staking claim after sun drops to be fighting over scraps. Ain't a battle they'll win out here. Squirrels are daytime beasts."

"Oh," I say.

Just me and Jackie out here tonight. Remi's been running around looking for a new place to live, what with the tape from Slaba's eviction notice's still stuck to the front door wood. Nobody's seen James-Peter for most of a week.

Jackie says we're robbing Nardo out of principle, principle and so we can use the profits from selling Folks' product to get us a new place. Make so much that we can live far as possible from South Shore. Not to mention that Nardo's got it coming to him for beating Westside upside the skull with that tire iron last year, then turning around and shooting up the place on Phillips (Remi gave up trying to convince Jackie otherwise this weekend past). And stealing off his woman so ugly that Jackie couldn't even get it up to sneak his backdoor loving in while Nardo was gone? That sealed Little Folks' fate.

"On top of that," as he explained it to me in a living room still splattered with glass, "you still owe me for fucking up, that never got paid back proper. It ain't like you got a choice but to roll out." His pronouns were all "us" and "we" until Westside started talking about debt accruing.

Jackie tunes my radio to this all-hip-hop station toward the middle of the dial. He lights the cigarette his lips grasp and nods his head. After one puff, he blows smoke into the air's chill.

"Roll down your window," I say.

He uses the cigarette's flickering tip to point at the dash-board. "Air's on. Besides, it stinks like the dead out there."

"Don't get them ashes in my ride."

"This buggy-wagon? Four on the Floor Dead. Ain't nobody told you what that shit meant before you bought this crap?" He cracks the passenger window and breathes.

My cell phone rings. Jackie plucks the cig between his lips and turns half of his face to me. "It's her. Get it. Don't feel like talking now."

The mother of Nardo's children speaks before hello slips from my mouth. "Westside?" she asks.

"No," I tell her. "This is Tommie."

"Who?" I repeat myself but dead air breaks our connection. "He's on his way. Said he'd be home in twenty minutes. Give him fifteen, he'll be there."

I nod without speaking and remember to ask, "What color is the car?"

"Gold, convertible. Nine-three. Prettiest thing you see pulling up in that lot, I tell you." She speaks fast, but the voice isn't full of vengeance. The woman's sound is sweet and soft to soothe ears full of Camel smoke, no matter her words. "Reach up under the spare tire in back. That's where he keeps shit hid on the road," she says.

"Thanks," I tell her and let go the button.

"What she say?" Jackie hums smoke at my steering wheel. "She ain't asked to talk to me?"

"Said to bring her some burgers." I point to his window. "Got my car smelling like rot ass."

"Told you so."

I reverse from the weeds and spin the Escort to face this parking lot's twin entrances, one off 95th, the other opening east onto Jeffrey. "Watch that way." I stare at the Walgreens across 95th. "And put the window back down. Don't smell so bad over here."

I touch the king's .38 taped to my kidney and Westside Jackie Lowe does just like I told him to do. Just for this moment, I pretend like I'm in control of what happens in this parking lot.

                    *   *   *

"YOU SAID A gold convertible, right?" Jackie spits.

Nardo swoops into the lot from 95th Street, the Saab's top down and its stereo beating the same melody-less rhythm as my dashboard speakers. Little Folks wheels past the Castle, but not before I see a thin bandage covering the opening where Weidmann slapped him with handcuffs. I drive around the restaurant as he stops the gold ride in a space near Jeffrey Boulevard.

Little Folks brushes a hand against his untucked shirt as he climbs from the car, checks himself in the windshield mirror before walking off. He's clean tonight—the shirt is a blue that shines to match both the Saab's gleaming wax job and the leather of his square-toed steppers. His pants are baggy, pleated and creased, just out of the dry cleaners. Both ears sparkle moonlight, too, with the reflection of diamond pebbles dangling from the lobes. He walks across the lot whispering into a microphone strapped to his face though he stares at the tar beneath his steppers.

I park two spaces north of his car and Jackie touches my hand against the steering wheel. "Let him go," he says. I breathe. "I'll holler at the fool after he comes out."

Westside pounds a metal rod against his open left palm now—a shimmy, or a crowbar maybe, bent at the pounding end. He laughs without looking from the red and purple lines in his hand. "You watch me," he says. "I'll be over there waiting."

Westside tiptoes strides across the lot, metal swinging behind his back though no one pays him mind. The drive-through line winds underneath the viaduct at Jeffrey and this rap station beat rises from every third car, only to rain back down on us. I touch the radio's off button, but no matter, rap pounds louder. Jackie stops his strides outside the restaurant entrance, propping himself sideways against grimy tile to hide in plain sight.

I breathe humidity through these vents, wet air and meat and onions grilling on the Manor corner to clog my nostrils. The tape holding the king's Saturday Night Special to my gut snaps loose. I press the strip back onto my body hairs, but the adhesive is all dried.

Nardo walks through the restaurant doors with a white-and-blue sack in both hands, his diamonds blinking against my rearview mirror. He holds the family dinner underneath his right armpit as he turns, and his face twists even before he knows who follows.

"What up, my brother?" Jackie's voice is just louder than the bass beat. "My nigga?"

"What up?" Nardo says. His eyes fill with this same fog of memory from the corner of 98th and Crandon.

"Ain't seen you in a minute," Jackie yells.

"Yeah," Nardo mouths. He walks on to the gold ride, but still looks over his shoulder. "Been a while, player."

I can't hear them now, as their reflections pass outside the mirror's frame. I watch through the driver-side window as Jackie leans toward the White Castle bag for Nardo to see the beige scar that runs above his spine, keloid skin left by the doctor who stitched his tire iron wounds.

"You remember this, don't you?" Jackie's loud again.

"Shit's hard out here in these streets," Nardo mouths as he points to the bandage above his eye.

"You ain't never lied about that," Westside says just over the bass beat, right hand rubbing the end of the rod.

Little Folks slings the hamburger sack to the convertible's passenger seat, and his hands are free. So when metal does drop from Jackie's left side, Nardo raises his forearm in time to catch the first blow. He spins on his ankles and tries to run from Westside's follow-up swing but his escape is without balance, and Jackie has Little Folks' spine fully crouched to pound.

Jackie pauses and stares at the convertible's floor. "You was gonna shoot me?"

Moonlight vanishes against Nardo's ears as Westside puts this bent metal cross on the corner hustler's back once, then again. By the third swing, I don't see the shimmy falling out of the night anymore, just this breeze angling downward like in the comic books. On the fourth, I hear the disks in Nardo's

back splinter as Little Folks drops to the tar. Quick, I hear
them, before the music beats and rains.

I take the .38 from my stomach, watch useless tape fall to
the lot's ground as I step out of the car. I want to see what's
come of Nardo, but I don't make it far before intestines boiling
rot steams into my throat. I pass the rear license plate, and air
warms in my lungs and all about my head. Onions and cheap
meat puff from the Castle and the top of my body buckles. I
squeeze the gat at my side, and I don't feel in control of a goddamn thing right about now. I'd laugh at a controlling thought
if opening my mouth wouldn't surely let rot and everything else
inside free, only so that I could collapse face-first in my own
vomit.

I do make it past the drop-top's trunk without falling
though, watch Westside swinging again on this clean corner-
hustling little man. Nardo doesn't scream or moan—no tears,
and little blood, shows. When the steel cut above his eye opens
and fresh trickle leaks against his ear, Little Folks raises his
right hand and waves to surrender or beg mercy or ask
whomever looks down on us for forgiveness.

And Westside Jackie does stop swinging just as my bile's
bubble quiets. Jackie asks Nardo, "What'd you say, huh?"
though Little Folks is silent. Remi's half-brother reaches between the pleats of the man's clean pants and doesn't stand
until car keys and an alarm remote dangle from his thumb. He
throws the key ring my way, but I let it drop to the lot. I'm still
watching Nardo's hand wave. "Take his shit."

"Please—" Nardo mutters.

Jackie looks at the empty air above the Saab before he swings his shimmy against the windshield just once. A single crack spreads slow across its glass and Nardo's quiet again. "It's all even now."

The car's alarm shrieks, clearing this part of the lot, though we hear these noises each night in city air, crying and dying to interrupt our dreams. I open Nardo's trunk and push aside newspaper and old clothes and cardboard to find the spare tire compartment. Just as the mother of Nardo's children said—right here beneath a slashed tire—three cellophane-wrapped packages wait. Two of cleaning detergent–white powders, the third of green paper stacks. All three stand tall and reach deep as the mass Bibles at the Ascending Queen, taller and deeper than the ragged blue book mamma carried to her meetings Uptown.

"It's there?" Jackie asks.

I nod without speaking, but the trunk blocks me from his sight. He asks again, and I tell him that I've found the stash, but he can't hear my answer for the Saab alarm. I stand from the trunk finally with white bundles in either hand.

"Damn hard on these streets." Westside struts from Nardo's dented body and snatches the coke from my right fist.

"Ain't that Nardo's ride there?" This voice comes from a place we can't see now, echoes beneath the alarm and inside this commercial break. *"Look there! Nardo's down."*

Soles pound tar from the east, I think, but I really can't tell for certain. They may be pounding from all around, even racing down from the train track weeds. I reach into the circle and grab the cash stack with my free hand, just barely make it to the Ford behind Jackie and his swinging shimmy.

Jackie points to the Saab chain dangling from my left. "Leave the keys," he says. "You forgot her burgers."

I toss the key chain to the place where Little Folks moans low, and snatch the hamburger sack from the drop-top's passenger seat. Nardo's nine millimeter pokes from underneath the driver seat, steel shining bright as the Saab, more hard power in it than in the king's popgun for sure. My stomach bile bubbles low.

We dump the stash underneath one of Dawn's warming blankets in the backseat, and a new song plays and I don't hear or see any soles running now. The Escort's cylinders churn one by one as I twist the ignition in my right hand.

I kick the .38 from the space underneath my accelerator, listen to Westside Jackie direct me through the lot and on to the place where the mother of Nardo's children lives. Jackie grabs the warming blanket as he talks, rips a stack of cash from the third cellophane package, and stuffs bills on top of the stink of grilled onions.

BEHIND A TORN SCREEN DOOR, the mother of Nardo's children is orange-skinned, and her face glows, though her left cheek is still swollen the color of a blood blister. She wears a green-and-blue T-shirt that hangs to her knees and her eyes glow bright, though I can barely see the whites. One of their sons stands at her hip—except for his own wet eyes, he is in the father's image.

"Is he all right?" she asks.

"No," I say. She snatches the sack from my underarm,

checks the contents, and turns into their home. The boy stands for just a minute longer though, eyes drying, and he waves. The mother nods and snatches him by the elbow before slamming their door against the tips of my shoes.

As we drive from the Manor, Jackie wants to know if she asked about him or said anything about the money or food. I tell him "no," and that she seemed to be crying.

＊　　＊　　＊

JACKIE WANTS US to call him "Jay Lowe" now. No more "Westside" or "Wild-Wild" or "crack monkey," no more "Jackie" even. Just Jay Lowe, not like the Puerto Rican mammie singer either, so we better not be cracking no jokes. "Jay Lowe," he says, "Jay Lowe, Jay Lowe, Jay Lowe, that's my muthafuckin name. Just Jay Lowe." Says a real player should walk around with a real player name. That's what he is now, what we all are: players, the real kind.

I walk through what used to be the Xbox room but is empty now except for the television and VCR James left behind. I see headlights in the alley through the kitchen window, beaming high between that narrow path and moving too fast to spotlight Nardo's two packages and the unwrapped cash stacks spread on the table.

I breathe the stirred breeze from the alley behind their kitchen and grab a stray piece of cellophane wrapper from the floor, where it slaps against the door frame's wood. Only as I raise the coke packages over my head do I notice the videocassette propped between cabinet door and wall, waiting on a stovetop shelf. The cassette has no label, and no recorded tape spools in either of its black casing's windows, but this is the film of my apple. Wasn't me who left her in this place, but soon as I see the minicamcorder cassette jammed into the tape case's open end, I know this is her. And I know now that Jackie never made copies of Weidmann getting loose with a Black child, and that all his loud talk otherwise was like everything else in this place. Hot, bluffing wind blowing, stinking and rotting-up the air.

I move my apple from her hiding place, not to keep the tape for myself or to destroy, nothing so noble. I move her to make space for Nardo Wakes' Memphis dope. Drop the packages back on the kitchen table and tear this cellophane sheet again to use for wrapping the tape case inside. I find my apple a better hiding spot—underneath the sink and behind the rusted pipes where Jackie's rats scurry—and there's plenty room for Nardo's stash on the top shelf now.

I separate the pile of cash into three mostly even stacks, and then stuff the third at my waistband's rear. A strand of tape still sticks to my kidney, and I blink before remembering that I left the .38 on the Escort's floor. A single motorbike headlight buzzes along the alley path as I leave the kitchen, and I let myself feel like a rich hustler with five thousand dollars cash pressed against my ass.

"So you gonna turn the place into a crack house?" Remi asks from the center of the living room. Jackie stands near the staircase, and Cleopatra's poster is gone from the wall now—it's nothing but a wrinkled paper ball in Remi's hands now.

332 | Bayo Ojikutu

"Got twenty-five days till Cook County shows to dump every-thing on the lawn."

"Ain't shit to dump," Jackie says. "Nardo and his people'll be over here to get back what's theirs before too long."

"Glad I don't have to tell you that," Remi looks at me cross-eyed. "About time. You just left him in that lot—"

"What else was I gonna do?" Westside asks. "Take the clown to the emergency room?"

Remi shakes his head slow. "Long as I don't have to come home and find hypes fixing on top of my bed. Got enough problems. Looking to sign on a new place before Slaba brings the torch over here himself, then the bulldozer to drop town-homes right on top of our burnt-up heads." He stares at Cleopatra in his fists. "Need to move that powder to somebody who wants to deal with it."

"What baller's gonna deal with us like that now?" West-side Jackie stares through this window almost ready to crumble. "You were the one who talked about putting money into a ki one day, making some real loot. Got two kis now, Rem-Dog, two for free. We gotta do it now. Lucky Luciano money's back there waiting on us."

I sit on the pastel couch and the cash stack rides up my back. I smear a white speck left on my wrist into the uphol-stery. "What about Primo?"

Jackie giggles high and long, sound rising into the landing above the shack's staircase. "Who?"

"King Lonnie's nephew," I say, "Smoove the Shark."

"'Primo Smoove the Shark,'" Jackie sings, before laughing louder.

"Primo got chased off these corners." Remi tosses the movie poster from right to left, but stops just short of juggling her. "Vicelords scared him away—all the nigga slings now is cash plus points. Ain't touched the blow since we was still in high school."

"He was the man back then," Westside praises.

"Not anymore."

"He tried to buy off me," I tell them. "Before I got arrested. Met with him down on Fifty-fifth. Not a dime bag either. He wanted me to get him a pound or more to move off Fifty-first Street. He told me times was getting hard and he needed to get back to hustling. Said that we all got bills."

"And you didn't tell nobody?" I don't look at Remi as he speaks. Instead, I press the couch stuffing into the bullet holes between my legs.

"I'm telling you now," I say. "He wanted to deal with me cause we had history."

"Old Primo trying to run con on a square," Westside croons, "that's all."

"Yeah," I say, "that's what he was doing."

"Call him," Remi says. "You didn't think none of this out before you took yourself to Ninety-fifth Street with a tire iron, did you?"

I lean away from the couch's backrest and point into Jackie's corner. "It was his idea."

"That's who the fuck I'm talking to," Remi says.

"Fooled you fools," Westside smiles without laughing. "Even had your cousin leave the White Castles with Nardo's girl afterwards."

He folds his arms and leans on the banister, posing. "So?" Remi asks.

"Dummy—once old Nardo gets in and sets sight on them empty burger boxes all over the living room, he's gonna know exactly who tricked him out. And he'll beat that tricking ass ho worser than he did the first time."

"And I'm the dummy?" Remi stares at me, but neither of us speak as air blows down from the landing to stir this tape sliver from some unknown place. "Take two days, maybe less, for Nardo's old lady to run her mouth to the wrong somebody, then them Manor cats to find their way over here to slash and burn, and save Slaba the trouble. Maybe less. That's as long as we got—call Primo, Tommie. You've got a number on him?"

"I'll get with the king," I say. Remi touches my shoulder barely, and I rise from the couch.

"Y'all ain't running out on me, right?" Jackie asks as I push against thin wood to leave their home, forgetting that the door swings inward to open.

19

M Y MOTHER GOT laid up in '71 and never went to college—that was the real inspiration behind me making it down at Southern Illinois University. Old girl used to remind me how she'd sacrifice to bring me to this earth every day of my young life. Swore how her disappointment in self swole right in tempo with the seed in her belly back then. So much so that mamma got all tied and knotted and cut after she'd pushed me out, just to make real sure I was her last living mistake.

Old girl used to get high and slap the mess outta me, flat side of her palm etched with tales of the dreams she'd forgotten just so I could live. Her and those colored folk in the picture frames on Remi's wall—who sat in and marched and took bloody beatings and swung strung and chopped and sprayed and shot to make certain somebody could put educated initials after "Simms." How she decided somewhere between wine, smoke, and slap that, no matter the disappointment and the forgotten desire, she'd put all her mind and love into making sure her one and only seed understood the sacrifice and followed through on promise's struggle. Just so I'd respect education and responsibility and the right to never hear anybody ever call me "nigger"—anybody except the lush who born me—and have it stick and burn. Educated souls who remembered and appreciated couldn't be "niggers" in the world outside these Four Corners, after all.

So I started off majoring in business down at Carbondale, figuring that as the best route into the insurance trade, only to mostly fail those first two years. That was what a good Afro-American from the city was supposed to do once we left the Corners. Fail, same as those folk in the black-and-white pictures did at first. Failed and struggled and sacrificed to set us right on the path. So I'd better struggle some to overcome and put the abbreviated title at the end of my name with brimstone pride. Burning like I meant it, just like Tory B. Moore calls himself *E-S-Q* and means it, and Elroy Murphy, *Cons.: Tommie Simms, B.A.*

Secured my job in insurance just like I wanted, hired mostly because the world was still busy acting all affirmed. And I moved on up, not struggling quite as much for the time being. Just took the steps my mother and all the rest of those folks put there for me to take—moving-on-up folks, moving and colored so many jive-ass hues, not just black and white these days. Telling jokes all the while, the higher we climb the funnier they sound through our fat lips. Until we hit the top, on the thirty-second floor, and our scalps hurt from the pounding and I rub my pain without smiling because the circle still guffaws at me, and it hurts.

Then we struggle some more, just to stay up there with the weight of fifty-one stories buckling the ceiling over our heads.

Maybe this way, me and my B.A. will remember that we're really not up so high when the floors do come tumbling down, and we'll run fast knowing there exists a chance that we might make it clear in time, before the top ceiling drops and we're buried with the souls and angels. We won't run back up that stairwell either, not to save the others like Jesus and Spider-Man and the pimp daddy in his July leather trench did, not now, won't run that way while brick and glass drop on our low-down floor. We'll escape out to the place where ruins billow smoke. Mamma didn't born no fool, and colored folk didn't go through all that struggle just for me to get buried in rubble. May have seemed like it in the pictures—maybe that's what those folks thought they were doing back then even, who's to say—but suicide couldn't have been the end goal.

"God is good," I'll say when I make it from the rubble, just like the circle fiends chimed in Mamma's Uptown meeting room, and as the greasy-forehead church clowns sing now. Our God is good, once and again in the chorus. As payback for all the struggle, the Lord won't let me climb up higher than thirty-two in the Global Mutual tower with my B.A. from SIU because He knows floors thirty-three to eighty-three are all coming down. Tumbling too fast for occupants to dream of running free fast enough.

So I make it out to the city's end, where I find all the bleeding and lynching and floating and pretending and joking and running and surviving, it's all about two bags of crack and twenty-five thousand dollars cash in the trunk of a drop-top in the White Castle lot. Over in that smoky Manor, I do call myself "nigger" (but with an "a" instead of an "er," I say it—as do most of the dark folk today). Niggas trapped in frames that don't move anywhere at all. Because the part of the struggle where we'd never hear that word is lost in the moving on up. We only use this choking "a" instead of the "er" to pretend otherwise while fighting to stay in the picture.

Aughta leave that cubicle space looking over Wentworth Avenue tomorrow. I'm only on the third floor in Pharoah Pugh's Chinatown office, but no matter, it is still waste. I just earned almost one sixth of a year's salary from Nardo's trunk—if I'd lasted through the whole fiscal year on their third floor, that is. Including the dope and cash I left inside the shack's cabinet, there was just about what I grossed during my very best year at GMIC. If in a few weeks, Manor Folks wage their struggle and collect what initialed negroes spend three years striving for, only for these hustlers to stuff their earnings underneath a flat tire and get it taken by clowns with tire irons and alley popguns. If I still drive on now with a good part of my income squeezed between my ass and the dusty cloth upholstery of a rusted-out Ford, then this half-assed cubicle struggle is even more joke than waste.

Some of this cream, I'm paying back to my old girl for bailing me out of the 63rd Street cage, most of it I'm handing over to my old lady and baby girl, for that's where it would have gone if I'd survived eleven more months behind cubicle walls, and to pay it out to them now is only right.

At least I know truth, so when I escape I won't try sprinting heroically past floor thirty-two, but not down to the corner curb either. Just in a circle, I'll run. Figure if I keep moving like so, the crumble won't have much of a target to drop upon, and maybe if I run fast enough, the birds will get too confused to swoop on my head and snatch my nappy crown. The ruin's smoke will catch up no matter what, but I will keep on until the ground collapses underneath my soles and there's nowhere left for escape. Eventually I'll drop down in that pothole—eventually—but until then I won't be getting anywhere running like this. Nowhere up, nowhere down, but the Four Corner air won't smell so bad breathed in circles, and I will just be.

✳   ✳   ✳

"WASN'T LOOKING FOR nothing this heavy." The Shark wears a Kangol hat just like Westside Jay Lowe's, except that his is maroon and rests straight at the top of this skinny head.

Had to arrange this meeting in Greektown's back booth before running. Remi, who says he hasn't tasted their lamb meat in some time, licks his thumb of grease and meat shreds as he looks up from the serving tray. I sit across the table, watching his back as he sops grease and speaks. "Trust me, ain't no loot in ganja these days. Recession's been hit—fools need real coping dope to get by. We're all suffering," Remi says.

"Ain't gotta tell me about the condition of the times," Primo says. I catch Emilio the busboy watching us over the top of Primo's Kangol. It is past two o'clock on a Tuesday night, and the seating area is closed now, but I paid Emilio fifteen dollars to let us sit here. I don't know why he's staring now.

"Forty large is a lotta scratch even on a good day, ain't it? We're playing like we some Rocka Fellas here or what? Pimp-ass

Slick Willie ain't the prez no more—no use in wasting time pretending to bling-bling these days. Only sissies and fools bling like diamonds once the sunlight shines."

Remi spits meat from his teeth and smiles clean. "You tried to run game on my cousin here? Is that what you did, Primo?"

The Shark doesn't glance this way, though I sit just opposite him in the back booth. He hasn't spoken a word to me since taking this seat. He stares blank-faced at the chipping wall behind me instead.

"Remind this brother about your meeting on Fifty-first Street," Remi says.

"Fifty-fifth—" I correct.

The Shark cuts me off. "I came to your cousin trying to do some business together. Looking to help a square who ain't got a clue, ain't even wet at the tip from getting inside any real guts. Was between me and him, what I was trying to do there, one nigga to another nigga. That's what I thought. Didn't know the other nigga was dealing from a bitch deck. Else I woulda never tried to help his ass."

"Hey, hey, fool, ain't nobody—" I interrupt the Shark now, though I sit closer to him than I do cuz.

"You shut the fuck up." Primo's pointer finger juts over Remi's serving tray, aiming between my eyes.

"Don't point at him like that there." Remi speaks softly, for Emilio still watches. Cousin leans his head against this windowpane looking on Jackson Boulevard, and he sucks his thumb. "You got no right, Primo. Shoulda come to me or Jackie."

The Shark's eyes dart behind his spectacles, right to left at the two of us. "I respect you boys. Was only trying to reach out to a brother I thought maybe needed a guiding hand. Life is damn hard in the '02, we're all desperate. Ain't a good point in time to be throwing a fresh buck in the wild. Square like your cousin get skinned to the bone out here."

"Yeah," Remi says in this wandering way. "Shoulda come to all of us if you were looking to do something. You know better."

"Went to the man who seemed like maybe he was in need." Primo shrugs. "Forgive me for giving a goddamn. Just a few pounds of weed is all I was after. Few pounds, few thousand scratch. Puff-puff."

"So you saying you ain't got forty to put down now?" Remi's done sucking and sopping. His hands move with the words, massaging his point into air. "Between you, the king, all those Lords running with you? You can't do it?"

"Funny how we gotta sit here and pretend still. No matter that we're closer to the sun coming up than we are to when it set on us," Primo says. "Who're we pretending for? Ain't nobody watching niggas no more. Nobody cares."

Emilio stands beside the cash register, bouncing on tiptoes to peek over the shish kebab display case. "Just say you don't got it, but tell me if you still want it," Remi says. "If you want it, maybe we can work something out for you."

"We spend all this time pretending for muthafuckas who don't know nothing about us no ways."

"What the fuck are you talking about?" Remi eats the last lamb shred found beneath his pita bread. "Thirty-eight K—"

"You can step on this right and flip it for three times over down in Washington Park," I say.

The tip of the Shark's finger points to the plaster behind my head. "Your cousin don't know what he's talking about, does he?"

"No," Remi says. I swallow my mother's frustrated noise.

"So why do I hear him talking here?" Emilio flips burgers on top of the grill, though there is no one here waiting for food. Three racks of lamb stand still at his shoulder. "Thirty-five, and we can do business together," Primo says.

"For two kis? Maybe Tommie's a square—maybe—but you *are* gonna make some nice cakes off this here."

"That's between me and the hypes," the Shark says, "not me and you. I ain't the needy one here. You got something heavy you gotta get up off your hands. Ain't strong enough to carry it yourself. No shame in that. I'm always looking to help a brother when they're in need—that's my way. But I ain't taking shit off your hands for free. I'm doing you a favor." Primo adjusts the eyeglasses at the bridge of his nose. "Now I can get up out of this dirty place, leave you with your bitch-ass cousin, your blow, and your friends from Jeffrey Manor, or you can let go all this pretend, wannabe bullshit, and let one man help another man. All up to you, fool."

Remi squirms against the booth and twists his bottom lip between pinched fingers. "You can have it by Friday?"

"Gonna be out your way to check on Uncle Lonnie. I'll get with y'all after that."

"Big bills," Remi says.

"No problem, brother: thirty-five G's in Grants and Franklins. Shee-at, I can pretend to bling good as the next nigga blings at two in the morning. Just don't look too close at

me a few hours from now." Primo offers his rippled hand,
open palm to the window, only to Remi though. "One day,
we'll all sit in front of each other and there won't be no lies, no
hustle, no rap, or no fake shit, then I'll be able to reach out and
help you young players and still walk outta here with my back
turned to you in trust."

"Be a good day," Remi says.

"No double-talking sharks?" I laugh. "Not in this world."

"Maybe in heaven," Remi agrees.

"May be," Primo says. He stands over the booth table,
staring at the remaining pita scraps on Remi's tray. "See you
fools Friday."

The Shark walks three sideways steps before he does turn his
back on our corner and exits through the back door. Behind the
counter, Emilio bites into his burger without looking up from the
sizzling grill, and the lamb racks turn on their columns ready to
serve, though we're the last customers in Greektown tonight.

✻ ✻ ✻

BEEN NO MAH-JONGG players on the block for two
weeks. My forehead taps against the cubicle's windowpane. I
wait with eyelids drooping halfway down over the pupils. Anx-
iety pulls skin back into my head though—I can always count
on some form of fear to bring me to weary senses. I blink to
clear sleep's crust from my eyes. Today is Thursday, and the
hustlers gotta come out soon. Before these last two weeks,
Thursday was always collections day in Chinatown.

"You have a visitor, Mr. Simms," the receptionist's voice
rings through unseen speakers, "a Mr. Rooks."

I push the mess of paper to my desk's far corner, searching for the telephone. Three forty-five the phone's clock reads, too late for this. I dial Gladys' extension instead of pressing the intercom reply and she answers without saying my name.

"'Mr. Rooks,' you say—what does he want?" I ask.

"He has no appointment, sir," she mumbles. "Says he's just checking in with you."

"Brad Rooks?" Gladys is silent. "White guy with stringy hair slicked straight back?"

"Mr. Rooks." She whispers the name. "Are you in a meeting, Mr. Simms?"

"Send him back."

The unmarked collector's Taurus rolls to the curb down on the Avenue. I push the pile to my desk's far corner, hidden against the Wentworth view—yet there is no need in pretending for Brad Rooks. Inside the tall building, in its management bathroom, and in the parking garage, he pretended for me, not the other way around.

Brad's reflection approaches in my view. He passes the cubicle opening and falls into the seat under Dawn's picture without waiting for my invitation, though he knows better. I turn, wait for him to roll the chair forward and block my opening, but he doesn't move from the cubicle wall.

"What's going on?' I ask.

"Tommie, that's exactly what I came here to let you know." His smile is all bone and yellow.

"Okay—"

Brad's head doesn't gleam today. He's let the hair grow and

wrapped the ends with a rubber band at his neck. He presses strands down to the scalp now, though not a one is out of place. Once he's secured the ponytail, he unbuttons the top two suit jacket buttons and smooths the tie against his dress shirt until I can't tell where shimmering tie silk ends and shimmering shirt silk begins. "First of all, how have you been? Even old friends shouldn't skip over the formalities of courtesy."

"I'm fine," I say. "I can't complain."

"Your wife and your daughter?"

"They're good." I sigh and glance at Dawn's picture. "I'm just working, guy."

"So I see." He stares at the paper pile.

"And you?" I spit, tilting my roller chair toward the window.

"I'm glad that you asked. 'Great' doesn't begin to describe how I'm doing, Tommie," Brad says. The fake jive learned from the radio dial's right end is gone from his words. "I left the company as of the first of the month, just before the holiday."

"Sorry. More layoffs?"

"No, no, no, Tommie." Brad laughs and his tie slips out of line with the shirt's pattern. "Nothing of the sort. Things are getting better out in the world. I know that it's hard to tell from way down here on Cermak Road, but the market is looking up these days. We've got a real storm coming soon, folks anxious about their security and livelihoods. What else is an insurance policy with a reputable company but an umbrella to carry around when you know the downpour's coming? The minute we start bombing those motherless, lunatic cretins back to the hell in which they belong, and that storm starts, once it happens, there'll be a line of folks scared of drowning lined up at the front door of every Class A provider in the business. Volume may even trickle down to a place like this."

"So why'd you leave Global?'

"Time to start up my own thing, Tommie." He tightens the rubber band. "Six years in the business, feeding off the scraps in the fat cat's litter box. This cat wants to be fat, too, don't we all?"

"That's the goal," I say, and feel my lips spreading.

"I'm opening my own office on the North Side, under AHI's banner."

"American Heritage?" I say. "Good company."

"Yes it is—best place for a guy trying to establish himself in the field. Can't beat this opportunity for independence."

"Congratulations." I stretch my lips wider, up into either cheek to show that I'm not hating like the king and James-Peter and Westside claim that I hate. Stretch and nod my head slowly, but I can't help but grab the Bic next to my uncovered keyboard and tap it against the desk's edge.

"Can't beat American Heritage, and I won't forget a guy who reached out to me, looked out when he could've blinked me from the old memory banks."

"Who's that?"

"You, Tommie, my man," Brad's right shoulder dips past the cubicle opening as he gets to jiving again. "Didn't owe me a damn thing, but you got with your boy, just to share that thing with me. Like a down brother should—did a right turn by me, Tommie. Most fire tree I've come across in this life. Got laid and mad splayed off those spliffs, my brother."

"Shhh—" I point to Dale Gefangen's wall.

"There's no one back there, Tommie. I looked," Brad tells me. "Just me and you."

I point toward the path outside my cubicle. "She hears everything."

"I can't forget your kindness." He sits straight-backed in the roller chair again. "You looked out for me back then: one right turn deserves another. I want you to come on with me at AHI."

I blink this last speck of sleep from my eyelash without speaking, then tap the pen three times on the keyboard space bar. Its noise is higher and not so hollow there.

"You'd be my top broker on-site. In the first desk my customers see coming through the door. Offices down on Sheffield, Tommie, that's a nice neighborhood. Nicer than this place by a good bit. Better salary, I'm sure. No insult intended."

"None taken." My mouth shakes from its stretching. Brad nods at the shady stitching of my tie, and smiles in pity. "You're offering me a job because I sold you some weed?"

"Don't be so humble. It was fire weed you sold me," Brad says, and his face is straight and blank now. "But not just that, Tommie. Your knowledge of the field and talent for combing through the finer details—the 'nuances,' like they say in the tower—probing and combing and asking all the important questions, that was always held in high regard at GMIC. You have an aptitude for this, and a true interest, it seems."

"Either that, or I fake it good," I repeat.

"Either or, as long as it seems true. That's all that matters in these places," Brad continues.

"I like it here at Pharaoh Pugh," I say, for I haven't figured Brad Rooks' hustle just yet. He could very well be the ratting bitch Westside warned me of back before he was Jay Lowe. I hadn't taken the thought seriously before watching the pattern of Rooks' tie show against his body. "Not too far from home, so it's a peaceful commute unlike way north up there. Just got adjusted to the office environment. Found myself a nice view of the street."

"Looking down on Chinatown?" he smirks.

I laugh. "Your place on Sheffield, ain't no tall buildings over there. What kinda view you got?"

He smooths the tie straight and unseen again. "I figured you might want to come under a better umbrella, Tommie. You know what kind of company American Heritage is. I know what this is: a friggin joke."

"Shhh—"

"It's just me and you, brother. We're looking to bring you on at a better salary than this place could possibly offer. You can do right by your family, almost like when you were up on the thirty-second floor."

I touch my back where the cash stack carves into my spine. I shift the bills' sharp edges down toward my ass. "I'm good, Brad. Appreciate the thought, but I'm good, just making it okay."

"This is a chance for a talented broker such as yourself to move back up. Up, then out into independent opportunities under the AHI umbrella. After all"—Brad's empty hands spread wide to stretch the sheen of his suit. He smooths the ends of his hair as my cheeks deflate—"isn't this what we all want to be in the end?"

I keep tapping the Bic against the desktop until I lose count and time. There's no more air to swallow in this place, so my guts warm and bubble. "I'm good, Brad," I say.

He lets loose the guffaw circle version of my mother's frustration sound—"u" before "g" from his glossy lips—as he presses palms against his thighs and stands from the roller chair. I flinch when he reaches into the suit's jacket's inner pocket. "You think about it, Tommie. Great opportunity to get out of this place. Think, and you call me."

I take the ribbed business card he offers, pretend to read its script as Brad backs from my cubicle. "Thanks," I say.

"No," Brad salutes before turning into the exit path. "Thank you. Best I ever smoked."

I wait to hear Gladys whispering good-bye to Brad at Pharaoh Pugh's exit. Once her wrists start jangling, I push the paper pile back to my desk's center, then pause to glance through my window. Only the black tire streaks show on Wentworth's pavement.

Gladys appears in the window reflection, and her bracelets ring now rather than jangle. I turn to the cubicle opening, finally reading the card between my fingers: *Bradford Rooks, American Heritage, Licensed Independent Broker.* The rectangle spins cutting circles once I toss it toward the wastebasket, spins and bounces off the cubicle wall to drop on top of trash scraps. "I'm going home now," I stare at the pointed ends of Gladys' high-heeled shoes. "Don't know how I'm gonna make it back to this place, Ms. Tucker."

"Tomorrow?" she asks.

"Afterwards—"

Her gasp is too sudden for the sound to be real, and her ringing arm rises to her breasts. "What, they're looking to bring you back downtown? Back on the top floor with your lake view?"

I glance at the rectangle fallen to the wastebasket's surface and roll my eyes. "I've got a view at home, Ms. Tucker, remember? Been looking at the water my whole life."

"Congratulations," Gladys says, and this smile softens her facial creases. "Good, college-educated brother such as yourself. I knew you were too good for this place, all along."

"No," my eyes roll from the trash scraps, to Dawn's picture, "I'm not good enough."

Gladys rubs her neck and the leering lines return. The color of her skin brightens as her palm pushes blood through veins. "But you haven't made it to Trinity with me yet."

"I'm a Muslim, Ms. Tucker. Thought I told you that." I smile now, mean for my lips to spread phony as her gasp.

Breath does leave her now, in one swirling puff that clouds my window. The receptionist's hand drops to her hip, and she loses balance, stumbles back into the pathway before she grabs the edge of the cubicle wall to keep herself standing. "No, you've never said that. I wouldn't have bothered you. Are you in the Nation with the Minister, or one of those other ones?"

"Born and bred Sunni," I shrug, then let my lips stretch as I pat Gladys' hand against Dawn's wall. She flinches, ready to jerk herself from my touch before she remembers official office etiquette. "We try not to discuss our religion these days. Hard times, what with Bush and the planes and the flags and the bombs, and all our goddamned oil. Hell of a time—just waiting for this tide to pass. I thought I mentioned this to you already though. I do trust you so, Ms. Tucker."

"You told me no such thing." The jangling hand pats her chest, searching for oxygen now. "But it's good that you trust me. That's what I'm here for, Mr. Simms, trust."

"Good. Name's Tommie, by the way, with an 'ie.'" I reach toward the cubicle opening with open fingers, and the receptionist peeks into Dale's empty cubicle, then gives me her left hand. I stroke the palm though, seeking to soothe her life lines full of worry. "That's how we Muslims spell the name. I still respect your god, after all, I just don't call him *God*."

Gladys forgets our etiquette and tosses my hand toward the desk, freeing me to push this pile beyond the computer keyboard. I snatch the wastebasket from Dawn's wall, in time to catch the 8x11 dumpings before paper splays about company carpet. God's wasted trees, wasted properly. I toss the basket against the far wall and watch blood pulsing in Gladys' face. "You'll be back tomorrow then?" she asks.

"Yes," I say. My back teeth bite mamma's frustration noise, but the sound bites back and spills from me. "Got nowhere else to go now. I'll be here, long as I can make it back."

Gladys' right hand rises from her chest to the nose, where she scratches and jangles again. She smiles at her fingernails' touch. "You be bless-ed till then, you here, till tomorrow morning," she says, and I just now notice how the receptionist sounds like my mother's fiends in their meeting circle with that word crossing her lips, "blessed."

20

THIRD TIME AROUND this circle, birds finally understand I ain't going nowhere. They soar just beneath clouds now, turning mocking circles not as small and mean as my freedom run. They are birds after all—they're pigs, too, yes—so God gave them these wings to fly high and grand. That's from the Religious Studies–Science and Faith in Environmental Biology course I took in Carbondale, after Remi left. Hawks and eagles and desert vultures soar, just like in the Old Testament, but not like the pigeons and gulls squawking babble and bumbling low in purple sky over here by the lake.

After Global Mutual let me go, I'd watch them fly and circle on the cable box animal shows—at least until most of my brain cells died from the sitting, and I flipped the channel to *Oprah*. So much dead matter still in my head now that I don't remember if these birds even truly count as animals. The cable narrator (or the religious studies professor, one of them, dead matter blocks clear recollection), his fake Anglo-Saxon accent spoken from high up in the nostrils, he did once claim that hawks and eagles and vultures do not fly their circles over free-running souls for the sake of the insult, nor for some evil joke told at our expense. He said that the birds have taken on a challenge instead—tracking overhead, timing our pace and dropping their bombs just right, or swooping down with dead precision once they've figured the way of our path, no matter that we targets keep moving.

I stand in place on Remi's porch. The sun drops slow—faster than it faded a week ago, slower than it will next week. The neighbor's Lexus rolls past the handicapped spot where my Escort rests, rolls and stops reluctantly in front of their brick flat. No doors open. I can't see through the SUV's windows, for each glass shield is covered in pitch-black tint still wet with sealant glue. The flat's front door opens and the man of the house steps onto their stone porch, propping the door with his heel. His porch is protected by an awning that juts from brick, casting shadow over the father and across much of this concrete that leads to his home. Dark light covers the For Sale sign that stabs from their lawn, its red, white, and blue poster board swinging with the east wind, in and out of the shade—

"4 bedrooms, 3 full baths, Jacuzzi tub, brand-new appliances, priced to sell—Remax. Above the Crowd."

The father reaches across the porch steps, but the SUV still does not move. He turns once he finds that he can stretch no further and catches the door with his off hand. I don't notice at first, but he stares at me with square boxed eyes.

"You live there, too?" he asks in this high-nosed voice. Like the *Animal Planet* narrator and the Carbondale professor—clean and flat and proper, from nowhere and everywhere.

"No," I say. The word blows with the breeze off unseen water. "My cousins."

The Lexus still hasn't moved. "Oh. Figured they might've left by now."

"Not yet. They're looking." I mean to snarl, but the blond-haired man stares without blinking. I point to the poster board. "Where you all going?"

He turns to the concrete path and he does reach further across the steps. "Back to Naperville," he says, shrugging at the word's flat sound. "We tried, you know?"

"Yeah." I hear my snarl this time. "So did we."

"This place isn't ready," he declares. His wife leaves the truck carrying their empty-eyed boy. "Not yet."

"No," I say, "never will be." The mother scurries up the pathway, skipping over crevices and between cement blocks so as not to trip with the boy child's weight. They reach the porch safely, and the father touches her shoulder and pushes his family inside. The front door closes at their backs without another word spoken.

I look to the flat at Phillips Avenue's northern end. Its windows hang empty—no peeping Ricky and Marisol dance the samba under stainless-steel pots today, no music playing at all—and the flag sticker and Brinks logo are joined by another sign. This makeshift placard reads Llamamos Policia. Then, because even us college boys barely remember the meaning these days here north of 79th Street, We Call Police.

✻   ✻   ✻

REMI LEANS OVER the keyboard in his private space, though the computer cords rest twisted and scattered nowhere near electric outlets. He stares into this powerless monitor, moving the mouse on its pad without clicking buttons. Josephine hangs from the wall, still the finest woman I've ever come across, and Dizzy's cheeks spread swollen over the mighty blowing holes even in shadows, but no notes float about the room. No jazz and no rhyming, no hot-combing naps, no Black bulls toppled, no shimmying and sexing, just hanging lifeless ever since Remi snatched Cleopatra's poster from the living room wall.

"Where's Jay Lowe?" I ask.

Remi doesn't speak at first, too busy swerving his impotent mouse in circles. "Don't call him that stupid shit. His name is Westside, same as it ever was. Who knows where he took himself. All I know is Ameritech cut off my Internet, I can't play the dungeon game, and he's got my truck someplace running out the gas."

"Y'all found someplace to go?"

"No more 'y'all' here. James's long in the wind. Jackie, I'm done with him. Nothing but bloody trouble in that soul."

"Family. What can you do?"

"Gotta make it past this." He leans over the chair's backrest and his cheeks fill with almost as much air as Dizzy's. "Can't live with him no more. Only end up gone bad. James-Peter did the right thing."

"So where you gonna go?" My question dances a frightful jig into my own ears.

"Not far. Saw a place south and over west a ways, near the Ryan. One bedroom, outside the corners, still nearby. Kinda." He stares at Ali posing over Liston. "Fuck was you thinking rolling to the Manor with that fool?"

"He's your brother," I say. The crack of my spine hurts—I switch the cash stack's resting place. Don't feel so rich carrying what's left of my cut now, I ain't nobody's player. I just keep this loot at my waistband because I can't walk around with a .38 on me, and these cutting bills do make me feel protected. "Made some scratch, paid back some debt owed. Could make some more off that powder back there. Good deal, the way I look at it."

"That nigga Primo ain't got no money—not thirty-five thousand kinda money." Remi turns to the black screen and laughs. "See how he was hemming and hawing, spinning fool circles in that joint. That's a hustler caught with his drawers down, telling tall tales about how big his wad is just so we don't look right there between his legs and peep the little pee-wee swinging in plain sight. Ain't heard from him since he walked out the booth. I said 'Friday,' didn't I?"

"Tomorrow is Friday."

"Last week, Friday," Remi corrects. "Damn near a week's passed. Ain't heard a peep from the guy. Have you?"

"I'm just a square," I remind him. "What do I know? Ain't seen nor heard from Folks in the Manor. You were wrong about that, too."

He clicks both mouse tabs twice and the monitor screen picture is unmoved, black and still as three A.M. "Hope so," Remi says. "Ain't looking to be right."

"Where are they?"

"Don't know." His answers trails. He glances at me without shifting in the chair. "You told Tarsha how you came about that loot?"

"Nope."

"She knows," Remi says, "I bet you. When I'm gone, don't waste time running around with Jackie."

I look through the windowpane. "I'm thinking about quitting Pharaoh Pugh."

"Shit. Why?" The mouse clicks.

"Job's a waste," I say. "What's going to Chinatown getting me? Bullshit paycheck, half-assed cubicle. Just a fool, picking lint out my pocket every day, that's all. Fuck else it's doing for me? I ain't no hero."

"Quit? Shit—" He shakes his head without looking at me. "Ain't told Tarsha that either have you?"

"Nope." Headlights shine in the room's window, then disappear, though no vehicles pass on Phillips. "Gonna leave her a piece of the take though."

"Need to go home, Tommie." He speaks to my back, for I'm searching for the headlights in his window view. "Only get all fucked up out here. Nothing but fools, clowns, and maniacs running around these streets. Got two lovely ladies waiting on you."

I press my cheek against the empty windowsill. "So when you leave this place, you ain't taking us with you?"

"Gotta keep living," Remi repeats just to make his final point.

*   *   *

YOU CAN'T HEAR that alley door swinging open from the kitchen. But wood banging against the chipped frame, this noise crashes ears in all corners of the shack. Closing without opening and echoing to warn.

"Cool out," Remi says, "that's him."

"Jay Lowe?"

"'Jackie,'" he hisses.

More than two feet press against the kitchen tile though, more than two lungs puff air in the shack's rear as cabinet doors slam and cooking pots crash and ring against a stove burner. "Hello? Might's well come on out now—"

Remi hears the squawking and clanging, too. He scoots out of the office door's sight line.

"We're waiting for you," the second voice calls as I open the window between Lena Horn and Jackie Joyner. Push it up to this crack where clumps of lead paint jam the wood.

It's too late now, besides. The office door creaks open without bringing light. Funky air and a shadow disconnected from its source seep into the room. Nothing new shines on us here, but I do see the siren-less Crown Victoria and the green van parked just past the north tower, at the 78th Street intersection.

Preacher Phil Friday's nine-millimeter steel shows in this doorway shadow first, then the little bald cop's outline. But his face is covered in a red-and-green Christmas ski mask, narrow slits freeing beady eyes and ears and nostrils for air. Phil puts the steel on Remi, and cuz stands with his hands raised to the ceiling, backing into Mahalia's corner.

His laughter spreads the mask where his brown lips show. Phil drops the nine to his side and waves at Remi with his free hand. "You boys hear us calling for you?"

"Fuck you want?" Remi asks, though we know. Phil steps into Mahalia's corner, pistol still relaxed. He pushes cuz's hands together over her picture frame. Once he's done, he waves me to the corner. The cop feels me up without raising my arms or spreading my legs. When he gets to my cash stack, he gropes and squeezes and traces the bill's outline against the small of my back.

I try to back away, but he snatches just over two Gs out of my backside without bothering to flick through the bills or glance at the Ben Franklin faces—just stuffs my cut down next to his own ass. The office space is almost all black now, Josephine and Dizzy have disappeared into the walls, taken all the rest with them. Phil Friday's counting hand is busy pushing a nine into my right temple.

"Sweet mother of Jesus," he says, as his free hand rubs cash against his spine, and his gun leads us to the rear. "Jig is up, my brothers."

WEE MAN SITS in Westside Jackie's chair, just before the stovetop. White powder rests atop the Formica, serving as the kitchen table's centerpiece. The cellophane bubbles popped under Wee Man's claw as Phil leads us into the kitchen, but no one touches Nardo's dope now. Holy offerings, these packages, on an altar, is how Wee Man described the white powder before taking Jackie's seat.

Remi sits nearest the alley door, just across from me—I can't watch his back here. It is all in front of us, anyways. Phil Friday stands over the stove, his pistol nudged against the cash at his backside, freeing both hands to swirl the pot full of water over the burner and set its flame. Both cops still wear their Christmas knits. These pigs ain't hiding who they are, but they still don't bother to unmask themselves.

"What the hell were you gonna do with all this?" Wee Man asks, pointing to his altar offering.

"What is 'this'?" Remi asks. "I don't see nothing here, Mr. Officer."

Their laughter reflects in the pilot light's flicker. "Which one of you is the col-lege boy, remind me."

"It's that one." Phil lets go the fire dial to point at me.

"But both of you are a couple of friggin physicists."

"Chemists," Phil Friday says and the water boils and the two of them laugh louder. "Some clown-ass chemists."

"On my beat," Wee Man says.

"Beat that," says Phil and their guffaws turn into little girls' giggling fit. They laughed like this while inside Kamisha, too, on the digital view screen.

"What, you think you're some kind of Colombians, in the cartel? One minute, all you want to be in the Mafia with the dagos, the next, you're Pablo fucking Escobar. What's next—you'll wanna be motherfucking black Osamas from the Four Corners ghetto? Fucking losers."

Remi coughs. "We don't see nothing here," he repeats. "Don't know what you're talking about, Mr. Officer."

"Gonna be some terrorists, down with bin Laden," Phil croons. "Or Allah maybe don't bling-bling bright enough for them—"

"I don't see anything," I say.

"Terrorists, huh? I can imagine that," Wee Man says.

Steam rises from the rice pot, lit by these glowing flames. "Dumb fucking niggers."

Preacher Phil's laughter quiets. "Hey, hey, that's enough of the n-word, Mike. Come on now."

Water bubbles and cellophane pops under Wee Man's hand. He sighs and looks my way. "You fellahs are gonna have to excuse my insensitivity—sorry, partner. Was a time when that word never passed these lips, no matter how much I heard it coming up as a boy. Then I joined the force and lost all my patience and couth and sensitivity. Sorry, Philly Boy."

His partner's Christmas mask shines in these flames, too. "Not your fault. Shame of it is, you get out on these streets and it's damn near impossible not to see them for what they act like."

"Don't worry, boys—you don't mind me calling them 'boys,' do you, Phil?"

"Fuck it. Can't help it. 'Boys,' 'niggas,'" Phil says, then repeats, "fuck it. Call um like how you see um."

"Don't worry, boys. Phil talked me out of shooting you. Not worth all the bloody time and effort. What'd you call it Phil, thought it was funny how you put it. 'Overkill,' was that the word? He said killing you boys would be overkill. Thought that was a funny thing to say. We can't claim my partner ain't looking out for his people, can we?"

"Can't never say that," Phil chimes.

"Take what you found," Remi yells to hide the begging in his words. "We don't see nothing. Just go."

"Thanks for giving us what's already ours," Wee Man laughs and rubs the crown of his mask. "What I can't figure is how come you didn't let us know you had this waiting on us in the first place, after how I got your cousin out of his bind."

"Guess we ain't but a bunch of niggers," Remi tells the pig. "Should know better than trusting dumb fucking niggers, like you say. How long you been over here?"

"Don't say that goddamn word out your mouth, boy—" Preacher Phil Friday yells and swings the cooking pot at the back alley door, sending boiling water from the metal in a spray of red, yellow, and blue. Steam drips from the fire and bursts holes in the cocaine's wrapping. I yelp and snatch my arm from this Formica as the water touches my wrist. My skin blisters and bursts without making this cellophane popping noise. I hold on to my burn, and the rest of the steaming water flies over us without breaking apart. Boiling stream flows solid in air before crashing into Remi's face, where flames sizzle and bubble no more.

My cousin screams and grabs his cheeks with both hands—holding on to keep his skin from peeling away from the bone. He presses his skull together but tumbles to the kitchen tile as Phil Friday runs more water into the pot. Wee Man curses and laughs as Remi rolls underneath the table.

He's still screaming and biting his palm though. The moans of my own pain are swallowed by his grumbling and rolling moans and the echo of the last unanswered question to leave Remi's lips before he boiled—"how long you been in this place?" All of my hurt leaves in the mist trailing from his burn and circling about us, just above cracked kitchen tile.

I drop to the floor with him and ask a fool question under his yells. "You okay, Rem?" When he doesn't answer except to keep begging for the return of time past—two minutes, God, that's all he needs, just long enough to get out of the way— I shake Remi at wet shoulders and ask another, "Can you hear me?"

He screams louder.

As boys, we'd run along Rainbow Beach come sunset— racing and chasing south to north on sand rock hard to the foot. One time, Remi and his winged ankles were whipping me good until he tripped over a brick chipped loose from the wall protecting the Corners from winter tide. Laid him out in a circle of bottle remains left from some soul's empty Wild Irish pint. Remi fell, then slid along sandy shreds until cracked glass ripped open the long stretch of skin joining his left knee to his heel. He screamed then just as he screams now, calling out for his dead mother and his long gone daddy and his unknown Jesus and his corner-hustling uncles and the king in his booth and for me, he called out for me back then last of all. Too loud for the sky to make sense of his babble—just this begging painful prayer roaring, garbled by desperation, could be heard. His sound swirls about the lakeshore, louder with each spin, swirling and searching for an answer that ain't about to come from this place. Nothing we can do to soothe his pain, not a damn thing to stop the blood. We ain't saviors, none of us. We weren't saviors when he bled, we ain't heroes as he burns.

"Where's this goddamn videocassette tape, Tiny?" Wee Man bends toward my ear and whispers so that I hear him no matter Remi's screams. "Give us the tape and we'll let *you* see."

I snatch Remi's hands from his face, and look on skin hanging on to his skull, wrinkled and blistered and bubbled, yes, but still there. The face though, his face just ain't black anymore. Skin's burned red, like the festive red-trimmed seams of these pigs' masks, or no, even as I stare at him, red changes to the maroon cancer that spreads from the roof of my Escort. Blood red, like my wife calls it. Bubbles swell and burst where his left lid used to be, and this face that was clean and dark pops, and he bleeds. Pus leaks from fresh holes, from the old ones, too—trickling from nostrils and the cracks in the scaled remnants of what were thick pink lips. No blood and little life left in this place, just leaking. The remaining right eye opens and though this pain leaves him winded, he sees whatever thoughts float across my pupils as I look upon him. And this one last scream vomits from down deep inside the gut.

"One more chance, Tiny, tell us."

I won't look at the pig. This pig is death, that's what hides behind the masks, death or something near. No, I look at Remi. My cousin hurts, means he's alive still. So, I scream, too, and when I do answer Wee Man, my words are louder than them all. "Go away," I howl, and the bird-pig reaches into his Velcro hiding place.

I hear the front door swinging open in the living room, swinging and slamming against the bullet-holed wall. And the sky over the alley blinks, though no rain is set to fall tonight. Weidmann lets go the steel waiting in his windbreaker and turns to Phil Friday. The preacher cop looks up from his burner and the water boiling there to glare at the kitchen doorway through black slits.

"Who's there?" he asks.

Then "Who's that?" though all that answers him is more rainless lightning blinking in the alley.

Flames jump at the pot's sides as the pigs wait for something more. Phil Friday grabs the cocaine altar offering as Wee Man draws his nine, and death does go from this place, fleeing through the back alley door and peeking over its shoulders with terror streaming from mask slits.

Remi's lungs empty of air now, and he is silent for a long moment. I wait for the ignition of Weidmann's lightless Crown Victoria and the green van though, their engines roaring and tires screeching off 78th Street. The headlights beam over this empty tabletop and the kitchen flame as death swerves in two mad circles before speeding west, away from our train tracks. Remi swallows the pus-wet end of his scream.

"Don't choke," I yell at this face of scales and blisters. When I'm sure the pigs are long gone, I rest my cusins's head against tiles and stand to snuff out the stovetop flames and stop the water's boil.

"Jackie," I call out, but no one answers—Jay Lowe isn't here, I know. Still, I walk to the shack's living room as the sky blinks one more time, stare as the riddled door slams inward against their walls, blown by the same foul air I've been breathing my entire life. Air blowing and swirling about, swinging doors open but trapping me here. Forever here, or at least until its purple poison settles cancer into my lungs to leave me dead as the fish floating on lake waves. "James-Peter?"

I scan the wall where the poster hung, and the pastel couch with its ripped holes, and the stairs to the shack's second floor, but nothing moves except for this air. "Who's here?" I ask, sounding just like the fool bird-pigs. I fix on the landing shadows above the staircase where I hid and watched them swoop, listening to all that's left of Remi's screams in darkness leaning down, these pus-filled moans bouncing about from the kitchen.

"Just me," I say.

21

THE PANTHER PASSED THROUGH my dreams when I was a child. Always left before sun shined, though I'd cry and beg for it to take me along. I wasn't longing to do panther-ish things in the dark like the beast, no, just didn't want to be left all alone in the Corners.

Cat walked on two feet as a man, but its skin was covered in brown and black fur to the flapping tail underneath its ass. He'd stand in my bedroom doorway so I could watch him through crib bars. Growling and leaking drool from his fangs, not out of hunger or bloody intent. Growling and drooling because that's what cats did back then.

The panther hoofed forward a bit, paused before bouncing a second step, then lurched back as it reached with its claw to touch the crib bars—reaching forward and stumbling backwards all at once. Yellow eyes took in my bars, jaundiced with fear, though wood protected it from me and me from it. But the panther flinched and stumbled and howled in some faraway pain just as it came near. Maybe the beast caught its reflection in my eyes, or the fear floating there, or maybe the whole damn dream played out for the panther in full, projected in right to left across yellow squints. Whatever he saw hurt the panther plenty—its own eyes shined wet as its hoofs retreated to the doorway, where the panther drooled and growled soft. My stomach boiled as I begged the beast to try coming near again, crash down these bars, for they were built only of splinters. Snatch me with those claws like panthers are supposed to do bloody prey. Take me with it, so far away.

Instead, the beast turned from the entry with drool drying at its fangs, and bounced off on hind legs too short for remaining upright. Its tail swayed east to west as it lurched to my mother's room. The panther growled and chuckled before slobbering new spit and disappearing behind her walls.

Then I'd hear the life-giver moaning in my dreams, like I'd never hear her moan with the wannabes from the plant floor years later; while the beast bayed at moonlight beaming through our Four Corner windows. Sounds full of nothing that resembled pain except in its echo.

Only as the panther passed my room again did it speak its true four-legged intent, pausing not to growl or spit or even to stand and watch me. Through dripping tears, I peeked that the panther wore a black leather coat tight to its fur, cut short so the hem fell just before the place where the tail swayed. The beast stood and bounced off, as cats do when their hind legs are too short for the rest of the body in a world that's duped them into walking upright. Left me behind bars though I begged with reaching arms, and cried as its whisper made some kind of sense before my eyes opened.

"Hush, my little man," the panther growled before leaving,

which was all it came to do in the first place: leave. "Brace yourself for falling when you stand. And you look after your mother now, you hear?"

I STAND IN DAWN'S DOORWAY, but all I can see inside the crib are warm blankets strewn where her head is supposed to lay. I don't move closer to the child, not due to fear. Ain't like I'm scared of beasts and bars or anything of the sort these days. I don't move because the child does not sleep here. Her bars are empty and the nursery is blue dark. The doorway provides a clean view of the beacon shining in the meeting place though. I see it perfectly. The beacon's the only thing that ain't nightitme out there. Its light at the lake's end shines a half-second again at a time, and there's not a damn thing to be scared of in this place.

I walk the hallway to our bedroom—Tarsha lies here at least, waiting on me or escaping this place inside her own dreams. I sit in the crevice at her side, after checking sheets to make certain the child doesn't sleep in my place. The only light in our room is the blinking alarm clock and my wedding band, and the shine of her dreamy smile spreading and blinking, too, as my ass squirms on top of cotton sheets.

I lean toward her, but she switches toward our blocked window view to the north. Maybe the light reflected by my band pierced her eyelids. Maybe. My heart thumps twice, loud to shake the bones before sinking into my stomach. I lean across her shoulder, and she still smiles. Her lips keep spreading, and player pride demands that I stand from this crevice and leave her to some orgasm-less wet dream. Yet some other kind of power pulls my lips to her ear.

"I wanna be there, too," this force whispers through my lips.

Tarsha's smile winks away as she turns onto part of her back and chokes on the end of sleep. She moves just enough that I need not lean to see her lids batting crust from sight.

"Tommie?" she says, as if she can't focus to see me clearly. "What'd you say?"

I sit on top of my ring finger and watch the time blink, for there's no beacon here. "Said where's the baby at?"

"Dawn?" Tarsha says, stretching bare arms over her head. "At your mother's. It's *Survivor* night."

I look at my watch. "You didn't pick her up by now?"

"Thought you were coming home—" her answer trails. She turns from the red clock numbers.

I stand and walk to the doorway, as the clock reads 12:57. "What are you dreaming about?"

Tarsha peeks over the shoulder without moving her back or her eyelids. The lids stay down to protect her from the hall-way's light. "You," she slurs, "back when we were kids."

She is lying, reading from her own sweet script. No matter, my heart does leap back into my chest and stays there to beat. I smile wide and foolish, though she faces the opposite wall and dreams in her own world again.

"I love you," I say. "My debt is all covered, just like I promised. Told you I'd be back, Tarsha. I'm going to pick up Dawn, but I'll be back."

"Come home soon." My wife's voice is full of open-lidded life now, at least it sounds so in my ears. Either Tarsha is awake, or this pulling thing that keeps me here has me duped. Either way, I do hear her, and believe, when she slurs, "Yes. I love you, too, Tommie."

✳   ✳   ✳

PRETENDING IS JUST the way we come to deal when we want to dream a place outside these Corners. Greatest dope to ever course nappy veins, this make-believe. You don't even see pretend fantasies—or smell or know them—before they've seeped inside the mind and wiped the hurt away, so that we can handle the reality. Not like smoking crack (which folk only do once imagination is all spent, left them no tool to pretend with), not like this pipe. When we play make-believe, we got no clue how high we are until the eyelids open and the ceiling gets to tumbling. That's the only way fools living on low-down floors get buried along with the rest of the souls. So high pretending and slow-blinking crusty dreams away, too damned high and groggy to run to safety. Pretending behind closed eyes, though this place is already without light.

The time for make-believe is over once I fix on the flame jumping out of a pipe made of TV antennae wire. This conk-headed, ponytailed molester holds it to my life-giver's lips. You can't pretend anymore when your baby cries in a high chair because she's swallowed cracked air—stale and flat and milky white—into virgin lungs. The child breathes and swallows and screams as she watches her grandmother stripped to pink bra and thin T.J. Maxx skirt hitched up to her knees. Watches grandma suck the ass of an antenna. Suck, suck, swallow, and puff, this milky smoke burned out of the readiest of ready rocks.

My mother is a fiend, I see, whatever that means. But she's my old girl, so I pretend otherwise just to get by, almost high as she's been getting by all these years. And Doreen's been getting mighty high all right, but she never left me behind bars on the Four Corners—except to slave for Henry T. Ford out in the south suburbs, back on that day I burned down our home. And she didn't even mean to leave me alone then, my love, and that's got to count for something, no matter this made-up dope she smokes.

I'm done with make-believe now. Should've given it up years ago, all the way back when I was a boy; should've choked good sense into her just like I'd planned. After we moved to this apartment from Merrill's ashes, my mother hung matching portraits on our new living room wall to remind us of the fire from which we came—two black velvet screens painted with brown faces peeking from shadows and streaming tears. Wallace glances at the portrait to the left, just over his head, of a crying baby boy while the life-giver's flame shoots past the other, this twin chubby-faced girl who screams between smoke trails.

My mother's lips burn. Can't pretend now, my nigga. Look, see, even as Wallace the crackman molester feeds rock smoke to my love with the pipe in his right hand, his left palm plays kinky with the rusty knee where she bounced me as a boy, that same knee where she rocks Dawn to dreams in the nursery room. As he tricks out my life-giver, the living room's thirteen-inch color TV plays a rerun of *Good Times* on its dusty screen. The pictures blink and fizzle because the crack pipe is made of the UHF antenna circle. In the screen's corner, blue letters flicker and announce, "Up Next on Channel 26, *The Jeffersons*." And I hear their theme song swirling churchy make-believe behind my eyes—"*. . . to the East Side . . . to a Dee-lux Apart-ment . . . in the Sky-I-HI-I*" as the Manor rock smoke seeps into my blood, leaving me nearly high off this contact cloud myself.

Another flame jumps from mamma's lips, touches the living room ceiling. But this here fire ain't a lifesaver at all, nothing like the flames twelve-year-old boys light with matches to burn down homes. No, this crack rock heat is the very end, singeing a hole over our heads. My feet won't move from the living room's rug as the flame jumps high and alone, freezes me here between my baby screaming and my old girl blazing. The both of them swirl about underneath this sucking hole.

I can't step forward until *Good Times* ends and my mother moans—at Wallace sliding his hand underneath that skirt or at the boiled rock that settles in her blood, whichever, the life-giver moans low and sweet. Low, sweet, and long as she moaned when my factory-floor uncles came, but not so full of life and howling love as she moaned underneath the swaying-tailed man. I've heard this cooing and settling sound around here before, but I'm frozen still.

Her sound doesn't last though, for soon enough, she watches me in the corners of eyes filled with reflected flames. She sees me frozen in that crackle, and the noise of frustration slips through her lips, forward, and then back.

"Gu-ugg," the high life-giver sings, "ug-ugg—" and finally, I do move.

I lift Dawn first, for her tears spill and the child brought none of this onto herself. Just got born into shit, is all—swimming up in it and trying to stay alive at least until the rest of us fools die. Then maybe she can start all over again and breathe clean air.

I touch my child's back, rubbing her to soothe. When Dawn is quieted just a bit, I untape my .38 from the left kidney. The molester and my life-giver are so high up now that they don't pay mind to me or to the TV, just enough to pass that fresh pipe back and forth between burned lips.

The pretend jig is all over once I open my eyelids to look upon Wallace the crackman—so far gone that he stares square in my face, feeding my mother rocks with one hand and pulling her panties down with the other. He glares this way no matter the .38 handle gripped in my left hand, duct tape dangling from steel and tapping against my trigger finger's tremble.

"What're you doing here, boy?" Creamy smoke spills from Wallace's lips as he speaks. No hateful curses spew from these low-lidded eyes though. "You bother us."

I rub Dawn at the crown of her loose curls and she does stop crying finally, bites into my T-shirt instead. I rock her twice on sneaker heels, then rest the child on the apartment's shag rug. Sweet baby girl does stay on her feet, too, no matter these clouds she breathes. And when she does fall, just like Tarsha told me, Dawn drops her palms to the floor first, bracing for the impact of collapse.

I reach into the crackman's clouds and take hold of his shoulder bone. Drag the bastard molester to foot, but Wallace does not fight, not my touch at least. All he does is pull back to snatch the twisted UHF antenna from my mother's lips and tuck its burning filter into dungaree pockets.

He is a tall man with bones that carried solid weight last Thanksgiving, as they did a few months back when my mother started bringing him around again. All of that weight is eaten away now, so as I drag him to mamma's front door. His feet leave the carpet and he floats in my fists. I lift the man as I lifted my child, without meaning to, and the life-giver reaches for her crackman with one hand, pulling pink cotton panties up her thighs with the other.

I open the door and toss Wallace into the hallway. Now he turns and stares with mostly clear eyes. I point the .38's muzzle at him—this is an unnecessary act, for I could breathe on this wisp and blow him away, but hustling lessons tell me the Coles Avenue crackman will understand the end of an alley pop-gun best.

"Fuck you think you is, boy?" Wallace slurs. "You bother us."

I cock the .38's hammer. "Get the fuck outta here, mutha-fucka—come back to bother her, and I'll put caps in you."

He laughs. "Nigga, I dare you to shoot. You bad, nigga? Shoot me now then, cause I'm gon be back tomorrow, nigga, get me some more of that thang. What you gon do bout it? Fuck you, ne-gro—"

"Don't come back here." I wave the forefinger of my free left hand, for I was wrong: the crackman does not understand. "I'll be waiting right here, muthafucka. I'll blast your ass."

"Who you gon blast, fool?" He cackles now. "Fuck you

376 | Bayo Ojikutu

gon blast me with? That thing? You gon stop me from getting me some of that sweet kitty cat, you best find you a real gun, boy. You ain't bout to do shit with that. You so bad? I dare your ass to shoot, punk." Wallace spreads his arms and leans his upper body back at the waist, waiting and begging.

"Muthafucka," I say, my bottom lip shaking. Then I repeat, for weakness's sake, "Don't come back here."

"I dare you, boy." Wallace yells, near toppling to the hallway carpet. I hide most of myself behind my mother's front door, only the king's .38 facing the crackman now. But I listen to him cackle on. "Didn't think so," he says, and turns to stumble on toward the elevator, his pocket trailing smoke as he sings Bill Withers in sweet harmony.

"*Ain't no sunshine when she's gone / it's not warm when she's away . . .*"

Mamma's draped the couch's slipcover over her shoulders to cover her breasts. I wonder if she was already fiending back when she nurtured me with these dull mounds. Smoking rocks with the wolf maybe, as I rested in her womb. Am I a born crack fiend just like Westside Jackie Lowe? But thank God, no, crack wasn't even around the Four Corners in those days— over on the West Side maybe, but not in my South Shore. This ain't in me. I tuck my Saturday Night Special into the waistband, and I remember that they used to call ready crack rock "freebase," back in 1972 anyway.

I lift Dawn from the carpet, rest her head against my shoulder and rub the scalp, though she doesn't scream anymore. I walk back toward the apartment door, but my mother pays me no mind. She's caught up staring at the crying boy in the velvet screen picture.

"I tried, you know," she slurs, "best I could. I did."

I want to say "I know" or recognize her effort, but Dawn coughs against my shoulder blade and my mother sips wafting smoke into her throat. Instead, through the pursed corners of my mouth, I say, "Thank you."

The words spewed, I close the door on my life-giver and trip past Wallace with Dawn's head pressed into a warm place. At my back, I hear my mother moaning and gurgling louder, and I run faster.

*   *   *

HOSPITAL HELD REMI for two days, no matter the ill sight of his burns—just long enough for the welts streaked across the forehead to stop leaking and flatten into his skin a bit. They put him out on the 75th and Stony Island bus stop once the social workers figured out my cousin's insurance card was fake, just like the Ascending Queen nuns did me when tuition checks started bouncing, except that Remi had pus-stained bandages still wrapped around his skull.

He's lost the left eye altogether. Doctors at Cook County concocted a sliced metal plate with a pencil mark dotted in the center for a temporary eyeball. They'll scoop the slimy remains of the left from his head and pop glass into its permanent place, as long as the welts in his right iris heal before a week passes. Otherwise, he'll walk around wearing sunglasses for the rest of his life, saving the world from looking upon scorched and dangling lid skin. No use in disgusting the innocent, seeing world with such horror, and no use in wasting a good glass eyeball on the uninsured and totally blind hustler either.

It's Saturday night. Cousin Remi's got three days to start seeing something from the right eye.

"You know what it's like," Remi speaks to Jackie, not asking really, sounds to me like he's reminding his half-brother. They sit in my cousin's private office—five more days before the county sheriffs come to put them out, and they still have nowhere to go. Remi's computer is already at the 76th Street pawnshop, replaced by the VCR that's connected to the television James used for Virtua Fighter. I enter the room and stop just behind the third folding chair, opened and empty at my cousin's left hand. The end of Remi's gauze dangles next to his earlobe. Jackie's changed the bandages at least, for no pus stains this white wrap.

"No, I don't know," Jackie says, brushing lint from his brother's shoulder. "What is it?"

"Ain't black, figured it'd be black. You know, when you imagine blindness—if you ever think of such a thing—always figured not seeing would be all black and quiet," Remi says. "I mean, right now there's nothing behind the bandages. But when I pull um down to peek through the slits, it ain't black no more."

"You ain't supposed to take the wrap off yet," Jackie scolds, his hand still at Remi's shoulder. "Doctors said so."

"It's all gray light," Remi continues, his head shaking so the gauze tape swings. "Something's up inside the light, just can't fix on it to know what it is. Hear every goddamn thing, too.

And it's all louder. Ain't no kind of peace here. Always thought if I was blind, God'd give me some quiet in exchange for losing sight. But I hear the goddamn rats running in these walls, right on top of my head. Remember when we moved to Phillips Ave., how we'd make fun of that blind old lady used to live across the street? She'd run out to the curb and get to swinging her cane cause she thought we was standing right in front of her. But we was way over here on our side of the street, remember?"—he laughs alone—"It's like that. Light on in here now?"

"Yeah," I say and the two of them jump from their folding chairs.

"Don't be sneaking up on us, fool," Jackie snaps. He looks at me with rolling eyes as the television screen blinks. "Your cousin's here."

"Tommie?" Remi pats the third chair and the bandages smile. "Sit down."

"Can't," I say, "I'm on my way. Just checking on y'all."

Remi laughs low and tired. "Used to be I'd look at them faces in the frames"—his finger aims for the wall, but he points at the ceiling's corner, just above the doorway. "Malcolm and Harold fighting the pigs, like I shoulda done Weidmann, like a man's supposed to do. Old lady getting rich, straightening out naps. Old boy jiving and rhyming, and Dizzy blowing that jazz. And this one, what's this one's name shaking her ass in straw?"

He points through the window glass, out on the avenue and Jackie frowns at me, waiting for the answer. "Josephine," I say finally.

Remi snaps middle finger to thumb real smooth. *"Josephine*

Baker." The bandages spread, seams smiling with scalded lips. "Finest sugar I ever laid eyes on, Josephine Baker. My fault, I don't remember who else hangs there—can't recall. Used to look at Josephine and know there was something better out here, somewhere. They're all the same gray now."

"Remember that flick they made about the ol girl." Jackie's words giggle as he stares at the frozen woman. "Honey they had acting like her on the cable station—she was fine. This skeeze on the wall? She's all right."

"I don't know," Remi's voice wanders. "Can't call it. I forgot the faces already."

"You all right, Cuz?" I ask. I feel the left side of his head, and his bandages tingle in my palm. This is the first time I've touched Remi since carrying him into that emergency room.

"Can't be talking like that there, Rem-Dog," Jackie begs. "Gotta act like you trying to see a little something. They ain't gonna give you no glass eye if you're rambling like a hopeless gimp."

The sound from Remi's bandages is more of a chuckle this time. "Know where I got these pictures from?"

His left hand pats the empty seat again, but I step backwards, toward the doorway without answering his question. Jackie stares at me and shrugs.

"You know?" Remi repeats.

"No," I say and glance at Liston playing comatose under Ali's victory pose—loser faking he's knocked out after the Mafia told the monster to tumble. The world was in need of more Black heroes back then, see, not monsters.

"Jewtown," Remi tells us, "way back before they moved the open market east. Picked them up around the same time your col-lege sent me back home."

He speaks each word quieter than the last until the final syllable is a whimper. "Wasn't my college," I reply, much louder.

"You went there," he says.

"So did you."

"You stayed," he tells me. I see skin hanging loose through the bandages where his eye melted, crusting and pulsing all at once. "After they made me leave, you stayed up there."

He points through the windowstill. "Down there," I say.

"What?"

"We was downstate in Carbondale," I correct. "I stayed 'down there.'"

"Whatever, nigga—you stayed. Was gonna be a teacher, you know. That's what I wanted to do if they had let me stay up there. My mamma always said teaching's what she shoulda done. Old girl woulda liked to ah seen me in front of a class-room maybe."

"You know it was Primo who done this," Westside Jackie blurts, his eyes fixed on the flickering TV screen. "Ratted us to Wee Man. Knew y'all shoulda never gone to that guy."

"Set us up just like we did the fools on the Corners," Remi says. "That's how it goes, ain't it?"

"Guess so, yeah," Westside murmurs now. "I hate fucking rats. Gotta make sure Primo gets his, now. *That's* how it goes for real."

Lids drop over my eyes. "I'm sorry," I say, and I do mean it, sorry for staying down there in Carbondale after they sent Remi away.

I expect him to remind me of the foolish way of apologies, useless and unnecessary in their emptiness. But he's quiet now, as he's forgotten the faces. I press my eyelids closed to this lightning flashing and fluttering in the window so my dreams aren't all sunset anymore either. Visions are all fuzzy gray behind my lids instead, just for a moment. When I peek, Westside Jackie has pressed the VCR's play button to bring full light and static to the screen. Flashing and breaking and fading until gray dots come together and form a clear picture—

My apple is bent over on-screen, palms pressed to the living room hardwood—this digital lens recorded the specks of dust between her fingers. Cleopatra and Officer Weidmann hang over her pimpled shoulder blade, the bird-pig entering the child's womb from the back. Kamisha's baby fat jiggles in that young, firm way as he pounds. Her face twists and the screen shrinks, camera closing on her eyes, and her flat mask begs for some kind of saving. She wants to smile somewhere behind eyelids, too, no matter the color of her dreams. Smile without me or any other soul knowing what brings her this joy. She won't tell me about her dreams after she's emancipated. My apple just needs help getting to that free place.

"Together, me and you," she hustles shadows, "we can end this life of pigs and prey, let birds swoop down from stank air without worrying, cause we've got eyelids to hide our dreams."

When I don't answer this time, apple looks over her shoulder and moans as this bird-pig pecks her bloody, faking gut-boiling bliss so the cop won't know how much he hurts. No matter what King Lonnie says about honeys and .22s, there is a power to her "pant-pant" noises. Remi and his half-brother guffaw with their hands hiding the throb at their crotches—my apple letting loose such noise is beautiful and funny to them. No matter that between the two, only Westside Jackie sees how Kamisha's baby fat shakes tight to the bone.

Remi pats the folding chair's cushion, waiting for me to join them. I turn from the screen and its fuzzy gray though, before the bandages brush against his earlobe. I leave them, my cousins and the mostly nude Josephine and the TV screen and my sweet apple, leave them to themselves.

The rest of the shack is dark, even the wall where the old queen hung in leopard skin and leather. Outside the shack, night's fallen on the Corners, though light still flashes where the sky meets water. I take quick steps past the new north tower, along 78th Street in the same direction as James left us, fast as I can without running. Like I told my mother once in a dream, men don't run from these Four Corners. Not how I see it—we look to the lake, where we come close as we can to the blinking beacon. I walk east toward that meeting place then, headed home to my love.

About the Author

BAYO OJIKUTU lives, teaches, and writes in Chicago, Illinois. His short fiction and creative nonfiction have appeared in various collections. He is a faculty member at DePaul University, and has been a visiting lecturer with the University of Chicago's Creative Writing Program housed under the school's Division of the Humanities. His first novel, *47th Street Black,* won the Washington Prize for Fiction and the Great American Book Award.

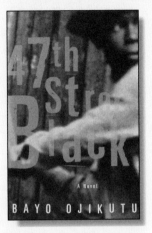

IN THE EARLY SIXTIES, 47th Street is the heart of black
Chicago. JC and Mookie are high school dropouts, playing
stickball in the street, when they stumble upon the corpse of
the area's black liaison to the mafia. Where others would run,
Mookie sees opportunity, and in no time he and JC are working
for Salvie, the local boss. Their rise in the gangster-driven ghettos
is as swift as it is brutal, and within a year, they are the most infa-
mous figures on 47th Street.

As JC and Mookie alternate telling their stories, both the
neighborhood and the two men's lives hurtle toward an explosive
confrontation with injustice.